DIAMOND HEAD

DIAMOND HEAD

A NOVEL

Cecily Wong

HARPER

An Imprint of HarperCollins*Publishers*

For Read, who never let me quit.
For my parents, who planted the roots and let me grow.

HarperCollins books may be purchased for educational, business, or sales promotional use. For information, please e-mail the Special Markets Department at SPsales@harpercollins.com.

FIRST EDITION

Designed by Adam B. Bohannon

Library of Congress Cataloging-in-Publication Data has been applied for.

ISBN 978-0-06-234543-1

15 16 17 18 19   OV/RRD   10 9 8 7 6 5 4 3 2 1

AUTHOR'S NOTE

It was important to me that this novel be as historically factual as possible, but there were times when I preferred a personal encounter with Hawaii and its history over what I learned in my research. I chose locations close to me—neighborhoods where my grandparents live, where my parents were raised—even if they did not yet exist in the history of Oahu. At times, I favored my grandparents' details of war, or the foods they ate, or the way they dressed, over what I read in historical reports. This novel is an exploration of an island with a complicated past, informed by family narrative, history, and, occasionally, a conflicting collision of the two, which resulted in my own invention.

DIAMOND
HEAD

CHAPTER 1

November 1964
HONOLULU, HAWAII

Inside the car, it smells like hibiscus. It was his mother's idea; something subtle, she told him, but fresh. Something alive. As the man pulls from his driveway he is grateful, just this once, for his mother's meddling. He breathes in. Already, the sweet smell is working on his nerves.

The man turns on the radio and immediately turns it back off, before he can even hear what's playing. He thinks of what he would prefer, if he were them, and turns the dial again, softly to the local station that plays old Hawaiian meles. The strum of ukuleles and the warm thump of an ipu drift through the car as he presses the gas, accelerating through a yellow light at the end of his street.

He's finally gathering himself, relaxed enough to tap a single finger on his steering wheel, almost to the beat. The traffic is light, which lightens him as well. In his line of work, in East Honolulu, the flow of the road is his greatest adversary.

The man pushes through four changing lights and arrives at their house in record time—a whole minute faster than his final trial the night before, when he slowed before the drive and looked at his watch, right before the hand struck midnight. This morning, however, is the first time he pulls past the stone wall and through the open gate. It's the first time he sees the full façade of the house, which is painted grey and is low and flat, wider than he imagined, as somber as the day.

As he steps from his car, it occurs to the man that his shoes are smudged. There was money in the stipend for a shoe shine, but he spent it instead on three white handkerchiefs, square and identical, which he placed in his glove compartment, just in case. He was a driver, he told himself. His shoes were seldom scrutinized, hardly ever on display. If the grieving women began to cry, he could offer them a proper handkerchief. But now the man questions himself. He squats and wipes the dirt off with his fingertips, cursing.

The shape of the house is a horseshoe, the entrance hidden in the center, recessed between two identical wings. The two sides jut forward, wrapped by long windows filled with wooden blinds painted white, all of the slats tilted shut. The door is white as well, with a gold bell, a gold knob. He hears no sound from within as he rings.

The driver's watch tells him he's almost exactly on time. They should be expecting him. As he waits, he steps back from the door and loosens his hands, which he realizes have formed fists when without warning, the knob turns and the door begins to open. The space before him widens and there she stands, stately, elegant, quietly stern. She looks just as he thought she might, but older. She's aged some since the picture they ran last week. Her skin is thinner, especially below her eyes, where it stretches like damp rice paper, revealing the delicate veins.

"Good morning," the driver says, nodding, taking the opportunity to avert his eyes, to let them breathe before lifting them again. "I'm your driver. Peter Choi."

Amy Leong smiles. Her face lifts in the corners of her mouth and eyes but she looks exhausted, almost pained from the effort. She nods and turns, walks briskly down the hall.

When she returns, seconds later, she is accompanied by her teenage daughter. *Theresa*, the driver reminds himself, as he becomes suddenly aware of what he is seeing—stricken by a sight he had not prepared for, something no one warned him about. Amy Leong's daughter is extremely pregnant. Her belly protrudes uncomfortably as she shifts her weight between her heels, her arms swaying beside her, balancing her with each laborious step.

She's a pretty girl, he decides, like her mother. Her dark hair is pulled back tight on her head; a white dress stretches over her stomach, falling above her knees. Without thinking, the driver looks for a wedding ring but does not find one.

"Good morning," he says again, stepping backward from the entrance.

"Hi," Theresa says. She cannot be more than eighteen.

With swift, eager steps, the driver strides toward his car. Already, he's overwhelmed. He wants to be back in his seat, facing forward, his focus on the road. He opens the back door and smiles lamely as the women slide in, his mind searching for something, anything to say to put them at ease. He comes up empty.

They cross the valley floor in silence, the low hum of the radio alone in its efforts. Even between the two women, not a word is uttered. They hug the eastern coastline, headed south, the wind off the Pacific bending the palm branches overhead, pushing the clouds, streaking the morning sky. As he reaches the country club, he knows from his run-through that they're halfway there, about to begin their approach to Diamond Head. Carefully, he lifts his eyes to his rearview mirror and catches Amy Leong turned to her left, toward her window, dark eyes narrowed against the rising sun. Like her daughter, she wears white today. A silk dress with long sleeves wraps around her tiny frame. It reminds the driver of a photograph, printed nearly twenty years ago. A double-page spread, he remembers. A white dress. Fireworks streaking the night sky behind her. They were from the same neighborhood, he and Amy Leong— Kaneohe, over the mountains on the windward side of the island. When the story came out, it was all their neighbors could talk about. Amy Leong's mother-in-law had long funded the Kaneohe school system. It was through her, the Lin Leong scholarship, that the driver had sent his daughter to college. He had meant to say that, to say thank you, but now in the silence he feels his mind fumbling, his chance slipping away.

Amy Leong shifts her gaze and the driver turns abruptly back to the road.

They cross through into Kahala and the land flattens, the rust disappears. Walls made of brick, of moss stone, of bright terracotta, of chocolate teak, of glistening koa begin to rise, guarding the houses that lie behind them. Flowers appear in long pendants, tiny and periwinkle, plump and magenta, dropping from the trees above. The base of Diamond Head spreads before them and the driver takes his left, the shape of the volcano guiding his path, drawing them closer to what he seeks: the odd curvature of land that cuts into the crater, the only one like it, a spectacular anomaly on an island teeming with surprises. Seen on a map, it's unmistakable. The base of the volcano forms an oval save for a piece on the southwest side where there is a mouth, a fortress sealed by an iron gate.

To their left the ocean crashes, gargles, foams onto the pale sand and the driver knows that it's too late. Anything he says now will seem strange. He can't comment about the weather, can't ask about the specifics of the arrangements; he's failed to execute the lead-up, the words he'd planned before saying his thank-you. They're almost there. He fights the urge to slow the car, to elongate the last stretch so he can think of a solution, but he doesn't.

He rounds the bend and at once it appears. A mammoth gate extends between the ridges of the crater, five hundred feet of solid wrought iron, towering above the lampposts before it. The driver slows beneath its shadow.

Bohai Leong
    Born July 23 1902, Died November 16 1964
    Age 62 years
    Born to Frank and Lin Leong in Guangdong, China
    Bohai is survived by his mother, Lin Leong, his wife, Amy
Leong, and his daughter, Theresa Leong

There's an announcement posted to the gate. Amy finishes reading first and reaches for the bell, but her daughter stops her. Theresa's hand extends absently, wrapping around her mother's wrist. Her eyes remain on the fluttering paper.

"Sixty-two," she whispers to her mother. "Dad was fifty-four, why does it say sixty-two?"

"What?" Amy replies, her hand still hovering over the bell.

"Sixty-two," Theresa repeats, her finger flicking against the announcement. "It says sixty-two."

"I don't know." Amy exhales. "Hong was in charge—she wrote it. I suppose she thought it might be better this way. People—*Leongs*—aren't supposed to die before sixty. Chinese superstition. It speaks poorly of the family."

"So you agreed to this?"

"I didn't agree to anything, Theresa. I'm just telling you what I know."

Theresa releases her mother's wrist and presses the bell herself. The gate opens inward and the low rumble of the motor vibrates throughout her thoughts, rattling them into something they're not. She thinks of all the ways she could win against her mother, all the ways her mother could be defeated. It'd be so easy, Theresa's mind coaxes, with just one slip of the tongue. She closes her eyes as the gate latches into place and the vibration halts. Stop it, she warns herself. Let it go.

The women step beyond the gate, where the garden looks as it has for decades. The thick lotus drifting gently in the silver ponds, the glossy stones, the red pavilion—painted white today, for Bohai—it's all as Amy remembers. Astonishing, she thinks, how money can slow the passing of time, erasing the years of growth and change and damage, painting over them when they begin to show through. A family might fall, but with a sweep of a lawnmower, a sprinkling of fertilizer, a garden can preserve the dignity that a family has lost. It can restore the pride that they can no longer find.

She wonders if it can recognize her today—if the garden knows she's Amy. She fights the urge to speak with the lotus, to whisper to the pond, reassuring them that she's still the same girl who arrived with her father in nylon shoes, all those years ago. That despite how it might look now—and she knows how it looks—she's not altogether bad. Not entirely selfish.

Amy pauses. She lets the heels of her shoes sink softly into the grass.

Framed in the doorway of the great house, dressed in a white blouse and trousers, Theresa can see Hong arranging a basket of lisee. Her hands work quickly for her age, deliberately, positioning the small envelopes of lucky money so that their painted images face forward. Next to the lisee there's a second basket, a mountain of hard candy to give mourners as they arrive. Something sweet to lessen the bitterness of death.

Watching Hong work, Theresa forgives the old woman for faking her father's age. In Hong's careful hands, Theresa sees the complexity, the desperation that accompanies losing a person whose entire life you have witnessed, have followed across two continents, from difficult conception to unexpected death. Hong was there the entire time, quietly serving tea, wrapping the family's skeletons in lucky red paper. She's the only one left who can remember Bohai's real mother.

Bohai's real mother. In Theresa's mind, the funeral announcement appears. Her father's face, pale and clumsy, and the words printed below. *Born to Frank and Lin Leong.* She absorbs the second lie, lets it fill her, amazed that within such sparse words her family has managed so much dishonesty.

"Are you ready?" Amy asks. Theresa realizes that her legs have stopped moving.

"Right," she says, her palm pressed to the underside of her belly. She wonders if her mother realizes, if she even cares. It was she who had told Theresa, the day after her father passed, of his elaborate inception, of the complications that had followed. Now, as she climbs the stairs to the entrance of the great house, Theresa wishes that she had known sooner. Theresa wishes a lot of things.

Theresa

It's the morning after; we've just come home from the hospital but neither of us can sleep. My mom's on the dock. She's sitting on the edge, her feet skimming the water, a cigarette lit between her fingers.

At first, she doesn't see me. I walk up from behind; she lifts her arm and inhales, blows smoke out over the marina. It catches in the mist and drifts downstream, gone before I reach the end. Her shadow, precise beneath the early sun, is long and thin. It cuts across the beams of wood, perfectly still, perpendicular.

I sit beside her and she doesn't move, but she doesn't make me ask again. She takes a final drag and stabs the end of her cigarette into her ashtray.

This is what she tells me. This is what I know.

1909
GUANGDONG, CHINA

In Chinese tradition, child naming is taken very seriously. When a baby is born, it is first given a *milk name*, or a *little name*, consisting of either two syllables that repeat, like LingLing, or a nickname, like Little Pearl. The baby's parents, in close consultation with the baby's grandparents, will spend the next month carefully selecting the child's given name. This is not a simple process. There are many rules and traditions in Chinese naming practice—dozens of lucky names to consider and even more inauspicious names to avoid. It is considered inappropriate to name a child after any famous or well-known figure, and highly offensive to name a baby after an older member of the family, or even a distant relative. If the new child has older siblings, the parents must consider the names that already exist and name the child something to create a balance or relate the siblings in some way. My father was the oldest child of his family, named Bohai, or *elder brother of the sea*. He was the first son, but they hoped he would not be the last. In a way, my father's name was an aspiration, a plea for more sons. He was never enough; from the day he was born, from the time he was named, my NaiNai and Ye Ye were hoping for someone else.

My entire life, I've called him Maku. When I was little, I learned the Hawaiian word for father: *makuakane*. The word was too long, so I pronounced what I could and it stuck. *Maku* doesn't mean a thing, the ultimate blasphemy to the Chinese tradition, but after decades away from China, these things, like so many others, begin to fade.

Maku was born in 1909, in the province of Guangdong, to his father's first concubine. The word *concubine* coming from my mother's mouth startled me, but she assured me that it was common for a man like my Ye Ye. At least, that's what Maku had explained to her. My Ye Ye took a concubine after my NaiNai lost her second child—*a second girl*—and was determined incapable of bearing any children, let alone sons. I'm told she went a bit mad that day, pleaded with the midwife to *check again, please, check again* as they removed the stillborn from the damp room. She pulled at her hair, clumps of limp black strands falling from her head in her weakened state, more deceived by her child's gender than the absence of life. My NaiNai swore it would be a boy, swore she felt his sex the minute he was conceived.

A male feels sturdy in the womb. He sits low. He craves salt.

My NaiNai spent the last five months of her pregnancy patiently resting in bed like a good Chinese wife, nurturing the seed in her womb, coaxing it to be firm and masculine, praying endlessly for a boy. She named him Fai, secretly of course, reasoning that a named child could not be taken from the earth, desperately hoping that a boy named Fai could not emerge a girl. But after the second day of labor, it was a girl who fell from my NaiNai's womb, slowly and deliberately, and it was then, in her despair, that my NaiNai thought to find her husband a concubine.

Her name was Hailee—fourteen years old and unremarkable, intentionally plain faced, sold to my NaiNai for less than what she spent on Sunday dinner. A single photograph remains of Hailee and Maku—Maku barely a month old, Hailee barely a teenager—tucked away deep in a chest in Maku's closet. I found it two years ago, when I was in high school, looking for my birth certificate among the neat, yellowed stacks of mementos. I didn't know who she was at the time, didn't understand that the baby was my father. All I remember is thinking what a sad face she had; square with small features, her grey eyes seeming to fade behind her eyelids, her cheeks faintly pock-marked. I brought the photo from the closet and held it beneath a lamp, taking her in. She was too young for such old skin.

Maku was born without complications. Hailee had asked for her mother, as Maku was her first child, but was denied—not by my Ye Ye, who offered to pay for the trip, but by her own mother, who wrote to tell Hailee that she no longer belonged to their family, warning her to be silent during delivery else evil spirits would swarm the newborn child. My NaiNai took her mother's place, standing behind Hailee as she gave birth to my father, to the first Leong son.

Hailee bore Maku while squatting, in one of the back rooms of the house, accompanied by a midwife and a doctor. Heeding her mother's advice, Hailee made no sound during delivery, but she fainted with her last push, falling backward from her shaky knees, hitting the wooden floorboards in one solid motion. The doctor picked up Maku, wiping the warm blood from his face with a square of white cotton, and handed my NaiNai her son. He was born healthy, to a soundless room, a gold necklace slipped around his neck before the umbilical cord was cut—tying his life to the necklace, instead of the cord.

The month that followed Maku's birth was riddled with quiet anticipation. Thirty days of rest, thirty days of prayer, thirty days of protective clothing and herbal fluids. The house felt fragile, as if too much activity would make the gold-rimmed windows shatter, as if too heavy a step would crack the marble floors. My Ye Ye, who spent most of the year away on business, stayed home for the entire month, methodically puffing on cigars in his library, he too silenced by Maku's newborn presence. Hailee was kept in a room by herself—the same room where she bore Maku—where she was fed pig's feet and boiled eggs to build up her strength and prepare her milk for the baby. She cried every night, quick, subdued whimpers from under her grass-colored quilt. She slept endlessly in her disheveled state, piling her unwashed hair on top of her head, going days without setting her feet on the wooden floors of her room. The doctor came every day to check on mother and child. As the thirty days came to a close, Maku became strong—his skin turning from pink to milky white—and Hailee developed a fever.

I'm told that the one-month festivities were spectacular. Red and gold balloons filled the garden sky at sunrise to signal that the waiting period had passed. My Ye Ye's personal jeweler came to the house to outfit Maku in gold bracelets, heavy enough to keep him anchored to the earth. Guests arrived from six provinces to attend the ceremony, from as far away as Chengdu, each bringing with them a thick red envelope filled with lucky money for the newborn child. The great hall of my grandparents' house had been waiting years for an occasion of this magnitude—capable of seating seventy guests, with room for three dozen servants to sweep the hall of empty plates after every course. There were thousand-year-old eggs to celebrate fertility, salt-and-pepper squid caught that morning, chilled duck with mahogany-colored hoisin sauce, and *yi qi tong*—shark fin soup, a favorite of my Ye Ye's and a rich indulgence for the rest of the party.

My Ye Ye spent most of the banquet running a porcelain spoon through his shark fin soup, admiring the soft cartilage as it floated through the mushroom-scented broth. My Ye Ye was a man who took great pleasure in luxury. That's what Maku used to say. He was a self-made millionaire who came from nothing, who gave himself his first taste of shark fin at the age of twenty-eight.

Maku and Hailee slept through the festivities, tucked away in their separate corners of the house, the lively party a murmur in the background. Maku had a nurse by then; his care had already been transferred to Hong. Hailee was needed only for breast-feeding, and even for that she wasn't required to leave her room. One month marked the day she could finally wash her body, comb her hair, clean her teeth. But Hailee did none of these things. She continued to sleep, under the warmth of her green quilt, as if the month were not yet over.

Hailee's fever persisted for six days after Maku's one-month celebration. Each day, the doctor arrived at the house with stronger remedies and more exotic herbs to help soothe her febrile body. Hailee soaked through her blankets each morning, waking up in a damp, twisted pile of linen. At first, she called out for her mother, begging her to save her from her own body, from her hot, aching limbs and the bile that emerged from her stomach almost every hour. Then she called for Maku—her son—to bring her comfort as she passed through into the next world, as Hailee was sure would soon happen. She dreamed vividly, her tenuous state transporting her mind to faraway places. She dreamed of open fields, the heat of her body warming all of her visions and coloring them with an intense fuchsia glow. She dreamed of frogs, thousands of them, leaping within the tall field grass, their legs extending far below their bodies. The frogs comforted her, sending a chill through her body when they plunged into the cool water ten at a time. Sometimes the frogs would call out—all at once—creating a deafening cacophony of low gargles and high-pitched chirps. The sky would turn a blistering crimson as her body began to swelter, and the frogs would begin to multiply. She tried to catch them, one at a time with her sweaty palms, but they would always slip through, teasing her with their fat bodies and slippery exteriors. She chased them, her aching limbs now thick and powerful, flickering against the electric-colored grass as she ran faster and faster. On nights like these, Hailee would run until her thighs were sore, beads of toxic sweat running down her temples, her sheets soaked through to the mattress.

As many times as she asked, Maku was not permitted to see his birth mother. Her room was moist and putrid, the smells of death hanging heavily in the air. The doctor said that if Hailee didn't infect Maku, she would certainly scare him with her nonsensical mumblings and violent outbursts. So Hailee died alone. On the eleventh day, no one in my Ye Ye's house was disturbed by the screams of Hailee's vivid dreaming, of her awaking in a pool of icy sweat. The doctor found her splayed out on the floor by the foot of her bed, her face pressed into the smooth wood boards, her arms outstretched as if trying to catch something.

According to my mother, it took five years to realize that Maku wasn't normal.

He wasn't abnormal, exactly. There was nothing wrong with him; no disease, no demons, no tangible defect to blame. He was simply reserved. Modest. Shy. As a baby, my NaiNai and Ye Ye used to boast about his even demeanor. Maku never cried or howled, never spit up his food, never whimpered at the touch of a new hand cradling his body. My Ye Ye said that he would be a fine businessman one day—a scrupulous trader who would carry the family's business into the next generation. Hong would joke to the servants that she'd never had it so easy, that raising Maku was like raising a stuffed doll.

Everything Maku did was meticulous. He didn't crawl like other children. The day Maku decided he was ready, he raised himself onto his feet and walked, all the way from his crib to the nursing chair, steady as a horse. His first words were not a jumble, left to be deciphered by doting parents who have memorized the sounds of their baby's gargling, but short, clear words. He refused to repeat what he could not yet pronounce. Even at this stage, my NaiNai and Ye Ye were proud.

My son can walk without crawling and speak without stumbling. Soon he will learn without instruction and make money from nothing.

For the first five years of Maku's life, he was prized as the golden child—attending lessons all day, always the first to eat, and never addressed by his given name, Bohai, but rather Zhangzi, or first son. For those first few years, my NaiNai and Ye Ye would have given him the world: anything he desired, regardless of the hour or the expense. But of course, Maku asked for nothing.

As the fifth year of his life passed and Maku grew into a boy, the sparse words he was once praised for began to concern my NaiNai and Ye Ye. He spoke less and less, using his voice only when spoken to, and even then, replying with one word answers, or quick sentences strung together in the most efficient way. He stayed in his room, reading the same books over and over, stacking them back neatly on his shelves. My Ye Ye, seeing his son's interest in stories, brought home dozens of gold-bound children's volumes from his travels, wrapped in silk bows with exotic places painted on the covers. And while Maku always said thank you, graciously but without excitement, the expensive new books remained on the top shelf of his bookcase, untouched and unopened, while he continued to reread his favorites. The heroes of these stories were furry and four-legged; they often lacked people entirely, deficient of swords or ships or perilous adventure. The rabbit would cross the meadow, finding a new home. A family of sheep, newly fleeced, would enjoy summer on the farm.

In spite of his lessons and constant nurturing, Maku never quite displayed the qualities of a good Chinese first son. It was a strange situation for my NaiNai and Ye Ye: a young boy encouraged to be arrogant and superior, who had three maids chasing after him at all times, would push in his own chair after dinner, read in his room instead of practicing sports, and daydream throughout his lessons— though he would always apologize afterward. He was a gentler boy than my Ye Ye intended to raise, his definition of masculinity tied to the wildness of his own youth. My Ye Ye would shake his head and mutter that he might as well have had daughters. My NaiNai agreed. *What a strange boy.* It was during this fifth year that my Ye Ye started going away again, for weeks at a time on business trips to the north, finally leaving behind his first son.

Even in those times, my NaiNai and Ye Ye were considered quite wealthy, having made a good name and a good bit of money in the shipping business. They lived in Guangdong—a large, teeming region in the south of China—in the capital city of Guangzhou, or what my teachers call Canton. Guangzhou holds one of the busiest trading ports in all of China, east-facing and enormous, named the Silk Road on the Sea during the ancient dynasties. I'm told that my Ye Ye is infamous among the men of that harbor, that he set a record for annual cargo that has yet to be broken. It was here, in this port city, that they raised my father until the age of five.

A considerable portion of my NaiNai and Ye Ye's money was amassed during wartime, sending out fleets of ships to Russia and America filled with what my Ye Ye called toys, but which I imagine were tanks and antiaircraft artillery. It was typical behavior: he could spend the day shipping a hundred thousand tons of lethal machinery to the enemy and be home in time to enjoy dinner with his family. Business for my Ye Ye was about money, not about friends or politics or principles. He had a way of making shady dealings seem legitimate, of downplaying even the most illegal or corrupt of transactions.

I'm told my Ye Ye had many German acquaintances. *Freunde* he called them with his subtle Chinese accent, *friends*. But these were friends that never came to the house, were never called for tea, and were not present at Maku's one-month celebration. These were business *freunde*, who called late at night asking for my Ye Ye in their heavy, guttural language. My Ye Ye spoke perfect German—perfect French and English, too—which he studied every night in his library. Languages enchanted him. The verbs, the syntax, the colloquialisms, they delighted my Ye Ye like a riddle that he alone could solve, sharing the answer with my NaiNai and Maku every night at the dinner table, insisting that they study linguistics as well. There was nothing that pleased my Ye Ye more than executing a perfect joke in a foreign language—making a whole table of Europeans laugh with his wit in their mother tongue. He felt powerful in his language, confident in business and socially poised. A cosmopolitan man is what he called himself, his loyalties lying somewhere between China and Spain.

It was Europe he sided with during the Boxer Rebellion, a decade before Maku was born, when his own people were fighting for freedom against Western influence, religion, and the ever expanding opium trade. For many Chinese the Boxers were heroes, but for my Ye Ye they were barbarians, thieves, hooligans. He was never a patriot, always a capitalist, looking into the future and picking the side that favored his enterprise. Even his brother, Shen, four years younger, had been secretly training in Shandong, learning martial arts and practicing calisthenics to prepare for the revolution. Occasionally, Shen would send a message to the house asking my Ye Ye for money, imploring him to support the Chinese effort, telling him that his training made him immune to swords and capable of dodging bullets. My Ye Ye was always courteous, he would always reply to the frantic messages but he would lie to his brother. He would tell him that money was tight, or that it was impossible for it to safely reach Shen without being traced back to my Ye Ye. Afterward, he would complain to my NaiNai.

They've brainwashed my brother, filled his head with demons and nonsense.

But my Ye Ye was a rational man. He understood that his cynical patronizing would stop the messages, cutting off his one line to both his younger brother and his source of classified information. So when news came from the north, announcing that the Boxers were moving toward Peking, my Ye Ye already knew. He'd received a message from Shen the day before, telling him of their plan to storm the foreign embassies, sending an aggressive message of Chinese nationalism.

It seems that Shen was a man who suffered from passion. He had passion in excess, always jumping from one cause to the next, never satisfied with his current endeavors. He felt the injustice of the world so minutely, so intimately, that he couldn't help himself; he had to do something, no matter how insignificant or futile. And my Ye Ye knew this. He considered Shen's fixations to be like a disease, chronic and incurable, which is why he still indulged him. He still read every word his brother sent. He still responded, treating Shen as if he were a sick patient, already on his way out. My Ye Ye knew that by the next message, Shen would be on to something new; each cause more precarious than the next, until he eventually met with death. At the very least, my Ye Ye wanted to receive those final words.

But in Shen's last message, telling my Ye Ye of the Boxer's plan, there was something very surprising. In the brief telegraph, Shen skipped the usual topics. There was no allusion to government conspiracies, no talk of his supernatural powers, not even a reminder about social responsibility. Perhaps more surprisingly, this was the first time that Shen did not ask for money.

He had just married, he wrote to my Ye Ye. He had met a girl and he was in love.

My Ye Ye placed the paper down. He paused. To be a single man following the precarious path of a revolutionary was one thing. But to involve a woman, a young lady—with that, my Ye Ye took issue.

Don't worry, brother, read the final line. *We've trained hard and prepared well.*

What happened next was exactly as my Ye Ye predicted. The indiscriminate massacre of foreigners, the deaths of hundreds of Chinese Christians, the torching of buildings, the escalation of political tensions—it was all just as he had foreseen, and every morning my Ye Ye skimmed the headlines of the newspaper, skipping the articles, already knowing what they would say. When my NaiNai began to lament the loss of so many Chinese Boxers, my Ye Ye remained stoic, speaking only words of frustration.

The Chinese are too nearsighted. They think of nothing but war and violence, not understanding the good of trade and alliances, of new religion.

For the eight weeks that the Boxers occupied Peking, my NaiNai and Ye Ye awaited a message from Shen. They knew he was within the city, fighting with his quickly falling comrades, his brother in the south the last thing on his mind. Pamphlets and newspapers showed pictures of executed revolutionaries, left bloodied in the middle of the street, dead with a single bullet through the chest. *He can dodge bullets and is immune to swords*, my Ye Ye said, repeating his brother's words with a quiet laugh as he sipped his morning tea. My NaiNai, who was fond of Shen, flew into a rage.

"This is how you speak of family? This could be your brother!" she exclaimed, throwing the newspaper picture at my Ye Ye. "Does that make you laugh? That your brother may be dead while you chuckle over his words?"

My Ye Ye held his tongue after that, growing more and more silent as the days passed without a word. He read the newspapers now, looking for Shen's name in the lists of the dead, but he was never there.

My Ye Ye had not seen his brother in a long time. They grew up together along the Yellow River, moving from village to village with their father as he searched for work in the wheat and maize fields. Their father was not a skilled farmer, but more than that, he was not a man who cared to work. Like clockwork, he would meet the overseer of some small settlement and beg for a job, offering his sons as additional labor, making promises of exceptional harvests and new ideas for irrigation and superior crops. Then my Ye Ye's father would drink and my Ye Ye would work, planting the seeds and collecting the dry corn, hauling water, sorting for quality and checking for diseases and rot. Shen was ten, old enough to work, but he lacked my Ye Ye's focus, his appetite for something better. Shen held a fierce loyalty to their father, willing to lie to the overseer about his drunken state, his perpetual absence from the fields.

In the fall of 1887, when my Ye Ye was fourteen, they had been living along the river in the north of Shandong for almost six months. The overseer had taken a liking to my Ye Ye and requested his assistance on a trip to the highlands to find mountain yams. His wife had been complaining of kidney pain and there was word of the nearby growth of a medicinal root. The journey took three days, westward to the holy ridges of Mount Tai, and it was there, high on its crest, that they were told of the flood. The dykes had broken in Henan province to the west and had overwhelmed the banks, spreading violently, swallowing the settlements, leveling the houses, consuming everything in its path; the animals, the people, they were swept away like dust by a broom, razed in a mighty, biblical flash. Very little remained, they said. Everyone was gone.

That day was the first time my Ye Ye thought he had lost his brother. He went nearly a decade thinking this, venerating him at the ghost festivals, burning paper money and trinkets to send him in the afterlife. Until one day, when my Ye Ye still lived in Shandong, Shen appeared at his doorstep: a full-grown man, looking into his brother's face like looking into a mirror. They embraced in the doorway without a word, and I'm told that was the last time my Ye Ye cried.

But the next morning, after a celebratory meal of jiaozi dumplings and long beans and endless pours of rice wine, Shen was gone. He slipped out of the house in the early hours, while the others slept, leaving a note on his blanket, still warm from his resting body. *See you next time*, it said, the fat strokes of his characters like a small child's. My Ye Ye was devastated, quietly and profoundly heartsick for weeks, quiet at dinner, distracted at work, until Shen returned and my Ye Ye realized that this was how their relationship would be. Like their father, Shen was a nomad: appearing and disappearing, never staying longer than a few days, off to chase the revolutionary dream, to rid China of the evils of Westernization, to overthrow the Qing, to practice martial arts, to learn to eat fire, to destroy Christianity, to join the next group of men with a dozen swords and a righteous cause. My Ye Ye had little choice in the matter; he simply had to keep his door open, his life moving.

Once a year, every year, my Ye Ye asked Shen to come live with him and his family. My Ye Ye knew a change of environment would do wonders for his brother—that a warm bed and regular meals might keep him safe forever. My Ye Ye, however, refused to force Shen into change; he knew that under duress, Shen had a tendency to rebel, like a child, against all things good and conventional. But this last message had been different. My Ye Ye couldn't kick the feeling that something had shifted, that his brother had changed. Shen wrote that he'd like his wife to meet his family—that after the occupation of Peking was over, he would finally make the journey south with his new bride.

CHAPTER 2

November 1964
HONOLULU, HAWAII

Hong stands in the entrance of the great house, her square frame lit from behind, her hands clasped before her as she watches the women approach.

"Looks healthy," she says, smiling, gesturing at Theresa's stomach. "I think a boy."

"She still won't tell me," Amy replies, embracing Hong at the top of the stairs. "Can you believe that? She still won't tell her own mother."

"It's a surprise," Theresa says, the words automatic now. She repeats what she has told her mother, nearly every day since that morning in September when she went to see Dr. Ho, the Chinese birth chart specialist. Theresa had asked her mother to leave and Amy had waited outside, pacing the empty parking lot as Dr. Ho made his calculations, as he found her lunar age and matched it to the time of conception, sliding his prediction across the wooden table.

"I want it to be a surprise," Theresa says again as she leans in to touch her cheek to Hong's.

"Let her have her little secret," Hong replies, winking at Theresa. "Soon enough, we will all know."

The old woman takes Amy's hand and turns it over, opening her palm and placing a piece of candy in the center. She gives a second piece to Theresa. Hong wraps her own hand around Theresa's, letting the heat from their palms fuse, softening the thin sugar shell between them.

"Eat," Hong tells them. "Life is a dream walking. Death is a going home. Let it be sweet."

Hong unwraps a piece for herself and together, the women place the candy on their tongues, letting the honey flavor melt and chase away the bitterness that came before it. The taste comforts Amy; it soothes her in a way she had not expected.

"I can't tell you how indebted I am to you," Amy tells Hong, biting into the center of her candy, cracking it open so that its strength can fuse to the bottom of her teeth. "I don't know what would have happened if you weren't here. It would have been a nightmare. It would have been impossible."

Hong shakes her head dismissively, swatting at Amy's words with her hand.

"These things I do are for the family but I do it also for myself. It's not easy to accept but death is a gift. Bohai was too young. Yes, he was too young, but we are lucky," Hong says, her voice dipping on the last word, a low rasp exiting through her flat, thin lips. "How lucky it is that we can say goodbye, don't you think? It does not always happen like this. We are not always so fortunate, not always able."

Hong pauses and Theresa can hear the candy in her mouth, making a hollow sound as it clicks against her teeth. Her hair is entirely white now, but on Hong, these bright wisps of colorless hair look less like a sign of age and more like a reaction to something inside of her—something entirely good and pure—as if her body is unable to produce a silver or a grey. The skin on her face is padded with a fleshiness that leaves most women her age. The only indication of Hong's fragility is in the lids of her eyes, which slope downward toward the outer edges, dragging on her face when she frowns. Theresa notices this now, as Hong considers her words.

"He would have liked to be here today," Hong says, looking past their faces, above the garden, beyond the iron gate. "He would have wanted to do the rites." She speaks with a measured regularity, her words slowed by both caution and intention. "He came to me last night, you know? In my sleep. He comes every night since Bohai passed, and he tells me that today he cannot be here, but he is wait-ing." She pauses. "He is waiting to greet Bohai when he arrives."

Hong smiles and the heavy slope of her eyelids disappears.

Theresa stands between Hong and her mother, her ears lit, her mind suddenly ignited. She isn't sure; she's racking her memory, not yet entirely positive, but Theresa thinks—for the first time in the entirety of her life, in all the years she has stood between these women, their conversation like layers of impenetrable, maddening encryption—that maybe, just maybe, she understands what they are saying.

It startles her at first. She thinks again; she reconsiders. It's become almost second nature to Theresa, to be excluded from the conversa-tion, for the subject matter to be decades old, for those around her to allude to people without names, to events without dates or context or clarity. Theresa is used to it; the padded dialogue that reminds her of her absence, of her separation from a lifetime already lived is like white noise, so impossible to grasp that she's almost stopped trying. But today Theresa thinks she hears it differently. Since her father passed, since the stories began, she's made a point of listening.

Her eyes move to Hong's wrist, to the white bandage wrapped around its soft circumference. She knows what's below it. She remembers Hong in her parents' living room, almost six months ago, extending her hand, showing Theresa the stained cloth that has lived on her body since she was seventeen years old. *I was younger than you,* Hong had told her. *Can you believe that?*

Her parents had been gone that afternoon, off brokering her future in Kaimuki. That's what she'd told them when they had left, glaring, glowering as they got into their car and drove away. Theresa was miserable, two months pregnant and still in her pajamas at noon when there was a knock at the front door.

"What are you doing here?" Theresa had said.

"I took the bus" was Hong's response. She looked so strange in their doorway; away from the house on Diamond Head, she appeared to be from a different era. With her short white hair, her high cossack collar, she looked like a figurine of an elderly Chinese woman.

"Sorry." Theresa paused. "Do you want to come in?"

"Yes." Hong nodded. "Yes, I do."

Hong walked through the front door, down the hall and toward the living room. Theresa had wondered if she should change out of her pajamas. She had wondered if her parents knew that Hong was there, but she hadn't asked, because something told her that they did not.

On the coffee table, Theresa collected her cereal bowl from earlier that morning and moved it to the sink. She ran the faucet as Hong sat on the couch.

"Can I get you something?" Theresa asked when she returned. "Water? Are you thirsty?"

"No, it's okay," Hong said, patting the bag beside her. "I have my own."

"Okay." Theresa sat on the couch across from the old woman and began thinking of a way to ask her again what she was doing there, how she had managed to show up half an hour after her parents had driven away for the entire afternoon. But Hong spoke first.

"I have come to tell you a story," she said, straight-faced, entirely serious.

"A story."

"Yes. It's a very old story. Maybe older than me." Hong smiled, pointing to her face, holding her finger to her cheek. "Laugh," she encouraged Theresa. "It's a joke."

Theresa had laughed, unexpectedly, for the first time in many days. It was a strange laugh, prompted yet sincere. She had always enjoyed Hong's company, what little time they'd shared, just once a year when the Leongs gathered to celebrate the Chinese New Year. It was tradition for Theresa to help Hong in the kitchen, preparing and arranging the sweetmeats in their elaborate porcelain boxes as the adults gathered in the great room. She could recite the seven sweets in her sleep, had memorized their symbolism and given a presentation in the sixth grade: lotus root for friendship, squash for a long line of descendants, carrots for wealth and prosperity, coconut for a strong relationship between father and son, ginger for continuous good health, melon seeds for fertility, and lotus seeds for the protection of sons. It was with Hong that Theresa felt her heritage most strongly—a connection to a country she had never seen, to a language she didn't speak.

Amy stayed out of the kitchen, greeting Hong when they entered the house and immediately retreating into the company of her mother-in-law. But as soon as they left the Leongs' party, on their way home to sleep before the next day's celebration in Kaneohe, Amy would always question her daughter. Had Hong said anything about her? Did she seem healthy? Did she seem herself?

"Now," Hong said to Theresa, nodding on the word. "Are you listening?"

"Yes," Theresa said, wishing they were in the kitchen, that she had something in her hands to busy herself.

Hong cleared her throat and leaned forward, so far that her chest reached nearly to her knees. She folded her hands in front of her, stretching them outward, and then she straightened, vertically, releasing the air in her lungs. Finally, Hong settled back into her spot on the couch and gently, methodically, she began her story:

One evening, in a street lit by moonlight, a young boy meets an old man. This man is Yue Xia Lao. He is the old lunar god of matchmakers and marriages. Lao explains to the boy that every man is attached to his future wife. He says that every man is connected to his destined match by an invisible red string, tied around both their ankles. This string, he says, connects destined lovers, despite time or place or circumstance. It can stretch and tangle, but never can it break.

But be warned, Lao tells the boy, not all will find their destined match. Stay on the righteous path, do good deeds, and only then can you be united with your true and perfect companion.

Then Lao points to a young girl on the street. He tells the boy that this girl is his true love and destined wife. The boy, he is too young to be interested in a wife, so he takes up a rock and throws it at the girl. It strikes her in the face. The girl cries and runs off. She clutches her eye; she turns into the alley and disappears. Yue Xia Lao shakes his head and scolds the boy. You have unsettled the forces of fate, Lao tells him. You will see that these misdeeds change not only you and your future, but also the generations that follow.

Years later, when the young boy becomes a man, prosperous and respected, his parents arrange for him a marriage. The night of the wedding, his bride waits for him. Her face is hidden beneath the wedding veil. The man lifts the veil and finds that his wife is a great beauty of his village. Her face is perfect. She has even, milky skin, a soft mouth, eyes that echo a hundred shades of blue. She is flawless, except for an adornment that she wears on her eyebrow. The man asks his wife why she wears the adornment and she replies that when she was young, a boy threw a rock at her. It struck her face and left a scar. She wears the decoration to conceal her embarrassment.

His bride is the same girl shown to him by Yue Xia Lao, fifteen years before. She is connected to him by a red string and fated to be his destined match.

Hong had yet to blink. She held Theresa's gaze throughout the entirety of her telling, as if reading the words in the whites of her eyes. And Theresa hadn't looked away. The rhythm in Hong's voice kept pace like ocean tides, crashing steadily to its natural pulse. Theresa couldn't find a place between Hong's words to interject or look away, not even once, not even for a moment.

"A red string can never break," Hong continued. "A whole life, it can pass, while you are married to the wrong person, living with a knot."

Theresa's blood slowed. Could she know? She panicked. How could she already know?

"A knot?" she asked as the blood rushed to her face, sweeping through her veins, unbalancing her. "What do you mean?"

"A knot," Hong replied, dipping her head. "An affair. A forced marriage. A concubine. A prostitute. These things, they are knots in a red string. They are punishments for mistakes. You see, a red string with no knots, it moves like Chinese silk. It slips through mountains, weaves through cars and trees and railroad tracks. It can swim across an ocean and cross three countries to reach its destined match. But a knotted string, it is very different."

Theresa swallowed. The saliva caught at the bottom of her throat. She forced it down with a gulp of dry, swollen air.

"With time, with neglect," Hong continued, "a knotted string becomes stiff. It becomes like sandpaper and then like wood, stubborn and rigid. And as the knots collect, the chance that you will find your match becomes so small, because who can cross three countries with lengths of wood tied to their ankle? Who can swim for miles with such a burden? Do you understand what I am saying?"

Theresa drew in her lips and slowly, inhaled through her nose, trying to spread oxygen throughout her body. She hoped it would stop her from crying, from giving away her predicament entirely. She understood exactly what Hong was saying; she nodded her head.

"Good," Hong said gently. "There is just one more part." Her voice continued like this, softly, as if compensating for the words that she would say next.

"See, these knots, they do not depart when you do. This is where the most confusion lies. These knots are passed, from mother to daughter, from a father to his son. So that the more you lose your way—as the knots gather, as they sprout, the harder you make it for your children to find love, and for theirs after them."

Hong paused and her eyes were entirely clear, like two snow globes whose particles had settled to the bottom.

"You hate me," Theresa said, lifting her eyes from Hong's crystal stare. "You hate me, too. I get it. I do."

"It is the opposite!" Hong replied, straightening. "Last night I dreamed of fish. I saw your child, I saw your face. You're frightened, Theresa, I know you are but I have come to tell you that you still have a chance. You have one knot, just one instance of weakness, your red string is still strong. You have so much, Theresa, if only you do not lose it. You must not tie yourself to him, you must see what lies beyond."

"But the wedding—"

"*Wedding?*" Hong repeated, her mouth suspended around the word.

"You didn't know?"

Hong's face slackened. She hadn't known.

"Listen," Theresa began. "I appreciate you coming down here to talk. It means a lot to me, it really does, just to know you care. But a fairy tale isn't going to save me from this. I wish it could but it can't. And I don't mean to offend you, but do you think *an invisible red string* can save me from this amount of fuckup? I'm sorry." Theresa shook her head and raised an apologetic hand. "I'm sorry, I just feel like it's a nice story and I'm glad to have heard it but really, has a red string ever done something real for anyone?"

Hong looked up and something substantial, something vibrant crossed her face, like a flash of accidental brilliance.

"I have one more story," Hong said, leaning forward once again as a smile spread below her cheeks. She raised her hand, her open palm. "Just one more," she said, "and I will answer your question."

Hong

I can see from her face that she wants to be alone. Bohai's daughter sits in her pajamas. They are green and made of a shiny material that looks uncomfortable for sleeping. But she will listen because I am old and because I have asked her to listen. I will not waste her time. I will tell her the best story I know.

1900
GUANGDONG, CHINA

The journey was unthinkable.

They told me time and again that I would not make it. They said I would be taken, tortured, raped. That no one would take pity on a Boxer's daughter, on a Boxer's wife. And even if, by some miracle, a spirit soldier did appear, pulling me along from sun to moon, finding me a patch of earth to rest my body, I would surely starve—shrivel like a lemon peel under the August sun.

I traveled sixty days, Shen's voice in the hollows of my ears, in the pads of my feet, the tug of my red string pulling me onward. As if he knew he would die, he left me with a single name—that of his only brother—in the province of Guangdong, a place I had never been, their spoken word like a taunt, a jumble of sounds just beyond my reach. The night the liberation attacked, blasting through the wall with their heavy cannons, the sounds of men screaming like fireworks in flight, Shen demanded that I memorize his brother's name, made me promise that if anything went wrong, I would find his family in the south. And so I did. If not for my own salvation then for his; to deliver the news of his departure to his only relatives, so that his soul might eventually find peace.

Sixty days I walked, the landscape changing with every week. I kept my silence throughout, offering myself one indulgence, a single question when I felt it was time. *What day is today?* I would ask a stranger—always a woman, a mother with a child, a girl with a small load strapped to her back. I chose them carefully, searching for faces with bumps on their chins, a sign of kindness, a lucky omen. Tuesday, they would reply, or Thursday or Saturday, and I knew only then how much time had passed.

In the sixth week, the weather changed; it slowed me down. The hot temper of the south, the fire element—I began to feel the changes I was warned of. During the day it rained, and when it stopped, the dampness hung in the air and on my clothes, sour smells of mildew lifting from my flesh. The dry, flat land of the north was replaced with rice paddies that lined the roads, sinking deep into the earth, collecting the rain, bright green stalks reaching higher than my waist. At first it struck me as beautiful, the change of colors and smells of fresh shoots and foreign manure—but as night fell my mind changed. It was filthy sleeping on the soggy earth, my clammy body wishing for arid land, baked hard and dry during the summer months.

The women changed as well. They were darker and smaller, their eyes wider and larger than my own. When I summoned the courage to ask the day, my words were met with confusion, with strange liquid sounds, with silence. I listened to the language change, discerning what little I could, and the less familiar it all felt, the more I knew I was getting closer—that it was time to use the paper Shen had written for me, his brother's name, the numbers of his address in small, sturdy strokes. I began to show the paper, shyly at first, which was met with dismissal, then more boldly, the damp desperation seeping through my fingers as I held out the paper, pleading for help.

It was a man. An old, rumpled man with an eye that drooped lower than the other looked at the paper and back at me, his good eye narrowed. He held my gaze for a long time, chewing at his lips, his teeth mostly gone. Finally, he pointed to his right, down a wide road that led to a neighborhood of houses. He grunted, pushed me in that direction, and I think I ran, emboldened by his answer, the paper flapping in my hand, searching for the house that Shen had described, with three large brass bells that hung above the door frame.

When I first laid eyes on his brother's home, my knees as weak as loose hinges, my breath short and hot from overuse, I thought the old man must be mistaken. It was the grandest home I had ever seen, larger than anything I could have drawn on paper, more beautiful than my imagination. It rose two mighty floors, the rounded windows rimmed with gold, the fat shingles of the roof painted smooth and red, the bells exactly as Shen had described. I waited on the street for a second person to pass, this time a woman, who nodded her head as she read my paper. Indeed, I stood before the home of the shipping Leongs—the honorable Leong Fu from the north. The way the woman looked at me, I felt such shame. The way I smelled, the way I looked, the way I grunted my comprehension like a wild beast; suddenly, I saw myself in her eyes. At once, I was aware of where I was, overwhelmed by the vicinity of my task.

I remembered a wooden comb at the bottom of my rucksack. I crouched on the dirt road and nearly fell, dizzy from hunger and fatigue and heat. I held myself up with my right hand and reached my left into the bottom of my bag, feeling for the dull teeth of the comb. And despite my torn clothes and the smell of rust and pigs that clung to my skin, I combed my hair.

I walked to the front door, step by step, my stomach twisting. I could feel the lining tighten under my racing heart. My legs had carried me for sixty days, across a country torn by war and violence, yet these last ten steps were the most uncertain. I knocked on the wooden door, my knuckles growing white with each strike.

I heard footsteps, then the sound of the doorknob turning. I realized I had stopped breathing. The door opened and a young girl wearing servant's clothes stood in the large frame. The look on her face did not change with the sight of me.

"Hello," I said in strained Cantonese, flattening the sides of my trousers with my hands, reciting what little Shen had taught me. "My name is Hong. I like to speak with Leong Fu."

Now the look of the girl's face changed. Her eyebrows rose with surprise.

"Leong Fu?" she said, and then something else, her words dipping with a heavy, difficult vowel.

"Hong." I said my name again, pointing to myself. I began to forget my words; my head began to cloud. "Wife. Leong Shen. Brother Shen—" The girl stopped me by raising a hand into the air. She began to shut the door, bowing her head slightly, when I heard a different voice.

It was a question, followed by footsteps. A thin hand stopped the door from shutting and pulled it back open. Now a second woman stood in the doorway.

She was lovely. Her arms, long and graceful, bent like branches of cherry blossom. The slender bones in her neck and her collar stuck out beautifully. She wore a long lavender dress that fell from her square shoulders and she was so tall—as tall as me but different in every other way. Where my cheeks were padded and soft, cramping the shape of my narrow eyes, rounding my face, the woman before me had skin both even and tight, as if washed smooth by the southern rain, bathed in milk, scrubbed with pearls. The hue of her skin was darker than mine, like the color of damp sand, creating the look of shadows, of angles as it stretched across her wide forehead. A sign of prosperity.

For a moment, I forgot why I was there.

The woman said Shen's name. Her eyes were as wide as a child's.

"Yes," I said in my native Mandarin, but I didn't recognize my own voice. I stood there silently, looking into this woman's eyes, everything I had planned to say falling from my head and dropping to the ground. I felt empty.

"Who are you?" The woman asked cautiously, repeating it in Mandarin, the syllables slow and unnatural. "What is your name?"

"My name," I tried to remember, "is Hong." I spoke with painful difficulty; the woman nodded me gently along.

"I come from Shandong. I have traveled for days without water or rest to bring your family news of Shen." I paused and saw behind her a long, dark table. In the middle, there was a display of golden flowers. I took a forceful breath.

"Shen was my husband. We were married before the revolution." I held out my hand to show her the silver band on my finger. "Shen has been lost to war," I said, and the words came out exactly, like the words of a poem recited a thousand times. I had practiced them in my head since the beginning of my journey. I needed to be calm when the moment arrived.

The woman's face was softer now. Her hands had let go of the door. Now she pressed the tips of her fingers together.

"I am Lin," she said, "wife to Leong Fu. We waited news of Shen and here it arrives. Please." The sound of my language in her mouth, broken and difficult, made me wish desperately that she would speak Cantonese, that I could hear the voice that matched her face.

Using both hands, Lin pulled the wooden door wider. I stepped through the frame and suddenly it felt like a spring day. Within the house, the floors were cool and fresh. Clean air circulated through the wide hallways. Beyond the front door was the long, dark table, where, with gestures, she explained that we would meet once I was bathed and dressed. She turned to her girl servant and gave her quick instructions before turning down a corridor.

The girl led me down the opposite hallway and into a small bathroom lit by windows covered in thin white paper. She filled the bathtub with water that steamed and smelled like roses. She draped an earth-colored shirt and trousers over a wooden chair and the door clicked behind her.

I was so tired, so heavy from emotion and travel that I could barely understand where I was or how I had gotten there. I undressed quickly, eager to feel clean. I sank into the deep tub, the hot water collecting the filth from my body, swirling shades of brown and red around me. A square cake of soap sat on a stand beside the tub; I worked it into my flesh, digging the smooth edges of the bar into my back, my arms, my thighs. I held my breath and sank under the water. I closed my eyes and thought about never coming back up.

I thought about the cotton slippers the girl had left for me, and then the pair I had arrived with—the shoes I had left outside the front door. The right side had been tied to my foot with a piece of twine for the last two hundred miles. I had learned to walk with a limp, dragging my right foot along the country roads, kicking up the dust with my sole, afraid that the twine might break. No one stopped to help. Not a soul. In a way, they were right: no one took pity on a dirty Boxer's wife. But I was not taken, tortured, or raped. And for that, I was thankful. I came up for air.

I stood and let the water drip down my naked body. Pieces of my filth stuck to the sides of the tub. I would clean it later, I thought to myself. Lin was waiting. I dressed slowly. It was strange to have such soft material against my skin. I turned to leave but when I saw the dirty tub again, I couldn't help it; I had to wipe the inside. I used my old shirt, the one I wore closest to my body that was least soiled. I wet the cloth and removed the bits of dirt from the sides of the tub, dipping the shirt in the brown water, squeezing it out and wiping again. When the largest marks were gone, I hung the shirt on the edge of the tub. I opened the door and walked carefully down the hallway, the cotton slippers like walking on moon cakes, and toward the long, dark table.

When I got to the dining room, I almost fainted. Lin sat in one chair, drinking tea, a steaming bowl of soup to her left. To her right, at the head of the table, sat a man who was an exact copy of Shen. He was better dressed, his arms and cheeks padded with extra flesh, but in his face, in those thick eyelids, that strong jaw—all I could see was my dead husband. I bowed, trying to calm my nerves. I did not expect to see him there. Lin stood up and said it wasn't necessary. And please, I should have the bone marrow soup, it would help me regain my strength.

I sat and brought the hot soup to my lips, the gelatin fats rising to the top. It was the first taste of real food since Peking. I had been living off the scraps of pigs, breaking into their pens at night and eating their leftovers. It was mostly rotten cucumbers, raw sweet potatoes, wet piles of spoiled rice. The first two weeks, my body rejected the scraps and the bits of old food rose from my stomach the next morning. But soon enough my body adjusted. It became grateful for what I could give it.

The bowl touched my lips and didn't come down for a long time. The broth smelled of onions and tasted of beef; fatty, delicious marrow and bits of meat cooked for hours in its own juices. Ribbons of cabbage arrived at my lips. I slurped them like noodles and they melted in my mouth. Heat flooded my body and swam through my veins, first coating the lining of my stomach, then filling it, overflowing and running to my shoulders, my ankles, my fingertips. I ate greedily. My head cleared as I reached the bottom of the bowl. It wasn't until Mr. Leong began to speak that I finally brought the bowl down from my mouth.

He had Shen's voice.

"I understand that you are my brother's wife," he said in perfect Mandarin. "Lin has also told me that Shen is no longer with us." He paused and I put my bowl on the table. He looked down for a moment and then spoke again, his voice gentler now. "If you are willing, I would like to know everything. Anything you're able to share, Hong, I'd be grateful to hear."

I looked up at him, holding the last bit of soup in my mouth. I felt it coming back up with the thought of remembering, of trying to explain what had happened to Shen. My eyes remained on Mr. Leong's face, following the lines I knew so well. They were almost identical; the even cheeks, the heavy brow, the thin mouth. I imagined him as Shen; my beloved Shen. He had said my name and I almost believed it.

"Okay," I said. I swallowed my soup and wiped my mouth. "Okay." I pressed my fingers to my forehead, letting them rub into my skin for a moment. I imagined we were in heaven, Shen and I. He wore a shirt made of silk as we sat in our beautiful home, at our long, dark table, as I reminded him of the details of our love. I thought of him and I knew where to begin. I took a deep breath and brought my fingers down from my temples.

"Shen was my fated match," I began with a force that surprised me. I was ready to speak, to be heard after weeks of silence. "I am certain of this. He is the final resting place of my red string. I feel it with every nerve in my body, every beat of my heart; I will never find another man." I pushed my bowl to the side, the bones left on the bottom, determined to tell our story. "We were introduced two years ago, in the springtime, at a secret society meeting for the Fists of Righteous Harmony. My father was a leader."

Mr. Leong leaned back in his chair and folded his arms. I knew right away that he disapproved of the cause.

"We weren't troublemakers," I insisted. "My father was a farmer—a good man. My mother died in childbirth while delivering me, and we were all each other had."

He nodded. His face was kind.

"Three years ago, we were plagued with a terrible drought. Our land dried up. The crops stayed in the ground, and what little grew began to shrivel within days. We knew we'd lose everything if it continued—if the water refused to come. But then, as if our prayers were being answered, it began to rain. We were so happy; it was the rain that we thought would save us. Our land began to soften, sprouts began to appear."

There was a hope in Lin's face that made it difficult to continue. She held her breath, her eyes wide and expectant. Her expression strained as she listened, following my words; I wondered how much she understood. I paused, turning my gaze downward, looking instead to my own fingers.

"And then, like a curse, the rain would not stop. For three months we watched our crops flood and drown. My father sat in the fields, in the rainstorm, weeping for hours, his body as frail as I've ever seen it. We had no choice but to leave for the city and find food.

"And it was the right decision, because in Qufu, our luck changed. My father met a kind man named Wei who gave us a room in his home, who paid us in return for small jobs, and with time, he told us of his cause; to rid China of the evils of Western-ization, to stop the flow of opium, to end the spread of foreign religion—of Christianity."

I hated the words as I said them. They sounded so stupid after what I'd lost—everything did; the cause, the rituals, the training. But I didn't know at the time. At the time, it felt like salvation.

"Soon my father was practicing martial arts every day with Wei. His body grew powerful, his mind enlightened. It was the first time I'd ever seen him happy—truly happy. Together, they began holding secret meetings in the basement of Wei's home. Among the Boxers of Qufu, my father and Wei were well respected.

"And that's how I met Shen." I looked at Mr. Leong and blushed. He was listening carefully, his hands resting on the table.

"Shen had come to the spirit possession ceremony one evening. My father was leading it for the first time, with Wei. Shen was the youngest man there."

I was captivated by his presence. I was overcome by a feeling that is still difficult to describe. It was exactly how I had always imagined love would be, fiery and immediate; a magnetic heat that connected our two bodies from across a dim room, a sensation that could burn through continents and oceans until it found its other side.

But how could I explain that to Mr. Leong? I shook the heat from my thoughts and pushed forward.

"The men began their trance. They handed their bodies to the gods and began preparing themselves for the ceremony. I'd seen it a few times before: the jerking movements, the outburst of words with no meaning, the wandering eyes. I was allowed to watch, from a wooden stool in the corner, but not to speak. I served water and warmed liquor, which the men drank at the end."

"Liquor with men?" Lin spoke for the first time, her words harsh and sudden. She leaned forward in her seat.

"Oh no," I said apologetically, shaking my head. "I did not drink with them."

Mr. Leong interrupted me, turning to Lin to explain her misunderstanding.

"When we first married," he explained, looking back at me, "Lin was lectured in Mandarin but she never took to it. She preferred to learn English and she's quite good. But please, do continue. The spirit possession. I've heard of it before—I'm interested."

I looked to Lin and she smiled tenderly, a quiet understanding passing between us, allowing me to go on.

"It's a test of will and strength," I explained, repeating my father's words, not knowing how else to describe it. "To prepare the men for battle. To defend themselves against the use of deadly man-made weapons; guns, swords, fire, cannons. A powerful Boxer was said to be able to give his body to the spirits. And the spirit would inhabit his soul, providing protection against these things. The night Shen came, they were passing a scorching rod that had been heating in the basement furnace.

"The men stood in a line, as they normally did, shaking out their arms and legs and repeating the incantations, waiting for my father to hand them the hot steel rod. Shen was the fourth in line. I couldn't stop looking at him, watching the muscles in his arms and the strength in his jaw."

I had prayed at that moment. I prayed that he would be able to complete the task, that his hands were as strong as his mind. Because if he didn't, somehow I knew that I would feel it too. I was convinced that if Shen was burned, my hands would blister as well.

"When his turn came," I told them, "the first three men crying out but managing the rod, Shen took it silently. He stood still. He tightened his fists and the smell of burning flesh filled the basement. My father and Wei looked panicked. They wanted to remove the rod from his hands but they were unwilling to break his trance. Shen began to jerk forward, the rod pulling him around the basement, his arms leading his body in sharp, uneven movements. He cried out; a scream with no words, throwing his body against the wall next to my stool, the back of his shirt tearing as he slid against it, never letting go of the rod. By now, the other men had broken their trance. They ran from his path, afraid of the spirit that possessed him. My father and Wei ran to Shen and took his shoulders—pressed them against the wall. He began to shake, his arms still stretched out in front of him, holding the rod on both ends. Wei grabbed a broomstick and raised it above his head. He shouted an incantation and with all his strength, he struck the rod in the middle, trying to knock it from Shen's hands, but his hold was too tight. Wei tried again, bending for strength while my father held Shen's body. *Whap. Whap. Whap.* He hit the rod three more times before it fell to the floor. Shen's hands were red with blisters. He fell to his right side, his chest pounding, his hands still in fists."

I had climbed to the top of my stool, crouching on the small sur-face, afraid to get in Shen's way. I remember the smell of his burning hands. I remember telling my father and Wei that he should stay with us; wanting more than anything to see him again.

"Shen woke up in a panic the next day in Wei's sitting room, both hands bandaged like fighting gloves. My father and Wei sat above him, excited to question him about his vision. I hid on the other side of the wall. I had been there all morning, waiting and listening to their chatter. Whenever I could, I would peek through the doorway, trying to steal a look at him. When Shen finally opened his eyes, I was watching. He sat up suddenly and began to speak."

There were ribbons, he said, *thick crimson ribbons filling the air.*

"They weaved in and out of clouds. They touched the heavens. I needed one. They were the most beautiful things I have ever seen, each of them weightless, formless. I tried to grab one but my hand went right through it. I reached for another and it melted, its scarlet dye dripping down my wrists. I had to have it, so I chased them, snatching at ribbons as they froze, cracked, dissolved into thin air. And then I saw a girl—a girl I've never seen before, sitting beneath a lemon tree. She was barefoot. I called out to her for help but she didn't respond. She stood—reached out her hand to me—and from inside her sleeve came a red ribbon, tumbling to the ground, unraveling in my direction. She ran away. I ran after it, throwing my body on the ground and capturing its tail with both hands. It threw me into the air but I held on. It thrashed my body from side to side, slipping through my hands, sending a heat through my pulsing palms, challenging me to let go . . .

"At that moment, my legs had carried me into the sitting room, consumed by Shen's vision. I wanted to get closer. I wanted to see his face again. He looked up at me, in the middle of his sentence, and our eyes met and locked.

"'*It's you,*' he said, his bandaged hands pushing his body upright. '*You're the girl.*'

"My father turned, followed by Wei.

"'Hong?' my father said, standing. 'My daughter?'

"I started to walk backward, alarmed, afraid that my father would be angry. But Shen spoke first. He fell off his bed and onto his knees.

"'Master. Shaman. Fellow Boxer,' he addressed my father, his head bowed almost to the ground. 'It's fate. I can't explain it. Your daughter is the girl beneath the lemon tree—the barefoot girl. I ask you as a man who has seen beyond himself, please. Let me marry your daughter.'

40

"We were married the next week. My father was very fond of Shen and he trusted his vision. Sometimes I think that I willed him to see me under that lemon tree. That I felt for him so much that first night, I must have slipped into his mind."

It was quiet for a moment after that. Lin fell deep into her seat, her lips pressed inward, her eyes staring at the golden flowers in the middle of the table. She had understood enough.

"Shen believed in the revolution," I began again, feeling warmed from his vision, sensing him close to me after reciting his words. "He truly believed. He taught me about politics and read to me from books. He wanted a different kind of China; one where a family wouldn't starve during a drought or be forced from their home in a flood. He explained that the government was on our side, how the Empress Dowager had announced her favor for the Boxers. No more Westerners in positions of power. The end of foreigners deciding how we should live, threatening our culture. With the support of our government, we weren't just a clan of peasants in a basement. Everything changed. We were legitimate. We were fighting for the national cause. And at the time, it was the most exciting thing I had ever experienced.

"After we won the first two battles at Langfang and Beicang, Shen thought we could do anything. He and my father thought we were ready for Peking, to invade the walls of the Forbidden City and overtake the foreign legations. And I was so in love, I believed him. I cheered them on.

"The Empress knew our plan—she was within Peking and she promised to protect us. She believed in our cause, and I believed in Shen. He had grown so close to my father and Wei, the four of us had become a kind of family. Preparing for Peking felt like planning a trip; it brought me such joy." I looked to Lin and spoke slowly, pleading to her womanhood, trying to make her understand my foolishness, if even just a small piece.

"I was never interested in the martial arts or the fighting. Let the

41

men fight—I would mend their wounds, wash their clothes, tend to the children. I liked being a part of it. I wanted to be a Boxer more than anything. I wanted to belong to the cause.

"The day we invaded the city, I was told we were twenty thousand strong. We marched together in a mass, wearing red turbans and sashes, beating on gongs and blowing horns as loud as thunder.

"The noise—it was deafening. It sounded like a stampede of animals instead of people. The men pulled their swords from their sashes and waved them in the air, calling out from the bottom of their throats. As we drew closer to Peking, their calls became even louder. They were shrill and maddening, competing with the sounds of our instruments. Then the women around me began to stamp their feet and I felt the earth vibrate and I no longer needed to move my legs. The mob carried me, pushing me forward with their bodies. We were moving as one, exactly as Shen had said China should be, and I remember how powerful it all felt. There were so many of us. Shen and I smiled; he held my hand as we were carried along. It felt like we were floating.

"And then I heard gunshots. From above the great wall guns began to fire. I saw one of our men fall and get crushed by the crowd. I remember the horror I felt—the way my heart stopped at my first sight of death. I wanted to turn back but it was too late. I looked behind me and saw a million people, a sea of red flags and turbans, but now they looked angry. Shen hooked his arm around my waist and pulled me along. 'Don't worry,' he said, 'I promise to keep you safe.' And so we continued.

"That first night went as planned. We made it into the Imperial City and surrounded the foreign embassies. We had taken over the inner wall. Shen and I were in the middle of the crowd, so we got through easily—I saw no more death that night. We had a party in the evening around an enormous fire. We stole the foreign flags from around the square and burned them.

"It all seemed so harmless—I believed it was for the national cause! But three days after we invaded, a group of our men set fire to the British Embassy, and then the Hanlin Academy, and soon after we were exploding the French Legation and taking innocent prisoners."

Nightmares of the violence had followed me throughout my journey south. Images of foreign wives screaming in languages I'd never heard before, being pulled into the buildings we had taken over.

"It was so much worse, so much bloodier than either of us had imagined. My father and Wei had separated from us. They were called upon as advisors for the occupation. By the second week, I had no idea where they were. Every day I watched someone die. And it wasn't just men. I walked past young children—daughters— among the remains of buildings exploded by cannon fire. Every day, it destroyed me. I had to get out, and Shen agreed. But there were no safe exits. We had to be smuggled from the city, and for that, we had to wait in line."

Even then, I remember that I thought we'd survive. That night, the night we decided we had to escape, Shen removed the turban from his head and ripped it into long strips, taking a piece of red fabric and winding it around my wrist, knotting it twice.

"I remember," he had told me, tying a second red band around his own wrist and taking my hand, pressing his palm into mine. "I remember the day we met. I remember my vision. I won't let you die."

I looked down. The fabric was filthy and smelled of damp places and endless dirt roads. But I knew I'd never take it off—that Shen's fingers had tied those knots to last forever and it was now my job to make sure they did.

"The eight weeks that we spent within Peking were hell. I felt like a monster. Shen and I would climb a cypress tree against the north wall and hide for days, bringing our rations with us, saving our eyes from the horrors below. We imagined that we were somewhere else. We talked about my father and Wei as if we knew they were alive. We said they were having tea with the Empress. They were planning a way to save us. We would tell each other stories—stupid, made-up stories that went nowhere and had no ending. We decided on our children's names—three boys and a girl.

"It may sound strange," I said to Mr. Leong, "but in that tree, over the sounds of gunfire and screaming, I fell even more deeply in love with you—r brother."

I brought a hand to my mouth as soon as I said it. I'd been looking so intently at Mr. Leong, imagining Shen, that I'd forgotten who I was talking to. But Mr. Leong just chuckled.

"We look alike," he said. "Ever since we were boys."

"I'm sorry," I said, my cheeks growing hot. Mr. Leong put a hand in the air.

"Please," he said. He was still smiling. "It's a compliment. Shen was always more handsome."

I had no idea how long I'd been talking, but the first pot of tea was empty and the sun was about to set. The servant that had made my bath came from the kitchen with a full kettle and a plate of small cakes. I was grateful for any offering of food, and I had not eaten cake since my wedding. I stopped speaking when she entered, but Mr. Leong wanted me to continue.

"The tree," he said, "the cypress."

I nodded, remembering my place, feeling as if I were remembering a fable and not the story of his brother's death. My husband's death. I nodded once more, precisely, as if it were an order.

"One night, when we were hidden within the branches of the cypress, we heard a cannon blow through the outer wall. We heard the screams that followed. We thought it might be the liberation.

"It was in that tree that I memorized your name," I told him. "I learned where you lived. Shen made me repeat it over and over again. Our plan was to find you together, but if something went wrong, he demanded that I go alone."

I paused after that and closed my eyes. I said a quiet prayer. I knew Shen would be happy I was there. He would be so relieved that I had made it.

"By the afternoon," I continued, "we had both fallen asleep. We had learned to secure ourselves within the cypress. We locked our legs around the thick branches and slept sitting up. We woke to a gunshot in the tree. A mass of branches fell to the ground and someone shouted in English, *Who's up there? Surrender immediately or we'll fire again!*"

I heard the soldier's voice echo in my head, the foreign words that marked the end of Shen's life screaming in my ears. That voice is burned into my memory.

"Shen's sword had slipped from his sash and fallen from the tree. We had given away our hiding spot."

I stopped, unwilling to finish. It was the first time I had talked about it. The first time I had been forced to find the words to describe what had happened to Shen and it all seemed so meaningless. I felt so much more than I was able to describe, and the words I had chosen sounded empty in my ears, not worthy of Shen's life; barren, hollow sounds that told half of a story, a fraction of the heartbreak.

Lin leaned forward in her seat. She held her hands together in front of her mouth, waiting for me to continue. What could I tell her? That I was done? That I couldn't go on? I shook my head and willed myself to finish. This story, this ending was the purpose of my journey.

"Shen was frantic. He knew they would fire again. They would fire until they killed us both. I clung desperately to my branch. He grabbed my shoulders and made me face him. 'What is the name of my brother?' he demanded, but I didn't want to answer. I shook my head and began to cry. He repeated it, his fingers digging into my skin. Finally, I said it. He kissed my forehead and he jumped from behind the branches. 'No fire!' he yelled in his best English. But they didn't understand him. They thought he was a sniper. He was dead before he hit the ground."

There were tears in my eyes, gathering along the edges, ready to spill over. Hate was not nearly strong enough to describe what I felt for that soldier; his voice, his gun, his haste. Nor was it strong enough to describe my feelings about war and everything it stood for. All of it had been a terrible, worthless mistake.

"I opened my mouth to scream but nothing came out. I know it was Shen keeping me quiet. He was keeping me safe. I clung to that branch with all of my strength and my body began to tremble. Tears fell down my cheeks and caught in the leaves, and the leaves of the cypress trembled with me. I held on tighter, begging my limbs to be still, pleading with my eyes to look away from Shen's body. But he was right there, right below me, and I couldn't look away. I stared into his lifeless eyes for hours, whispering to him from my branch. And when the sun went down, hidden by the night I screamed as loud as I could."

The table was silent for a long time after that. I could hear the cook washing dishes in the kitchen. The servant came out with candlesticks. She lit them. She left.

"Shen was a good man," Mr. Leong said eventually. "I could have done more."

Lin touched her husband's hand.

After the foreign liberation arrived, men from eight different nations came pouring into the Legation Quarter, trying to rescue their fallen embassies. Somehow, with their arrival the city became even more disgusting, even more violent and savage than it had been in the eight weeks before.

Peking, the city known for silks and precious stones, porcelain and gold, became a thief's paradise—a hellish place for godless men. And without any policemen, everyone became a thief. The British tore apart the homes of rich Chinese families and stole everything of value, selling it at auction in front of their ruined embassy. Russian soldiers walked through the streets with wheelbarrows filled with furs and porcelain vases. I saw an American diplomat, dressed in a suit, running with a dirty rice sack filled with gold and jewels clinking together. And it wasn't just the foreigners. Our people stole too, and because we knew the city so well, we were perhaps the best at it. But there were such shortages of everything—food, clean water, clothing—that it seemed the only option was to steal and to trade for survival.

I told the Leongs how I escaped the city through the drainage canal under the wall. It was easier to get out then. All the soldiers were busy raiding. I spent a day looking for my father and Wei, but it was hopeless. Peking was an impossible, dirty tangle of confusion and crime. I had to save myself. Even the Empress had been smuggled from the city the week before; even she had left us.

I told them of my sixty days' walk. Of the hundreds of people who passed by without a single offer of help. But I survived, and I knew Shen had been watching over me.

The sun had set hours ago. The tea had been refilled three times. I was exhausted, but there was one last thing I had to do.

"I am a hard worker," I said, my eyes turned down to the table. I felt suddenly shy. "I learn quickly and I do not complain. Please." I looked up to Mr. Leong. "I see that you have little help and I know your family is only growing. I could be of service to you and Lin and the others. I have no place to go. I ask not for charity, but for a position in your house. I promise I will not be a burden."

"We would be honored if you would stay," Mr. Leong replied, his words coming swiftly. "Lin and I are the only two here. Children will come, but for now it's just us."

Lin smiled softly, her damp eyes catching the light of the candle. Without looking at her husband, she turned to me, putting her hands on mine, her fingers touching the red band around my wrist. "Please," she said. "Please stay."

CHAPTER 3

November 1964
HONOLULU, HAWAII

It's nearly ten in the morning. The sun sits below the trees but it's rising, as it does each morning, through the two-story windows of the great house. It softens the leather of the furniture; it reflects on the glass tables. Today, light fills the house in blinding abundance. As the sun gathers strength, growing in height, it must contend with a chorus of lightbulbs, scattered and lit throughout the great room. Today, there is a brilliant glow from within the windows, so that the house appears to illuminate the day.

At the head of the great room, there is a polished mahogany table. Atop the table lies a casket made of koa, and within that casket lies the dead man. For now, the casket is closed, but Amy knows that soon enough she will see her husband. The liquids in his body will not be his. The color of his skin will be somehow wrong. His eyes will be closed; he will not see her. Amy tells herself these things as she enters the room.

An aisle has been created, down the center of the rows of identical chairs, as if today were a wedding and not a funeral. At the mouth of the aisle, Amy pauses, and although the chairs sit empty, she decides to walk around them.

"Come this way," she says to her daughter, guiding her around the back. Then Amy waves to a man who sits to the right of the coffin. It's a strange wave. Her open palm rises to her head and immediately drops, as if she thought she knew the answer but suddenly forgot.

Theresa follows behind her mother, but her eyes trace the walls of the great room. The framed photographs of the family, almost life-size in their proportions, still hang on each of the four walls—but today they are wrapped, like oversized presents, in thick white paper that creases sharply at the corners. The photos on the wall, the faces framed within them, the memories they hold are not welcome today. They complicate the feeling of mourning; they chatter too loudly for a funeral.

Theresa stares at the largest photograph, the one hanging above her father's casket, and she narrows her eyes, searching her mind for some kind of hint. She sees her Ye Ye in black and white; it comes to her suddenly. Behind that paper, he sits reading the newspaper at his dining room table. His fingers wrap around a cup of coffee. Amy's father took this photograph; for the first time, Theresa makes this connection. As her thoughts flee her, latching on to something small, she closes her eyes. She tries to make her mind as blank as the paper. She will not be defeated so early, she tells herself, and turns her mind to something else.

Scrolls, Theresa finds, some of them fifteen feet long, occupy the remaining wall space. Thick, black lettering, their strokes made with a full sweep of an arm, adorn the narrow, colorless paper. The sheer whiteness of the room, the dozens of lit bulbs, makes it difficult for Theresa to concentrate. She wonders if that's the point—if perhaps these spotlights are a kind of human bleach, cleansing the body, purging it of anything dark or stained or hidden. Theresa reaches out a finger and traces the outline of a character. Without thinking, she picks one with a line that rises and plateaus, falls and crosses back again with a flick of its tail. She watches the light shift on the surface of her fingernail.

"Kaipo," Amy says, as the man beside the casket stands. He leans over to kiss Amy on the cheek. He places a hand on her shoulder and squeezes tightly, wrinkling the material beneath his palm.

"You look great," the man says.

"I look terrible. But thank you."

"The priests are here. Both of them. And so is my mom. Theresa," he says, extending a stiff arm, patting her strangely on the shoulder. "You're getting big."

"Yeah," Theresa says.

"Is your, um, fiancé coming?" he asks, looking more at Amy than Theresa.

"Theresa did invite him," Amy tells him, "as a kind of truce."

"I'm not holding my breath," Theresa replies, shifting her attention away from them. She holds her eyes on the corner of the room; she picks a focal point and tries to breathe. She tries to let it go. The way her uncle looks at her, the way he greeted her with an outstretched arm, as if afraid to touch the wreckage, it's worse than Theresa imagined. Her Uncle Kaipo has always brought out a strangeness in Theresa, a physical insecurity. Handsome and magnetic, Kaipo was in the middle of his second divorce, both of his wives Narcissus Pageant Queens, wiry and perfect, their easy poise unfathomable to Theresa, disconcerting. Now, Theresa wishes that she could disappear. In her current state, she feels older than her uncle, uglier, messier: all of it amplified within the great room.

"How is she?" Amy asks the man. Her voice is low, heavy with air.

"Oh"—he pauses—"she's all right. I picked her up this morning— tried to convince her not to come. At first I tried to pretend it was just another day, you know, see if she might have forgotten. But she was waiting for me, dressed and everything. I couldn't talk her out of it."

"Do you think Hong's upset?"

"I talked to her. I think she understands. Of course, she doesn't want Mom to see Bohai like this, but I think she understands."

"Where is she?"

Kaipo sighs. His hand reaches to his hair, still thick and black, and combs through it. The jacket of his suit rises with his arm.

"Honestly, I don't know. She's been everywhere. She's been walking the house since this morning, just room to room, touching things, sitting down to rest. She's not talking, though. At least not to me.

"Listen," Kaipo says, his eyes shifting between the two women. "If you wouldn't mind, would you take a look at what she's wearing and tell me if it's all right? There're going to be pictures and I want her to look, you know, healthy. I don't want any extra shit from the papers. Press hasn't seen her in twenty years and I know they're desperate for an angle."

"God," Amy says, touching her temple with three fingers. "I didn't even think of that. I should have asked. I should have had something made for her. I can't believe I didn't think of it—"

"Amy," Kaipo interrupts. "It's not your fault." His closed lips form a half smile. His eyes are entirely still.

"Right," Amy says, nodding. "Okay, so I'll see you in a while, then. Don't worry. We'll take care of it."

"I appreciate it," Kaipo says, nodding as he leaves.

"He's such an asshole," Theresa breathes as they move from the casket.

"He's not an *asshole*, Theresa. He's old-fashioned. It upsets him to see you like this."

"*Old-fashioned?*" Theresa repeats. "Two divorces in six years is considered old-fashioned now? It's like he thinks it killed Maku. Like Maku died because I got pregnant."

"Stop it," Amy orders. "Please." She pauses. "Just let me think for a minute."

Amy's first thought is of Bohai's old room upstairs. She imagines his mother standing by his window, her fingers resting quietly on the sill.

"What do you think?" Amy asks her daughter, hesitating at the bottom of the stairs.

"I guess." Theresa shrugs. "Seems like a good enough place to start."

They climb the wide wooden staircase that curves to the second floor. Theresa uses the banister for support, drawing herself slowly from stair to stair. They take a left at the top and continue down a long hallway, past half a dozen identical doors, all of them shut.

For Theresa, her father's childhood room could lie behind any one of these doors. She'd have to open each of them and look inside to know for sure. But Amy knows this corridor and its many rooms, unchanged since before she was married, and she takes brisk steps to the end of the hall, to the second-to-last door on the left.

She knocks.

"Mrs. Leong?" Amy calls gently through the door. "Are you in there?"

When no one answers, Amy twists the knob. Slowly, she opens the door.

Inside the room, the air is stale and static—perfectly so, as if it's being used for preservation. The double bed, made up neatly, looks like it hasn't been slept in for years. The sheets are starchy and the creases of the pillowcases look permanent, like they'll never wash out, no matter how long they soak or how much they're ironed. The bed is flanked by two colossal bookshelves without a vacant space between them, the colorful spines of hardbacks crammed together in organized rows. This, Theresa thinks, is how she knows that the room was once her father's.

There is no one in the room, but Amy notices an indentation at the foot of the bed—a circular shape where the blue quilt dips slightly into the mattress.

"I think she was here," Theresa says, reading her mother's thoughts as she touches the hollow with two fingers. "Or someone was."

Amy can feel particles begin to rise from the carpet as their bodies stir the air. Already, they are disrupting the space, depositing bits of themselves in the silence. Their skin, their scent, their breath—they're leaving so much behind. They're displacing what little remains of her husband. Amy's lungs go still; her body tenses, drawing her skin closer to her, willing it to stay her own. She turns slowly, careful not to exhale, and leaves the room. Theresa follows and Amy closes the door behind them, pulling on the knob to tighten the seal. She breathes.

"Has it changed at all?" Theresa asks as they stand in the hallway. "I mean, since you and Maku lived there. Did it look like that?"

"I—" Amy pauses, her hand still clutching the knob. "It's exactly as I remember, actually."

"It's so weird, imagining you guys here." Theresa touches the doorframe and fits her fingers into its vertical grooves.

"It was very brief. We weren't here more than a month before we moved to Hawaii Kai."

"I know," Theresa says.

Amy nods, once. Her lips press firmly together.

"Come on," she says. "We should check the other rooms."

They follow the hall back to the staircase, knocking on each closed door along the way and peeking in when no one answers. As Amy suspected, each of the rooms is empty.

At the top of the stairs, they make the decision to descend, to look for her in the kitchen and the sunroom and out back by the waterfall. But when they reach the bottom, Amy hesitates. She looks in the opposite direction, down a hallway lined with dark wooden panels.

"It wouldn't make sense," Amy tells her daughter. "After your Ye Ye died, Kaipo told me she never goes down there, but I don't know. I feel like it's worth a look."

Theresa nods. Together they walk to the end of the corridor where the passage splits in two. To the left there is an open archway; to the right are double doors. Amy reaches for the knob and finds that it's locked.

"It's Kaipo's now," she says absently, standing before the double doors. "She can't be in there. She doesn't have a key."

"Mom," Theresa whispers. She's turned in the opposite direction but her arm extends behind her, grasping at her mother. "Mom," she says again.

Amy turns, and through the archway she sees her.

In the study, all the lights are switched on. The lamp on the desk, the chandelier above it, the sconces that line the paneled cherry-wood walls—they all seem to be pointing at what's taking place on the floor.

There's a trail of white paper that leads from a row of shelves behind the desk to where Mrs. Leong sits on the floor with her knees pressed to her chest. The bits of paper are various sizes, some as large as a full crumpled sheet, others like paper rubble, like mismatched confetti. Along the path, framed photographs lie scattered in the chaos. On the shelf, a mostly unwrapped frame lies facedown. On the desk there's another picture, fully exposed. As Amy moves closer, she sees more and more of the silver frames, unwrapped and strewn about on almost every surface.

In the middle of the brightly lit mess, Mrs. Leong sits with a photograph held close to her face. She clasps it with both hands. She stares at it with a blank intensity.

"Mrs. Leong," Amy says softly, knocking on the open door. She's ten feet away but the woman does not look up.

"Mrs. Leong," Amy says again. She's close enough now to reach down and touch her. "It's Amy," she says.

"Can she hear us?" Theresa whispers behind her mother.

Amy shushes her. She lowers herself to the ground, placing both palms on the floor to steady herself.

"Mrs. Leong, I've come to get you. I've come to bring you to the funeral. Would you still like to come?"

Mrs. Leong's fingers tighten around the picture frame. Amy watches the tips of her fingers grow white and softly begin to tremble. Still she does not look at Amy.

"What do you have there? Can I see? Is it all right if I take a look?"

Amy removes her shoes and sits on the ground. A bit of paper clings to her ankle. Amy shifts her weight toward the woman and takes in her face. It summons a memory, both faraway and entirely vivid, of the last time they were together like this. She leans in closer to see the photograph the woman holds in her hands and is met by a picture of her husband, taken on the afternoon of their first meeting.

Bohai is reading in a wooden chair, perfectly upright. He's completely immersed in the pages; his cheeks are flushed, his mouth faintly agape.

"Have a look," the woman says suddenly, extending the picture to Amy. She presses the frame into Amy's chest and clears her throat. "Here," she says. "Have a look at my son."

Lin

1914
GUANGDONG, CHINA

Frank's resolve to move our family to an island I could barely pronounce came without warning at the end of 1914, and my immediate reaction was panic. He had arrived home from a six-week business trip to the north when he called me into his library. On the map we had received as a wedding gift, a small group of islands was circled. Slowly, Frank traced his finger along the route that we would take across the Pacific Ocean.

I wanted to react. I wanted to tell Frank that leaving China was completely out of the question. But I couldn't find the strength. Each time I formed a sentence in my mind, readied it on my tongue, a tightness grew in my chest and expanded into my mouth, blocking the words from their exit. Recently, it had been this way. Bohai had just turned five, and it seemed his silence had begun to invade my body as well. I couldn't change my son—I had tried in every possible way and failed in even more—so perhaps it was not Bohai who needed changing. It was a thought that never left me. Perhaps it was I who was incompetent, a woman incapable of mothering. As days passed and my son remained unchanged, I felt my failure swell and multiply. There was a voice, one I had silenced for many years, that now whispered to me at all times of the day. You are unworthy of this life, it said. It was all a mistake.

We no longer spoke of Bohai, Frank and me. We spoke of very few things. Frank had begun to travel again and was gone most days of the month, far away from the silent house that reeked of our disappointment. When he returned, sometimes I wouldn't know for two or three days. He would sleep in his library and leave early the next morning. Sometimes a suitcase on the floor or a teacup in the basin would be the only sign of my husband's homecoming. Hong would find the suitcase and tuck it into a closet; she would wash the cup in the basin and say nothing. She was the only person in the world who understood the fragility of my mind and the peculiarity of our situation. She knew how easily I could drown in that teacup, how simple it would be to suffocate in that suitcase.

But that night, Frank had woken me. He had taken my hand and I had blushed in the dark of the corridor as he led me to his office, where he told me of Oahu and his plan to move our family there.

"Years ago, I took a shipment there and I always said I would return. There's an ancient volcano unlike anything I've ever seen before, Diamond Head they call it. It's magnificent. An old home to the Hawaiian gods, and soon it will be our home as well."

I remember looking at the map and hearing his words, my thoughts still hanging in the dark corridor, when I thought our encounter would be different, when I confused the urgency in his eyes with desire. When Frank spoke the words *move immediately*, I realized what was happening, and the heat coursing through my body became thick and slow. My legs lowered into a chair and the only thought that remained in my defeated mind was how foolish I had turned out to be.

"It wasn't a simple decision," Frank said, sitting himself. "But with time, you'll come to understand why."

"Can't I know now?" I asked softly, using my voice for the first time. I felt completely powerless, pathetic. So much of my life hinged on the decisions of this man, and I could barely find the strength to speak, to ask him why. *Virtuous*, I heard my father's voice in my head, reciting his favorite proverb, *is a woman without knowledge*.

"It's complicated," Frank replied, his eyes shifting to the map.

"Okay," I whispered. "But just tell me," I said, my words pushing through the narrow passage, unable to stop. "Am I being punished?"

I closed my mouth and immediately regretted my bravery. I

couldn't look at him. I felt the presence of his body across from mine as I sat in silence and shame, imagining him growing angry at my question, pictured a hand rising above my head, a slap across my face as my father would do to my mother. Moving to Hawaii was not a punishment. A swollen eye and a fractured arm and no doctor in the village was a punishment. A mother who continued to wash dishes and laundry, who served meals while her arm grew swollen and disfigured, was a punishment, but not this.

We sat there, the single candle lighting our stillness, and I waited for my husband to become my father. But he did not.

"Do you remember the year we were married?" he said, his voice gentler than I had expected. It surprised me. I nodded, my body still rigid, but I did not look up.

"That same year," Frank continued, "just before Shen passed, two German missionaries were killed in the north. In Shandong." He paused and I watched his right hand reach to his desk, to smooth the corner of his map. "Their deaths, they were violent and the Germans were angry. They demanded that the Chinese government provide them with reparations for their loss."

I didn't understand. Why was he telling me this? What did any of it have to do with Hawaii? I remember looking at the map and finding Germany, seeing that it was nowhere near the islands Frank had circled. Be still, I told myself, and listen.

"The reparations came in the form of land," Frank continued. "Kiochow in Shandong was given to the Germans on a ninety-nine-year lease. And with that land, they built an enormous ship port. The port of Tsingtao."

Frank paused at this moment, and slowly I raised my eyes from the ground. He was staring at the map, his thick eyebrows pushed together in difficult contemplation.

"Lin," he said, his shadowed eyes meeting mine, "we are friends of the Germans, and they have been very generous to us. Our business, our money, it comes in and out of three ports." He raised three fingers, his knuckles facing me, swollen and worn. "There is the German port at Tsingtao; there is the port here in Guangzhou, and there is one other." His index finger cast a long shadow across the map, trembling softly in the dim light.

"When the Germans received Tsingtao, the British leased their own port in Shandong—nearby, on the north side of the peninsula. The Germans were building a naval base, gathering manpower, bringing in soldiers from their country, and the British didn't like this, so they built their own port. For months there has been rumor of war, Lin, of a German invasion, and the British, with their Japanese allies, wanted to make sure they were prepared."

Frank nodded his head, once, his stare ripping through me.

"Some men, they choose to align themselves with one country; they choose to pick sides. I have never understood alliances. There are too many variables to consider, too many trivial issues. So I choose to make friends with whom I wish. The British and Japanese treated me just as well as the Germans, so why should their distaste for each other mean anything to me? To my business?"

Frank held my gaze. His eyes were exhausted, delicate red webs extending from his pupils to the outer edges, but they were determined. He wanted me to understand. He wanted me to know that Oahu was not a punishment. Without a single blink, he continued, and I felt a surge of the old confidence I once shared with my husband.

"Last week, something happened. There was a surprise attack. The Japanese and British invaded the German port and they seized Tsingtao. I had no idea. I was already at sea and the news couldn't reach me." He was gathering intensity, his voice growing more powerful, rawer with each word. He paused now, allowing himself to breathe.

"I took my shipment as I normally would, north first to Tsingtao, then to Weihaiwei—to the British—but when I got to Tsingtao the British were there. The Japanese were there. And when they saw me, when they saw my ships, they were angry, Lin. They made threats. To me, to our family."

I was clutching the hem of my nightshirt, my fingers cold and rigid, pearls of sweat gathering along the back of my neck. I never knew what my husband did, exactly. I knew there were ships involved, dozens of them, and he would transport things from country to country. But my understanding of money, of business, was shallow at best. At my parents' restaurant, where I worked as a girl, the exchange was simple. A plate of food for a yuan. A pat of rice, a piece of fish—I understood this to be business. What my husband did, how he traveled and bartered and came home exhausted, all remained a mystery. There was no cooking, no creating, no producing of goods to be sold. Instead, Frank had a briefcase. He had paperwork. A few times, early in our marriage, I thought about asking, but how would I phrase it? How would I ask without revealing my position, that I hadn't the slightest notion of how these collections of paper made him rich? And then, when I lost my babies, my girls, I stopped thinking of it entirely. Who was I to be asking of money when I could not produce the single thing we lacked?

"Lin," Frank said. "I fear we are entering a war. I fear for our safety and I know that if we wait much longer to make our move, we will run out of options."

I looked at my husband and, for the first time in our marriage, I saw a nervousness that made me uneasy. Suddenly, I understood that this had nothing to do with me or Bohai or a marriage that could not produce sons. This was a force greater than my daily anxieties. And as my husband took my hand in his, blew out the candle, and led me back to our bedroom, I knew that I would follow him to that group of islands, to his ancient volcano, secure in the secret we now shared, the information he had entrusted in me. That night, I believed that the red string was guiding our fate.

The next morning, I went immediately to see Hong. Slowly, I led her into the idea, showing her the photographs of Oahu that Frank had left for me.

"I won't go without you," I insisted as she studied the photographs, her flat lips shut in careful thought. "Do you see the water? So clean you can see to the bottom! Imagine a life there—so close to the ocean."

"It's a photograph," she said finally, handing it back to me. "It's a beautiful photograph."

I couldn't believe that was all she said. Since the rebellion, Hong no longer believed in China. She spoke poorly of our country, calling it a leech that preyed on its children, a nation of slaves. To my surprise, she showed an interest in English, the Western tongue she once considered evil. She attended lessons with me and my tutor, learning the language with a vengeful determination. She never said it, but I knew she saw English as the link between Shen's life and his death. Had one of them spoken English, just enough to yell through those branches, enough to slow the soldier's gun, Shen might still be alive.

So with a gentle approach, I expected she would be willing to leave; I thought she might even be pleased. What I did not consider, however, was Shen. China was where Shen's body lay. To leave China meant abandoning the spirit of those who had passed, and as much as Hong felt China had wronged her, she would not agree to that. She would not leave her homeland for a house near the ocean. She would not trade her loyalty to Shen for a row of pretty sugarcane.

A life without Hong was a half-life. I'd imagined it on many occasions, and each time a bitter taste filled my mouth. Since the day Hong arrived at my husband's door, I felt that she had been sent to me, and I to her, to ease each other's journey into the unknown. When I lost my daughters, Hong was there, quieting my madness, assuring me that fate had intervened, that it had nothing to do with my own deficiency. She would not allow me to use the word *barren*, would not let me neglect my appearance, reminding me that without desire, without intimacy, there was no possibility of sons. While I poured my soul into Bohai, Hong ran my household with a deft hand,

and when Hailee died, it was Hong's composure that allowed me rest. She was more of a mother than I was able to be, loving Bohai easily, without the constant need for validation, without the complications that plagued my mothering, that colored everything just a little black.

I needed her; we all did. In my mind, there was no possibility of leaving Hong behind. So I forced her hand. I told her the one thing that frightened her more than anything else in the world. War was coming, I said. I told her war was coming and we were all in danger.

"Is this true?" Hong asked, her square face revealing only a portion of what I knew she felt.

"Frank says it is." It wasn't a lie, I told myself.

"I need time," Hong said, her thoughts far away. "And I'm late for the vegetables."

Hong walked away from me and continued her usual routine, shopping for the evening's meal, stripping the linens, watering the houseplants. But that afternoon, without a word, she closed herself into the prayer room at the end of the hall. From the corridor, I could smell her lighting incense and burning long, thin joss sticks for her loved ones. For Shen, for her mother. Through the door I could hear her praying, repeating words of sorrow and forgiveness. Hong remained there through the evening, cutting paper into houses and clothing and jewelry, bringing a match to the figures and sending them to the afterlife. After dinner, I knocked on the door and joined her. I kneeled with her in the sandalwood smoke and held her hand. I brought her a roast duck and a pyramid of sweet cakes to lay on the altar. At midnight, I left her alone to pray and I knew that she had made peace with her family. I knew that Hong had decided to come with us.

We left for Oahu six days later, aboard one of Frank's enormous freighters, all of our belongings piled on top of one another. There was no time for order or method. Items were placed in whatever container could hold them and transported immediately to the ship. We sailed for eighteen days across the Pacific Ocean, Frank's fleet of ships following behind us, along the same route that my husband had traced with his finger the week before.

We reached the shoreline in the early morning, when just half the sun sat on the horizon. The light was soft and reassuring, as if it had been waiting for us to arrive before extending its mighty beams across the ocean. A gentle glow spread along the water's surface, popping in cobalt and deep shades of silver, glinting like the facets of a sapphire. But more than the light, it was the skyline that captured my breath. Looming above the island was a mammoth silhouette, dark and magnificent, that rose in a circle around a crater. Its base sprawled in every direction, delicate ridges filled in with light, extending into the ocean, peaking in unequal heights like the crests of a crown, sparkling, studded with jewels.

From behind me, the sound of Frank's voice, the touch of his hand on the small of my back.

"It really looks like diamonds, doesn't it? The British, when they stumbled upon this crater they thought they'd struck it rich. Even when they realized their mistake, they still named it Diamond Head because of the headlands. It's magnificent, isn't it? The way it juts into the sea?"

Frank's arm extended across the volcano's silhouette, his eyes squinting in the low sunlight. His voice was hot on my neck, warming his words with an intimacy, an energy that felt brand new. How long had it been since my husband spoke to me this way? Early in our marriage, I remembered the enormity of his patience, his gentle focus, his ability to stir desire within me with the most ordinary words, from a single touch. His breath, just warmer than the breeze, just damper than the mist, reached across my skin, suddenly alight.

Clouds, thick and milky, the density of smoke, took flight above the volcano. They spread in the shape of a V, giving way to the apricot sun, blazing, dreamlike.

"There are few things in life as beautiful as a fresh start," Frank whispered, wrapping his arm around my waist and pulling me into his chest, sheltering me from the wind off the ocean, pressing me into his eager heartbeat. "This will be ours."

Looking at Diamond Head as the glow rose behind it, breaking through its crests, I felt the same distant, foreign heat swelling in my own body. We wanted the same thing, Frank and I. Without ever discussing our failures, our fears, or our hopes—Frank knew. He found us an island; he found us a way out. It was clear to me he remembered what we had once shared and was fighting to get it back. He hadn't given up, not yet. And on those crystal slopes, in the safety of its sacred shadow, I saw our chance. I closed my eyes and opened them again, my damp vision confirming my mind's enchantment, its reality.

Our ship docked in Honolulu Harbor and I stepped off the wooden planks of the gangway, entirely overcome. The breeze—the warm, sweet winds that came off the water—could not be captured in a photograph. Neither could the smell; a powerful blend of flowers and fruit, sand and salt water. Every part of the island seemed to sway in harmony; the thick leaves of the palm trees waved to one side and then bent to another. And the sand, like freshly milled flour, was even whiter than it was soft. I couldn't believe a place like this existed, and neither could Hong, who stepped onto the dock and smiled wider than I'd seen in a long time, her teeth exposed, her surprise unmistakable.

It took Frank just three days to find what he sought. He came to the hotel to get me, riding a lean black horse, a cowboy's hat on his head, a roll of paper tucked in the saddle. Taking my hand, he lifted me behind him, handing me my own hat, wide brimmed with a blue satin ribbon. *You're going to love this*, he said, kicking the horse as he called out, a sound I had never heard from my husband's mouth. My smile grew so large as we galloped across the flatlands, I was certain Frank could feel it behind him.

My hat flopped with the gait of Frank's horse, my heels gripping the leather stirrup, wishing I could throw my right leg over the saddle and ride like a man. I envied the control it gave, the ability to turn and gape at everything we passed, without the fear of losing balance. Everything was new, wild, and unexpected. I felt like the heroine from one of Bohai's books, a woman on horseback in a new frontier: a white dress, a handsome man, a mission to find land. I never imagined the sun could feel so clean against my skin, so dry and hospitable, nothing like the damp heat of southern China that soaked through clothes and hair and sent people indoors. The salt from the ocean lifted into the air and sailed through the breeze, and when I licked my lips, it was all I could taste. Clutching Frank, I closed my eyes—just for a moment, just to breathe without the distraction of sight. To smell the scenery change as we moved through the countryside; my words, my mind, failing my senses.

As we reached Diamond Head, we rode past a handful of homes already built in the area, mostly by white families, Frank explained, on large lots that faced the ocean. We slowed through them, Frank pointing, telling me about George Macfarlane, a businessman and member of the king's staff, who owned the enormous estate at the base of the western slope, and James Campbell, a man rich from sugar, who had the two-story house that Frank called a Victorian, with a porch on the ocean, lifted by stilts. They looked so foreign, so white and symmetrical, so different from the homes in Guangdong. There was no gold, no red, no statues or ponds or protective gates. Western homes were left unguarded. Their front doors open to the street.

We rode south through a park—Kapiolani Park—the land changing from wet to dry. Our horse stopped to drink from the wide, winding streams near Waikiki before heading to the eastern end of the park, dry with shrubs and trees, where Frank said a racetrack once stood. He fell in love with the open space, the tall hanging trees and the flat expanse. It reminded him of the great parks of Europe—he described them to me as we rode, landscaped with brilliant flowers and orchards and fountains with marble statues. The Hawaiian park had none of these things, but give it time, Frank told me. They were building a zoo and an aquarium; the open fields would be used for baseball and polo and public music. Before Bohai turned ten, we would be strolling the promenades with parasols, resting among the gardens.

The afternoon sun began to break and I'd nearly forgotten the day's purpose, so absorbed was I by my enjoyment of being on horseback. We rode through a large parcel of land that cut through the base of Diamond Head in the shape of a U, its mouth facing outward. Removed from the ocean, it was protected on three sides, cradled by the walls of the volcano. The land rose slightly toward the rear, with the curve of the incline. Frank slowed the horse. For the first time, he brought it to a halt.

He dismounted first, before lifting me by the waist, lowering me to the patchy ground. Without a word, he pulled the rolled papers from the saddle and flattened them against the flank of his horse.

A sketch of an enormous house, taller than it was wide, spread across the beige paper. Arrows and tiny numbers were etched in pencil, drawn along the edges of the building. The walls of the house appeared to be made almost entirely of glass, rising along the cliff of the crater, positioned in the exact spot where we stood. *Three floors*, Frank said, his finger tracing its height. More than any other home on the island. A gate would close us into Diamond Head, blocking the entrance of the U, shielding our pond and our garden of lotus, fully formed in my husband's mind. We would have no neighbors, Frank said, so earnestly I laughed at him, looking around me, not a single home in sight. He looked up at me, his eyes narrowed, somehow serious.

"And for you?" he asked.

"What about me?"

"You must have something of your own. Anything you want, I'll build it."

"Will this house not be large enough for both of us?" I joked, forever amused by the extravagance of my husband.

"Really, Lin," he insisted. "Something frivolous. A closet with a dozen mirrors. A bathtub the size of the moon. A queen's throne. A waterfall."

"A waterfall," I said suddenly, mimicking his ridiculousness. "I would like a waterfall."

We looked at each other, trying to hold our faces straight, waiting for the other to call a bluff. But neither of us did.

"Say no more." Frank smiled, tipping his hat. "I'll get you the bathtub, too."

Construction began the next afternoon. Frank gathered the crew from his ships, men he'd brought especially for this task, unloading materials and tools from the cargo we carried. They laid the foundation as Bohai, Hong, and I spent our days across the inlet in Waikiki, at the Moana Hotel, relaxing in the shade of the striped cabanas and taking our meals in the white-glove dining room. The hotel was filled with couples and families from California, brought to Hawaii on the Matson cruise ships, their pale skin exposed in bathing suits and flowered shirts, fully unbuttoned, unashamed. Those first few weeks were simple and luxurious. Hong and I enrolled Bohai at Oahu College—the old Punahou, the best school on the island—practicing our English with the other mothers, going shopping for clothes like theirs, with prints of plump flowers and checkers and dots.

With Frank gone most of the day and no household to run, my unburdened thoughts turned quickly to Bohai. It occurred to me that if anything could change my son, it would be the tranquility of this island. He could be tempted outdoors, encouraged to explore his new home without the prying eyes of our old neighbors. He could learn to swim in the warm, peaceful waves right outside our door. He could ride his bike along the empty country roads, would grow strong and wild like the island that surrounded him. Since that night in the library with Frank, since our moment on the deck of his ship, I felt a renewed sense of determination about Bohai. Everything was not broken; there was still time, still hope, and I refused to give up yet. Some of my fondest moments with Frank were spent with Bohai, watching him grow, and I wanted to give Frank that feeling again— that first bubbling of pride and excitement over a life that would develop and follow in his mighty footsteps.

I began to take Bohai to the beach every morning. I woke him early before school and dressed him as the sun rose. I coaxed him onto the sand, allowing him careful steps into the gentle waves, his tiny body silvery and frail. Within seconds, the water would knock Bohai from his feet. *Get up*, I would yell, so determined to right my son, *you can do it*; but even weeks into our exercise, my son could not find his balance. I held his hand, day after day, as he panicked in the water and fell to the sand, his difficult breath expanding beneath exposed ribs. As much as we practiced, he made no progress, but still I forced him. I didn't know what else to do. I would make him try again and again until he was red-faced, panting and exhausted. On our way back to the hotel, I would talk to him about how to improve the next time, his timid head nodding silently as I spoke.

When Frank returned in the evenings, sitting after a long day of work, he would ask about his son, and without hesitation, I would lie. I would tell my husband that Bohai was a natural—that in the water, he was fearless just like his father. It became second nature for me, lying about my son, boasting of his progress with stories entirely made up. I began to recite the opposite of what had actually occurred. If Bohai ran from a starfish, I would say he picked it up; he threw it into the ocean. The morning he swallowed too much water and stayed home from school, I said we'd lost track of time, that he was so happy in the waves that I couldn't bring myself to leave.

We had so little time together, Frank and I, with the construction consuming so many of his hours, that I didn't want to spoil his mood with our old grievances. The house was almost finished. Frank said it was a matter of weeks, and I reasoned that in our new home, our new life, I would double my efforts, triple them. Whatever it took, Frank would have his son.

The announcement came on a Wednesday. Frank arrived at the hotel and loaded us into a carriage, and without explanation, we knew that the house had been finished. Hong and I, we'd spent three months speculating on what it would be like, drawing pictures of the rooms on the hotel's stationery, begging Frank for clues. For three months, he kept much of the house a surprise, not allowing us to visit until the final reveal. Even in the carriage and as we stepped out onto the unfamiliar land, he had us blindfolded until the last minute.

"Take them off," he instructed, and I'm told our reactions were identical. An open mouth, an open palm rising to cover our amazement. Our necks bent backward to take in the structure's height, squinting from the sun's reflection off the massive windows, each of them taller than two lengths of our bodies. It was everything I hoped it would be and nothing I'd ever seen before, nothing like what I'd understood from Frank's drawing, both alarming and dazzling in its grandness, its strange shape and delicate formation. I took three steps backward and almost fell, suddenly aware of what I was hearing, the crashing of liquid, my waterfall.

"Do you like it?" Frank asked, his smile threatening to consume his face, and both palms returned to my open mouth, trembling; I nodded like a lunatic, warm tears falling in disbelief.

We moved into the house on Diamond Head and almost immediately, as if the proximity to water had worked its magic, Hong blossomed.

By the spring she had made friends with all the Chinese vendors at market, cooking all the food she was accustomed to back home but with a touch of the island's offerings. In her new kitchen she made her chicken as she always did. She boiled the bird in soy sauce and ginger, garlic and sugar, but now Hong used only cane sugar from a nearby plantation. Now she called it *shoyu* chicken, the Japanese term the island preferred. Her soup broths, her prized recipes, suddenly had seaweed floating along their surface, sticking to the egg noodles she rolled out on the lanai table, sitting down, facing the ocean. Instead of pomfret, Hong steamed mahimahi. Instead of fried shallots, Hong garnished with spring onions. She picked up new recipes at market, from the Japanese and Filipinos and Portuguese, making strange dishes like green curry with shrimp and pork adobo with potatoes and peas. On Sundays Hong made haupia custard from fresh coconuts, grating the meat and squeezing the milk from the shreds, toasting them and saving the brown flakes in tall glass jars. The soft, creamy dessert was our family's favorite, gone before Monday.

Frank insisted that we all speak English, even at home, with the exception of when Chinese was needed for business or market dealings. Hong and I complied; we complained but I think we enjoyed it. It was the first time we were both speaking a language not native to our tongues. It felt fair, leveling our abilities. In a new place, a foreign land, I supposed that I owed her at least that. But during that first year she surprised me. It was I who grumbled about the strangeness of islanders while Hong recited her English verbs, as she wove hala leaves into baskets for ripening her mangoes and lilikoi. Even Frank became Frank that year, shedding his Chinese name for something more American.

Bohai turned six in the spring and Frank and I bought him a bicycle. It was Frank's idea, encouraged by Bohai's progress in the water. We chose a red bike that we hoped would be lucky. We said it would stir fire within him. That day we took home the most expensive bicycle in the store, tied a gold bow on the handlebars, and left it in his room while he attended school. When Bohai returned home that afternoon, Frank was in his study. At first I thought to get him, wanting to present our gift together. But then I decided against it. I remembered that what I told my husband each day was a lie. Bohai was the same boy he'd always been, and I had a feeling I knew how my son would react to his birthday gift.

Indeed, Bohai walked into his room and stiffened. He moved

slowly to the bike and touched it with a single finger. Turning to face me, he said *thank you* and stepped carefully around his present to get to his desk. He appeared somehow frightened by it, somehow threatened by its presence. For three days, the bow stayed on the handlebars until I removed it myself.

It's difficult to say if we made progress that year. I grew so tired of forcing my son to do things he did not enjoy, and then lying to his father, claiming that he had. It was an exhausting game, and at the end, Bohai remained unchanged. Settled in the house, I knew even Frank was wise to us. I feared the old silence creeping back up; I dreaded its arrival, could feel its threat to our new home.

But then a miracle happened.

One morning in the middle of November, I woke up with a terrible nausea. I walked slowly to the bathroom, to find the herbs Hong used to cure my headaches. As I walked down the corridor, I felt a familiar faintness in the side of my head, clutching it as I stumbled onto the cool tiled floor. Opening the cabinet and looking at the small medicine jars, I felt my stomach churn and rise. I doubled over and vomited in the basin below me, my hands gripping the sides, my open mouth trembling. I knew this feeling—I had been through this before, but I could not believe it was happening again. I shrieked into the basin, my heartbeat pounding in my eyes, and I knew it was a boy. I just *knew*. My nights with Frank, they'd been different in Hawaii, his appetite for me ravenous and new. He barely took the time to undress me now, unable to wait, capturing me as I stepped out of my morning shower, calling me into his study, shutting the door, taking great pleasure in enjoying me in his new home, whenever he could. In Guangdong, I used to worry about Frank and his desires. I feared a second concubine, another woman, but in Hawaii, those thoughts vanished. It was impossible; no man, even one as potent as my husband, could juggle such a full act. And the way he touched me, the way he left my body raw and electric, there was no doubt in my mind that it was a boy growing within me.

Kaipo was born the next summer, our second summer on the island. No one would say it at the time, no one dared speak the words for fear of upsetting Bohai, but it was undeniable to anyone who knew my family. Kaipo was the first legitimate Leong son, the only male to come from my womb, the child my husband feared might never arrive. I gave birth in a hospital for the first time, and when the doctor revealed it was a healthy baby boy, I wept and wept, overcome with delight that I was able to give Frank what he had wanted for almost two decades. That I could, in some way, begin to prove myself worthy of this man, of the life he had chosen to share with me.

From the age that he could walk, my husband took Kaipo everywhere he went. They drove to the harbor together almost every day, and then, when Kaipo began school, every afternoon and on the weekends.

It came as no surprise that my husband's attention shifted from Bohai to Kaipo, but oddly enough, the arrival of Kaipo also brought balance. Kaipo's presence seemed to ease Frank's anxiety about Bohai. My husband had two sons now, and he seemed no longer troubled by Bohai's strangeness. In truth, Bohai's simple needs were a relief, as Kaipo grew spoiled and threw tantrums, demanding expensive toys, then motor scooters, then fast boats and ridiculous cars. On the rare occasion that he did speak, Bohai was always the voice of reason. By the time they were teenagers, I was certain that my husband felt blessed by his fortune. Kaipo was his heir and Bohai his steady hand. Kaipo was the face of the new generation and Bohai the insurance.

As the boys grew up, they developed a curious relationship, one that I could have never predicted. Bohai, nineteen and painfully shy, as tall as his father but thinner than a matchstick, would take the advice of his twelve-year-old brother. I once walked in on them in the bathroom, Kaipo running a comb under the faucet, preparing to give his brother *a haircut like Richard Dix*. I had to give them credit, Bohai's hairline was always a decade older than his age, but at nineteen it was very similar to the movie star's, receding at the part, slightly wavy. I insisted that we go to a proper barber and the boys agreed. Kaipo presided over the haircut, instructing the barber to use more wax, to allow the hair to dip at the front, to comb the sides tighter to his brother's head. The ladies, he told Bohai, were going to love it; he would have a girlfriend in no time.

But of course, Bohai did not attract a girlfriend with his new hair. The kids at school teased him, not to his face but to Kaipo's. They called him Old Man Oil Slick, asking Kaipo if he was actually related to his brother. Kaipo punched a classmate that day; the principal at Punahou called the house to explain that while Kaipo had been provoked, it was policy that he be sent home. It was that afternoon, alone with a fuming Kaipo, that I learned how cruel the kids were to Bohai. How protective Kaipo felt of his brother. When Bohai returned from school, he wouldn't talk about it, not to me or to Kaipo. He simply washed the wax from his hair and combed it back the way it had been. Kaipo actually apologized for embarrassing him, for leading him astray, but Bohai didn't seem upset. It's not your fault, he told his brother.

Still, Bohai kept his distance. Frank and Kaipo oversaw my husband's shipments. They spent most of their time at the harbor, directing deliveries and inspecting the condition of the boats as they docked after a long journey. Occasionally, Frank would ask Bohai to join them, but he never would. He preferred to stay in the study, where Frank and Kaipo would hand him thick stacks of paperwork that he would read and organize and file. I think Bohai was happy with this arrangement; I really do. I think he felt relieved by Kaipo's presence. He was no longer the single heir to my husband's dynasty, the only one left to carry his name. Quietly, it seemed that Bohai had resigned from his position as first son. He continued to carry out the family duties; he did plenty for us, he worked all the time, but without any of the spotlight he deserved, any of the attention he hated so much.

In a way, it broke my heart, watching the two of them. Kaipo was exactly like Frank, a mirror image; they were effortlessly charming, liked by everyone. People talked about Bohai; in private, they asked each other what was wrong with him. There was a quiet strength in Bohai that was constantly overlooked, always eclipsed by his brother's bravado. I never knew how to talk to Bohai about it, and when I finally made my attempt, it only seemed to bother me. I rambled for twenty minutes about how difficult it must be, how unfair, and when I asked for his thoughts, Bohai simply shrugged.

We're different. That was his answer; that was all he said.

When Bohai was twenty-four, it occurred to me that my son could be homosexual—that his strange affliction stemmed from an unnatural desire within. It came to me in a dream, a nightmare. Like in scenes from a movie, I saw Bohai living a double life, happy with a man like him, understood at last in a way we never could. I watched them read books and go on walks and every so often their hands would touch, their fingers would meet and intertwine. It wasn't until I awoke that I realized what I had seen. I sat there wide-eyed and flustered, caught between recalling the images and denying them entirely. Immediately, I left the bedroom, afraid that Frank would hear my thoughts. I feared him waking to my face and sensing Bohai's queerness beneath my discomfort. It felt so real; I needed to leave before I gave something away.

Was it possible? I had no idea. I didn't know the first thing about men with such issues. I'd have to ask, but I was certain I never would. I wasn't sure what outcome bothered me most. Either Bohai would confirm my suspicions, and I would be forced to carry the weight of his confession, or he would reject it, and I would be back to where I began, still searching for what plagued my adult son. The thought of either option only added to my anxiety, so I chose to do nothing. I confided nothing in Hong, who had a firm take on my son's personality. *Let him be*, she'd said to me time and time again. From when Bohai was a little boy, Hong believed in the beauty of Bohai's nature, that a good man finds his way. She scolded Kaipo regularly, raising her voice, questioning his whereabouts well into his twenties—but with Bohai, Hong kept quiet, raising her voice only to defend him to me. Hong wanted something better for Bohai, which irritated me throughout the years, jabbed at something sensitive, because beneath her words I heard how happy his life might be without the chains of his family, without the burden of us.

Later that month, when I'd almost erased the images, when my memory of the dream had become hazy and distorted, Kaipo brought his new girlfriend home for dinner. Her name was Nanami and she was a Japanese girl, small and doll-like with narrow wrists and wide eyes; she gave a light, quiet laugh after Kaipo said practically anything. At great expense, we had sushi brought to the house that night. It was Kaipo's idea. He wanted to show Nanami how easily he could eat with chopsticks, how he had learned the Japanese names for yellowtail and mackerel and sea urchin.

I felt the dinner was going especially well. Frank was enjoying the fish and the sake and Kaipo was putting on a lively show, acting like an announcer as he called playful attention to Nanami's perfect technique.

"She studied at the royal academy of sushi," he told us, as Nanami extended her black lacquered chopsticks to a piece of fleshy salmon. She lifted it from the center with the narrow tips of her instrument, dipped it gently into the soy, and placed it on her tongue. She smiled, close mouthed, and it appeared as if the sushi had vanished.

"It's spectacular," Kaipo whistled, putting down his own chopsticks. "I can't eat any more. I feel unworthy. You deserve the rest."

Nanami laughed and so did I. Bohai ate slowly, selecting one piece at a time, chewing each mouthful much longer than necessary. Then, from across the room, the phone rang and Bohai jumped. His saucer of soy sauce shook and spilled onto the tablecloth.

"It's for me," Bohai said abruptly. He pushed himself from his chair and walked swiftly from the dining room. As the table grew silent around me, I realized it was the first thing he had said all evening.

Bohai never received phone calls, and he especially never received phone calls on Friday nights. Something was wrong. I needed to know who was on the other end of that phone and I was certain, absolutely convinced that it was a man. At once his face returned to me, his hands, his fingers.

"Excuse me," I apologized to Nanami, rising. "I just remembered. I need to give Bohai something for his phone call." I could tell from Frank's expression that he found my explanation odd, but he held his tongue.

"Oh, please, go ahead," Nanami replied, and I left as quickly as Bohai had.

In the next room, I picked up the phone as softly as I could. I held it to my ear, air stale in my lungs, and heard a dial tone. It had only been a minute, maybe less since the phone had rung. How was he already finished? I put the phone down and, without any plan, I went searching for my son.

On the second floor, next to Bohai's bedroom at the end of the hall, I saw that the bathroom light was on, the door slightly ajar. I walked on my toes, advancing toward the pillar of light, listening for sounds within. I heard water, running steadily, echoing inside the small room. I pressed my back against the hallway wall and peered through the opening. My son was slumped over the sink, splashing faucet water against his face, muttering to himself and spitting into the basin.

Get a hold of yourself, he said softly, shaking his head into the sink. It was so quiet over the running faucet that I almost missed it. *What's wrong with you?* he asked himself, collecting a handful of water and throwing it against his face. He kneaded his fingers deep into his skin. His mouth was open; liquid dripped down the sides. With his eyes closed he breathed deeply. He sucked in water and expelled it violently, shooting it through his lips like a whale's spout.

His desperation startled me. He asked the question like there was something terribly perverse about what he was feeling. He spoke to himself without an ounce of hope, without a trace of understanding.

I couldn't help myself. My legs started moving; I walked through the door.

"It's okay," I said, placing a hand on his back. Bohai jolted upward. Water spilled down his face, soaking the front of his shirt.

"What? What are you doing here?" he stammered.

"It's okay," I coaxed. "Whatever it is, just tell me. I want to know, whatever it is."

"Nothing," he said, stepping away from me. "What are you talking about?" He reached for a towel to dry his face.

"Bohai," I pleaded. "I know there's something you're hiding and I think I even know what it is but I need you to say it. Just once, don't make me guess. Just say it to me, please, Bohai. Please."

Bohai went quiet. He went still.

"How," he began, stumbling slowly, "how—do you, I mean, what do you—" He began to panic. His breathing began to quicken. "Does Kaipo know?" he asked abruptly. "Do you think she knows?" His brow furrowed in distress. He looked horrified by the thought.

"Of course not," I insisted, but then it occurred to me: the enormous discrepancy between our words. It didn't make any sense. "Wait, what?" I said, but he just stared back.

"Are you," I tried, but I couldn't finish the question. I knew it wasn't right. At that moment, in the middle of my thought, I knew that I had it completely wrong.

"Nanami," I said, the surprise hitting my mind and my tongue simultaneously. "You like *Nanami*," I said again, my voice lit with disbelief.

Bohai shushed me. He walked past where I was standing and shut the door completely.

"It's not a big deal," he said, pressing his back against the wood, his arms spread outward as if I'd try to escape. He looked intently at me and I stared back. I couldn't believe it; I really couldn't. Bohai wasn't homosexual. He liked Kaipo's girlfriend.

"No, no, of course not," I remembered to say. "Of course it isn't."

Silence spread between us. I didn't know what to say. I was afraid that if I spoke, I would sound excited, which would seem at once strange and inappropriate. Bohai had to speak first. I couldn't find a way to do it.

"I'm sick about it," he said finally. "It's terrible. She's sixteen. She's Kaipo's girlfriend."

"It's normal," I countered. "She's a nice girl."

"Please, don't say anything, not even to Dad. It's humiliating. It's bad enough that you know."

"I'll never say a thing," I promised. "I understand, I do. And it's not a big deal."

I caught my reflection in the mirror and realized I was smiling. I immediately stopped. I swallowed, tried to contain my joy. I felt so much hope. For twenty-four years, I feared that my son was devoid of desire. He never showed an interest in girls, not once had I seen him affected by a woman. But there it was: a normal, visceral response to a female.

Bohai would be all right. It was an amazing, spectacular thought. My son was a late bloomer but with a bit of help, a bit of prodding, he could still lead a normal life. He would date, marry, have a family of his own—for the first time as his mother, I was convinced he was capable, that for the most part my son was a regular man suppressing his desires. A shy boy born to a powerful man, stunted by the burden placed upon him. But he could deny himself for only so long. In my mind, there had to be a tipping point, and soon enough, Bohai would break free of his mental restraints. I hugged him, his wet shirt pressed against mine, and left the bathroom to return to the dinner table. And I never said a word, not one, not even to Frank.

The years slipped by like water from a leaky tap. Year after year, they continued to drip, until suddenly my sons were grown, and Bohai was turning thirty-three.

The number took me by surprise. Its largeness, its significance hit me all at once. I began to recall the years before, the birthdays that had come and gone, feeling like an idiot as I numbered them in my mind, shocked by how much time had passed. In the last ten years, we'd been through so much change. Just as Frank predicted, the neighborhood had filled around us and with it came invitations to parties at the Dillinghams' La Pietra, to polo matches on Kapiolani's lawn, to tea on the roof garden at James Castle's Kainalu mansion. Our schedule was more hectic than it had ever been in Guangdong; the people in Hawaii gathered for any occasion, threw parties simply because it was Friday, because the moon was full, because the weather was pleasant. On the days that we had no event to attend, I began a charity league with a handful of women from the neighborhood. With a monthly allowance from Frank, we threw fund-raisers for the public schools in Kaneohe, for supplies for the local children. I told Hong I understood what she said that day, about being a Boxer, about being a part of something real. It was the first time I had a cause of my own, an opportunity to help my new community, and I threw myself into it, satisfying something within me that running a household never could.

Meanwhile, I realized suddenly, I had neglected my own child.

I looked at my son. I studied his face for traces of change or desire. I watched as he blew out his candles in three timid breaths. He served himself the smallest slice of cake, passing Hong the last fat corner, and ate in silence as chatter filled around him. His body was still thin, his skin still white. His body showed no sign of the island that surrounded him. Even his hair was combed neatly to the side, parted on the right, just as he'd worn it as a boy.

Bohai was on the path to loneliness, it occurred to me for the first time since that night in the bathroom. I felt my heart swell to the size of a melon, heavy with guilt. How had I let this happen? How had I let myself attend parties and fund-raisers, blind to my son as he grew older and more alone? I had forsaken my duty as a mother, as the person closest to him, who perhaps understood him most. Yet again, I realized, I had failed Bohai.

I retired to bed early that evening, my guilt so large I could think of nothing else. I was sure things would change for him, but they never did, and the only person I could think to blame was me.

Bohai wasn't mine. It was a thought that occurred to me less and less. I loved him as if he were my own. Still, I wondered if this fact had anything to do with my negligence. I let my mind reel, my thoughts traveling in wasted circles until, at long last, sleep overcame me.

Hours later, I woke suddenly to a face, my hands clutching at the mattress as I pushed myself upright. It rattled me deeply, shook me in a way that no other dream had. The face, it was thin and sallow, flesh sunken beneath her eyes, where her cheeks were meant to be. She lay there expressionless, her skin reduced to a frail wrapping that spread across the bones. She looked used and wasted until she was finally discarded.

It was my fault. All at once, it came to me.

I had given Frank a concubine. I had let Hailee into our lives, invited her into our bed, tangled her into our fate. And was it not I, too, who had sought her out? After years of misery, of disappointment, was it not I who found her? Hailee, fourteen years old, her body barely a woman's, had been knotted into our family's string, and worse yet, that knot had made a child.

Bohai was the product of a knot; he was the result of a mistake; my mistake, my impatience, my desire to please, to distract Frank from my failings. My meddling, it destroyed Hailee. It left Bohai strange and luckless: a clumsy, half-formed version of a son who would later come.

How had I never seen it before? Left alone, Bohai would never find his destined match, because his fate began as a tangle. And if it was I who had tied the knot, it was I alone who could set it right.

How did the story go? Was every person in the world born with a red string slipped around their ankle? Was every man given a destined match? Or was it possible for a string to become undone, for a person to get skipped in line—sentenced to a life without divine attraction?

Without question, I felt the presence of my own string. From girlhood there had always been something inside me searching for a companion. I never imagined he would be anything like Frank, but I knew he was out there, our fates drawing nearer. Even then, the dark years behind us, I felt extraordinarily blessed by my tremendous fortune.

But what if there was no push and pull at your ankle, no yearning to cross oceans or climb mountains to be with your match? Was it possible I had twisted Bohai's string beyond repair? Could it be too late, my son's match come and gone? I shook my head and settled back into bed, careful not to wake Frank. *How ridiculous.* Of course there was a woman for Bohai.

I simply had to find her.

CHAPTER 4

November 1964
HONOLULU, HAWAII

Theresa watches her mother's face change. She sees Amy's features dim, gradually, as if a dial is being turned, lower and lower, that connects to the clarity of Amy's eyes, to the pigment of her skin, as she takes in the photograph that Mrs. Leong holds out to her. On the floor of the study, the women sit in absolute silence so thick that it slows everything about the room.

Theresa can't see the photograph. She stands by the entrance, shifting her weight from foot to foot, alternating the pressure on the pads of her swollen feet. She's thinking. She's racking her mind for something to say, something with the power to shatter the wall that sprang up before her the moment her mother removed her shoes, the moment she lowered herself to the ground. They're fading into the photograph. It seems to be draining them, casting a somber spell over them both.

Theresa's immediate burden is clear; she repeats it to herself in steps. First, she must get her mother off the ground. Second, she must return the day to her father. A series of steps, a mission, a final obstacle course—Theresa thinks of the day as such. Stricken with intention, single-minded, in the preceding days Theresa's anger has eclipsed her grief. It's wrong, she tells herself, she knows it is. But until she finds her answers, Theresa can't relent. She needs to know how much she must hate her mother, needs to understand to what extent she is responsible for the day, culpable of wasting a life so much worthier than their own. Theresa's anger brings her strength; it separates her from them; it acts as a higher power, a catalyst to shake the truth from a family she barely knows. A family who makes her feel at once childish and irrelevant. Her fear remains the same, compounded within the mighty house. What odds, what *tiny* chance did she expect, competing against a thousand ghosts?

Speak up, Theresa commands her father, sending her words down the corridor, closing her eyes and trailing behind to ensure their safe arrival. *Just this once, Maku, you have to speak up!*

"My son," Mrs. Leong says, turning toward Amy for the first time. "He never learned to ride a bike."

"What?" Amy says softly, lifting her eyes from the photograph.

"A bike. He had one, but he never learned."

"Oh." Amy pauses. "I didn't know."

Theresa opens her eyes and watches Mrs. Leong nod as her mouth forms a frown. Wrinkles, thin yet deep, extend past the corners of Mrs. Leong's lips, so that her sadness drags to the bottom of her face.

"Mom," Theresa says, but it goes unanswered. She tries again, her voice lingering in the silence. Amy does not look up.

Steadying herself, Theresa counts to five and tries to visualize a pool of cool, fresh water. She lets it fill her, and when it reaches her fingertips, Theresa pushes herself from her spot near the archway. Her father's day will not carry on like this, she tells herself; she must move it forward. For once, she will not allow him to be lost among her family's psychoses, their voices always louder than his, their shadows forever larger, more important.

Theresa walks swiftly past the women, taking large strides toward the desk behind them. Without a word, she lifts a trash bin, and with her free hand, Theresa begins to tidy the room. She doesn't know how else to start, how else to clear the space of its stubborn clutter. She grabs a piece of white paper from the desk and throws it into the bin, followed by another, crumpling it between her fingers. She reaches for a third and then a fourth, smashing the paper and shoving it deep within the trash can, letting the sound fill the room. Theresa looks to the floor, where the women still sit, and sees that her movement makes no difference to them. They sit motionless, as if they are the only people in the room, completely blind to her effort. She needs something louder to shake them, something disruptive to break them from their trance.

With an outstretched arm, Theresa heaves her torso across the desk and sweeps all the paper into the basket, knocking over a paperweight and a stapler, sending loose pencils flying off the edge. The pencils click against the floor, one after the other, as they scatter in different directions.

"Theresa!" Amy exclaims, turning around. "What are you doing?"

Theresa does not respond. Instead, she follows the trail of paper away from the desk, bending over and filling the bin. She collects the photographs as well, holding them to her chest and replacing them backward, quieting their voices. She's making noise now, plenty of it, ripping the paper before throwing it away, punching it down into what she's accumulated. *Go*, she orders the ghosts, shaking the bin into the air. *Leave him alone.*

"Theresa," Amy whispers sternly, reaching out her hand as her daughter passes, trying to slow her down. "What are you doing? What's gotten into you?"

"Hand me that," Theresa says, pointing to the picture her mother now holds.

"Theresa—"

"Hand it to me," she repeats. Theresa's voice is harried, agitated but not unkind. Hesitantly, Amy gives her daughter the photograph.

"Do you think she looks okay?" Theresa asks, nodding at Mrs. Leong, who is staring at a patch of carpet near her foot. In her right hand she holds a pencil that has rolled beside her.

"What?" Amy says, shaking her head.

"How does she look," Theresa repeats. "That's why we're here. Do you think it's okay?"

Together, they turn and look at the old woman.

Mrs. Leong is dressed in white, as she should be. A linen blouse stretches across her front, pulled tight across her chest—so tight that the material gathers beneath her armpits in distressed wrinkles. Her shirt creases along the soft folds of her middle, and Theresa can tell by the stiffness of the lines that she's been in the same position for some time. She sits in cropped pants, also creased around the width of her hips. They're loose, like men's pants, and they cinch at her waist with a drawstring that's come undone. Her hair is long and limp, falling around her face in a thin sheet. It has more color than Hong's but it lacks all signs of life. The tone is patchy and dull. It has none of the magic Hong's possesses.

"She was never like this," Amy whispers, rising from her spot on the floor and turning away from Mrs. Leong. "Even at her worst, she was still so beautiful."

"I know," Theresa says, her mind pushing forward her earliest memory of the woman, of the small room with the single bed, the single dresser. The old woman had sat in a folding chair wearing a navy pantsuit, emerald earrings, her hair pulled into a neat chignon. When Theresa hugged her, quickly, clumsily, she'd held her breath. Her NaiNai smelled of smoke and heavy rose perfume.

The women pause. They both know the answer, but neither can find the solution.

"She can't go out there like this, can she?" Amy asks.

"I don't know." Theresa shakes her head. "Does she have anything else here?"

Amy frowns, looking past her daughter.

"If Kaipo would have said something earlier . . . I could have gotten something for her—I could have made her something."

Theresa breathes, her head growing light. She feels the irrelevancies of the day crawling along her skin, threatening to get below it. She's upset with Kaipo for not saying something earlier. She's angry with herself for forgetting an iron. The creases on Mrs. Leong's clothes seem insurmountable, as if her crumpled appearance could deny her father the peace he deserves.

"Really, though," Theresa stammers, getting ahold of herself. "She looks fine. She's a little wrinkled but it's a funeral, for God's sake, it's not a—"

"I have an idea," Amy interrupts, raising an open palm. She turns to her daughter. "Stay with her a minute, okay?"

"Mom, it's fine," Theresa insists, but Amy is already walking toward the archway.

"I'll be right back," she calls over her shoulder. "Stay right here." She's gone before Theresa can refuse.

Alone with Mrs. Leong, Theresa is met with a silence she feels somehow obliged to fill. Recently it's unnerved her—a complete absence of words or sound. Whenever she's alone, Theresa plays the radio. The sound it makes doesn't matter—advertisements for soap or a dozen wind instruments, it makes no difference, she's not listening. When there's no radio, Theresa will run a faucet. She'll flush a toilet. Silence is her greatest regret. It reminds her of her father and all the spaces she never filled, of all the words she wishes she had said but now must keep to herself.

"Don't listen to my mom," Theresa says to Mrs. Leong, pacing the space in front of her. "You look great. You're almost eighty, for God's sake, we should be celebrating, not trying to get you into a pair of heels. It's just that there's going to be press here and I know Uncle Kaipo and my mom want you to look perfect, you know? Like how you were before—"

Theresa's eyes dart toward Mrs. Leong. She shuts her mouth and swallows. A moment passes and nothing happens, nothing changes. Mrs. Leong sits with her knees to her chest, her expression the same blank sorrow, as if watching a tragic movie she's seen a thousand times, during which she no longer feels the need to cry. It occurs to Theresa that she has never been alone with this woman, her NaiNai. It occurs to her that her NaiNai may have no idea who she is.

87

Carefully, Theresa closes her eyes and sees a yellow building, a porch, a warm can of guava juice. She was young, maybe six, no older than seven. Her mother had promised her a day at the beach, the best beach she knew of on the North Shore of the island, but before they could swim, they had to make a stop. An hour later they slowed before a yellow building, and outside on the porch sat Mrs. Leong, *her NaiNai*, Amy told Theresa, *Maku's mother*. Her NaiNai was very sick, Amy explained; she had been sick since before Theresa was born. They approached her slowly, Amy introducing them both by name, and for exactly one hour they sat with the old woman, Theresa fidgeting in her chair, her sweaty palm warming her can of juice. Her mother talked for the entire visit, about what Theresa has no memory, but her NaiNai didn't say a word—that, she remembers. The old woman's lips, as if sewn together, never moved, never opened to take a single breath. Afterward, they drove straight home and Theresa didn't ask about the beach, rattled by the smell that still clung to her skin, by the silent old woman who lived all alone. As far as Theresa remembers, after that visit, they never went back.

Quietly, Theresa opens her eyes and studies Mrs. Leong's face, her heart beating softly in her ears. She lingers on each of her deteriorating features, first her chapped mouth, then her nose, sprinkled with age spots, tracing the woman's face upward with difficulty, a conscious effort to keep them steady. None of it is familiar to Theresa. Whenever she saw her NaiNai, just once a year in this very house, Theresa could look for only so long. The tall, waxy-skinned woman smelled so intensely of a small room, of old belongings and the sickness her mother had yet to name. Every New Year, as soon as she could, Theresa retreated to the kitchen with Hong. It was barely her on that porch all those years ago, her young memory so faint it seems almost dreamlike when she recalls it now, always in tableau, never in film. Theresa finds she has no memories attached to the old woman's eyes; she remembers nothing about her skin. And as she allows herself to finally blink, Theresa finds that the thought calms her. She finds that their total strangeness is encouraging. It grants her some bravery. Theresa takes a breath and reaches inside herself once again, extracting everything that she feels for this woman who sits on the floor, this woman whose life Theresa now knows intimately without having exchanged a single significant word.

"Um," Theresa says, clearing her throat. Her voice sounds brash and childish. She hates that it's her, making such a sad attempt—that she's this nervous before an audience of a single stranger.

"I want to say that I think you're an extraordinary woman." She pauses. "I know that doesn't mean much, coming from me. In fact, you probably have no idea who I am and I hate that." She shakes her head. "I hate that I was scared of you. That a part of me still is."

"But I'm learning a lot this year," Theresa whispers, afraid that her voice will break. "I've learned a lot about opportunities and what happens when they go unused. I know we don't have a lot of time before my mom comes back, so here it is, my opportunity to say that I admire you. Your story, your strength. I wish I could hear it from your mouth."

The woman has yet to look at Theresa, to recognize that she is speaking. Theresa fights against her instinct to give up. In the silence, it's easy to see her NaiNai as a piece of furniture, a lamp or a chair to which words make no difference. She fumbles through the quiet and finds her mother's voice, hears her simple advice. *Just speak.* To be acknowledged, she told her. That's all her NaiNai wants. Theresa breathes.

"I've been thinking about you since Maku died. I keep coming back to you, thinking that you might understand." Theresa looks at the old woman, barely able to dress herself, and searches for a way to say it.

"I spent my entire life with him and it's as if I never knew him, like I never tried. This whole time I thought he was fragile but that's bullshit." She shakes her head. "Maku was a thinker. My father was a mathematician. There was nothing *wrong* with him, not like people said. He gauged his decisions with logic, he chose with numbers."

Theresa steadies herself. She feels the heavy beat of her heart, tries to slow the pace of her breathing. When she speaks of her father, it happens intrinsically. In her defensive approach, her aggressive tone, she feels the need to preserve her father as the man she sees him as now: wronged, his life far worthier than his end. But more than anyone else, Theresa thinks sadly, as she has often in the preceding days, the woman who sits before her—this vacant, broken woman— understands something of her father's burden. Even now, twenty years later, her NaiNai has not been released to death. To this day, she endures a penance so much larger than her crime.

Theresa tries again, her voice full of collected air, as steady as she can.

"The odds of this family, they're horrifying. There's a punishment for every doubt, a humiliation for every weakness. Look at you, look at Maku. Where does it end?"

Behind her, Theresa hears her mother's heels click against the wood of the corridor, growing more pronounced with each step. She breathes, pressing a hand to the underside of her stomach.

"What I'm trying to say is," Theresa whispers to the woman, leaning toward her as Amy appears in the archway, "what I'm trying to say is that I think I understand what happened to you. I think I can understand a piece of how you feel."

Amy walks across the room and Theresa straightens. Her mother holds a hanger with a crisp, white collared shirt. It's a man's shirt, and almost instantly, Theresa recognizes its style.

"It's Maku's," she says instinctually.

"It is," Amy replies. "I knew he had some shirts still in his old closet. I think this might work."

Amy squats and shows Mrs. Leong the shirt, holding it to her side.

"This is Bohai's shirt," Amy tells her. "He wants you to wear it today. What do you think?"

Mrs. Leong extends her hand, cautiously, and takes a bit of material between her fingers, rubbing them gently together.

"Here, let me help you up so you can put it on."

"Bohai," Mrs. Leong says, nodding once.

"Yes," Amy replies, taking the woman's hand and helping her slowly from the ground. Mrs. Leong's eyes stay on the shirt. Her fingers have yet to release the piece of sleeve that she holds.

"Theresa," Amy calls. "Help her with that sleeve. Like that, but bend her elbow. Exactly. Okay, now just hold her arm and I'll do this one. Mrs. Leong," she says, taking the hand that clasps the second sleeve, "I need this part, okay?" Amy peels the woman's fingers from the shirt and helps her into it. She tightens the drawstring at Mrs. Leong's waist and ties it into a bow.

"There," Amy says, stepping backward. "You're perfect. Just one last thing."

Amy reaches both hands behind her neck to unfasten the double strand of pearls she wears. The necklace is connected by a thick jade clasp, edged in gold; a wedding present. She wraps it around Mrs. Leong's neck and the effect is immediate. Mrs. Leong looks dignified. In her son's shirt, in Amy's pearls, it seems entirely possible that this woman was once the head of an illustrious family.

How strange, Theresa thinks. How remarkable, how terrifying that a lifetime can hold this much change, can stretch to this level of distortion. Theresa watches her mother with Mrs. Leong and suddenly she hears the photographs begin to chatter. She hears a whisper between her ears, rising in volume, growing from a single voice to five, to ten, to a chorus of mouths from within the silver frames, all of them sounding their horror, echoing their suspicion.

The photographs and all their memories, they can't believe it either. *A fraud,* they chatter, *a waste. A terrible, catastrophic mistake.* And right away, Theresa knows; these bitter words, this fiery lament, they're speaking of her mother.

Theresa

1922–1942
KANEOHE, HAWAII

A is for Amy, my mother, the first letter of the alphabet and the oldest child of her family. My mom's sisters, Beverly, Camilla, Denise, Eileen, Francine, and Grace, all followed, born in alphabetical order. Her three brothers, arriving with the second half of the girls, were not named with the same precision. It didn't matter, my mom would say; there weren't nearly enough of them to lose track. They lived in Kaneohe, on the windward side, in the country. *Poor* is a word that my mom dislikes, but that's exactly what they were. Poor, cramped, simple people, twelve of them under a single roof.

She grew up beneath banana trees, plagued with discomfort. The fruit from the banyan made her sneeze; the sugarcane, with its long, untidy stalks, gave her a rash; the dense, coarse crabgrass made her eyes water, her lids swell, her vision blur. My mom learned of allergies in the sixth grade and swiftly she bundled all her grievances under the safety of that word. Octopus trees, palm grass, club moss, ferns of any color, size, or texture. She had a brush with each of them, and she was allergic to them all.

It was always stories with my mom—believable ones too, which made my job as her daughter so much more difficult. She told them with the conviction of a man on death row, confident in his plea of innocence. With her words, my mom rewrote years of her life, tampering with her experiences, altering her motives. It was easy for her to live in her mind, I see that now. No one bothered her there; no one could tell her that it wasn't true.

It's safe to say that the nature of my mother's stories altered over time; that with each new stage of life came a different purpose for narration. In her youth, she used her words to avoid things she disliked. A bad bicycle accident would prevent her from ever having to race the neighborhood kids—so she stole her mother's eyebrow pencil and drew perfect scars along her elbow. I wish I could, she told her friends, *but look*. Her face gave nothing away; her eyes sloped with genuine regret. Her lies came easily because in her mind, in the balances that weighed her right and her wrong, they were not considered lies. My mom spent and saved her words like gold, like precious stones, playing them strategically, saving some for difficult times to secure a certain outcome. The modification of words, of feelings and experiences, were simply tools that she hoped might pry her from the life that she was born into.

As my mom got older, she'd make her own clothes and swear they were a gift from a rich relative, hand-sewn and monogrammed in foreign silks that felt more like polyester. In high school, she wrote an essay called "My Other Sister," in which she told the story of her identical twin sister, born two minutes after her with the umbilical cord wrapped around her neck. Her teachers, unwilling to verify the details of a stillborn child, didn't know what to make of it so they gave her an A. They passed the story among the staff and by the end of the semester they all looked at her differently, sympathetically.

I never inherited my mother's penchant for stories. In a way, there wasn't space. I was the vessel, the holding tank for hers, and for the longest time I didn't mind. She fell into these moods; I'd find her on the couch after school, drinking a glass of wine, waiting for me to come home. If I had a sibling, this would be something we'd both understand, that when you walked through the door and saw her sitting there, when you heard her call your name before you even removed your shoes, she was deep within her mind. She was feeling sorry for herself, I realize that now. For hours, she had been playing the reel on repeat, waiting for something to pull her from the depth, and usually it was me.

Theresa, she'd say, and I would think of my homework, what was due the next day. These afternoons, they didn't happen all the time. Months would pass, happy months where wine was saved for dinner and I came home to an empty house, my mom out grocery shopping or playing mah-jongg with my aunties. These afternoons, they didn't disrupt my life. It was an obligation I was happy to indulge because listening to her stories was the only thing my mom ever asked of me.

I remember one afternoon now, clearer than the rest. It was a Monday after a weekend in Maui, after three days at the beach. I was eleven and my mom had bought me a new swimsuit, a magenta two-piece with nylon fringe that sailed as I ran along the water. Maku was shore fishing—an activity that was made for him. He could stand there for hours, his khaki hat tight to his head, his back perfectly straight, effortlessly still as the ocean surged before him, as the sky broke from orange to lavender.

Maku never caught a lot of fish, but he always hooked something: a snapper, a goatfish, something brilliantly gold or tiled red and white, shiny like a kitchen floor. When he felt a bite, he'd yell for me. Until recently this was the loudest I'd ever heard his voice— my name from across the beach. *Come quick!* And I'd run as fast as I could, tassels whipping against my skin, my father's gentle call like a sergeant's command. He positioned me in front of him, my hands on the pole, his hands wrapped around mine, and we slowly reeled in the most dazzling fish I'd ever seen. It was small, barely longer than the length of Maku's hand, but its scales were like jewels, emerald and sapphire, glinting from the water that ran down its surface. It was a fluke, Maku said, and I thought that's what we'd caught. But it was a mahimahi, a deepwater fish, a baby, an accidental catch. We had to throw it back, Maku told me. Before it died, before it shed its brilliance for a murky grey.

The Monday after, when I returned from school, my mother told me about a boy she knew as a child, a young boy from the North Shore who was the small town's expert on fish. She led into her story as she always did, with a loose connection, as if the story were really for me. *Seeing as you're interested in fish now*, she'd begin, and I'd take my place beside her on the couch, nodding. The boy's uncle was a local fisherman, she told me, and he taught his nephew all he knew. But soon enough, the boy surpassed his uncle, spending all his time in the ocean searching for new fish, memorizing them below the water so that he could draw them when he surfaced. With a notebook of lined pages and a set of colored pencils, he drew dozens of fish. Bigeye ahi with its long, yellow fin; ruby-colored snappers; flat, silver papio; powder-blue parrot fish; pancake-faced stingrays; rainbow schools of ta'ape; scarlet, venomous menpachi; snakelike o'opu; electric-orange a'awa; razor-toothed ono. My mom listed these species with remarkable ease, sipping her wine between descriptions. The boy's uncle would look at his drawings and identify the fish until the boy knew them himself, could match his findings with his homemade encyclopedia. And it wasn't just fish he gathered, wasn't just drawings he made. The boy was an expert on coral, diving deep into the reefs to study their formations, gathering the dead pieces from the shoreline. He made art with the odd, blooming figures of calcium, securing them against lengths of driftwood and selling them alongside his uncle's daily catch. My mom got lost in that story, more so than she usually did, remembering the name of a fish mid-sentence and derailing entirely, forgetting where she'd left off. As she spoke, barely looking at me, I realized that on these afternoons she simply needed a body to sit beside her. I could have been anyone, anyone who loved her enough to listen; anyone but Maku.

Because all these years, there was one story my mother kept to herself. The most fantastic, the most unbelievable of all her tales was the one she never told me, not until Maku died. It linked too closely to her reality; it stained her storytelling with significance, her cast of characters pulled from a genuine past.

The story of her life, the story of my family, of its ghosts, of its magnificent rise and decline—she locked it all away. She tried so hard to erase it, and in my mind, in the part that still believes I know something about my mother, that little fact changes everything. It's what I can't shake; it's what makes me believe it might be true, might have happened exactly the way she finally told it.

My mom grew up in the basement of a shared duplex. There was a single bedroom where my Grandma and Grandpa Chan kept their mattress on the floor, surrounded by boxes that rose to the ceiling, crumpled and misshapen, too full to close. The living room, the only other habitable space, was separated in two by a sheet. Three boys slept on one side, the seven girls on the other. Geckos were ushered through the screen door as if they were guests, twelve pairs of dirty slippers tracked through the hall and into the bathroom, which itself was used as a storage space—broken toys and rusty tools stacked higher than the toilet tank. When my mom was younger, when there were fewer of them, she attempted to organize the developing clutter. She remembered the clean spaces of her youth; she wanted them back. But as more and more siblings appeared, year after year for more than a decade, my mom gave up. Her thoughts began to wander beyond the needs of her struggling family. Her home shrank and her ambition grew. On the rare occasion she was forced into the fields to work with her siblings, my mother made daisy chains. She wrapped them around her head and fanned herself in the shade.

It was a neighborhood joke that the Chan family was run like a caste system. My mom filled in the highest ranks with my Grandpa and Grandma Chan. Next came Beverly, Camilla, and Denise, always in the middle. They trailed three years behind my mother, separated by eleven months each; it was just enough space to be counted differently, apart from my mother, after the honeymoon. The boys came next, climbing the family ladder as they got older and older. When they were boys, my Grandpa Chan was reluctant to see their value. He had hoped for sons early in his marriage, but after the arrival of four girls, I suppose the thought of sons lost its romance. The boys were merely mouths, bigger and louder, but as they grew older, my

Grandpa Chan embraced them. He began to see their value—not in the traditional sense, as heirs or guardians of the family. His pride was more selfish than that. They were proof my grandpa's seed could produce *men*.

The last of the girls, Denise to Francine, were known around Kaneohe as the Raggedy Chans, each of them dressed in ill-fitting clothes, passed from one sibling to the next. So it was not strange to pass my grandparents' house and see my youngest aunties on their hands and knees, weeding the crabgrass from the edge of the yard as my mother sat on the sidewalk, cutting up mangoes and watching them dry in the sun.

I like to think that, because of her favored position, my mom was beautiful, but it's difficult to say after meeting her sisters. My Auntie Camilla, my mom's middle sister, could not go anywhere without some loudmouthed moke chasing after her. Camilla was gorgeous, which became clear at the age of eight when her hair turned a honey color. Her eyes followed in turn, lending her the appearance of a mixed girl, an exotic hapa haole. For years she was the talk of the neighborhood. Where did her looks come from? Most days, my Grandma Chan looked crazy at best. Her clothes were never her own, she cut her hair herself, rarely wore a bra. The neighbors agreed that an affair did not fit into her lifestyle—or her temperament for that matter, which was harried, almost desperate in the way she moved from task to task. Then Eileen was born and she looked so much like Camilla. By the time she turned six she was fair and tall, her legs longer than most of the boys' at school. The rumors stopped after that, because what kind of woman bore ten children in ten years and went searching for more?

If Camilla and Eileen were beautiful, then my mom was not. Her hair was dark, her features decidedly Chinese, her waist thin but mostly square, almost boyish. She had no hips, barely any breasts, but unlike her sisters, unlike her mother, my mom took pride in her appearance. She grew her hair long, she kept up on fashion, she painted her nails, rubbed cream into her elbows and knees. She still does these things. She's never stopped caring about what people think.

While her friends drank beer and smoked menthols on the beach, my mom spent most of her teenage days in Diamond Head. She was cleaning the estates of families with names like Miller and Moore, Warren and Robinson. She hated it, but there was a certain understanding between my mom and her parents that quitting would devastate them. Most of her earnings my mom spent herself, but she always replaced the milk when it ran out. She could always be asked for a few dollars to turn the electricity back on.

Those big, shaded houses in Diamond Head, sitting up against the water with their open lanais and wooden floors, made my mom sick with envy. She would pace the length of the entryways. She would spread her arms as wide as they could go, basking in the sheer amount of space that two people could afford. She opened the double windows and let in the breeze, allowing the wind to whip against her face, taking in the smells of plumeria and salty ocean, basking in the luxury of elevation.

"It smells different in Kahala," she once told Camilla.

"Smell it good while you're there because at home you're *pilau* like the rest of us" was Camilla's response.

It had been two years since my mom graduated high school in 1939, from a Catholic school in Kaneohe. Naturally, she was the first to finish, walking across the high school gymnasium with leis piled up to her ears, but she was also the last. She was the only Chan child to receive a diploma. Most of my mom's sisters, my Alphabetical Aunties, dropped out of high school when it began to get difficult. It started with my Auntie Camilla in the ninth grade. She was hired as a waitress the summer before her freshman year and she never went back. The money was too good, she told my Grandma Chan. Then there was Auntie Denise, who dropped out early when she failed algebra two years in a row and was told that she'd have to take summer school. The rest of my mom's sisters were too young to consider quitting yet, except for Beverly, who was almost as diligent as my mom, and made it halfway through her senior year. It's my opinion that she would have made it the whole way too, right to graduation, had the war not broken out first.

It happened on a Sunday. It was quiet and still and entirely unexpected, that's what anyone will tell you about that day. My mom was on the earliest bus into Diamond Head, yawning freely, alone in the very last seat. The sun was beginning to rise, lazily extending its beams from behind the Koolau Range so that the very highest ridge seemed to be illuminated. There was another person on the bus, an old Chinese woman with cropped hair wearing men's corduroy pants, sitting with half a dozen chickens fluttering in a metal cage. She was already seated when my mom got on, in a middle seat, her short legs dangling off the plastic bench. She said hello in English, with a bit of irritation, knowing that my mother did not speak Chinese. The lady had asked her many times before,

"You speak Chinese?"

"No. Only English."

"You look Chinese."

"I am Chi—"

"But you no speak." And with that, she would turn back to her chickens. My mom never forgot these encounters. She's told me at least a dozen times about this woman in the corduroy pants. It bothered her, it really did. *Am I to be blamed for not speaking Chinese?*

For my mom, it was the same routine every Sunday. Occasionally, my Grandpa Chan would ride with her, getting off by his photography studio in Waikiki. She loved it when he came along. He would point out different buildings along the route, telling my mom what used to be there, what had changed. He always had some fact or theory to share with her, which made waiting for the sun to rise a little less tedious.

But that day, my mom was alone—just her and the chicken lady heading toward the southern coast of the island. The woman would get off with her chickens on South King Street, in Chinatown, where she would peddle her birds at the Oahu Market. By this time, the bus would be more crowded, the seats sprinkled with passengers on their way to early mass or a weekend job, so the chicken lady would have to squeeze into the aisle, her cage brushing up against the sleeves of strangers, a haole woman shrieking as the birds toppled from one side of the cage to the other.

"Is that allowed?" the haole lady yelled to the bus driver, looking around for support from the other passengers. "An entire farm on the bus!"

When the bus erupted in support, my mom cheered too.

Her first appointment was at the Darling estate, east of Diamond Head in the district of Kahala. The Darlings were a military family, Mr. Darling a commissioned officer with the United States Navy, Mrs. Darling spending her days and her military allowance at the Waialae Country Club, and both children—a boy and a girl—attending Punahou. They came from California, stationed on Oahu for just a year but by the way they were living, my mom told me, it seemed that they would be staying much longer.

The Darling home sat high on two acres of land, overlooking the soft waves of Kahala Beach. From the street, the house was hidden, guarded by a solid iron gate with gold Hawaiian etchings of fish and flowers and stick figures with spears. The first time my mom saw this gate, she thought that the Darlings might be local—perhaps a Japanese family with a strange last name. But they were haole, Mrs. Darling a platinum blonde in a silk *mu'u mu'u* with a turquoise hibiscus trim. The day they met, she greeted my mom with a perky *Aloha!*, lingering on the first *A* for far too long. She was ridiculous, my mom decided immediately—but she was kind, treating my mom as a guest who happened to dust their bookshelves and iron their shirts.

Behind the entry gate was what my mom described as a hotel

entrance. A circular driveway was cut into a perfectly even, pea-colored lawn, its edges sharper than you could draw with a compass and protractor. The palm trees, lingering formally around the perimeter of the yard, blocked the views both in and out, and a fountain, made of white marble, was planted in the middle of the circular driveway. A four-foot koi spouted water from its mouth. High above the front yard sat the main house, positioned atop a wide set of stairs with gleaming bronze banisters.

My mom rang the doorbell at the gate, checking her watch: 7:50. Ten minutes early. Akio, the Darlings' groundskeeper, came immediately to unlock the gate.

"Good morning, Amy-san," he said with a quick bow, ushering her through the gates and locking them again. "I'm happy to see you well." He was flustered, which was unusual, his familiar fingers fumbling through the brass keys. Instead of walking her to the front door as he usually did, he led her up the steep side steps of the property that wrapped around to the backyard. He took them two at a time, his small legs straining with each upward lunge, and when they reached the top, he was short of breath.

"Oh, Akio!" my mom exclaimed, seeing a newly blossomed bed of birds of paradise, her favorite flower. "They're incredible."

But instead of looking at the flowers, Akio looked to the sky, scanning the morning clouds for something—perhaps rain, my mom thought. He looked to the north. My mom looked too.

"Akio, it shouldn't rain today. The clouds are going north. I watched them the whole way here."

She squinted, shading her eyes with a cupped hand. She strained to see what was in the distance. There seemed to be birds, faint black dots emerging from between clouds and disappearing again, flying in a loose V shape as they migrated closer. They flew between the mountain ridges, dipping lower and lower, heading in their direction at a steady pace. When they became the size of fat mosquitoes, swarming in the distance, my mom asked, "What are they?"

Akio was silent, his usually expressive face washed of all emotion. He was white, almost transparent, the skin of his cheeks as thin as parchment. He was watching the birds, studying them, the dark pupils of his eyes tracing them steadily in the sky. Suddenly, he dropped to his knees, the top of his head hitting the dewy grass, and he began to pray.

Ten ni orareru watashitachi no Chichi yo,
mi-Na ga sei to saremasu yo ni.
mi-Kuni ga kimasu yo ni.
mi-Kokoro ga ten ni okonawareru tori
chi ni mo okonawaremasu yo ni

My mom stared at Akio, startled by his strange reaction. What had changed in the last thirty seconds? An ordinary greeting, a clear sky, a flock of birds—a routine that had played out most every Sunday morning for the past two years. But now Akio's body was doubled on the grass. His shoulder blades heaved with the force of his panicked voice, with sounds my mom realized she knew. They were so familiar. She searched her mind. She closed her eyes and isolated the rhythm of his words.

The sound of a hundred voices filling a small chapel, a steady hymn—the weekly mass from her years of Catholic school came to her suddenly. It was the Lord's Prayer. Her mouth began to move, forming the English words against Akio's momentum, stammering over the prayer called out so often in despair.

My mom dropped to her knees, putting her hands on Akio's back and shaking him, gently at first. *Akio, what is it? Are you all right?* And then, when he would not respond, more firmly: *Akio!* But he continued.

Watashitachi no hi goto no kate o kyo mo oatae kudasai
Watashitachi no tsumi o yurushi kudasai

Again, my mom looked to the sky, to the place from which Akio seemed to be withdrawing, squinting, one hand blocking the morning sun, the other pressed against Akio's shoulder when she realized that they weren't birds. She stood, breath still in her lungs. They were planes, still in the distance but expanding, growing larger and more defined as they headed west. She could hear them, faintly, the low gargling of propellers. The army was doing maneuvers, she told him. It was normal; it happened all the time. But my mom could not deny the dread that seized her, looking again to the kneeling man. Akio chanted as if possessed, thick lines of sweat racing from his temples, his compressed body rocking like an anguished child.

Watashitachi mo hito o yurushimasu
Watashitachi o yuwaku ni ochi irasezu, aku kara o sukui kudasai

She yelled. *Akio! What's happening? Tell me what's happening!* But as the last syllable exited her lips, her question was answered. The deep reverberation of explosions punctuated the morning air, sending the sound of thunder pulsing through the island—to the top of the Darlings' home, throwing my mom backward, legs fumbling below her as she gaped into the distance.

Dark, heavy clouds of smoke arose from the ocean, billowing high above the ridgeline, rapidly swelling and expanding from the rippling flames below. What sounded like machine guns, with rapid fire, blasted from beneath the smoke and sharp metallic cracks popped like fireworks in the air. The sound of bombs falling, which my mom never thought she'd recognize, was undeniable—a high-pitched whistle dropping from the planes, audible only between the slam of explosions. She covered her mouth to keep from screaming. Her breath returned in short, violent gusts.

The curve of the island blocked her view of what was exploding. She thought of her family, their faces appearing swiftly in her mind as she looked north to Kaneohe. None of them were beyond that ridge.

And then she remembered Akio, still huddled beside her, his voice juddering now, enormous.

Watashitachi o yuwaku ni ochi irasezu,
aku kara o sukui kudasai.

My mother crumpled to the ground, fear overwhelming her panic—her disbelief—and did the first thing that came to her. Her forehead met the grass, the smell of the earth swarming her senses as the Lord's Prayer came tumbling from her mouth, her words matching Akio's in rhythm but not sound. She held herself firmly, arms wrapped across her chest, clutching her shoulders, heart beating in her throat. Akio wept and so did she, his tears falling decisively, as if dedicated to someone. My mom cried silently, instinctually, she tells it, the moment painted with an unsettling intimacy. Together, they prayed, high above Kahala, as the Second World War began.

I understood very little of what would come, my mom told me. *I understood very little of what it meant.*

At last, the bombs subsided. Akio raised himself to his feet quietly, heavily, his forehead damp from the dewy grass. He removed the keys from his belt and placed them on the patio table. With his eyes lowered beneath him, Akio turned to my mother and he bowed.

"Forgive," he said, his voice barely a whisper, before walking to the stairs and descending slowly, taking them one by one until she could see him no longer.

My mom was dismissed that day as well. In the end, the Darlings saw little difference between Chinese and Japanese. But she left willingly, my mom told me. She was forever changed by what she had witnessed in their backyard, grateful to never return.

After the bombs fell and President Roosevelt declared war on Japan, my Grandpa Chan found himself with a problem he'd never had before. All around town, the government was seizing the assets of businessmen. Storefronts and trucks and desirable supplies were taken overnight and donated to the war effort but my Grandpa Chan went unnoticed; for once in his life his insignificance served him well. The government, the army, they had little need for a single room with a single skylight, so my Grandpa Chan went about his regular business, reopening his photography studio the very next week, met with a sight that in all his years, he'd never once encountered.

A group of a dozen men was gathered outside his door, smoking cigarettes and checking their watches. Soon, my grandpa had too much business, far more customers than he could handle alone. The sudden outbreak of war sent a tidal wave of young men through his studio doors. They were willing to wait in line, willing to come back, willing to pay twice what he normally charged for a sitting. A clock had begun; there was limited time before departure, and every soldier, desperate to be remembered, wanted his portrait taken before being shipped abroad.

It was my Grandma Chan's idea that he hire my mom. Grandma Chan saw it as an opportunity, a way to get them together again. My mom had been looking for a job since the Darlings, but no family wanted her, not yet. The island was still fragile, doors locked, people suspicious. They jumped at the sound of a dog barking, ducked to the starting of a car's engine. Houses near the harbor were abandoned, families fleeing to the safety of relatives in the north and east of the island, hunkering down three and four to a room. Rumors flew of a second attack, a follow-up, the Japanese angry that they had not damaged enough.

My grandpa knew this, and even so, he resisted.

"Amy will find something else," he told my grandma. "She always does."

"So that's your solution?"

"Amy doesn't want to work for me."

"And how do you know that?" my grandma asked. "Did you ever ask her?"

"I know."

"It must be nice," she snapped, "knowing everything, always being so right."

"Iris, please. I'm tired."

"You're tired," she repeated, her voice flat, incredulous. "You've been letting your daughter pay your bills for two years and you're tired. I suppose you're too tired to care about your daughter? You're her *father*, Joe. Do you understand that? You're the adult, not her."

"I just don't think it's a good idea."

"Fine." My grandma stood up from the table. She pressed her fingers against its greasy surface. "Another disappointment—she'll be so surprised!"

"What did you tell her?" He leaned forward, concern dawning for the first time.

"I lied." She paused. "I told her that for once in her life, her father wasn't thinking of himself."

My Grandpa Chan was a peculiar man. Stubborn as an ox, to this day he remains unchanged. I realize now that my grandpa Chan's peculiarities, while peculiar, were not unique. My grandpa was a poor man who resented the fact that he was not born rich. There was something in his blood or in his mind that taunted him, something delusional and entitled based in absolutely nothing. *The noble life* is what he called it, living properly, leisurely, devoting yourself to a fine art, like the children of nobility. When my mom was a child, he used to list the possible paths of her future: *piano, ballet, cinema*, encouraging her to choose an art from the age of two.

From a young age my Grandpa Chan developed extremely fine motor skills—teaching himself to steady a camera, to make an even stroke with a paintbrush—without learning the first thing about being a field hand or harvesting sugarcane or repairing a roof. Had he not been born to a family of farmers, his skills might have been received differently, but as a member of the working class, he was barely functional—something I suspect was more a product of choice than ability.

Little is known about my Grandpa Chan's past, about his parents. How he learned to work a camera, how he even came to possess one, my mother never knew. A single clue to my grandpa's humble beginnings lies in a black-and-white drawing, a memento he hung above his instruments. An enormous ship sits in Honolulu Harbor, three masts extended, the hull shaded dark with pencil, Diamond Head in the distance. The bottom corner reads 1862. His grandfather was one of the hundreds of Chinese men on board, a contract laborer headed for the sugarcane fields.

In a way, my Grandpa Chan tried to conceal his sense of entitlement, never vocalizing his bitterness with his mismatched life. Most of his thoughts he kept to himself, but that's precisely what they were: thoughts about himself, his suffering, the injustice of his life. And then the bills would be late while his ten children shared a dinner of kimchi and suddenly, quietly, my grandpa's inner aristocracy began to show. He didn't care. He didn't pick up extra shifts at the cannery or begin to sell valuables like the others in Kaneohe. For him, money was not something worth laboring for. Money was a blessing, a good fortune passed on from virtuous lineage, and the idea of sweating in the fields with the rest of the working class, saving pennies at a time, was a concept lost on him.

Many years ago, before my mom was born, my Grandpa Chan spent the entirety of his savings on a small space in Honolulu, on a busy commercial strip. He painted the walls ivory, he bought stools, he set up a cash register. He was going to be a photographer, something my Grandma Chan was very proud of at the time. She was convinced she was marrying a man of impeccable breeding—an artist, an aristocrat who could afford his own private studio in Waikiki. She never asked, never knew that with the purchase of the studio came the exodus of his money. There was a confidence in his eyes that comforted her, that made her believe recklessly in their future.

Together, they dreamed. He drove her through Waialae, asking her which estate she preferred, criticizing the slopes of their lawns and the colors of the stones that led to their driveways. He bought her plate lunch—her favorite *huli huli* chicken—and took her to the beach, telling her she was more beautiful than every woman who passed by their picnic blanket. He introduced her to cigarettes and showed her how to inhale, blowing luxurious clouds of smoke into the wind. They married quickly, two months after they met, one month after my grandpa purchased his studio. He promised her a ring, a real diamond set in gold. He even brought home a Sears catalog for her to choose from.

It was a genuine shock to my Grandma Chan when the ring never came. She rushed so deliberately into her life with my grandpa that I suppose she never stopped to question its reality, its sustainability. She became pregnant with my mom right after the wedding, which brought both joy and panic. My mother made the marriage real, forever joining them as parents, solidifying their decision to be together, to raise a child. But my grandma was ready, she told herself. Her daughter would have a different life. She would learn *piano, ballet, cinema*.

I'm told that the first three years of my grandparents' marriage were cheerful, their young delirium still fresh, my Grandpa Chan still doting on my grandma and my mom. He brought home malasadas after work and took them to see American movies when they were released on the island. He was obsessed with America, with U.S. history and popular culture. His future riches, his rise to greatness, lay in the hands of the young country, a land pregnant with possibility for men like him. So abundant was America that he hardly felt the need to try, as if living within her, knowing her history, was enough to succeed.

The photography shop was a mystery to my grandma. He told her it was doing well, always prepared with a story about a particular client or a job he had secured, depositing a couple dollars into her pocketbook as the grand finale. My grandma spent all her time with my mom, preparing dinners in their small kitchen, washing the sheets from their two beds, waiting for her husband to come home and make them feel like a family. The first few years of my mom's life were unlike any to follow, protected by a balloon of optimism, shaped by the chatter of eager parents.

But then came three more girls—arriving faster than my grandma could imagine possible. In the back of her mind, she knew that the structure of her life could not handle this kind of growth, that eventually the walls would burst. But she also knew that more children was a sign of prosperity, so she lied to herself, almost consciously, clinging to my grandpa's words, repeating them doggedly to herself.

This is just the beginning. The money will come. We must be patient.

So her life became an exercise in waiting. With the few dollars she received from my Grandpa Chan—her allowance never increasing with the arrival of more children—my grandma saved and bought an annual pass to the Honolulu Zoo in Kapiolani Park, taking her four girls there almost every day. She made them each a bento for lunch—still concerned that her children should eat properly—and they would picnic next to the single monkey housed there. Once, in a fit of motherly compulsion, my grandma bought all four of the girls a shave ice, delighted to watch them pick their flavors, licking at the sugary snow as they dragged sticks along the bars of the animal cages. But at the end of the week, the money was short. Their small extravagance made grocery shopping impossible. She scolded herself for almost a month. She never did it again.

My mom was the only one who didn't understand why she couldn't buy a treat every time she went to the zoo, why she couldn't have a candy bar at the drugstore. All the other girls were used to it, being told no, and soon enough, a divide rose up between the sisters; the one who came before, and those who came after.

My Grandpa Chan began to spend longer days at the studio, not to drum up business, but to obsess over the proper light needed to capture his subjects—of which there were few—to clean his lenses, to flip through catalogs and admire the newest cameras. His studio was his solace, a place where, between the hours of nine and seven, he could feel some kind of higher importance. Within those walls he was an artist. He worked alone; there was no one to tell him otherwise. And when he arrived home at eight, sometimes nine o'clock in the evening with no money to speak of, he made no excuses, he felt no shame.

"My art is not about money, Iris. It's a process. The greatest artists never made money during their lifetime—Kafka, Van Gogh, Bach—think about it. The money will come."

"And Kafka let his children starve?"

"Don't be ridiculous, Iris." He waved away her question. "Kafka didn't have any children."

When my Grandma Chan became pregnant with Eileen, her four girls already in hand-me-downs and my grandpa's photography business clearly failing—finally, she stopped deluding herself. She stopped waiting for what good might come. The intellectual wit that she used to admire, that she used to believe would bring riches and success, was now simply music to the maddening choreography of their marriage. She had been tricked, subdued for more years than she was willing to admit, her ring finger still naked, the Sears catalog yellowing beside her mattress on the floor. She didn't even have a proper bed, she realized with a wave of disgust, let alone a diamond. But as reality washed over her, so did the realization that she had allowed it. She had been impulsive and naïve. Why hadn't she asked about the money? Were her in-laws really dead, killed in a car accident as her husband had claimed? Why did she agree to live in a basement in Kaneohe when her husband kept a shop in Waikiki?

The questions hit her all at once, ricocheting, filling the empty spaces and creating a deafening metallic sound. She doubled over, clutching the child growing in her belly, and vomited on the plastic floor. All of it—the picnics on the beach, the Waialae mansions, the slow, lazy cigarettes—it was gone. Not that she ever had it, of course. She wiped her mouth with a kitchen towel, already dirty from last night's dishes, and decided at that moment to be satisfied—not happy, just satisfied. With time, she would conquer her mind. She would suppress her expectations and learn to find satisfaction in this life. It was her husband who taught her to desire—to want things she had never before considered. He was the same man who showed her immense disappointment, a feeling of failing at something that was never real.

She wondered if her red string was as brittle as she imagined, understanding in that moment that my Grandpa Chan was not her destined match. He didn't fight for her love; he deceived her—eluding the truth with his empty flattery. She tried to count how many times they had slept together, numbering the knots she had woven into her own fate, stopping when the number became too high and she was short of breath, imagining her red string wrapped around her neck, tied to her bedpost, knotted to her front door.

It's a story, she thought to herself, bringing a hand to her throat, coaxing air through her lungs as she began to think about the fable she was told as a girl, the consequences she now feared would be passed to her children. *They'll know better*, she whispered to herself. *It's a fairy tale,* she repeated over and again.

CHAPTER 5

November 1964
HONOLULU, HAWAII

The walk back to the great room goes slowly. Amy's hand rests on her hip, her elbow bent into a hook for Mrs. Leong to hold. The women are nearly identical in height, but Amy wears heels, white and leather, which lift her at least three inches. Theresa follows behind them, gauging their pace, studying the outlines of their bodies, the strangeness of their movement.

There is a cautiousness in Mrs. Leong's step. She creeps down the hall, her knees slightly bent, her feet skimming the floor. Her height, Theresa thinks, is her saving grace. It spares her from looking like a child, hiding from her parents, stepping lightly across the creaky floorboards to avoid detection. On first glance, Mrs. Leong looks simply like an aging woman. Her body has softened from lack of use, but she has remained slender. When she stands, Theresa thinks, there is very little sign of her weakness.

As they draw closer to the mouth of the corridor, the women begin to hear sounds. The echo of voices whispering, the careful, muted footsteps of visitors, the soft scraping of chairs against the wooden floor. It sounds exactly as a funeral should, and suddenly Amy is reminded of why she is here. It rattles her, the fact that she is capable of such delusion—that, for a moment, she really believed that the day's task had been accomplished. She had found her mother-in-law a proper shirt to wear.

Amy straightens. Her arm tenses and Mrs. Leong halts; her fingers tighten around Amy's arm.

"Sorry," Amy says instinctually. "Sorry—everything okay?"

Without looking at her, Mrs. Leong nods once. Her fingers loosen and so Amy continues. She lifts a foot and puts it down. She lifts a foot and puts it down. She repeats it in her head, calming under the structure of the words, able to breathe between the repetitions. Amy is grateful to be entering with her mother-in-law. She had not considered this scenario but now recognizes the way it will look to her guests—like Mrs. Leong chose her, trusted her for this important role. She feels the heat on her arm spread to her face.

As they reach the opening, Amy spots her family. They're already seated, one after the other in a middle row, her mother and father closest to the aisle. Amy's first thought is of her sister, who was the first phone call she made upon discovering that Bohai had died. Beverly came to the hospital immediately, and they stood together in the hallway, not speaking, barely looking at each other. It was also Beverly who had made her call Kaipo, six hours later when the shock had subsided. Amy had lied to him. She told Kaipo she had just found out, that he was her first phone call.

Amy's mother spots her. She stands, about to walk into the aisle, but Amy raises her arm. She extends a finger. One minute, she mouths, and her mother sits back down. Amy's mother looks to Theresa and offers a kind of smile, her mouth and eyes pulled upward by muscles that resist.

The room has mostly filled, the majority of chairs taken by people holding programs, their mouths busy with lucky candy. There is still time before the service begins and Amy knows that every seat will be taken. Seventy-five invitations and seventy-five acceptances. Amy couldn't believe it. It became a little joke between her and Theresa, each time the small white envelope appeared in their mailbox, that Bohai had turned out to be the most popular of them all.

Kaipo stands at the head of the room, at his place to the right of Bohai's casket. He holds his hands in front of him, clasped calmly together as mourners approach to drape flowers and leis across the coffin. Afterward, the men shake Kaipo's hand. The women kiss him lightly on the cheek. It looks like a scene from a black-and-white movie, Theresa thinks. It looks like somebody very important has died.

A number of eyes follow the women as they walk to the front of the room. Amy keeps her focus narrow, on the row of chairs to the left of the casket awaiting them, her pace still slow and deliberate. But Theresa looks out into the assembly of faces. She sends her eyes gliding over them, speeding across their features as she searches for his face.

Theresa wonders if she'll recognize him. Beneath the lights, in a crowd of people, seven months later he's bound to look different. And doesn't she? Theresa is enormous, almost fifty pounds heavier than the last time he saw her, the night she collapsed on the toilet, sobbing. Theresa extended the invitation as an olive branch, as a way of making up to her father. The white envelope returned with a check mark beside Attending, small and sharp, no signature. It was in blue ballpoint pen, easily written by his mother.

The women approach the coffin. Theresa doesn't see him.

"Is that my shirt?" Kaipo whispers to Amy as they help Mrs. Leong into her seat.

"Bohai's," she replies. Kaipo nods, studying his mother.

"Brilliant," he says, and Amy almost smiles.

"I have to go say hi to my mom," she says. "Are we almost ready to start?"

"Pretty much. I think the last of them are coming in now."

"It'll be quick, I promise."

As Amy walks down the aisle, greeting the seventy-five faces, nodding at a hundred and fifty eyes, she begins to hear an echo. Our condolences, she hears twice, such a beautiful funeral. It echoes three times, then a fourth. To these things she says thank you, sending her voice in their general direction, growing faint and warm as she makes the final steps to her mother's chair. Say hello now, Amy tells herself, and the task is through. After this, she can remove her mother from her mind, erase her from the day.

"Hi," she says.

"Amy," her mother replies, standing. "You look gorgeous—is this silk? Did you have this made?"

"Mom," Amy interrupts, her eyes piercingly still. With the smallest, briefest movement, Amy shakes her head. *This*, her mother's vanity, her inability to act appropriately when met with anything she finds shiny or lavish or new, is precisely why Amy has kept the families apart for eighteen years. Amy's mother has not seen Kaipo since Theresa was born. She has not entered the great room since before Amy was married. It's entirely intentional; caught between them, Amy feels her life dialed back to zero. She is twenty again, hanging on the word of her parents, the only two people in the room with whom she has not made her peace. She corrects herself; the only two still living.

"Did you get a program?" Amy asks abruptly, already unsettled.

"Yes," her mother says, flustered. "Yes, I have it right here."

"Good," Amy replies. "Thank you for sending the flowers."

Amy leans into the row, extending herself to greet her father and siblings.

"We're about to start, so I have to go back, but I'll see you afterward," she says. Amy looks each of them in the eye, starting and ending with Beverly, before returning to the head of the room and taking her seat between Theresa and Mrs. Leong. She looks at Kaipo and nods her head. He nods back and looks out over the mass of chairs. There is a body sitting in every one. He unclasps his hands and straightens the jacket of his suit. He clears his throat.

"Good morning, everyone. Aloha." He walks to the mouth of the aisle, acknowledging each section of the room. "Welcome."

The room quiets immediately. In the silence, the lights feel brighter to Amy—somehow intrusive, penetrating her skin in the flash of stillness. She feels like an experiment, something tiny and helpless being studied under a heat lamp.

"I want to thank you all for being here today," Kaipo says, and his voice is weaker than Amy expects, limper. It's too hot, she thinks, lifting a hand to the nape of her neck. It's far too hot.

"It means a lot to me and I know it would mean a lot to my brother to see you all gathered like this." He clears his throat again. He runs his right hand through his hair and Amy notices that his brow is damp. A sprinkling of mist dots his forehead, and when she looks closer, tightening her eyes, she is certain that the perspiration is accumulating. She is positive that Kaipo is just as uncomfortable as she is.

Amy begins to look for a fan. She thinks of how she could excuse herself, just briefly, so that she might find some air for both of them—for the entire room. She thinks of the relief a fan would bring. She begins to picture the rooms of the house, searching them for a fan that she could use. Bohai never used one, she remembers, so there wouldn't be one in his bedroom. None in the library. That portion of the house is shaded, she thinks. It always stays cool, even in the warmest months, even in July. There was no need for a fan in there. Amy begins to conjure the study when she realizes she's hanging off the edge of her chair. She's leaning forward, fingers clutching the wooden underside, and she is suddenly aware that Kaipo is still speaking.

Slowly, Amy lifts her eyes to meet her guests. All of them are looking at Kaipo. They're listening carefully to his words, their faces heavy with empathy, every drop of their sympathy real, their grief quiet and effortless. And the longer she looks, unable to look away, rapt by the sincerity of their expressions, the more it feels like an open palm, ripping across Amy's face. The more it feels like that same hand, reaching into her stomach and twisting, challenging her to feel something real.

And then it comes, something at once enormous and expected. Amy feels betrayed, not by the people before her, but by her own capacity to change. She promised herself, she swore that she would be better, that she would honor her husband in the way he deserved, in a way she could not manage during his lifetime. It's her failure as a widow—the same selfish, predictable failure that plagued her as a wife—to be present, *simply present*, at a moment as important as this.

"I've thought a lot about what I could say today," she hears Kaipo say. Amy takes a slow breath and leans back in her chair. *Listen*, she orders herself. *What's wrong with you?*

"As you all know, my brother was a man of few words, and so the task of choosing the right words for him today is not a simple one." Amy breathes again. It occurs to her that her husband lies ten feet away—that in a way, he is there, witnessing her failure, silent as always.

"And even as I stand here now, I don't know that I'll get it right. In fact, I'm fairly certain that I'll get it wrong. But I also know that my brother will forgive me. Forgiveness was easy for Bohai—I'm sure you've all experienced it, the enormous compassion of my brother. It was one of his most honorable traits, and it was something that I have always envied about him."

Kaipo pauses. His eyelids lower softly to the floor.

"Did you hear that?" he says, turning toward the casket. "I envied you, Bohai. I envied you in more ways than you know."

A moment passes. It's followed by a second, and Kaipo has yet to turn back around. His eyes linger on the coffin.

Seventy-five people sit silently, uncomfortably, unsure of where to look. Amy feels the urge to stand. Her legs tighten, compelling her to save Kaipo, to do something decent for her husband. But Amy realizes she has nothing to say once she rises, not a single comforting sentence. She will simply be standing. Her left leg begins to tremble.

"There was plenty to envy about my brother." Amy flinches with the return of Kaipo's voice. She exhales downward, slowly breathing into her body, trying to keep the hot air away from the others. She feels Theresa's hand extend to her lap. *It's okay*, her daughter whispers, and her face looks just like the others'. It startles Amy—that she may be the only person in the room unaffected by Kaipo's speech, the only one not listening.

"Bohai was a brilliant man. He saved this family from ruin more times than I'd like to admit. And he never told anyone. Even now, I don't think anyone really knows how important he was to my father's business, to what the business is today."

Amy takes Theresa's hand and squeezes it tightly. She feels grateful for her daughter, for her gesture, small as it is. To Amy, it feels like an offering. A hand extended, an indication that her daughter will not hate her forever. Amy allows it to soothe her, to lighten her, and it feels like carbonation—rising through her body, lifting her from the inside. *Thank you*, she mouths, still clutching her daughter's hand.

"But if I had to choose a single trait about my brother. If I had to pick one thing that I admired most, well—that would be easy, actually.

"When we were boys, I never could have imagined that Bohai's life would turn out this way. He never talked about wanting a wife or a family. He never showed much of an interest. But I think that was the beauty of what happened to Bohai. He met Amy and it was immediate, like lightning. I'd never seen anything like it, and I have to admit, I was a little jealous that it was so simple for them. They met, they fell in love, they married, they lived happily ever after until death took him suddenly. That was the only part that didn't fit. But I say with confidence, that if I have seen fate in my lifetime—if fate and destined matches and red strings and fairy tales are to be believed—then I saw it in the two of them. I saw it every time my brother was with his wife."

Kaipo pauses and turns to Amy. His entire face smiles with the exception of his eyes, which continue to grieve. Amy turns her gaze to her lap, to where she holds her daughter's hand, trying to keep it steady. A dampness presses against the back of her eyes. It is the first time today that Amy is completely aware that her husband is dead, and that she is at his funeral.

"After Bohai met Amy, to say he was overjoyed would be an understatement. It was joy in his own way, of course. He stopped working fourteen-hour days. He spent more time with us. He went out for drives. He came to the beach. And then they married and had little Theresa and again, my brother was so proud, so *happy*."

Amy closes her eyes. She doesn't know what else to do.

"Bohai shared a closeness with his family that I admired very, very much. He loved these girls. He lived for this woman from the day he met her until the day he died. And I suppose that's what brings me comfort when I think about the fact that he's gone. And I didn't mean to get so sentimental, so forgive me all, I'm almost done. But I just wanted to say—I wanted to remind you all, as the people who loved my brother—that he died happy. That he died loved, and that he was in love."

Behind her eyelids, Amy waits. She dreads what's on the other side. She weighs her options and does nothing, suspended in the dark, hanging there, letting it swallow her. When she can no longer deny that Kaipo's speech is over, when she hears the sound of bodies adjusting, of voices murmuring in hushed agreement—still, she does not open her eyes.

Mom, she hears. *Are you okay?*

She doesn't move. Her mind is far away.

Amy

My father's photography studio was one of the few on the island, and the only studio in Waikiki. Before I began to work for him, his regular clients were mostly babies and toddlers dressed in ridiculous lace dresses with matching bows strapped around their bald little heads. Sometimes it took my father four hours to shoot a single baby. He would obsess over the angle of the wicker chair and tilt the child's head in a hundred directions, waiting for the precise moment when the sunlight poured through the studio window. Usually the babies would cry and the toddlers would throw themselves to the floor before he could get his perfect shot and the parents would have to bring them back the next day.

At noon, when the sun is right above this skylight, he would say excitedly, his finger pointing upward as the parents bounced their exhausted children on their hip.

When I was younger, when my father was late for dinner, my mother would say that he was so slow to take those pictures because he preferred his studio to being home with us. *And who wouldn't,* she'd mutter, bending under furniture, shaking out the rug too many times, *the mongoose would not live in these conditions!* My father, when he finally arrived home at nine or ten, would say that his perfectionism was *merely a testament to his dedication.* He said it as if he were a legendary artist and my mother would never understand. Even at fourteen, I knew he was wrong. The way he always left us, the way he came home, like a silhouette, his form was present but never his contents. Everything important, everything he cared about, it seemed he kept in Waikiki.

Like a TV show with only one episode, it was always the same fight.

My parents would be in the kitchen, on the other side of the sheet that divided our house in two. I'd hear my mother whispering in her harshest tone while dishes clattered in the sink. I could always tell how distraught she was by how high the faucet was turned up, by the sound her dish washing made. If a cup smashed, it was an emergency. There would be tears. *God damn it*, she'd whisper, and I knew she was crying for the cup, because already there were so few.

Then, over the sound of running water, I'd hear my father respond with a joke. I wouldn't make out the words but his tone was enough. The faucet would turn off and my mother would be gone, wandering the neighborhood until she had cooled off. I had long suspected she was smoking cigarettes. When she returned home, she went immediately to wash her hands. But it made me happy to think of her smoking in the dark, taking long drags and blowing them sideways into the wind. My mother indulged in so few things; she deserved at least that.

But then the bombs fell, we declared war on Japan, and everything changed for us. It was strange that war could bring us such good fortune, but that's what happened. The beige phone in my father's studio, usually silent for entire weeks, would not stop ringing.

Every day, we found ourselves flooded with more clients than we were capable of photographing, and for that first week, I ran around the small studio apologizing and refreshing my smile, racking my brain for a solution. It frustrated me endlessly to watch men leave the studio without a portrait. They had come to us with money, real money, and we had turned them away. Each day I counted them; five lost clients meant fifteen dollars uncollected. That was a week's pay. Half a month's rent. More cigarettes than my mother could smoke in a year. And then I'd look at my father, who had been shooting the same man for nearly two hours, and I knew change was up to me. And I could, I told myself. In years of listening to my parents fight the same circular battle, never finding a solution, I had learned a few things. Money was a serious world, a masculine world—that's what my mother didn't understand. If I hoped for success, there would be no emotions, no broken cups, no walking away without an agreement.

"Think about it," I said to my father. We were on the bus, passing through Chinatown on our way home. "They don't care about the art. They're going to *war*. All they want is a picture that makes them look handsome, and I know you can do that in under an hour. Even with the curfew, we'd make more money than we could spend."

The island had just come under martial law, which meant that between the hours of six and six, we had to be off the streets with our lights out. The radio told us that a lit cigarette or tobacco pipe could be cause for arrest, as could the light from a radio dial or the flame of a kitchen stove. I took the warnings seriously, and every night I made sure we were home before the sun touched the horizon.

My father let out a low sigh and leaned his head back against the plastic seat.

"You weren't supposed to turn out like this," he complained. "Didn't I teach you anything as a child? You were supposed to be an artist!"

"And I will be," I interrupted. "But you need money for art. You taught me that, remember? So let's make our money while we have the opportunity. These are your own words, Dad! *Ability is nothing without opportunity*." It was one of his favorite defenses in battle with my mom. It gave the impression of humility, of looking for a solution without actually offering any. I pushed forward, watching him respond to this, his own wisdom.

"If the soldiers pay the three dollars, let them do what they want. Maybe some of them want to smile—"

"No smiling," he said immediately. He crossed his arms across his chest like a child. "Ruins my film. Makes the pictures look cheap."

"Okay, okay." I turned my head to the window and smiled. I knew he would say that, but I wanted to see how far he could be pushed. I wanted to know how badly we needed the money. It felt strange to be talking to him like this, somehow nostalgic for a time I faintly remembered, kindling something I knew was very nearly spent. All these years later, it was a beautiful, twisted thought. If the war sustained, if the soldiers continued to enlist, I might just meet the dignified man my mother claimed she married.

"So no smiling." I faced him, straight-faced. "But you'll seat the soldiers in half-hour slots, starting at eight. And I'll make appointments so you'll have to stay on track!"

My father paused, closing his eyes as if I had just asked him the greatest favor in the world.

"An hour," he said, his eyes still closed. "And those weren't my words, about opportunity. They were Napoleon's."

"Is that so?" I paused. "Forty-five minutes."

"Who raised you?" he cried, opening his eyes and turning to face me. He took my chin in his hand and turned it toward him, studying my face. "You can't be mine."

"Don't worry," I told him. "You'll have no problem claiming me when we're rich."

The next day we began our new schedule, and by the time we closed up shop at four, we had collected twenty-one dollars, which I'm fairly certain my father had never earned in an entire week, let alone a single day. He wouldn't say it, and I didn't expect him to, but I could see it in his face. He suppressed a smile all day as we collected payment after payment, the soldiers happy to be in and out in under an hour. It was satisfying in a way I'd never felt before; a pleasure I imagined was limited to being a man, able to make money from your mind and not just your hands. But it had nothing to do with being a man, I decided, and everything to do with ambition, with desire and opportunity. I could save my father's business; I could restore his name. Every dollar was a new possibility, a door that had been locked for our entire lives. My father's camera clicked and I saw a coat of fresh paint on our house—the whole house, the upstairs now ours as well. I saw a set of porcelain cups, a four-poster bed, a record player on a table large enough for twelve.

Every day, I thought of these things as I sat at the cash register. My duties as my father's assistant were limited. My daily tasks were usually finished by noon, so I spent most of my day entertaining the soldiers, chatting with them as they waited for their time slot. From this, I received a different kind of gratification. I was asked on dates almost every week—some of them good, most of them not. With the new curfew, the soldiers had to be creative with their proposals. I got asked to picnics and afternoon drives along the shore, shave ice and morning dim sum. My father would listen in on our chatter, smirking at me when he could. He gave each of my suitors a nick-name, like "Big Mustache" and "Small Uniform" and "Cheap Guy." He would quiz the men on American politics and history before let-ting them take me out, showing an interest in who I dated for the first time in my life. I didn't mind. Really, I think I enjoyed it. I liked the attention—not from the soldiers, but from my father, who had been absent for so long.

It was Big Mustache, or Henry Wong, who lingered around the studio one day, charming both me and my father. He had just sat for his photograph, and I had spent the forty-five minutes deciding whether or not I thought he was handsome. He was the first man with a mustache who had struck me as attractive, and while I con-sidered his other qualities—his big eyes, his full lips, his black hair that was both wavy and thick—I realized that he was looking back at me, too.

"Focus on me, son, not on the girl," my father instructed from behind his camera. "I know she's pretty but you'll just have to wait."

Henry laughed nervously and I pretended not to hear. Great laugh, I thought to myself as I shuffled together two pieces of blank paper.

After his appointment, Henry came to pay me at the register. And to apologize for staring, he said. He hadn't meant to, he'd just gotten a little distracted. I let myself smile and I could feel it grow. Henry was handsome. It wasn't the kind of handsome you would recognize in a crowd or from across a room. It was quieter than that but it was there, in the ease of his eyes, in the calm of his voice.

"It's okay," I replied. "I think I was a bit distracted, too."

Henry went silent. His hand was still on the counter between us, fingers resting on his three dollars. He looked at me as if he had something to say, but had forgotten how to say it. I held his gaze and waited for him to remember.

"I'd like to do this again sometime," he said. He shook his head, a shy smile escaping him. "I mean. Not the staring part. But maybe a date? I promise I'll wear something else." He opened his arms to display his uniform.

"Listen," my father said from across the room. He had already begun with the next soldier. "You can take out my daughter if you can answer one question. It's easy, really. Any soldier should know."

Henry turned to my father. He stood up straighter. "This is your daughter, sir?"

"That she is," he replied, squatting to get a new angle, camera pressed to his face. "Aren't you, Amy?"

"Yes, I am, Dad."

"So are you going to answer the question or not?"

"Yes," Henry said, turning briefly to me. "Yes, of course. Go ahead, ready when you are, sir."

My father cleared his throat.

"State the military experience of the American president, Franklin D. Roosevelt."

This question, I thought to myself. My father had asked it twice already. Only one of the soldiers had answered correctly and that date had been a complete disaster. We had nothing in common and he wouldn't stop rambling about fighter planes and midget submarines, mouth full of dumplings.

But Henry seemed like a different species entirely. There was something familiar about him, something compelling about the way he spoke to me. I thought about scribbling the answer on a scrap of paper and sliding it to him from behind the register.

Henry thought for a moment, his hands shoved deep into the pockets of his uniform. The soldier being photographed smirked at him and was promptly scolded by my father.

"None," Henry said suddenly.

"What did you say, son?"

"The answer is none. Sir. President Roosevelt has no military experience."

My father snapped a picture and turned around for the first time.

"Exactly right. You may pick Amy up at three when her shift is over. She must be home by five thirty. No exceptions! I don't want any policemen knocking on my door tonight." He paused for a moment, and then remembering his thought, he said, "And good luck out there. We have a president with no military experience command-ing a war." He turned abruptly to the soldier he was photographing. "Don't think I can't see you grinning!"

Henry looked at me and mouthed the words *Is he serious*, his face caught somewhere between shock and delight. *Completely*, I mouthed back. *See you at three*.

As promised, Henry came at three, pulling up in a black Ford coupe. He wore a white collared shirt and navy blue pants, both freshly pressed. I could tell he was nervous, and it made me nervous too.

"Back so soon?" my father said as he walked through the studio doors.

"She'll be home before curfew, Mr. Chan. And safely. I'll make sure of it." They exchanged nods and I knew my father liked him.

"Go on, then," he said, winking at me as I grabbed my purse off its hook and walked out the door.

Henry drove effortlessly, as if the gearshift were simply an extension of his right arm, the engine revving quietly as he made easy conversation. We were going to the Pali, he told me, in Nuuanu, and my eagerness for our afternoon soared. I knew what it was—a lookout at the top of the Koolau Range, a hidden piece of elevation. Something spectacular I'd heard of while cleaning houses, through the daughters, a place I'd never been because my family had never owned a car.

The Old Pali Highway was a throughway built a century before. It was the first road to connect Honolulu and the windward side of the island, famous for the eight hundred skulls found during construction, thought to belong to the Hawaiian warriors who fell to their deaths from the jagged cliffs above. The road was narrow, in places not wide enough for two cars to pass, squeezed up against the mountainside and shaded by enormous low-hanging trees, almost tunnel-like in their density. Along the cliff, emerald vines fell from above, leaves dangling off them like charms on a bracelet. I gaped out the window as Henry talked, trying to memorize what I saw, already wanting to tell my sisters.

Henry was not a combat soldier. He was an engineer, leaving for Europe at the end of the month to work on the telephone lines. He had two siblings, an older brother who worked in his parents' pharmacy and a sister—three years younger—who would like me, he said.

We slowed for a narrow turn, starting our ascent of the mountain, and I began to tell Henry about my family, all ten of them, their names rolling off my tongue in alphabetical order,

" . . . then Denise, Eileen, Francine, and Grace. Plus my younger brothers Rich—"

"Holy smokes," he interrupted, "there're boys too?"

"Three of them! You think my father would come home at night if there were only seven girls?"

"Well, hell," he said, his voice suddenly serious. "You're not making this easy on me, you know."

"What do you mean?"

"A father, a mother, three brothers, *six* sisters. How will I manage to impress them all? Maybe I can build you guys a telephone line. How about that? Will they let me marry you if I can build a telephone line?"

I looked at him, ready to object, but he was already looking back at me, the road ahead a perfectly straight line. The lowering sun flickered in and out of the car windows as we passed below the latticed branches suspended above, through fleeting shadows that broke into sunlight. "Moonlight Cocktail" was on the radio. I liked him a lot.

"I . . ." I began. "It'd have to be a pretty nice telephone line," I said instead, feeling my lungs expand into the crevices of my chest and slowly fall. I knew I should be careful—that a man who introduced the word *marriage* within fifteen minutes was usually the most fickle kind of man. His audacity should have scared me, but I didn't feel that way with Henry. It had the opposite effect; I felt courageous.

The car began to wind its way up the Koolau mountains, hugging the moss-covered cliff to the right, a perilous open expanse to our left. There was no guard rail, no barrier between us and the valley that grew deeper and deeper below. But Henry was steady with his car, maneuvering confidently as the houses below us turned into cluttered rooftops and the breeze drifting through the open windows became more forceful, emboldened with elevation.

"In the backseat, there's a flower," Henry said, pointing behind him. I turned and saw a single orchid next to two tin lunchboxes tied shut with a green ti leaf. "Lore has it that these two stones"—he pointed to the right as he slowed the car down—"are the bodies of Hawaiian goddesses, left to protect the Pali. Before we head back, we'll leave the orchid under a stone as an offering to them. Then we'll be ensured a safe trip down."

"And the lunch boxes?" I asked. "Did the goddesses ask for a snack?"

"Those are for us," Henry grinned. "But the ti leaf is to protect it from being stolen—by the angry spirits or by that other goddess. The volcano one."

I knew there were old ghost stories set in this place—stories told to us as children about tired men tempted off the cliff by a beautiful ghost, or cars that wouldn't start at the top and the hungry spirits who would attack the stranded passengers for food. Ancient wars were fought on these cliffs, hundreds of men dead, their ghosts left to wander. But they were stories; legends to keep us safe, to keep the folklore alive. So I couldn't help but ask, "Do you actually believe in this stuff?"

"Of course not," he replied, "but it's fun." He shifted as the hill got steeper and turned toward me, hesitating. "It is fun—isn't it?"

He looked at me with such sincerity, waiting for my response— waiting for me to confirm that I was having a good time—that I couldn't help but laugh at him. He had planned this entire afternoon for us; he had ironed his shirt, he had packed snacks. So far, it was the best date I'd ever been on and here he was, wondering if he'd done something wrong already. Happy laughter spilled from my mouth as I shook my head.

"Oh, come on!" he exclaimed, hitting the wheel with his palm. "I had to be inventive!" Now he was laughing too. "Your father didn't exactly give me much time to plan *and* you have to be home by five thirty! That's a lot of pressure, Amy."

I placed my hand gently on top of his as he shifted into gear and began to slow the car. "Henry," I said, the warmth of his skin finding an unexpected shyness within me. I pulled my hand away and closed it into a fist, trapping the heat within my fingers, suddenly aware of both of our bodies.

"It's perfect," I finally managed, my courage melting in my hand. Henry shifted once more and parked the car along a wide ridge with a clear view.

"Good," he said. "And here's the main event."

I stepped out of the car and walked slowly to the ridge. When I looked over the edge I was immediately overcome with the most extraordinary nausea. My knees trembled softly. I felt faint and rickety and breathless.

I'd never seen Oahu the way I saw it that afternoon at the Pali. The Kaneohe that I'd lived in my entire life was suddenly a cluster of homes and fields on the valley floor—my entire world reduced to a sprinkling of roofs and patches of land. I had never felt so insignificant, so meaningless, but in the most remarkable way. The land below was wild and immense. I never knew it existed, never understood how large the fields reached around my home, how the land rippled in blankets of shrubbery and thick canopies of trees. It was a clear day, wind shifting the radiant mist north, away from where we stood alone, the lookout completely unspoiled by sightseers. In the distance, gorgeous, silvery clouds hung over Kaneohe Bay, echoing my elation.

I thought of how easily I could fall; how my body seemed to be filled with air and if pushed, I might float, like I was perfectly weightless. I spread my arms and took in the mountain air; I closed my eyes. It was the closest I have ever come to flying.

"Do you like it?"

I looked behind me and there was Henry, one of thousands of people on Oahu, one of the tiny bodies occupying the toy homes below. But he wasn't just anyone, I decided. Not to me.

We stood at the ridge of the mountain, finding the roofs of our houses and our old schools and his parents' little pharmacy, letting the wind blow over our bodies. I told him where I was when the bombs dropped, about Akio, something I had told no one but my sister Beverly, afraid of implicating him somehow. Akio and his gentle manner, his prideful workmanship: I would continue to see him this way, refusing to taint our years together with the hour that brought it to an end. The way he cried, the way he prayed, expelling a heartbreak that had become my own—that I could still feel, telling Henry then, as I thought of Akio removing his keys, saw his sunken shoulders disappearing down the stairs.

Henry was at Hickam Field that day, right in the middle of it all. He told me how the marines were lying flat on their bellies, crates of ammo strewn beside them, shooting at the planes with their rifles.

"They were our own planes," he said quietly, "we were shooting them down. There was so much confusion, they didn't know what to attack. Our own men, they were taking off from Wheeler Field and we were shooting them down.

"They had me carry sand to put out the fires. Everyone not trained in combat was carrying sand, hauling it back and forth. When the Japs had dispersed and we took all the injured men to the navy hospital, they let some of us go. They told me to go and I went, didn't ask if they needed more help, if they needed hands in the hospital. Just got in my car and left them."

"I stole a pair of pruning shears," I said, words arriving without my consent. It was the strangest thing, instinctual, forceful. "I carried them all the way home, fingers clenched around the handle. I walked into my house and it hit me. Two parents, nine little siblings, and for the entire walk, my only thoughts were of myself."

We stood there for a minute, not saying a word, not offering the empty reassurances we'd heard from others. It was a comfortable silence, a safe space between us.

"Tell me more about the folklore," I said, looking up from my hands.

"You're hilarious," Henry replied, his eyes squinting in the lowering sun.

"No," I insisted, "I mean it. I'm interested."

He walked slowly back to his car and leaned against it for a moment. "Okay," he said, lifting himself onto the hood. "Let's see. You don't have any pork on you, do you?"

I hesitated. I couldn't believe he'd just asked me that.

"Honestly?"

"No way," he said, leaning forward on his knees, "and you were making fun of my orchid?"

I walked to the car and grabbed my purse, reaching to the bottom and feeling for the Spam musubi I had packed that morning as a snack. "I'm embarrassed," I mumbled, tossing it to Henry on the hood of the car.

"We have to get rid of this," he announced, studying my musubi in his hands. "This is dangerous material you have here."

"What are you talking about?"

"Pork god, Amy. Half man, half pig. If you don't toss this before we leave, the car might not start again and then you'll be stuck with me forever. May I?" I nodded. He cocked his arm back and the next second, the musubi was hurtling high into the air, arching over the ridge and disappearing to the valley floor. "Much better. And now you should understand," he reached behind him and grabbed the tin lunchboxes, "why I brought *poke*.

"See, the gods don't care about fish," he said, handing me a tin and a set of wooden chopsticks. I pulled on the ti leaf and opened the lid. Fat pieces of pink ahi and black sesame seeds were packed into the little box. It had been a long time since I'd eaten fish this fresh, this expensive. I lifted myself onto the hood of his car.

"Unbelievable," I said, placing a piece of salty tuna on my tongue, "Where did you get this?"

Since the attack there had been nothing like this available on the island, at least not to my knowledge. The fish markets dried up, their supplies going straight to the government. Even meat, the worst cuts like hamburger and liver, was a rarity. It was for the soldiers; they needed protein more than the rest of us. It had been weeks of Spam, Vienna sausage, and tinned beef. It wasn't such a leap for our family; we were used to cans and bags, skipping the expensive, perishable aisles at the grocery store. My sisters had already started a victory garden with the seeds from the state, growing cabbages and taro to sustain us through what would come. But *poke*, raw and buttery, fresh from the ocean—even before the attack, I'd never seen it on my family's table.

"I'm glad you like it," Henry said, lifting a bite of fish with his chopsticks. "My uncle is a fisherman on the North Shore, and every Sunday my mom makes a different *poke*." Henry paused. "You really don't remember me at all, do you?"

I stopped chewing and put my chopsticks down. The way he had said it—casually, but with so much intention. It made everything in my body slow. I could feel the piece of tuna in my throat, could trace the blood pumping through my veins.

"What are you talking about?"

"It was a long time ago," Henry said, looking down at his car. "We were kids on the North Shore. In Waialua."

"Waialua?" I repeated. I hadn't thought of that place in years. I hadn't been there in even longer. My grandma lived on the North Shore. She had a small house on the water and I would spend summers there before she died. I was nine.

"With your grandma," Henry said softly. "Do you remember?" He looked up at me and gently pushed my hair from my face. With one finger, he touched the outside of my eyebrow. "I think I gave you this scar."

I pulled away from him; I touched my face and I remembered a boy. I saw him at the fish stand, small and skinny. It was by the docks, a few houses down from my grandma's. She would send me to get her mahimahi on Tuesday mornings. It was all still there, a little hazy, but I remembered the wooden counter, the blue paint on the metal sign. My grandma knew the fisherman, and every week, he would put aside a fish for her, wrapped in newspaper. And he would have his nephew walk me home. It was Henry.

I touched my feet to the ground and stood from the car, walking to the edge of the cliff. That day, we stopped on the beach. We put the fish in the sand. I ran into the ocean and plunged into the water, holding my breath to thirty, counting slowly. When I came up for air, something flew toward me. A small, flat rock skimmed the water in front of my face and jumped up. It struck me and I started to bleed; I screamed. Henry had been skipping rocks. I ran from the water to my grandma's house. Henry hadn't followed. It was the last time I saw him. The next morning, my mother came and brought me back to Kaneohe. My grandma had passed later that year, in November.

"I'm sorry," Henry said behind me. "I didn't mean to frighten you and I'm sorry if I did. It's just when I saw you this afternoon I felt it immediately. Then your father said your name and I couldn't believe it was you."

Words escaped me, my mind buzzed with strange electricity. This whole time, I had been with Henry, the boy with the fish. The boy who walked me home, the boy who made me cry. I had thought about him the following summer, after we sold my grandma's house and I knew I wouldn't go back. I had missed him.

"Amy." Henry said my name and I turned around. He touched a hand to my shoulder and my body went cold—everywhere but my shoulder, where the heat from his fingers penetrated me. "Are you okay?"

"I'm okay," I said, remembering the low rumble of the ocean, the sound of water filling miles of open air. I saw Henry holding my fish, heard him telling me how he'd saved me the biggest one.

"You used to walk me home," I said.

"Every Tuesday."

We were so still. I was thankful for the wind, for the relief it provided.

"It's getting pretty late. I think I should get home."

"I scared you," Henry said as we drove. "I know I did. I shouldn't have said it like that. I'm sorry—it was stupid."

"No," I said. "I'm glad. Really, I am. It's just strange, you know—meeting you again like this."

"It's not strange," he replied, slowing the car as we came to a stoplight. "It's fate."

He let his words linger; he didn't take them back or apologize for saying them. He said it like it was a fact, like he had read it in a book.

I couldn't sleep that night. There was too much to think about, to remember. My mind flickered with images of that last summer, of Henry. I couldn't believe he had recognized me. The boy I knew had been quieter. Not shy—we talked endlessly. Handing me my grandma's fish, he would explain to me how it was special in some way or another. One week he told me the scales had stayed bright blue, even after it died, which was rare because they usually turned grey. I still remembered that fact, still remembered so much of what he'd told me. I had no idea if it was true, but every so often, when I ate mahimahi, I would think of its scales and of Henry and wonder if the fish had been special.

We had a secret inlet, a shallow bay hidden by naupaka shrubs where we would sit for hours after delivering the fish, keeping each other company as the summer waned on, when we would find each other there on Wednesdays and Thursdays, then almost every day of the week, both of us parentless, friendless. Henry had grown up on that beach, steeped in its lore, a story for every plant and animal we passed. Naupaka, he told me, was once a beautiful Hawaiian goddess who fell in love with a commoner. Henry's young voice returned to me, his fingers dragging a stick through the damp sand as we sat in the shade of the glossy plant found all over the island, unremarkable before that afternoon. The goddess Naupaka was forbidden to marry the commoner, so she took the flower from her hair and tore it in half, giving him one side, keeping the other. Naupaka's lover was banished to the mountains and Naupaka to the beach, which is why, Henry said, the naupaka tree blooms with just half a flower. Which is why the plant is found only on the beach or in the mountains.

He made me something, I remembered suddenly. I got out of bed and walked into the bathroom, started pulling boxes down from above the toilet. I sifted through three boxes filled with Christmas ornaments and old clothes and art we had made in elementary school. At the bottom of the fourth box, I found a piece of flat wood, facedown. I lifted it out and flipped it over. Attached to the front was my name, spelled out in long pieces of skinny white coral. It was perfectly constructed, the coral glued evenly to the frame, the letters expertly formed. A young engineer, I laughed to myself. We had collected the pieces together, I remembered now, Henry explaining along the way. *They're actually animals; they eat plankton with their tentacles.* We gathered them in a plastic bag we found caught in a hau bush. I had forgotten to take my pieces home and Henry had showed up the next day with my present.

I looked in the mirror and lifted my hair. The scar was barely noticeable, just a faint line, slightly lighter than my skin and shorter than my thumbnail. I was still mad at Henry when my mother had come to get me. I showed her the cut and she'd teased me.

It's the red string of fate, she laughed to my grandma. *Lucky girl, her destined match gets such a good price on fish.*

Afterward, as an apology, my mother had explained. As we rode the bus back to Kaneohe, she told me a story.

And even as the memories of Henry faded, I still thought about that old tale. I remembered the red string, hoped for my destined match. Was this fate? Even before I knew it was Henry, I knew there was something there. We felt connected; each time we touched, it had reached through me. I stayed up all night, lost in my memories, and the next morning I found myself sitting on my bed, staring at a blank wall from when breakfast ended to when lunch began.

"What are you doing?"

I looked up, snapping from my daze to see Francine standing above me. Her hands were covered in red dirt, her hair tied back with a handkerchief.

"What?"

"There's a guy out there in a black car. He asked if you were home." Francine shrugged and walked back outside.

I pushed off my bed and ran to the front door to look out the screen. There was Henry's car, and Henry, talking with my brother Richard. I rushed to the bathroom and studied myself in the mirror. I looked terrible, tired. I brushed my hair into a ponytail and pinched my cheeks to bring some life to my face. He was here.

"Henry?" I said casually, walking through the screen door. "What are you doing here?" I couldn't control how big my smile became. It surprised me, how scattered I felt.

"I'm here on official family business," he said with a smirk. "My mom made malasadas this morning and wanted me to bring some by. For your father, of course." He held up a brown paper bag.

"How friendly," I replied, feeling warm all over again.

"So how much does a car like this cost?" That was Richard, walking around the Ford coupe, squatting and examining the wheels.

"Well, it costs nearly an entire military bonus. If you join the army, you could get one too. But then, of course, you'd have to go to war."

"It's really nice," Richard said, kicking up some dirt with his foot.

"Can I show you inside?" I interrupted. Henry walked to me and leaned down, shaded his eyes with one hand.

"Is this okay?" he whispered. "I'm not crazy, I promise."

"I know," I said. "I just can't believe you're here."

I didn't mean to say it like that; I worried Henry would take it the wrong way, but he knew what I meant: I couldn't believe this was real. I couldn't believe he was here, physically—flesh-and-bones Henry from a childhood that had almost vanished.

"Me neither," he said, taking my hand. "Okay, let's go find that scary father of yours."

We walked through the one room, past the kitchen, and out the screen door into the backyard. My mother and father were sitting at the table, drinking instant coffee and not talking to each other.

"Dad," I said, closing the door behind me, "Henry's here and he brought us some malasadas." My father turned around in his plastic chair.

"Henry!" he said, standing up. "Congratulations! Five twenty-six—you got my daughter home early last night!" He shook his hand.

"Thank you, Mr. Chan. It wasn't easy." Henry handed him the bag. "From my mother."

My mother eyed Henry curiously. She stood and took the bag from my father.

"I'll put these on a plate," she said. "I'm Amy's mother. What a nice surprise on a Saturday." She was smiling when she walked back into the house. When she returned, doughnuts shimmering on a plate, she asked Henry about his family.

"We live nearby, in Kailua." He pointed behind him. "My parents have a small pharmacy in town. My father fills prescriptions; my mom does perfumes and soaps but only to fund her cooking. We like to say we sell drugs to buy food." My mother giggled.

"She used the last of her flour but she wanted you and Mr. Chan to have some. As a thank-you for the photographs."

"Well, these are some of the best I've ever had. Tell your mother she's a very talented woman."

"I will," he said, grinning. "She'll like that."

I looked at Henry and couldn't get over the fact that he was sitting in my backyard. It felt like a secret history, something heavy yet fragile that we shared. It was reassuring to see him in the light. He was real like this, not a memory or a stranger on the Pali. As I sat next to him, listening to the tenor of his voice as he spoke with my parents, I could feel myself slipping.

He didn't stay long; just enough for a malasada and a cup of coffee. I walked him to his car and he said, "Well, I knew if I didn't have something to do today, I'd ask you to come with me. And I'm trying not to scare you today, so I promised my sister I'd take her to the beach. But say you'll come for lunch tomorrow. My mom is making a feast."

I was barely listening. I was thinking about how much I liked his mustache.

"Yes," I said abruptly.

"I'll pick you up at noon, okay?" He leaned over and kissed me on the cheek.

"Henry," I said, as he lowered himself into his car. He looked up at me and I lost what I was trying to say. I stood there, trying to collect my feelings.

"Yes?" he asked slyly.

"Thanks," I whispered, when that's all that came to me.

Henry smiled as he started the engine. "No problem."

I stayed on the street, watching Henry drive away, and when his car disappeared, I felt an overwhelming urge to start walking. To make the distance between us smaller. I wondered if this was love, not meaning to wander so far but unable to stop myself. I wondered how long I could make this feeling last, if I could go to bed wrapped in this warmth, if I could spread it through a week, a month, an entire season. And then another feeling—a strange detour that I hadn't intended but couldn't help, feeling a certain sadness as the thought passed through my mind—that the way I felt for Henry that afternoon, there on the empty road in front of my house, was stronger than anything my parents had ever, in the span of their lifetimes, felt for each other.

I don't know why, but I assumed Henry's house would be much nicer than it was. I felt terrible thinking it, but after the fresh fish and the malasadas and the car, I thought that Henry's family must have some money. They did not.

We pulled up to a house about the size of my own; a little larger, painted a light blue with brown trim, the smells of soy sauce and Chinese five-spice hitting my nose as we stepped from the car.

We walked through a screen door and removed our shoes, Henry calling out to his family that we were there.

"Amy!" A plump woman emerged from the small kitchen smiling, wiping her hands on her floral apron and opening her arms to hug me. "I'm so glad you could join us!"

I leaned in to hug his mother, as Henry's father and siblings entered from the other room. *Paul and Margaret*, I reminded myself.

We exchanged hugs and handshakes as they ushered me into their small dining room, the wooden chairs around the table completely mismatched.

"Lunch is almost ready!" Henry's mother said before rushing back into the kitchen.

"I like your dress," Margaret said, pulling out a chair and sitting. "Where did you get it?"

"I like yours," I said, "and this dress?" I looked down and pretended to think, as if I hadn't spent the last twelve hours obsessing over what I would wear, "I made myself, actually."

"Wow," Margaret cooed, "it's really nice."

"Here we are!" announced Henry's mother, emerging from the kitchen with a huge ceramic pot, steam billowing from the top as she placed it on the table. She scurried back into the kitchen and reentered the dining room with a bamboo steamer filled with pork-and-chive shumai, a bowl of glistening baby eggplant, soft mounds of rice paper rolls stuffed with bits of dried shrimp, and finally, little plastic saucers heaped with sliced scallion and ginger and toasted sesame seeds. I could feel my eyes expanding as she continued to fill the small table.

"I told you," Henry said, "that's my college fund."

"For us," Henry's father started, "food is the most important part of family." He took the lid off the steamer. "And we like to think we're a very, very important family." He chuckled heartily.

"At least for now," said Paul. "With rations, we won't be able to eat like this for much longer. We'll run out soon enough." He reached his chopsticks across the table and picked up a shumai.

"Oh, Paul," his mother said, clicking her tongue and sticking serving spoons into the dishes, "you don't always have to be so *negative*. I have plenty saved in the freezer. It will get us through. Besides, Amy's here. It's a special occasion." She winked at me.

Henry's mother served me everything on the table, each dish accompanied by its own garnish, its own special sauce. I had never seen this much food on a family's table before, and Henry hadn't exaggerated; it was all spectacular.

Henry's father told me about the pharmacy, and that if I ever needed a medicine or a bandage or anything at all that he carried, just to let him know.

"Or a perfume!" added Henry's mother. "Henry, bring her down to the shop next week and I'll mix her a perfume!"

They were some of the kindest, most generous people I had ever met. I loved the feeling of being in their home, of eating their food and listening to their easy chatter. I wanted this for myself. I wanted this for Henry and me.

When lunch was over, I followed Henry's mother into the kitchen to help with the dishes.

"Henry has not stopped talking about you," she whispered, passing me a kitchen towel to dry the plates as she washed. "It's a shame he's leaving so soon. I know we'll all miss him dearly."

I nodded sympathetically. I had almost forgotten that he was leaving.

"When exactly does he go?" I asked, realizing that I didn't know myself.

"Next week Friday, dear!" She squeezed some soap onto a sponge. "I begged him to reconsider, but at this point, he can't. He'd have to give back that money and he already spent it on the car." She shook her head. "But he'll be fine. I keep telling myself he's not going to *war*. He'll be fixing telephone lines just like he does here and he'll be back in a year and—"

"*A year?*" I interrupted.

"Yes, darling, at least a year. It's not what I want for him either but he enlisted before all this Japanese stuff even happened."

I dried the rest of the dishes in silence, nodding along with whatever Henry's mother said, trying to keep myself from crying. *A year.*

I thought about saying goodbye to Henry and had to stop myself immediately. *Was this possible?*

When the dishes were done, we walked into the dining room, where the rest of the family was still talking. I must have looked terrible, because Henry stood immediately and took my hand, leading me outside to the back patio.

"Is everything okay?" he asked, sitting me on a bench against the outside wall.

"You're leaving on Friday," I said. "For a year. Why didn't you tell me?"

"I did tell you," he replied, putting a hand on my knee, "I said I was leaving at the end of the month."

"But next Friday, Henry!"

"I know." And that was all he said for a while.

"Amy," he said, drawing his lips in to moisten them. "I don't know how to say this without scaring you, so I'm just going to say it, okay?"

"I'm not scared."

"I've loved you since I was ten, okay? I've never stopped thinking about you and I'm certain I never will. A year seems like a long time but we can do it—it's only a year and I'll write every day. I know this doesn't happen for everyone, Amy. I know how lucky I am to have walked into your studio last week. Please. Tell me you feel it too. Tell me I'm not alone in this."

I looked at him and heard the ocean again. I felt warm and safe and nostalgic. Who was I to deny something that so strongly, so intensely resembled fate? I couldn't describe what I felt for Henry, wasn't ready to call it love, not yet. It had been three days, and the progression of my feelings startled me. But despite myself, I knew exactly what it was. It wasn't three days, it had been three summers. Henry was a constant in my life before I knew I needed one. When my parents went through their difficult time, when there were too many of us to care for and I was sent to Waialua, Henry was there. And he was still here, patient as ever, asking me to wait for him.

"It's not just you." I hesitated. I heard the words in my ears. *I love you, too.* So simple, so easy to give away—but I couldn't. I wanted to save it. "I feel it too," I said.

He put his hand on my cheek and lifted my head, leaning in to kiss me on the mouth. It was soft and gentle and warm. He pulled me into him, my body pressing into his, the heat between us melting my fear and apprehension.

We sat together on that bench, my head on his shoulder, until the sun began to lower and it was time to take me home. In the car, we kissed again, his hands exploring my body and my body eager to let him. I didn't want to go home. It was a terrible time for a curfew, a terrible time for a war.

Henry and I saw each other every afternoon until he left—from three o'clock until the sun went down. He would wait outside the studio in his car, always with some snack prepared so he could keep me out until dinnertime.

Except on the last day. On Thursday, he arrived on foot.

"I thought we could walk to the beach today," he said, taking my hand as we started toward the ocean.

"Are you packed?" I asked, not wanting to talk about it.

"Pretty much," he replied.

We stopped at a wall overlooking the sand and the water and the families below enjoying the sunny day. Henry squinted at me, the sun catching in his eyelashes.

"Can we sit here for a minute?" he asked. I nodded, putting my hands on the wall and pulling myself up. Instead of joining me, Henry put his hand in his pocket and removed a square black box. He opened it toward me; a small diamond ring sat in the middle.

"This is not a proposal," he said, taking the ring and removing my hand from over my open mouth. He slid the ring onto my middle finger.

"This is a promise. A promise that I will write to you as often as I can, that I will be faithful to you, and that when I return, I will work my ass off and trade this in for the ring that you deserve. And then, Amy, if you'll have me, I promise that I will marry you."

I began to cry.

"No," I said, "I can't accept this, it's too expensive. I can't," I repeated, beginning to take the ring off my finger, but he clasped his hand firmly over mine.

"It's not expensive enough, but jewelry isn't exactly simple to find these days and it's all my car is worth so you'll have to wait for something better."

"You sold your car?" I asked stupidly.

"Yes. I sold my car because I don't need it anymore. If I'm not here to pick you up after work, what do I need a car for?"

"Please don't go," I said, wiping my eyes, the diamond on my finger heavy and warm.

"I'll be back." His smile was filled with so much hope. "It's not forever. Remember that. I've waited so long already. This is nothing."

He raised himself onto the wall and sat with me. He took my hand in his. Together, we stayed like this, not saying a thing, until the sun began to turn lilac. I tried to memorize him. I put my face into his neck and breathed. He had a sweet, earthy smell, like grass in the morning, after the dew has settled. I studied the curve of the back of his neck, the soft bend that disappeared into his shirt. I touched it, tracing it upward to his hairline. His jaw, his wrists, his shoulders—I recorded every detail. I felt the warmth in his pulse. We stayed until an officer approached us, telling us to get home. Henry nearly started a fight with him. We'll leave, I told the officer. We're leaving right now, I said as I clutched Henry's shoulder.

In front of my house, he apologized. But he didn't need to. We both felt it; the anxiety of separation, the weight of the unknown. He kissed me in the pitch black, our fingers pressed into each other's body, trying to extract the last of one another. Then he disappeared into the dark, the unlit street swallowing him up as he made his way to his parents' house. I sat on the slab of cement outside my front door and held myself still, suddenly shivering, suddenly freezing.

The next day, my father let me come in late so that I could say good-bye to Henry at the docks with the rest of his family. He waved to me from the deck of the ocean liner, and when his face became indistinguishable from the rest of the waving soldiers, I turned away.

"So this is the ring," his brother Paul said to me, taking my hand and inspecting my finger. "It's nice. Not quite a car, but it's nice." I nodded and tried to smile.

On the walk back to the studio, I gathered myself, repeating in my head what Henry had said to me the day before. *It's not forever.* I could hear his voice so clearly. I could feel his hands on mine.

When I arrived at my father's studio, pushing open the front door, I found him in unusually high spirits.

"Amy! I have good news!" he exclaimed, not acknowledging my tears or Henry's departure. "We've received a very important job!" He took my hand and led me to the table where he had been taking down notes. I didn't respond. I was thinking about Henry crossing the Pacific at that very moment.

"It's the Leongs! A man called this morning asking if we could do a private sitting at the Leongs! Three hundred dollars, Amy! They will pay us three hundred dollars!"

"*The* Leongs?" I asked instinctually. I wasn't sure I'd heard him correctly.

"Yes, Amy, *the* Leongs. They saw one of my portraits in the paper. They want me to do a private sitting. A private sitting!"

"That's amazing," I said, fighting to keep the excitement in my voice. "Congratulations. Really, Dad. That's unbelievable."

And it was. Two weeks ago, this would have been extraordinary news. The Leongs played a hand in everything on the island, especially beloved in Kaneohe for Mrs. Leong's work in the schools. She raised ten thousand dollars the year I graduated, a record-breaking amount. Her name was everywhere: along the wooden shelves of the middle school library, above the door in the high school gymnasium, on the benches in the new community garden. Lin Leong threw parties; that's what I'd heard. She threw parties at their Diamond Head mansion and suddenly we had new textbooks and a water fountain and a white net on our basketball hoop. The Leongs were a private family and there was plenty of speculation about how they lived, about what it might be like behind the massive iron gates that concealed their home. I had read an article about it last summer. There were no pictures, but I remembered a quote: *Public in business, private in family, and victorious in both; the Leongs are living the life you wish you had, but you'll never know much about it.*

I thought of Henry. He'd be happy for my father, excited for my family. This could be what I needed, I told myself, a nice distraction, something to keep me busy as Henry sailed to Europe. And three hundred dollars was nothing to take lightly. It was an incredible fortune for us, I knew that. It was another step closer to a new beginning, another opportunity that I hoped would lead our family to redemption.

"When are we going?" I asked.

"Next Saturday," my father replied, "eleven o'clock." He smiled and I did too. I couldn't help it; it was the most honest show of happiness I'd ever seen from my father. It cut through my misery, a tiny slice of light.

The Leong home was located on the southwestern slope of Diamond Head, secluded within a curved piece of land that cut into the base of the crater, the only one like it. It was one of the first homes to be built there, my father told me as we left the house Saturday morning. While the other wealthy families were building homes in Waikiki, next to the ocean and near shops and restaurants, the Leongs remained within the protection of the volcano. They continued to guard their privacy.

My father and I rode the bus, getting off at Kapiolani Park and walking the remainder of the way south along the water to the western slope. I wore a floral shift dress with a white yoke collar and a lace hem I'd sewn on the day before. My father wore a navy suit—the same one he'd worn when he married my mother twenty years ago. It was the only suit he owned. We walked the final stretch in silence, both of us organizing our thoughts before we arrived.

As we approached the crater, its silhouette growing as we neared, blocking the rising sun, we knew immediately which property belonged to the Leongs. Just as my father said, exactly as I read in the article, a massive iron gate spread before us, longer than a football field, sealing an expanse of the volcano entirely hidden from the street. The gate was made of two layers of iron, one completely solid and flat, the second an overlay of metal rods, long and ornate, extending past the top of the solid slabs. The middle of the gate, where the iron formed an entrance, was flanked by a pair of large bronze pillars and atop those pillars stood two towering stone lions. I stood there, awestruck, taking in its astonishing height. The lion on the left was frozen in play with her cub; the lion on the right was posed with his foot on a ball. I'd never seen anything like it; even in Chinatown, the imperial statues weren't half as large as these. We paused, my father and I, looking at each other but saying nothing. There was nothing to say. Drawing a final breath, long and slow, my father straightened his jacket and pushed the buzzer.

A minute later, the gates opened automatically and we were greeted by a woman named Hong. Graciously, she ushered us through the entry and into what looked like an oil painting—the third rendering, flawless. A gracefully sloping lawn created different levels, the largest of which housed a silver pond surrounded by flat, oval stones and lavender lotus blossoms. Opposite the pond, on a higher level, was a Chinese pavilion painted red with a green roof, its open interior sheltering a day bed and a table with chairs, a tray ready for tea. A bridge, an arched stone overpass, reached over the pond and connected the pavilion to the lawn below.

More than the colors, I remember it was the textures of the garden that astonished me. Everything seemed to be so lush yet so precise, each element of the garden complementing the next. From ten feet away I could see tiny hairs growing on the stems of the lotus. I fought the urge to touch everything—the flowers, the grass, the lacquer on the pavilion—to see if it was real. I looked at my father. His fingers were running anxiously along the top of his camera and I knew he was fighting a similar impulse.

But Hong was two steps ahead of us, leading the way to the main entrance. Once again, I tilted my head back and took in the height. The crater, its honey-colored ridges lit with shocks of velvet green growth, soared around the property, gathering the sun like a funnel. Light poured upon the house, which looked nothing like how I had imagined it. In every possible way, it was more magnificent. Long, polished pieces of dark wood met at right angles to form giant windows that rose at least three stories. The windows were perfectly clear, so that I could see the pale, melon-colored walls of the interior—the most remarkable color I had ever seen on something so ordinary. Above, long glass balconies emerged from the walls of the highest floor, one for every room, displaying lounge chairs and sun umbrellas. It was brilliant; total privacy with a pristine view of the ocean, their balconies taller than any structure in front of them, nothing but Diamond Head behind. Below, the double doors of the entrance were painted red, already open. A low, warm light flooded the foyer.

I removed my shoes at the entrance, my nylon sandals looking small and cheap on the hardwood floors. My father did the same. Hong seated us on a low black sofa in the next room, where there was also a piano and an Oriental rug.

"One moment. I tell them you're here," she said, and exited the room.

We sat in silence, avoiding each other's gaze. I feared my eyes would give away the anxiety I was trying to suppress. I did not expect to feel so overwhelmed, but it felt like a secret world, a hidden society within a crater I'd seen a hundred times, never knowing what absurdity lay within. I began to compose my words in my head. *Good morning, Mr. Leong. What a beautiful home you have. The lotuses have bloomed splendidly. Mrs. Leong, what a pleasure to meet you!* It all sounded ridiculous, sitting in their modern living room, but there was no time to come up with anything else.

Mr. and Mrs. Leong entered from a hallway, Hong trailing behind them with a tray of tea. They were dressed neatly, Mr. Leong in a black suit with a high collar and Mrs. Leong in a black dress that brushed the top of her knees. They looked as regal as they did in the newspaper, but they were smiling.

"Photographer Chan! Marvelous to see you, thank you so much for coming to our home. I know it's an unusual request!" Mr. Leong walked to the couch to greet my father, who suddenly realized he should stand up.

"Mr. Leong," my father said, shaking his hand. "The pleasure is all mine. It's a great honor to photograph your family."

"Please, call me Frank. We're not so formal here. And who's this?" he asked, gesturing toward me.

"This is my oldest daughter and assistant, Amy." I held out my hand to shake his, and said the first thing that came to me.

"Good morning, Mr. Leong. What a beautiful home you have. The lotuses have bloomed splendidly."

Mr. Leong chuckled and glanced at my father, who was introducing himself to Mrs. Leong.

"I see you've raised this one well." He winked at me. "I will pass on your compliments to our gardener. You'll make him a very happy man."

From the same hallway emerged two more people, two boys—men, really—one wearing a bright red aloha shirt unbuttoned halfway down his chest, the other wearing a black suit like Mr. Leong's. Instantly, I knew which one was Kaipo. Over the years, I had heard his name a number of times, always good things; he was so handsome, so charming, so funny. I had even known a couple of girls he dated. But it never lasted long. He could never stick with any one girl—or at least that's what I'd heard. I pulled my eyes away from his exposed chest, wiping a bead of sweat from my hairline, telling myself to focus.

I looked at the second son, whose face I didn't recognize. He was thinner and older, more serious in every way. He nodded timidly as Mr. Leong introduced them. He did not lean in to kiss my cheek as Kaipo had. *Easy, son,* Mr. Leong joked.

The six of us sat down to the tea that Hong had prepared, and Mr. Leong began to discuss his ideas for the photography session.

"I want to capture my family as we are—not posing like statues as has become the fashion. I want candid photos, not everyone looking in the same direction and smiling like idiots." He took a sip of tea. My father nodded.

"Can I have a cigar, then, Dad?" Kaipo asked, spread across a black ottoman.

"If a cigar will capture the real you, Kaipo, then by all means." Mr. Leong made a sweeping gesture toward his son and turned back to my father. "Can you do that for us, Mr. Chan? I have the highest confidence in your work. I've seen your portraits in the paper—no smiling idiots." He raised his tea cup toward my father, who in turn raised his own.

"You will not be disappointed, Frank," he said, the Frank sounding like an afterthought.

"And, Amy? Are you on board?"

My attention was suddenly pulled back to Mr. Leong.

"Yes," I said abruptly. "One hundred percent." I shifted in my seat, the teacup rattling against its saucer. I was distracted by so many things—the enormous backyard I could see through the tall windows, the hot tea balancing on my knees, Kaipo's tan chest—but most of all, I couldn't help but notice that throughout the entire conversation, Mrs. Leong had not stopped looking at me.

"Well," said Mr. Leong, finishing the last of his tea and taking a bite of an almond cookie before placing it back on the plate. "Shall we begin?"

"Absolutely." My father put down his cup. "Why don't you all continue about your day, and Amy and I will be around the house taking candid photographs. How does that sound?"

"An excellent idea! I was just in the middle of a fascinating news article, so I think I will continue with that. You two have full rein of the house; take the best shots you can." Mr. Leong rose and began to walk into the dining room, where I could see a newspaper laid out across the table. "You heard Mr. Chan," he said, turning back and addressing his family, "go about your regular business." And then, realizing he should amend his last statement, he said, "But please, behave yourselves." He winked at me a second time and continued into the dining room.

We crept through the house, taking shots of the family. Mr. Leong read the newspaper at his enormous dining room table, dark and glistening, eleven empty chairs around him. Mrs. Leong fanned herself on the front lanai and knit on a window seat, the spool of yarn unraveled to the floor. Kaipo polished his car, his shirt fully unbuttoned by then, and smoked cigars in the study. And then there was the oldest Leong son, Bohai—the shy one—who was the most difficult to photograph, hiding behind a book almost the entire afternoon.

"Do you mind putting the book down, just for a moment?" my father asked him.

Without speaking, he lowered the book. He looked straight at the camera, his expression entirely pained. My father had yet to lift his camera. I knew he wouldn't take this shot.

"What are you reading?" I asked cautiously.

"Oh," Bohai said, shifting his legs against the chair. "It's about a whale."

"A whale? No wonder it's so large," I joked, trying to lighten the conversation. Bohai twisted his face into a strange half-smile.

"I don't think I've read that one," I said more seriously, pointing to the cover.

"You can have it." He hesitated, not looking at me. "I'll be finished soon."

"That's very kind," I said.

"Okay," he nodded. "I'll continue, then?" He looked to my father.

"Yes, of course," my father said. "Probably better that way. Please, don't mind us."

Bohai lifted his book and began to read. My father and I walked from the room but in the doorway, he paused. He squatted and brought the camera to his eye. Bohai sat in his wooden chair, his body slouched ever so slightly, his mouth parted as he read. My father shook his head, but still, he took his shot.

We walked the entire span of the house, peeking into rooms and looking for subjects to photograph. We snapped a photograph of Hong in the sun-drenched kitchen, peeling an orange while she stood at the counter. We found an incredible bathroom on the second floor with a porcelain bathtub larger than my parents' mattress. One of the bedrooms was lined with bookshelves, each of them crammed with hardbacks, which we assumed must belong to Bohai. Then we went into the garage, where we found three American cars parked side by side, all of them black, two of them convertibles.

"*Holy shit,*" my father murmured below his breath, shaking his head in disbelief.

It was Kaipo who put me at ease, who appeared from time to time to make his mother laugh, to put a cigar between her lips and make her pose like an Italian gangster. He insisted that I be photographed as well, helping me into the driver's seat of his car—which was not one of the cars in the garage, but a fourth parked in the carport. He retracted the roof and turned on the radio.

"Act natural," he warned, "or my dad won't hang it on the wall."

I understood why so many girls had fallen for his charm. He was mischievous and carefree—a rare combination of traits I decided only wealth could sustain. But even Kaipo could not pull my thoughts away from Henry. I looked at Kaipo and saw a million girls, all of them screaming for his narrow attention. I wasn't a screamer; I didn't like the odds. Men like Kaipo didn't have that kind of hold on me.

At two o'clock, we all sat down together for a light lunch of dim sum, which Hong served before sitting down at the table to eat with us. I remember thinking it was odd, that no one cared that the household help was eating just as heartily as everyone else. Then, as I reached for a third fish ball, I realized that my father and I were also employees, and I put my chopsticks down as Mrs. Leong began to ask me questions.

"Were you in school, Amy?" she asked.

I was used to people asking me this question in the past tense. All the Oahu schools had been shut down since the bombing and it was unclear when they would resume.

"I went to Kaneohe High," I said, "so I feel the need to thank you for all you've done."

"Nonsense, dear! Think nothing of it." She smiled, waiting for more.

"Luckily, I graduated two years ago, and since then I've been doing various kinds of work. But I think I'll stick with my father's photography for now. I enjoy it." I paused. I hoped it was a satisfactory answer.

"Congratulations, you made it just in time! So, that would make you—twenty, then?"

"I'll be twenty-one next month."

"Wonderful," she replied, dabbing her mouth with a napkin. Kaipo raised his glass to make a toast and everyone turned to face him. Except for us—his mother and I, we kept our eyes on each other, the two of us grinning, lingering in the warmth of each other's attention.

We promised to return the next morning with the photographs; we worked all through the night to develop them. The next day, Mrs. Leong answered the door and greeted us as if we were old friends, inviting us in for a drink.

"No, no, we really should be going," my father said, flattening the sides of his trousers. "I just wanted to be sure you got the photographs."

"Hold on," Mrs. Leong said, holding out a palm and starting across the room, "let me get Frank. He's been talking about the pictures since you two left. And if you won't stay for a drink then you must at least agree to come for dinner next week." Her finger was still raised as she disappeared down the hallway.

A moment later, Mr. Leong's voice called out.

"Photographer Chan!" he exclaimed, right arm extended as he walked to where we stood in the entry. "And Amy," he added, accepting the package of photographs.

"They came out great," my father told Mr. Leong, "even better than I expected. Your family photographs beautifully."

Mr. Leong whistled as he flipped through the stack of images.

"Tremendous work," he declared, "fantastic. Well, this one of Bohai will have to go and look at this one—who is this old man?" He chuckled, stopping on a picture of himself drinking coffee. Again, he winked at me.

Mr. Leong reached into his pocket and pulled out a thin fold of bills. He handed them to my father.

"Thank you, Photographer. And you both are to take Lin's invitation seriously." He pointed a finger at each of us. "We expect you here at dinner very soon."

I could see my father's hand tremble slightly as he removed his wallet from his back pocket, inserting the money as he tried to maintain the conversation.

"Of course," he replied. "We look forward to it."

Then, emerging from the hallway, something long and glistening draped across her right arm, Mrs. Leong rushed across the room and held out what she carried. It was a dress, apricot-colored and silk, with enough fabric to reach the floor.

"I had it made for me," she said, wrapping the dress in tissue paper and placing it neatly into a shallow box, "but what a waste it seems when I imagine how it would look on you! Of course it will have to be taken in, but really, it's going to be stunning."

She placed the box in my hands and my fingers, unsure of what to make of her extravagant offering, accepted with hesitation—before my mind could politely refuse.

"I don't know what to say," I said. "Are you sure?"

"Am I sure?" Mrs. Leong laughed. "Yes, dear, I'm absolutely certain—this dress was meant to be yours."

I had never even seen a dress like that before. In magazines perhaps, but never in person. This was the kind of dress you had to create, dictated from start to finish, every detail, every button, every stitch considered.

"Wow," I said. "Well, thank you. I don't exactly have a place to wear it but—"

"You'll wear it here," she interrupted. Her eyes flickered with energy. "When you come to dinner, you'll wear the dress."

She looked so happy, so eager to see me again. Too happy, I thought to myself. Why was she so eager?

"Of course," I managed, still holding the box with two hands, perfectly even as if it were filled with liquid. "Thank you."

"It's my pleasure," she replied.

On the way home, I thought about asking my father if he felt it was strange, if there was something peculiar about the gift or the way in which she gave it, but my father seemed just as happy as Mrs. Leong, just as eager. I thought of how to say it, how to make it sound silly, dismissing the question as I asked it. But as I tried to form my question, my mind fought back; it wanted what they had, it wanted to be happy, to feel worthy of our triumphant day. Mrs. Leong was a generous woman, I told myself; money like that, it came without explanation.

The next week, I sat at the cash register trying to write a letter to Henry. No matter how many ways I started it, I couldn't quite convey what I needed to say; that I missed him, that I thought about him constantly, that I followed men around town that looked like him from the back. I missed his family. I missed his mustache.

But then there were the other problems, like how I was beginning to forget the tone of his voice. And when I closed my eyes at night, I could only picture his eyes and his nose, a blank space filling in his mouth and his cheeks. I woke up often, in the dead of night, reaching under my mattress for the photograph I kept of him, straight-faced in my father's studio. I'd take it into the bathroom, study it under the yellow light, perched on the toilet seat until I felt entirely crazy. It had only been three weeks—not even a month—and he was already starting to deteriorate in my mind. With each sleepless night, more and more my memories of Henry became defined by that photograph. That uniform, that somber stare, I could imagine him no other way.

But I couldn't tell him that. How could I possibly tell him that?

"Amy," I heard my father call from the back room, pulling me swiftly from my miserable thoughts. "Come here a minute."

The back room was a place that I entered only when asked. It was my father's space and he felt protective of it. When I first came to work at the studio, he insisted that I understand how film was processed, and I spent hours with him in the darkroom as he explained each of the liquids and the importance of timing and cleanliness and temperature. But since then, the only time I went to the back room was when it needed to be cleaned, which wasn't often.

It was two rooms really, a small room with a metal table that held my father's developing instruments, and an even smaller closet, kept dark and cool, where the film was actually processed. My father was putting on blue nylon gloves when I entered, about to go into the darkroom.

"Amy," he said. And that was all for a minute. He examined his left glove.

"There is something very interesting that has come up, and I feel the need to discuss it with you." He opened a black canister that sat on the table, one of six that he used daily. I sat down on the spare stool.

"Come with me," he said, opening the door to the darkroom. I got off my stool and followed. He shut the door behind us and then, sufficiently shrouded in darkness, he began to speak.

"Mrs. Leong called yesterday evening. She was very taken by you, you know, Amy? She liked you very much."

I listened quietly. I knew this already—I had the dress as proof of her admiration, but it seemed that my father knew more. It seemed that perhaps he knew why. I heard him deposit a roll of film into the canister and pour in a glass of purified water to swell the gelatin. I knew the sounds well. He set the timer.

"I'm going to ask you to do something, and I don't know how you'll feel about it, but it's amazing, Amy. It's a tremendous thing for you to do." He inverted the canister and set it back on the table.

"Well, what is it?" I asked, my voice large in the small room.

"It's not that simple, Amy. It's a big decision, one that I'm not taking lightly, and—"

"Dad," I interrupted, my eyes finally adjusting to the dark. "Please just say it."

"She wants you to be a part of their family," he said abruptly, his hands still. "She wants you to marry her son."

"She wants me to marry *Kaipo?*" I asked, more astonished that Kaipo could not find his own wife than by the offer.

My father went silent. The timer went off and he poured the water from the canister, replacing it with a new clear solution. He looked intently into the canister, swirling it around in his hand. His silhouette was thin and delicate in the dark—he looked like a paper cutout. He could not look into my eyes. He set the canister on the small table and let out a deep breath of air.

"Bohai," he said finally. "She would like you to marry Bohai."

Now I was silent. *Bohai*, I thought in disbelief, and the sound of his name was jarring, like a sudden, careless swipe of a violin. Bohai had barely spoken two words to me that day, let alone given any impression that he would like to *marry* me. How could it be Bohai? And then I thought of the dress. Of course, I realized, it was so painfully obvious. Mrs. Leong—she had been planning this. This whole time, all the staring, all the curiosity, she had been examining me for her somber, elder son—the son in need of a wife. The dress was a bribe; of course it was. It was a taste of what would come.

"I know he's shy," my father continued, "but he's a good man. And Amy, wouldn't you like that life for yourself? Think of the opportunity."

"You can't be serious," I said, my voice lowering to a rasp. "You can't possibly be serious about this, Dad." My eyes shifted frantically, trying to get my father's gaze to meet my own but losing him in the dark. The timer began to beep.

"God damn it, of course I'm serious!" My father raised his voice for the first time, slamming the black canister on the table.

Tears came, all at once. They began to fall as I stood, realizing the gravity in my father's voice. He wanted this. He actually wanted me to marry this sad, lonely stranger.

"What about Henry?" I exclaimed, panic rising in the pitch of my voice. "I'm going to marry Henry!"

"I know you have feelings for Henry!" he interrupted. "I know this, Amy! But do you hear what I'm saying? Are you hearing *me*?"

The tears were still coming. I didn't know what to say. *Feelings* for Henry? He knew nothing of how I felt for Henry. My mouth filled with terrible thoughts, all the things I could never say; that he'd never known real love, that his marriage to my mother was a pathetic charade. He was a selfish, ignorant man who would always be miserable because he'd settled.

But then I thought of Henry and instead of his voice, instead of his hands, I saw the photograph. I saw myself in the bathroom, on the patio, all around town with that flimsy, worthless photograph that was razing all my memories. My teeth clenched as I summoned his face, his real face, his smile, the low tenor of his laugh, anything attached to flesh, to bone. If I could see something real, just for a moment, I was certain the feeling would return. And I would be right about him and my father would be wrong.

I gripped the table, infuriated, overwhelmed.

"Please, Amy, listen to me." My father reached for my hand but I retracted it. I glared as his voice trembled. "I may be an old man now," he said, "but I once had dreams of my own. I wanted to be successful. I wanted to be rich. I wanted to give you children everything you ever wanted. But look at me." He reached for the film canister, shaking it vigorously, violently, his arm thrashing through the air. Suddenly he released his grip and the container smashed against the wall of the darkroom. I heard the lid break open and felt the spray of the clear liquid exploding against the wall, the metallic smell of chemicals filling the room.

"Do you think I like this?" he demanded, slamming a fist against the table. "Do you? You think I don't know I'm a failure? My wife despises me, my children don't respect me—I know this, Amy! I know all of this!"

I brought a hand to my mouth and my tears stopped. I'd never seen my father like this. Not once, not ever.

"I have failed in so many ways." He paused, his head shaking slowly in the dark. "I was supposed to have a different life, and I fell short. But this could be our saving, Amy, don't you understand? This *will* change everything. You want children. Do you want to raise them like mine—twelve people in one basement? It's pathetic," he spat, dropping his head between his hands, his body shaking as he tried to contain his resentment.

"I want so much more for you, Amy. Go home. Think about it. If you won't, I will call Mrs. Leong in the morning. But I think you'd be making an enormous mistake."

Even in his lowest times, my father was a clever man, and he knew exactly what kind of thoughts would arise if I went home to Kaneohe to *think about it*. He wanted me to see the dirt, the leaks, the rust, the cracks, the daily battles that were my alternative. He forced me to consider what my future could realistically hold, coming from a one-room duplex in the country, from a family of twelve in a ramshackle basement.

When I arrived home, my sisters were in the front yard, poking at centipedes with sticks and collecting them in jars, all of them oblivious to the proposal I had just received. I tore past them, ignoring their hellos. I charged through the screen door and heard their voices stop, felt all their eyes following me.

I needed to write to Henry. I needed to tell him what had happened, and the decision I had already come to. I would not marry Bohai—*it was absurd*. It was insulting and arrogant and completely insane. I pulled a piece of paper from a folder under my mattress. I sat on my bed with my pen to the paper, lungs filled with sticky air, poised for my tirade.

Dear Henry, I began, and immediately I felt my grip on the pen tighten. I exhaled the heavy air and my fingers tightened again, this time so hard that I could feel the metal against my bone. What came next? How did I possibly begin? *Dear Henry, my father would like me to marry another man. Dear Henry, Lin Leong has approached me to be her daughter. Dear Henry, since you left I've become acquainted with the Leongs and their oldest son has proposed marriage.*

The thought alone was enough to induce panic. As I considered my words, it felt like they were being thrown into an abyss, disappearing as soon as I thought them. The paper taunted me with its emptiness, its flimsiness, its ability to simply get lost along the route and never arrive at its destination. With words like these, how could I trust a letter? How could I explain that my father had begged me— that for the first time in my life, I had watched him cry? And perhaps even more difficult, even more convoluted, that his tears had affected me somehow. I felt the weight of my entire family, all eleven of their miserable faces wondering *why, if I had the capacity to save our family, would I dismiss it so easily? Did eleven lives not outweigh one?*

Not to my father, I thought to myself. Not until now.

I began to mark the page. I pressed my pen deep into the blank paper and drew long, violent scratches that reached into the next page. I drew them faster and faster until I was furiously making lines, ripping the paper and getting ink on my thighs. And then I began to cry— disobedient, uncontrollable tears, ripping the paper in a dozen pieces, crushing the pieces between my fists and throwing them to the floor.

As my mind began to boil, as my thoughts continued to deepen and tangle, I heard the screen door open. I heard my sisters' voices, one after the other, as they entered the house. From my bed I watched the white sheet; I closed my fists around the last bits of paper and watched them march through. Denise held the jar of centipedes— dozens of them, crawling on top of one another.

They looked at me, sitting in a pile of torn paper, my knees marked with ink, my breath short from crying.

"What's wrong with you?" Denise asked as she tapped her finger against the outside of her jar.

"Yeah, what's wrong with you?" Like an echo, I heard it three more times. My vision began to blur.

"Can I just be alone?" I begged, trying so hard to control the pitch of my voice but immediately giving away my desperation. "*Please*. Can you just give me a minute?"

"Fine, fine," someone said, "but I need to check under your bed. I think that's where the magnifying glass is."

I sat quietly, stupidly; I willed myself to be patient. I waited for my sisters to clear out of my room—a room that was rightfully all of ours—when I heard my brothers come in through the back door. I heard them opening cabinets in the kitchen on the opposite side of the wall. I tightened my fists and felt my fingernails dig into the skin of my palm.

"We need water and all the cups are dirty." My brother Richard lifted the dividing sheet and walked through. "What's wrong with you?" He looked briefly at me and then at Denise, who was still holding the jar. "Ohhh, centipedes." He grabbed the jar and overturned it, releasing the insects onto the bedroom floor. He laughed, running in place so that the centipedes scattered under the beds and into the piles of dirty laundry and along the cracked baseboards and throughout the house. My sisters shrieked and jumped on the beds. The louder they screamed, the faster the insects moved.

I was the only one in the room who stayed still. I sat there silently. My tears had stopped. Five girls jumped on the beds around me, screaming as my brother taunted them. *This is my life*, I thought, blocking out the sounds around me. *This is it.*

It occurred to me that I was one of the centipedes, tumbling in the jar with the rest of the insects. All of them were ordinary; all of them were destined for the same miserable fate. What made me any different? Among creatures from the same place, raised in dirt, packed together in a single room, what determined an extraordinary fate? Was there such a thing for us?

Henry was not insignificant. Henry knew how to fish, he knew how to move electricity, knew how to drive, how to cook, how to love without fear, how to give just to give, without expectation or motive or agenda.

But did these things add up to an extraordinary fate? Or would we live off kindness and laughter, raising our children on hand-me-downs and vegetables from our meager victory garden? And me? I could clean houses. I could stay home and raise our children. I could wash our sheets, worry about our bills. And when my daughter got old enough, I could show her my high school diploma—my highest honor, my greatest achievement. I could tell her that it's difficult to change, that not all of us are destined for something great; that it's okay to be a centipede.

Silently I stood. I lifted the sheet and left the room. Bohai at least had a chance. I wasn't that stupid, wasn't so foolish to think that money didn't make a difference.

I opened the back door and found my mother on the patio. She lowered her cigarette.

"I need one of those," I said, pointing to the pack on the table, a sudden urge for something I'd never taken to.

"Tough day," my mother said, more as a statement than a question, handing me one.

"So you know." I lit the end and took a long pull.

"He told me last night."

I held the smoke deep in my lungs. I let it travel through my blood, up to my head, releasing it when it began to burn.

"What do I do?" I exhaled. It came out as desperately as I felt.

"I don't know." She shook her head. "It's not a situation I've seen before. Your father loves you. He wants something different for you." She paused.

"Amy," she said, blowing out a long trail of smoke, letting it linger in the air before swatting it away, "I'm not saying that what your father and I have is bad, because it's not. We care for each other. But sometimes you go your whole life not knowing what you could have been—*who* you could have been, if you chose something else."

My mother looked down at her naked ring finger. It was always something that made her self-conscious; it was something she spoke of only in times of true distress. She looked so vulnerable, so fragile and exposed as she spoke. She had thought about the situation all night, she said. She had not slept. When my father told her about the offer, she was overcome with a flood of conflicting emotions.

"I thought he was joking," she said. "I couldn't believe it was real—this chance to become instantly wealthy, instantly a *Leong*. And then, Amy, I thought about you. I removed you from the fantasy and thought about what this all really means."

I waited. I could feel her getting to her point, and I was fairly certain she had come to the same conclusion I had, if not something similar. I knew my father had been contaminated by our day at the Leongs. He had seen too much. We both had.

"Amy—I can't promise that you will be happy with Bohai, but you will be provided for, which in hindsight is almost more important than love. You're a remarkable girl—you always have been. Since you were young you've wanted something better, something extraordinary to touch your life. Here it is. I'd be lying if I told you I wouldn't do it myself—start all over and do it myself."

"And marry without love?" I pressed her, not believing for a minute what she was telling me.

"I married for love, Amy," she said slowly. "Or at least I thought I did. But things change. A lifetime is a long time—a terribly long time to give to someone because of something as impractical as love."

"As impractical as love?" I repeated, outraged now. I put my head in my palms and I could feel it again. The anger, the overwhelming frustration that this choice had to be made. That if I didn't choose correctly, I could waste the rest of my life wishing I could go back and choose again.

"Love fades, Amy. The heart, it wants one thing and then it changes its mind. Love is a fickle thing."

"Do you even know who he is?" I exploded, saving this fact, this bomb for the moment I needed it most.

"Who who is? What are you talking about?"

"Do you remember the boy in Waialua? The fisherman's nephew, the boy who used to walk me home, who threw the rock at me and gave me this?" I pulled back my hair and pointed to the scar. "Do you remember? Because it's Henry, Mom. After all these years, it's Henry."

My mother's face softened, but just for a moment. She was too caught up to care; I realized it immediately.

"Yes, okay, Amy, it's quite a coincidence—but what does it matter?"

"What does it matter? All the things you told me as a child—about red strings and fated matches and rocks and scars—is what? Something you made up?"

"Of course it's made up—*it's a fairy tale, Amy!* I wish my parents would have guided me. I wish I hadn't clung to some children's story like it was the truth! *Red strings*," she spat. "Wake up! Does this look like red strings exist?" She gestured frantically around her. "Tell me, Amy, does this look like a fairy-tale ending to you?"

My mother's breathing quickened. I could barely look at her. I lowered my eyes to the table and for the first time in my life, and with difficulty, I considered my mother's pain; the unmistakable regret and heartache clinging to her words. She was not the woman I had known in my childhood, strong-willed and full of life. In her voice I heard a panicked young girl, someone in desperate need of a second chance. I needed her to stop. It was one thing for me to feel this way about my parents on a bad day, when I searched for the worst of them. But to hear it from my mother?

I stubbed out my cigarette, my mother's words reconfiguring themselves in my head. *Was it true?* I looked at my mother and knew that it was. She had made her choice; she had chosen wrong. Now here she was, twenty years later, still wishing she could go back and choose again.

"These are your mistakes," I said to her, pushing up from the table and walking to the door. "Don't make them mine."

*   *   *

But I couldn't shake my mother's words. They clung to me like sand, eroded my confidence like salt water. For ten days, my mind became a hopeless, destructive tangle, as I traced my future with Henry and Bohai, trying to imagine an outcome that wouldn't end in regret, or poverty, or eternal damnation. For ten days, I shut out the world entirely. I existed only in my head, seeking advice from my parents when I felt on the brink of explosion and then scolding myself, wishing that I hadn't. Their conclusions were the same, as I should have known they would be. But still, I accused them of being selfish and heartless, slamming the door behind me as I left to roam the neighborhood, the empty hours taunting my every step.

On the third night—my parents' words howling in my head, reminding me that this decision would not always be mine to make, that the window of opportunity was rapidly closing as I drowned in indecision—I made a deal with myself. I would tell Henry nothing of the Leongs' offer and wait for a sign. If red strings were based on fate, if they were real and we were connected, then Henry should know that something was wrong.

It was a game I was certain I couldn't lose. Since Henry's departure four weeks ago, he had written to me at least three times every week. His words strengthened me. They instilled a confidence in me that what we were doing was right—that we were right. I was convinced it was simply a matter of time before I found the next letter in the mail; his perfect words would comfort me; they would pull me away from a decision that became more difficult with each miserable day. I believed Henry would know, and every morning I waited by the mailbox before work. But for an entire week, one Saturday to the next, an invitation to the Leongs' extended and politely, regretfully postponed—a letter never came.

I would not take this as a sign, I thought, after nine days passed without a word from Henry. I needed something bigger, a real sign, to push me in one direction or the other. Living with my mother and working with my father had begun to wear me down. My father had not stopped talking about the Leongs. I could feel his restlessness, his agitation closing in on me as the second weekend approached, knowing we could defer the invitation for only so long, his desire hemorrhaging. He made a point of telling every friend he had, every client he shot, about the Leongs' hospitality—and everyone agreed. Mr. Leong had a reputation for generosity, donating thousands of dollars toward supporting the war effort, appearing constantly on the front page of the newspaper. The fact that my family *knew* him— had been invited to their house—was already bringing childlike joy to my parents. And every morning, as the newspaper sat shamelessly on the kitchen counter, Mr. Leong's face staring up at me, I began to wonder if even I knew what the right decision would be.

And then, on a Monday morning, ten days of waiting already passed, my mind warped with agony and anticipation, I received a letter from Henry. I tore it open, eager to read his words and show it to my parents. By then, I felt almost vengeful, intent on sham- ing them with Henry's unbreakable devotion. My mother would be jealous—it was a terrible thought, but I wanted it. I wanted her to apologize. I wanted to hear her say that I was nothing like her— that in Henry, I had found my destined match. I read the letter right there, on the empty road next to the mailbox, growing more con- fused with each sentence.

Amy,

I'm sorry it's been a few days between letters; I promise I haven't forgotten about our agreement. I wish I were writing to you with better news and a lighter spirit, but war seems to be disrupting the entire world. What started in ████████ is spreading everywhere. The people I've met in ████ are suffering terribly and there seems to be a shortage of everything. Clothes, food, water, clean places to sleep—every day it changes me and makes me think about bigger things. It seems so long ago that we were in my car, far away from all of this. I miss those days so much, but now that I've seen what's happening ▓▓▓, I can't ignore it. Every day I think of you and hope that you are strong. There is so much uncertainty in the world right now and I pray that you will never be affected by this kind of ▓▓▓▓▓.

I received a letter from my mother yesterday. She tried to be optimistic but I could tell she's worried. The pharmacy is not doing well. There were problems before I left, and now she says that every day they lose money by staying in business. I don't know what will happen, but whatever it is, we'll get through it. But you might want to stop by if you can. I know they'd love to see you.

We leave ▓▓▓▓▓ today and head ▓▓▓▓. I will write to you as soon as I reach the next destination.

▓▓▓▓▓▓, Henry

I squinted at Henry's square handwriting, at the holes where the words had been censored—speechless. For ten days I had imagined his words; his confessions of being miserable without me, his plan to return early, his boredom abroad. But here it was; the shortest letter Henry had ever written me, most of the words not even concerning our relationship, every detail and location cut cruelly from the paper. I read it again, and then a third time, trying to extract every bit of meaning from his sparse words, holding the sheet above me as if the sky could fill the blanks. Turning the paper over, I searched for more, inspected the envelope and found the government tape used to reseal it; in my haste, I hadn't noticed at first. *Opened by Examiner 524.* I gripped the paper at its edges, willing it to fill me with warmth, to remind me of a feeling that was slipping away. But it never did, because it was a flimsy, worthless piece of paper and Henry was on the opposite side of the world, his location in the trash of some government office. I felt like an idiot, the letter now ripped in two places, the indentation of my thumbs proof of my insanity.

For a moment, I considered tearing it apart and burying it in the backyard. I could pretend that the letter hadn't arrived yet. I could wait for the next one—one that said something else. I wanted so badly to be right about us; I didn't want to believe that our connection was generic or familiar or anything less than fireworks and destiny and red strings.

But I had already read it—that was the problem—and just as Henry had written in his letter, now that I'd seen what was happening, I couldn't ignore it. War was real, as were its consequences. Henry and I had been playing in a world of make-believe, I realized for the first time, and reality was changing that. How stupid to think that he would continue to write me love letters while the world fell apart, as cities were bombed and homes destroyed and mothers and children went hungry.

Henry was the brave one, not me. While I wallowed in self-pity, Henry was seeing the world, witnessing its problems, finding solutions. To think he could help an entire country and I couldn't even stop the suffering in my own home? It startled me. It made the world expand around me until I was just a tiny speck, my love for Henry but a flash in the universe, a trivial occurrence.

I looked down at my middle finger. Henry's diamond ring—his car, his military bonus—looked back up at me. I thought about the starving families. I thought about Henry's family, struggling to keep their pharmacy afloat, and my own family, clinging to the hope that I would change things for them; that I would sacrifice my first love for the benefit of everyone.

The stone on my finger could help Henry's family, and marrying Bohai could help my own. It was disgraceful, I thought, to wear this ring while Henry's family went without. Henry's brother's comment at the docks struck me now. *So this is the ring*, Paul had said as Henry sailed away, studying my middle finger. I was so consumed with grief that I hadn't stopped to consider that Henry's family might be suffering too—not just from Henry's departure, but financially. And when Henry sold his car to buy me a frivolous diamond ring, I could only imagine how his family must have felt.

I walked back into the house, Henry's letter shoved into the pocket of my shorts, every crevice of my body lit with intensity. My parents had been right. I had been given a singular opportunity to create change—to combine my family's tarnished name with the most prominent household on Oahu; to bring my family some much-deserved, long-awaited happiness. If I stayed with Henry, it was only a matter of time before he grew weary of my dreaming. My desire for a life different from our parents' would seem arrogant; my decision to refuse Bohai and stand by Henry would create resentment within us both. In another life, it might have been different, I realized. Love was a luxury of the rich. They could afford to be wrong; they could change their minds as they wished. Of course it wasn't fair, but much of life was turning out to be a series of strategic choices. Play the game and perhaps you had a chance. Convince yourself that life was impartial—that we're all given an equal shot—and you'd drown almost immediately, sucked down the hole with the rest of the ordinary people.

I reached under my bed and found a piece of paper and an envelope. I wrote quickly, not stopping to read it until the very end. I wrote that I had not meant to be so selfish—that it had been a difficult time for me as well and I had realized that now was not the right time for my relationship with Henry. I thanked Henry's family for their kindness and apologized, several times, for whatever pain I was causing. And then, removing it from my finger for the first time, I slipped off my ring and folded it into the letter, tucking the package into the envelope and addressing it to Henry's parents.

"Amy?" I heard my name and looked up to see my father drying his hair with a towel as he emerged from his room, fully dressed. "Are you almost ready to leave?"

"Yes," I said, licking the envelope and sealing it shut. "And you can call Mrs. Leong. You can tell her that we'll be at dinner on Saturday night."

My father put his towel down and stared at me.

"You're sure?"

"I'm positive."

My father nodded once, disbelief in his eyes, shocked that after all the fighting—all the yelling and tears and terrible words exchanged—I had come around. I had made the decision to save us.

"You know how I feel about it," he said, suppressing a smile.

I closed my eyes and, strangely enough, I felt liberated. Calmness washed over me with the sealing of the letter. The burden of my indecision was released and I welcomed the clarity that replaced it. It was the right choice, I nodded to myself. I would be a fool to think otherwise. If love did fade, as my mother had warned me, if it was indeed fickle, it was simply a matter of time before my love for Henry became distant and small. Our relationship had been a whirlwind, sweeping me off my feet and leaving me disoriented. But now, with a little space, I realized that the best thing I could do for both of us was to release him. Henry would find someone else, someone better. I was sure of it. He would find a girl who wouldn't forget his face in five weeks, whose heart would not be tempted so easily.

And I, with the passing of time, would find happiness with Bohai.

CHAPTER 6

November 1964

Honolulu, Hawaii

The smell of jasmine and smoke opens Amy's eyes. She faces downward, her eyes in her lap, and Theresa's hand is gone. Thick ivory clouds hang suspended in the air, floating sideways, filling the empty spaces of the room and stifling its light. Amy lifts her eyes to the first row of chairs and finds that she cannot make out a single face. She is cloaked in smoke, and so are they.

She follows the haze to her right, to a table at the foot of Bohai's coffin where Hong is lighting joss sticks, one by one, with a wooden match. In a heavy bowl, lined with gold and filled with grains of uncooked rice, dark incense rises in slim sticks.

"Mom, are you okay?"

Amy turns to her left and sees Theresa still sitting beside her.

"Oh," she says. "Yes, I'm fine. I needed—"

"I know," Theresa interrupts. "I told Uncle Kaipo to let you be. I was just asking."

"I'm okay," Amy says. "Thank you."

Beside Hong, a priest begins to chant. He holds a small gong in his hand, beating it in front of him with a bamboo stick, its head wrapped in soft leather. The metallic sound reverberates throughout the room, shaking the smoke, keeping pace with his voice. The song he sings comes from his nose, shrill and beautiful, punctuated by the steady crash of the gong. His words are a prayer for Bohai. He calls out to the spirits, begging them to open the road for his departed soul, to grant him a dignified transition. The priest's chant, his melodic plea, marks the beginning of Bohai's journey into the next world.

Smoke oozes from the tips of the joss sticks, rising high in white, undulating lines. They seem to dance to the gong, flitting sideways and breaking in half when the mallet strikes the brass. When the last stick is lit, Hong blows out her match and squats below the table, removing a wooden box the size of a mah-jongg set. She holds it from the bottom with open palms, positioning herself beside the table like an imperial statue, powerful and motionless.

The priest's song ends with a high note, climbing in octaves, higher and higher until the final strike of his gong. When the ringing halts, the smoke becomes still.

"Let the family approach," the priest calls. "Let them offer their comforts for the afterlife."

Almost immediately, Amy rises from her chair. She is the first to do so, and at her new height, she finds that the air is clearer. The fog hovers above the heads of the seated, creating a soft blanket of clouds, separating the earth from the sky. She breathes in the placid air and hopes that the afterlife is something like this. A moment completely your own. A quiet place to breathe. Amy makes her way to the table, and when she arrives, Hong reaches over the top of her box and opens it toward her like a briefcase.

Within the container lie dozens of folded gold papers, the majority of which are cylindrical—paper wrapped into a circle and tucked inside on the open ends. Scattered throughout these tubes are silhouettes of golden paper houses, boats, and cars. There is a pair of pants and a pair of shoes. There is a trunk for carrying these things and a servant to carry the trunk. Amy takes a match from the table and strikes it against its surface. The flame stings the tips of her fingers; she tips it sideways. With her left hand, Amy reaches into the box and removes a cylinder that she holds to the flame, letting it catch fire and releasing it into the ceramic bowl below her. It continues to smolder, transforming from shiny paper to flakes of delicate grey ash.

Hastily, Amy reaches for another, lighting and releasing, sending the paper money to her husband. She burns three more, one after the other in quick succession, before her match has burned to the end and she must put it out.

There are many things that Amy would like to burn, none of them available in Hong's wooden box. She thinks of them now—locked in her vanity drawer, all of the words she would like to incinerate. But for that she needs a real fire. She needs a furnace that leads to nowhere, a flame with the power to simply destroy. She looks into the ceramic bowl, at the flimsy piles of paper remains, and knows that a single match can never do what she hoped.

Before this moment, Amy had thought that the burning of these papers would fill her somehow. She had asked to go first; she had requested to make the first offering. The fire, the smoke—Amy thought it a way to be close to her husband. She imagined it as a moment of clarity and repentance, her thoughts lifted with the paper, able to reach Bohai well before the gifts arrived. But as she stands before the table, inches away from her husband's body, Amy's mind is as white as the room. She burns the paper and feels like a fool, the first person to offer a worthless symbol, to sacrifice something of no value. Why did she think it would be this easy? It's a match, she scolds herself. It's not magic.

Amy strikes a second match and holds it to her face. She watches it flicker as it climbs the length of the stick. It's almost to her fingertips and she hasn't moved; she hasn't looked away. But as the flame kisses her skin, she drops it suddenly into the bowl. She inhales sharply.

"Careful, Amy," the priest says.

Amy looks into the priest's face and is stricken by the sight of him. This close, she's surprised by how he's aged since she saw him last, twenty years ago on her wedding day. The priest's skin hangs loosely along his jawline, rippling gently as he speaks. He still wears his hair long, gathered behind him in a ponytail, but it's greying, not at the roots but streaked throughout its length, which seems unusual to Amy.

"I'm sorry," she says.

"For what?" he replies, smiling. "I hope you didn't burn your finger."

"No, I'm fine." She nods. "I just . . . I think I'm done."

"Very well, then. If you want, you may see your husband now."

Amy hesitates. To her left, she sees Kaipo rise from his chair. Amy moves to the side and takes slow steps toward the head of the casket, where Bohai lies, padded by white silk cushions and exposed from above. When she can almost see his face, she stops. She closes her eyes and takes the last two steps. She searches for the thoughts that failed her at the altar, the words she was supposed to send with the smoke.

She waits.

She waits for a long time, but nothing comes.

Amy opens her eyes and almost chokes. She brings a hand to cover her open mouth, tries to close her eyes but they resist. Everything about her body, inside and out, grows weaker with the sight of him.

Bohai looks like himself. He looks almost exactly as he should, which frightens Amy more than anything for which she prepared herself. It reminds her of ten thousand mornings, of the last twenty years of her life, waking up next to the face she sees now. Amy stands there, waiting for Bohai to open his eyes. She waits for him to say good morning and push himself upright against the silk pillows. He's reaching for his glasses now; he's about to make coffee. There's something entirely ordinary about the way he looks in that coffin, something startling about the ease spread across his face, and suddenly, Amy realizes it's been six months. Six months, a summer followed by a fall, one hundred and eighty unique opportunities to explain, they've all passed since Amy last saw this expression.

Her husband looks serene in death. He looks relieved.

"It doesn't feel real," Amy hears behind her. It's Kaipo, his eyes resting on his brother's face. "Something about this family," he says, eyes narrowed. "Never a warning. Just out of fucking nowhere."

Amy nods.

"For me too," she whispers, before turning and walking back to her seat, passing Theresa at the altar.

As Amy sits, she thinks she hears Mrs. Leong's voice behind her—something short, barely audible, maybe nothing at all.

"Sorry," she says. "Did you say something?"

"I'm next," Mrs. Leong says, turning to look Amy square in the eye.

Amy's lips part, waiting for words, but a moment later she presses them back together. Who is she to tell her no?

"I could come with you," Amy offers.

"No." Mrs. Leong pauses, but that's all she has to say.

Theresa was supposed to be last. She is Bohai's only child, the youngest member of their family. But as Theresa walks to her father's casket, Mrs. Leong rises. She displaces a pillar of smoke and coughs. The sound is moist and raspy. With knees bent, her feet take slow, shallow steps toward Hong.

As the two women stand face to face, Amy wonders what Hong will do. She's already closed the lid of the box; the ceremony should be over, Mrs. Leong should not be last. As Hong has told the family many times, Mrs. Leong should not be present at all today. Under no circumstance, she has explained, should a mother be permitted to bury her child.

They stand, their solemn expressions unchanged, their collective stillness enormous—but something passes between them in the moment that they share, looking into each other's face. Slowly, Hong reaches her hand to the front of the box and lifts its cover.

Mrs. Leong chooses a cylinder, holding it lightly between two fingers. She turns to the burning incense and hesitates. She squeezes the paper softly, compressing it and releasing, allowing it to spring back into its natural shape.

"Lin," the priest says gently. "May I light it for you?"

Mrs. Leong jumps; the paper drops from her hand. She stares at the man, her pupils darting from feature to feature.

"Lin," the man says again, extending his hand, a match pinched between two fingers. "It's okay."

Between them, the dying joss sticks release the last of their smoke. Mrs. Leong leans in closer, bending at her waist, trying to get a better look at the man.

"She's here," Mrs. Leong says, her eyes lit with emergency. "I saw her. Hurry up. I have to get Bohai—she's already here!"

Lin

1942
DIAMOND HEAD, HAWAII

Bohai sat at his desk in the study, a dim lamp lighting the papers spread before him. Behind him, the sun began to set through darkened windows covered in crepe paper that extended from edge to edge of the wooden frames. With the declaration of military law, Hong and I had gone to the craft store and bought their entire supply, a dozen black rolls, and went immediately to work. From the outside of the house, a faint yellow glow could still be seen but how elegant it looked, how magical. Tonight, I needed magic.

Amy was here; the evening was in motion. She had just arrived with her father and she looked spectacular. I could tell by her appearance that she had taken my offer seriously. The dress was hemmed beautifully, her hair slicked back in a perfect French pleat. She had come to win my son, and when I hugged her at the entrance, I sensed a shaky understanding pass between us.

Now it was time to reach an understanding with Bohai. I looked at him from the doorway, from the small, dim passage that led to the study, and I felt such determination. Ready or not, Bohai would find some happiness of his own.

I said his name as I walked through the door. He looked up from his papers but said nothing. I sat across from him. I placed my hands on his desk.

"Photographer Chan is here," I said, "with his daughter, Amy."
Bohai nodded.

"She liked you, Bohai. Did you know that? She asked about you tonight."

"Okay," he said, without a trace of emotion. It was as if I had told him it would rain, or we would have fish for dinner. I was astonished by what little effect they had, my careful words. Perhaps he sensed it was a lie; maybe he didn't believe me. Whatever the reason, it was clear that flattery was not the correct approach. For this, I'd have to try another way.

"Listen," I said, lowering my voice as I leaned forward. "It's time. I know you know this, even if you won't admit it to me. But I'm telling you, Bohai: right now, right outside this room there is a young girl who is interested in you, and unless you intend to grow old and alone with your father and I, I suggest you take this seriously."

Now I watched his face soften. His eyebrows sank as he took in my words. This was the image I would leave him with. Old and alone, a middle-aged man still living at home with his elderly parents. It was working; I could see it.

"Okay," Bohai said, removing his glasses and setting them down. He looked directly into my eyes, which is something he did so rarely. Something had clicked. "Thank you," he said, and I fought every urge that came to me. I wanted to congratulate him, to jump from my chair and embrace my son, but I didn't; I couldn't. I knew it was best to remain calm. I could feel my limbs battling the impulse, tightening and releasing with excitement.

"I know you don't like crowds," I told him, "so I'll bring her here if that's okay." He nodded. It had been my intention all along to bring them together on Bohai's ground. He was most confident in the study, wearing his suit, surrounded by his paperwork. In the dim light, he looked almost powerful. He looked important.

"I'll be right back," I said, rising from my chair. "And don't be nervous," I added, reaching over and squeezing his arm before leaving through the alcove. "She likes you."

I found Amy with her father in the sitting room. As I approached, I watched Mr. Chan raise his whiskey to his lips and take a long sip.

"I've come to borrow your daughter," I said to Mr. Chan, placing my hand on Amy's shoulder. She turned, her face bright and cheerful, and fashioned a smile that revealed so much. It touched me somehow, filled me with something familiar. Behind her crafted smile was a mountain of anxiety hidden by courage. It was a good thing, I decided—a promising sign. She would need both in equal balance for what awaited her.

"He's so excited you're here," I whispered to Amy as we walked down the hall. "But you know how he's shy, so don't let that put you off. I know you'll get on wonderfully once he gets comfortable."

"It's no problem," she replied, her heels clicking against the hardwood floor. "I'm good at talking."

"Then it will be perfect." I led her through the passage and knocked on the open door of the study. "Bohai," I said, "there's someone here to see you."

Bohai stood immediately, banging his knee on the desk and shaking the lamp.

"Hi," he said abruptly. "Hi—wow," he gulped, pressing his hands to the knee he had hit.

It was the dress. The pale orange drew out the warmth in Amy's skin; the silk glided with her step, the slit up her left leg gave just a hint of what lay behind. My son was speechless—but not in his usual way. Bohai was dumbstruck. It was a different silence, a stillness fueled by desire.

Amy smiled—there was her confidence, growing as my son stared.

"Hi," she greeted him. I waited for more but that was all she said.

"Sit, sit Amy!" I gestured toward the two chairs. "Bohai, would you like to offer your guest something to drink?"

"Yes," he replied, still looking at Amy. He walked toward the small cooler and caught my eye. Then, with the smallest gesture, he nodded me from the room. With a flick of his head, he asked me to leave. "Thank you," he said, and I couldn't believe it. My son wanted to be alone with Amy. He wanted me to leave and it was I who wasn't ready.

"Of course," I said quickly, gathering myself. "I'll call when dinner is ready."

I walked through the alcove and paused in the middle, realizing how dark it was. *Would you like some champagne,* I heard. *That'd be great,* she replied. Slowly, I flattened myself against the bookshelves that lined the small passage, not yet sure what I was doing. To my left was a space, a narrow gap between two shelves into which I could easily fit. It was ridiculous, but they wouldn't see me, I thought; it was so dark. I could stay and listen. I slid across the shelf and into the space.

In the study, Bohai held the bottle of champagne, twisting the cork with his right hand. I held my breath; he'd never done it before. The bottle popped and I jumped. He filled two glasses and I told myself to calm down. To have confidence in my son.

"You look beautiful," he said, handing her a glass. I covered my mouth. *Thank you,* I heard. Amy was just outside my vision.

"Your mother gave me the dress, when we delivered the photographs. I'm glad she invited us to dinner so I'd have somewhere to wear it."

No, I thought; don't tell him the dress is from me. Don't make him think of me. I was sweating. But she was being honest, I realized, just as I had been with Frank. She was comfortable with her simplicity; I liked that about her. If I was going to stay, I needed to relax, to breathe, I warned myself. I pressed my back against the wall. Perhaps it was better if I didn't look.

It's from France, I heard Bohai say, *the champagne.* I could feel his mind working. *My father has cases of it brought in during the summer. He has a friend with a vineyard.*

Wow.

Do you like it?

There was a pause. I wondered what was happening. Then I heard a damp cough—Amy's cough, muffled by a hand or a sleeve.

Is there something wrong?

No, no. Another pause; I leaned forward, far enough to see Amy's wrinkled face, Bohai's worried expression.

"It's just," Amy said, "I've never had champagne before."

"Never?"

"Never." She shrugged. I fell back against the wooden panel. I smiled. It was happening already. *It's delicious*, I heard. Bohai was opening her world; she was opening his. *The bubbles, they taste like roses.* Bohai laughed and so did she. There was an urgency in the room, I could feel it from my spot in the dark. They had their own reasons, but they both wanted this. They were working together unknowingly, toward the same goal.

Your father's photographs were so nice.

It's easy to do in a house like this. Usually, we just have a white wall. We don't normally have a waterfall to work with.

Still. We've had plenty of photographers. Your father is the best.

Is that so?

Really. He is. And that waterfall. It's embarrassing. I've always thought it was too much.

I disagree. Your father seems like a man who deserves a waterfall.

It wasn't his idea, actually. My mom wanted it.

A pause.

But if you like it, then so do I.

He was trying so hard. I'd never heard so many words from my son in a single conversation. He was creating his own topics, searching for compliments. He had learned something from Kaipo. He was doing well.

I watched Amy walk across the doorway, stopping at the bookshelf that held the family photographs. She picked one up and looked at it. Bohai rose and followed. He stood inches behind her.

"We went to Indonesia, three years ago, the whole family," he explained. I knew the picture well. The six of us stood in front of a house on stilts with a thatched roof. Hong had been there too, but she had taken the picture.

"And this one?" Amy chose another frame.

"Maui. We go every year to fish. Do you like to fish?"

"I wouldn't know. But I'd love to learn."

I took a deep breath and withdrew into the small space, feeling my heart pick up speed. Their voices buzzed as I closed my eyes; I felt dizzy as my mind pulled me backward. It had been years since I'd thought about it. It was a choice I made. I hadn't needed to and so I hadn't, but in that instant it overwhelmed me; it shook the breath from my lungs. Amy's presence was unearthing memories, difficult emotions from a faraway place, buried for as long as I could manage. But watching her now, watching this, I couldn't shake the feeling that we shared something, Amy and I. We were cut from a similar cloth, given a similar chance. In this girl, in my dress, I saw so much of myself.

The year was 1900 and I had just turned seventeen. Thinking of that year, the smells of deep-fried bean curd and sweet moon cakes overwhelm my senses. Hot grease coats my nostrils. I breathe in and taste salt and fat and stale seawater. I had been working in the kitchen that summer, in my parents' restaurant in Guangdong, frying up pomfret by the hundreds in the steamy back room. I think back and it feels like another lifetime, another existence entirely. I see her in the kitchen, her hands calloused, her oily cheeks flushed, and I can hardly believe that girl was me.

I was their only child. It sounds so simple like that; such a predictable sadness, so easy to understand how my life might have been. Of course my parents thought of me as worthless, certainly they hoped for sons. These things are true, but I remember so much more than that.

Most every week, from as young as I can remember, my father would threaten to sell me. It wasn't unusual in our village; many daughters had been sold to the fields or to the households of wealthy families. The thought of going to work among women did not scare me, but my father knew this. He said he would sell me to an old, filthy slave owner, to a man with six child concubines. If I didn't obey him, I could disappear as easily as salt thrown in the ocean.

When he failed to scare me properly with slavery, as I got older and learned to hold a stern face, my father threatened to kill me. It was permitted in those times. If a daughter was too useless, or too disobedient, a father had the right to end her life to make his better. Rotten was my nickname, because I had spoiled my mother's womb.

I had left it barren and ruined, which, my father told me from the age of five, was a reflection of my soul. I didn't deserve to be wed, he had said, laughing as spit escaped through the wide gap in his teeth. Girls like me weren't suitable for marriage.

Perhaps I was rotten, I remember telling myself, gathering strange comfort from the word. In a way, it felt like an explanation. There was something growing inside me as I became a woman, something rebellious and hard. Sell me, I said to my father on my fifteenth birthday. I even repeated it for him as he stood above me, palm raised high in the air. He beat me into darkness that night, and right before it overcame me, I thought I might be dead. That night, I thought I had gone too far. When I awoke the next morning, my body swollen and raw, I remember feeling a terrible joy. Physical damage let our neighbors know what was happening in our home, and in a strange way, I saw it as a shame on my father. He had the strength to break bones and bruise skin, but not to kill. What kind of man would continue to break his only daughter—to let her heal only to break her once again? A coward, I hoped they would think.

When my body was battered, I was kept in the back kitchen of the restaurant. I tended the vat of hot oil, which is a stench that will never leave me, frying customers' orders and passing plates through the narrow door. It seems to me now that my father understood my game. Most fathers displayed the disobedience of their daughters, and I assumed that would happen to me. It was a humiliation that told suitors the girl was willful, to think twice before extending an offer. But my father was spineless, and I was never to be married. I was the hopeless girl with the saddest of fates, and so he chose to hide me from the pity of others. In the kitchen, my father knew I suffered alone. Tucked away without a soul to speak to, it was as if it had never happened.

It was on a Monday, during the last days of summer, that everything changed. My body had nearly healed and I was at the front counter again, when a young man came into the restaurant for lunch. He wore a Western-style suit made from a material that moved like water. It caused me to stare. He ordered salted chicken and sat on a stool near the only window, eating neatly while the other men looked on. He paid too much for his meal. He gave me a bill worth more than twice the amount he owed, and when I tried to give him change, he shook his head. He told me to keep it.

I took the bill immediately to the back kitchen. I gave it to my mother, who rubbed it between her fingers and held it above her head, checking for authenticity. We knew almost everyone we served. It was a small restaurant in a small village; even the vagrants we knew by name. It was usual for our customers to bargain down the price of their meal, to ask to put it on credit, or to trade for whatever they hauled in their suitcase. But to overpay—that had never happened before.

"Is it real?" my father asked. My mother nodded and handed him the bill, which he folded into the pocket of his trousers. "Stay in the back," he ordered.

My father was gone for a long time after that. An entire hour passed without a single order for food. The door to the dining room remained closed, and the noise on the other side seemed to fade. My mother and I picked through the day's vegetables, cutting out the brown spots and saving them in a pile for us to eat for dinner. We cleaned the bucket of fish, peeled the bag of shrimp. I had almost forgotten about the suited man when we heard my father's voice through the door.

"Lin!" he called, his large voice filling the kitchen.

My mother looked at me and then to the door, sitting perfectly still on her wooden crate.

"Go," she said. It was her virtue as a wife and her failure as a mother, always doing as my father ordered. Afterward, she tended to our wounds, always mine before hers, but never did she defend herself against my father, no matter what violence awaited us.

I wiped my hands on my apron and pushed open the dividing door. On the opposite side, it was absolutely silent. Every table was empty, dirty plates and used cups left abandoned, as if the customers had left in a hurry. The front door was closed, and when I looked closer, I realized it was also locked. My father sat at the only clean table, a thick stack of yuan in front of him, more than I had ever seen. Across the table sat the suited man.

"Come closer," my father called from his chair. He was smiling.

My legs refused to move; my mouth became dry. I couldn't pull my eyes from the money. A terrible, sinking feeling grew inside of me.

"What is this?" I whispered, my body trembling. My eyes would not move from that stack of yuan. "Who is this man?"

My father slapped his hand on the table and I quieted; my body stiffened. My father looked at the suited man. He bowed his head in humility and I understood that the money on the table was for me. He had finally done it. I had been sold.

"This man is Leong Fu," my father began. "He is in need of a wife. You will be his wife."

I couldn't breathe; I couldn't move. I felt too much fear to look at the man, too much weakness to face my father, who I knew was still smiling.

Heat rose through my chest and into my neck. It filled my head and burned the back of my eyes. I had pushed too far; I had caused too much trouble. My father had done exactly what I had challenged him to do; he had sold me, and by the appearance of the suited man, this would not be my last stop. I would certainly be sold again.

"No!" I screamed, falling to my knees in the middle of the dining room. "No, please, Father. I can change. I'll be different. You deserve a better daughter than me, please give me another—"

"Get up!" my father demanded. "You stupid girl."

"Lin." A second voice spoke. My knees shook against the hard floor. It was the suited man, and he knew my name.

"As my wife, you will be cared for. You will be happy."

I looked up from my spot on the ground, the man's words twisting wretchedly in my ears. Is that what he had told my father? That as his wife, I would be happy? Of course not; it was all a disgusting game. I wanted to spit on them both. I wanted them to trample me right there, to spare me the humiliation that would follow. My father looked into my terrified eyes and smiled his same cruel smile and I knew there was nothing more to say. That stack of money was worth more than a lifetime of farm wages. My father had gotten lucky and he knew it. He was so pleased with himself.

"Bow to your husband," he demanded.

I am a slave, I remember thinking. My fate was not my own; I had known this for my entire life. I closed my eyes and let my body take back its tears. Slowly, I rose, and I bowed to the suited man.

We sat in his wagon together, on straw cushions that smelled nothing of straw. It had a closed top and a door with a window that let in a small rectangle of light. As the wheels began to move I kept my eyes down and counted the knots along the panels of wood.

"I want to show you something," Frank said, his voice steady and firm. Beside me, I felt him moving. He shifted on the straw; I was almost certain he removed the jacket of his suit. Carefully, I stole a sideways glance. With one hand, he began to unbutton his collar. His fingers ran along the front of his shirt, undressing himself, and my body went cold. I prepared myself for a struggle. I pressed my fingernails into the

pads of my thumbs and knew that, given enough force, they were long enough to draw blood. I looked up to face him; his shirt was halfway undone, a triangle of his chest exposed. I dug my fingers into the cushions, piercing the fabric that contained them. If I screamed loud enough, I told myself, the driver would have to stop. He would have to come back and check.

Frank loosened the last button and pulled the shirt from his shoulders. I opened my mouth to cry out and shifted my weight to my feet—when I was met with a sight that silenced me outright. As if a heavy boot, held by its laces, had struck my stomach, I felt the air rush from my body. My mouth remained open but nothing came out. Frank was still. He didn't come closer.

"My own father," he said softly, his stomach rising with his speech, "he gave me these." He pointed to the longest scar that marked his body, one of half a dozen that marred him. It stretched from the right side of his rib cage to his belly button, stained deep purple along flesh that protruded faintly from his body. On the left side of his chest, below the muscle, broken blood vessels created a terrifying splattering. I recognized the patterns, the way the color faded along the edges, the deep, shiny pockets at the core, but I'd never seen it like this, on a body attached to a face. My parents didn't own a mirror and my mother was always covered.

"My father was a man with a temper as well," Frank said. "And I hated him." He reached for his shirt and pulled his arms through. He buttoned it from the bottom. "As you must hate yours."

I had shrunk into the corner of the compartment, my shoulders hunched in embarrassment. I felt that at any moment my father would jump from behind the wagon door and laugh at my stupidity. This day, this man, this story—it couldn't be real, he had to be testing me. How else could this man know all that he did?

"Long sleeves on a day as hot as this," Frank said, as if reading the words from my thoughts. "The bruise on your neck when you turned. The way you walk like your hip is healing from a break. I just—I couldn't leave you there, do you understand?"

Frank looked out the small window of the wagon. His eyes narrowed and I recognized something cruel in the way he stared, in the forceful, bitter way he swallowed. He was thinking of his father.

"You don't have to trust me, not yet," he said, eyes still focused beyond the window. "But I'm a decent man and I meant what I said in the restaurant." He paused, but

I knew what he referred to, because no man, no person had ever said those words to me before.

"I would like it if you were happy," he said. "From now on, I'm going to take care of you."

For the rest of the trip we said nothing. I could think of nothing worthy of saying. But the farther we traveled without stopping, without my father jumping from behind the wagon door, the more I believed that this man might understand something about me. That perhaps there was decency in this world.

I opened my eyes. It was warm in the alcove; the fabric of my shirt clung to my skin. I peeked through the open door of the study and exhaled in relief. Bohai and Amy were still there, sitting together behind his desk. They were laughing; their shoulders touched. The bottle of champagne was empty. I watched them, so full of excitement, and was reminded of the wonder I had felt as I realized my life with Frank would be nothing like the way I had imagined it.

Within a month we were married. He bought me a dress and my first pair of shoes. Because he knew who I was and where I came from, and knew that I could offer him nothing in exchange, our courtship was honest. Frank led me slowly through the transition, through the strange process of having nothing to having everything: a two-story home, a household staff, a garden, an indoor bathroom. Those first years with Frank, before the children and the war, for me they were nothing short of magic.

I looked at my son, at Amy. She was the oldest of ten, she told me the week before. They shared a room; it came out by accident. I had asked about her studies, if she had a quiet place to work, and almost immediately the idea came to me. All this time I had been searching in the wrong place. With the sheer power of money, I had been rescued, removed from my bitter reality and given another life. It could happen again—naturally, it could happen again. What stopped me from doing it myself?

I watched them at Bohai's desk, the two of them flushed and

delighted. Bohai was looking for something among his papers, his fingers flipping through the documents. *I know it's here,* he said, *I was just looking at it.* Amy watched him, thoughtfully, not saying a word. And then, turning her body toward him, she placed her hand on his.

Bohai froze. He looked at Amy, his mouth slightly open, unable to speak. Slowly, she leaned into him and their lips met and parted, their hands still connected on the table.

I drew back against the wall, not believing what I had seen. I placed a palm over my heart, pressed it into my chest to steady its beat, and a smile arrived, a secret laugh.

They must be married, I thought to myself. *It's the only way.*

The morning after the dinner party, I woke up with the sun. I checked the clock and walked to the dining room, expecting to find my son having breakfast alone. But he wasn't there. I rubbed my eyes and looked again. It had been years, perhaps decades, since Bohai had slept past six. Even as a teenager he would read at the table for hours before school began, before even the roosters knew that the day had begun. I tapped my fingers on the kitchen counter, waiting for an idea to come to me. When nothing did, I walked up the stairs and down the hall to my son's bedroom door.

I wondered if I should knock; I'd never been in this situation before. Softly, I tapped twice on the door. When there was no answer, I let myself in. Bohai was still asleep.

"Bohai," I whispered, sitting and placing my hand on his shoulder. He opened his eyes immediately.

"I overslept," he replied, rubbing his eyes and sitting up to face me.

"Nonsense, I just wanted to talk to you about last night. It looked to me like you and Amy got along very well." He brought a hand to his forehead and rubbed his thumb slowly into his temple. I considered my son's face, the same face that had caused me such anxiety mere months before. I considered the position of his body, the way his shoulders hunched over while he sat. His narrow eyes squinted with sleep; his bare chest was more defined than I remembered. There was something different about him and suddenly, I realized: he seemed masculine. For the first time in my experience as his mother, I was seeing my son as a man.

"Mom," he said, and then he paused. He shut his eyes to moisten them and opened them wide to meet me. "I think I love her."

It took me by surprise. I had expected resistance, or at the very least, apprehension. You're pushing too hard, I imagined him saying, you're moving things too quickly. I searched for words and found none. In thirty-three years, *love* was a word that Bohai used rarely, and when he did, it was only for family.

"I know," I managed. "Which is why I think you should—"

"I want to marry her," he said suddenly. He repeated it, I think for himself, as if it were the first time he had reached this conclusion. The sun was beginning to soak through the white curtains of his room. The two of us sat on his bed, a sliver of bright light between us, as we considered the words that had just been said.

"You have my blessing," I said simply, taking Bohai's hand under the sheet. "Of course you have all of our blessing."

I could feel my heart beating in my ears, my breath growing fast and excited. It was all happening so quickly I could hardly keep up. Finally, Bohai had reached his tipping point and in Amy he'd found his force, his strength, his prize. A new life was poised to begin, a fairy tale beginning to unfold.

I had always had concerns about Bohai. That was no secret. It made me feel foolish now, knowing how simply the solution had come. How easy it had been to set Bohai on the right path and see him finally happy. And I saw it in Amy, too. There was a quiet contentment that I knew almost certainly would turn to real love. Bohai was a good man, just as my own husband had turned out to be. I knew how the story ended. I was a living example.

Now that they were engaged, I began with preparations for the wedding dresses. I thought back to my own fitting in China, a day I remembered more clearly than my ceremony. The enormous mirrors at the tailor's shop were overwhelming to my seventeen-year-old self. I had never seen the full length of my back, never seen the top of my head and the tips of my toes in a single frame. I had seen a mirror before and I knew there was no magic behind it, but I couldn't help but wiggle my fingertips and watch the girl across from me do the same, accurate to the point of amazement.

I arranged for Amy and her mother to meet my seamstress at the house. Hong helped me set up the pedestal in the sitting room and position the three-paneled mirror. We opened the two sides and found ourselves standing before our reflections, two aging women preparing for a wedding. I had been married for just a year when Hong arrived in Guangdong, and the image of us together now was startling. Like the simplest function of my body, I gave little thought to how Hong had changed, how age and time had marked her. The years had washed over us, each new phase shinier, easier than the last until we had hardly anything left to worry about, to confide in each other the way we used to. Our relationship was different now, certainly, the intensity of our past left behind, but I never took for granted the importance of Hong, the necessity of her. The sound of her making tea in the afternoon, the old-world clink of porcelain cups against saucers, the smell of her sweet, black herbal tonics lined up along the low shelf of our refrigerator, the way she still covered her mouth when she laughed—these things anchored me to a place where I still had to fight, when I made my greatest leaps of faith. I cherished that about Hong, and I would always think of her as she was that day at my table, young, fierce, and determined. She was almost sixty now, her arms soft, her skin loose. I wondered how she thought of me.

The doorbell rang and I went to answer it. Amy waved at me nervously as she climbed the stairs, touching her cheek to mine when she reached the top.

"Mrs. Chan," I said, extending my arm to her mother, "I'm so happy to finally meet you!"

"Yes," she said, her small voice unsteady. She leaned in to greet me. "Thank you so much."

I led Amy and her mother into the sitting room, where my seamstress began immediately. She showed them the fabrics we had gathered, encouraging Amy to touch the colored bolts and hold them to her skin. Amy would need three dresses for the occasion, my seamstress explained: a white wedding gown, a traditional Chinese cheongsam, and a departure dress.

Throughout this ceremony, Mrs. Chan remained silent. She shared no opinions as we picked through the fabrics. She stood with her hands in her pockets, her lips pressed tightly together.

My seamstress began to take Amy's measurements and I went into the kitchen to find the tray of iced tea that Hong had prepared. When I returned, Mrs. Chan had left the pedestal and was sitting quietly on the couch, her hands folded in her lap, the pads of her thumbs rubbing anxiously together. I wanted to tell Amy's mother that I understood. That during my wedding preparations I had barely said a word, so frightened that I would say something wrong and have it all taken away. But now was not the time for such heavy matters. A wedding was meant to be a happy time, and what Amy's mother needed was a distraction.

"Mrs. Chan," I said, setting down the tray of iced tea, "have you decided on what you'd like to wear?"

"Me?" she said, her palm pressed to her chest as she looked behind her.

"Of course!" I replied, clapping my hands together. "You're the mother of the bride—your dress should be almost as beautiful as your daughter's. Amy, help your mother to the pedestal, please."

Mrs. Chan's eyes widened and moved to her daughter, as if asking her permission to accept my offer. It occurred to me that Mrs. Chan had no idea that she would be having a dress made as well. Amy smiled at her mother, stepping off the pedestal in a ball gown they had begun pinning, and walked to her.

"Mom," she whispered, putting her hands on her mother's knees. "Go on," she said, still smiling. "You heard Mrs. Leong, it's your turn."

Slowly, Amy's mother rose from the couch and took cautious, even steps toward the mirror.

"Mrs. Chan," my seamstress began, "I think a skirt suit in a royal blue would be marvelous on you." She walked over to the bolts of fabric, selecting a rich blue silk that shimmered as it unraveled.

Mrs. Chan looked at the seamstress but said nothing. She had stopped walking, frozen in her step, one leg in front of the other.

"Or we could make a dress—not too short, maybe lavender? Or a suit with pants if that would make you more comfortable." My seamstress paused and turned to Mrs. Chan for a reaction but her face remained stuck in the same faltering expression.

"We can make anything, ma'am, just say the word and—"

Amy's mother burst out laughing. Uncontrollable, girlish laughter tumbled from her mouth, a joyful gust of disbelief.

"This is really happening," she said, shaking her head and wiping a tear from the bottom of her eye. She looked at her daughter, then to the seamstress.

"Make me anything you like. No matter what it is, I promise you, it will be the nicest thing I've ever owned." She stepped onto the pedestal, still shaking her head, and stretched out her arms to be measured.

Bohai and Amy were married at the Royal Hawaiian Hotel in April 1942. I wish I could say it was a simple wedding to arrange, but it was not. In the months after the bombing, all of Oahu's best hotels were closed to tourists and private events like ours. They had made special arrangements with the military, which turned their hotels into a place for American soldiers to rest and enjoy the island. Frank suggested that we wait to hold the ceremony, as did Bohai when he became aware of the difficulties. But I wouldn't hear of it. I wanted the wedding right away. I feared that the passing of time would bring complications and mixed feelings about the joining of our families. I feared that if I waited too long, I risked spoiling Bohai and Amy's happiness.

I took on the task of arranging everything myself, faced with wartime decisions that I had never before considered. Despite the circumstances, it was important to me that I honor Hawaii with the marriage of my first son in our adopted soil. I drove to Waikiki three days in a row and walked the grounds of my favorite hotels. I imagined a ceremony in each of their ballrooms; in my mind, I arranged tables and flowers and guests. The space was not available for weddings, the staff continued to remind me, but I was determined. I decided on the Royal Hawaiian, for both its grandness and its rich history of housing Oahu's royal family.

I spoke first with the general manager, then to the owner. They told me the same thing. It would be impossible to evacuate all four hundred guestrooms for a private event. I tried to ask them in the way that Frank would, with equal amounts of charisma and authority. But I wasn't as convincing as my husband, and in the end, I needed his help.

"I won't need you for anything else," I told Frank at dinner. "I promise. I'll do the rest myself." He smiled at me and shook his head.

"I'll see what I can do," he replied.

The next morning, Frank called, and we were given a Saturday in April.

My original idea was a twilight ceremony—at seven thirty in the evening—honoring the Chinese tradition of wedding on the half hour, so that the hands of the clock move upward instead of down. The general manager of the Royal Hawaiian laughed, as Frank said he would, as he turned down my offer to outfit the hotel in blackout shades. We settled on an afternoon ceremony in the Coconut Grove, a quiet outdoor garden shaded by coconut palms, along the hotel's private beachfront. It would be followed by a traditional Chinese reception at the famous Lau Yee Chai across the way. We would begin at noon, Bohai and Amy drinking wine from a shared goblet a half hour later, and end at five thirty, with just enough time to drive our guests home by curfew.

It was a small wedding by Chinese standards. Flights in and out of the island had been suspended and all private planes had been grounded. The Honolulu airports were being run by the military. Frank considered bringing in friends from China with one of his cargo ships, but there was no time. The wedding day would arrive before our guests had crossed the Pacific and there was no possibility of rescheduling. So the invitations were sent only to our friends on Oahu. Three hundred in all: two hundred and forty guests from our side and sixty from Amy's. When she handed me her short list of names I encouraged her to invite more people. I told her she needn't leave anyone out.

"That's it for me," she said. "All from Kaneohe—so the good news is that we'll need just one big bus to take everyone home. It could be a way of saving money." She laughed nervously afterward and I felt so close to her. I knew her excitement intimately. I understood her doubt.

Our guests sat in bamboo chairs with fat red cushions, the chair backs wrapped in white silk covers and knotted in the back with a sweeping bow. The grass had been sprinkled with white pikake earlier that morning, so that its light floral scent could perfume the air and mix with the sweetness of the coconut trees. I had hoped to re-create that first feeling of Oahu—the awakening of all five senses that had greeted me in the harbor that morning. Frank had chosen a Hawaiian band to play quiet meles. They strummed ukuleles and tapped on ipus as our guests arrived and took their seats.

Bohai and Amy entered the Coconut Grove in red sedan chairs, each of them lifted off the ground by four friends, one at each corner. Amy's chair was covered in the front; Bohai was not allowed to see his bride until the last moment. They met at the mouth of the aisle, and slowly they were lowered to the ground. Bohai stepped down and took confident steps down the aisle. As he reached the end, the minister picked up a conch shell and blew on the opening, announcing the entrance of the bride. I had everything scheduled down to the minute, and I found myself watching the clock more than the event I had so carefully planned—until Amy emerged. From behind her curtain, Amy's ivory-and-diamond shoes touched the ground. They were followed by her hand, which pulled away the curtain as she slowly came into sight. The entire garden was silenced, including the priest, who stopped blowing on his conch shell abruptly, the air taken from his lungs. I had seen Amy that morning in her dressing room, as her sister removed the last of the pins from her hair. But in the final few hours she had transformed completely, and even I was not prepared for how spectacular she was that afternoon.

Her skin was as smooth as porcelain, her mouth painted red as a pomegranate. Black kohl traced the outsides of her eyes, one of them covered by a red lace veil. The train of her dress was endless, an entire bolt of embroidered silk trailing behind her as she walked down the aisle. And the final piece—a long, delicate strand of creamy pearls—was wrapped twice around her neck and clasped in the back with a jade brooch lined with gold. An early wedding present from Frank and me. I had picked it out myself and given it to her the night before.

Instead of a Chinese tea ceremony, Bohai and Amy exchanged leis in front of a kahuna, to honor the Hawaiian tradition, and shared a goblet of wine in front of the newly joined families. Bohai placed a lei of orchids around Amy's neck, catching a blossom on her hairpin. *Marriage is never easy*, the minister joked, and the sound of laughter, of the warmth of our guests filled the afternoon sky, blessing their union. Amy placed her maile lei around Bohai's neck. She ran her fingers along the edges as she pulled away. They held hands, they kissed, they became husband and wife.

Before we knew it, it was two o'clock and we were rushing Bohai and Amy to their bridal chamber in the hotel's presidential suite. They sat on the bed where they would spend their first night together, while Frank prepared the two goblets waiting on the table. He tied them with the traditional red string, and handed one end to Bohai and one to Amy, filling them with wine and honey.

As the mother of the bride, Mrs. Chan was in the nuptial chamber, sitting in a chair beside her husband. She had decided on a lavender dress with a wide collar and a thin silver belt. She looked lovely, so happy. Her eyes were bright and glossy as she smiled, her excitement glowing from within. It seemed to me that all the apprehension that Amy's mother felt on the day of their fitting had vanished in that moment, as Amy and Bohai toasted to their happiness. The red thread connected their goblets; it joined their lives and their fortunes.

When the wine and honey were gone, we met our guests at Lau Yee Chai for a customary nine-course Chinese dinner. The restaurant had been decorated lavishly. Thirty circular tables were arranged around the banquet hall, each of them dressed in a red silk tablecloth. The chopsticks were painted in gold leaf; the white cloth napkins were embroidered in black. Gold-and-crystal chandeliers hung from the tall ceilings and delicate strands of sparkling turquoise dropped below them. It was exactly how I had imagined it. Everything from the place cards to the temperature of the tea was absolutely perfect, and I couldn't have been more pleased. Then Amy entered the banquet in her second dress, a gold cheongsam with delicate silver embroidery, and I knew that all of our hard work had been worthwhile. That rushing the wedding hadn't, even for an instant, compromised the loveliness of their moment.

Dinner was served in traditional succession: shark's fin soup followed by Peking duck, cold ginger chicken and lobster with black bean sauce. When the plates were cleared, they brought out deep-fried oysters, steamed whole fish with chili and garlic, abalone and black mushrooms, roasted squab, and finally, salt-and-pepper shrimp. I had selected the menu with Hong. We sampled two dozen dishes before settling on our nine.

Mr. Chan happily fulfilled his duties as the father of the bride, walking from table to table to take the customary shot of whiskey. I watched all of Frank's friends and business associates shake his hand and congratulate him on the success of his daughter. They clinked their glasses together and cheered, sending a shot of whiskey down their throats. Frank joined him about halfway through the tables, announcing to each new group that Mr. Chan was a famous photographer, and as the evening progressed, his best friend. By the time Mr. Chan had greeted his last guest, he had finished half a bottle of whiskey and started dancing with Amy, his suit jacket abandoned on his chair.

This is the happiest day of my life, Amy whispered in my ear, her expression so sincere she looked like she might cry. Every inch of Amy's body sparkled, from the diamonds in her ears to the rubies on her shoes. She couldn't take a step without receiving a compliment or being presented with a red envelope filled with lucky money. As the evening continued and she began to drink, sipping whiskey from her teacup, I watched Amy give her mother the little packets of lucky money. Amy nodded and smiled and pressed the envelopes into her mother's trembling hands. I could feel her satisfaction; I remembered the disbelief. To have my own money, to be worth at least the amount in the envelope, was one of the most extraordinary realizations of my life. On my wedding day, I took my mother behind a dividing wall and showed her the money I had been given. *You can keep it for yourself*, I whispered. *You don't have to give it to him.* Of course, she had. But it didn't matter; there was enough money for two more lifetimes, and I, their worthless daughter, would always be the source.

At five o'clock, when the guests were full and the sun began to lower, Frank and I unveiled our final surprise, setting off ten thousand fireworks on Waikiki Beach. Traditionally, the fireworks are lit

at the beginning of the wedding, but I wanted to wait until the end—
to symbolize the excitement of a new life about to begin. The beach
was dotted with uniformed men, all obeying orders, a few upset
about the illegal extravagance—but every one of them looked up to
the sky, mesmerized by the neon explosions that rained down on the
ocean, against Diamond Head's towering silhouette. Frank and Mr.
Chan stood by the water, the slacks of their tuxedos rolled up to their
knees, a flask of whiskey passing between them as they tilted their
heads upward. Amy clutched Bohai's hand, their bare feet tucked
deep into the warm sand, watching beams of fuchsia and scarlet light
up the evening sky. And when Bohai's hand slipped from Amy's wrist
to her waist, her arms wrapping around his neck and sliding down his
chest, they quickly excused themselves over the sound of crackling
fireworks and ran barefoot along the beach, toward the honeymoon
suite that awaited them.

CHAPTER 7

November 1964
HONOLULU, HAWAII

Hong is the only one who hears Mrs. Leong.

It takes her just a moment, a single flash of contemplation, to match her old friend's words to a memory. And as Hong places it, slips the words into their slot in time, she understands precisely where Mrs. Leong's thoughts have fled.

Hong wants to smile but she doesn't. She doesn't want to be caught, doesn't care to explain its source; but on the underside of Hong's skin, in among the blood that still pumps through her body, she feels a gratitude, liquid and ethereal, that Mrs. Leong's mind has settled on that evening, that a happy memory has won out in the trenches of her old friend's mind.

Let her stay there, Hong decides. Let her feel the joy of her son, the thrill of his wedding.

"Sorry?" the priest says, leaning in closer. "Sorry—what was that?"

Mrs. Leong doesn't respond. She continues to look at the priest but her eyes move through him. Even across the haze of the smoke, the priest can tell that her focus is far beyond his face. So he turns to Hong, and with the darks of his eyes and the hesitation on his lips, he asks her what to do next.

"It's too much," Hong says, quietly enough so only he can hear. "Better to let her be—finish the rites. She's tired already."

"Of course," the priest replies, his brow slanting inward, creating a look of absolute understanding. "Yes, go ahead. I'll finish here."

Hong nods once and closes her wooden box. She tucks it under her left arm and places her right hand on the small of Mrs. Leong's back, guiding her away from the altar.

"Save your strength," Hong whispers, although she knows Mrs. Leong isn't listening. "Plenty of day still left." She hears her own words, her attempts at reassurance. She feels them travel from her lips to her ears and wonders if all along, she was speaking to herself.

Together, they walk from the great room to the kitchen. From there Hong can hear the priest's voice, beginning to chant anew to the rhythm of his gong. In her mind she can see the white-gloved pallbearers approaching the altar, lifting Bohai from the corners of his casket, walking him through the lingering incense, down the aisle, out the front door.

In the kitchen, Hong fills the kettle with water from the sink and places it on a front burner. She lights the flame below it. Before it boils, as steam sputters softly from its short silver mouth, Hong removes the pot and pours two cups of tea. She stirs one, patiently counting to thirty before allowing the leaves to settle. She blows gently on its liquid surface and hands it to Mrs. Leong, who stands by the kitchen door, looking out its small window.

It's a side door, opening to a pathway; the pathway leads to the garage. There's not much to see, some grass and cement, a thin bush of pink hibiscus. She's pulled the white curtain back from the window and simply stares, holding the porcelain cup with the tips of her fingers.

Hong returns to the stove, holding her open palm above the burner she's just used. She touches her index finger to a coil and thinks. With her right hand, Hong reaches for a baking dish in the cabinet and places it upside down on the burner. She places the kettle in the sink and runs cold water over the top.

"One minute," she tells Mrs. Leong, "I'll come right back." But Mrs. Leong doesn't move. She doesn't shift her gaze from the window.

Carefully, Hong wraps her hand around the doorknob at Mrs. Leong's waist and with two fingers, without a sound, she turns the lock. She tries the knob, just slightly to feel it resist, and exits the way they came in.

Back in the great room, guests have begun their exit. Kaipo stands at the front door, shaking hands and offering a shoulder for them to pat, to squeeze, to rub encouragingly on their way out. Already, he looks rumpled, like a child's favorite toy, passed among friends, ragged from overuse. Intuitively, Hong's feet start toward him, but before she can reach the door, Amy appears with Theresa at her side.

"What happened?" Amy asks. "I'm so sorry," she says, "you knew all along. She shouldn't have come."

"It's okay," Hong replies, not revealing what she knows. "She's with tea in the kitchen. She's okay."

"She was supposed to come with us. Should she still come with us?"

"I think it's best that you take her from the kitchen. Use the side door. And I will do the salt water." Hong nods once and turns, disappearing down the main corridor.

"Theresa," Amy says. "Go—tell the driver to pull into the side of the house. I'll get Mrs. Leong and wait for you there."

"Alone?" Theresa responds, her mouth suspended around the word. "Mom, don't make me walk through all of them. Please. You know how they look at me!"

"Theresa," Amy says firmly.

"Let me stay with her."

"What?"

"I'll stay with her and you can get the car," she pleads, breathless. "Come on, Mom, please. I don't know if he's here. I haven't seen him yet and if he is, I don't want to run into him right now. Alone."

Amy lifts a hand to her temples and kneads with her fingers, pushing them deep into the parallel grooves.

"Fine," she says, without looking at her daughter. "Go, then. Quick, before I change my mind." She waves her from the room but Theresa is already on her way.

Amy slips through the front door without much trouble. Keeping her head down and walking at a brisk pace, she deflects the stares that follow her. She moves too quickly to be stopped for small talk; she walks with enough purpose to be left alone. Twice, on her way across the garden, Amy looks up and scans the groups of gatherers. She searches for a young man among the middle-aged skin and dark suits of her husband's mourners, but she doesn't see him. At her daughter's prompting, Amy realizes that she hasn't seen him at all that morning. She looks a third time and knows that the last place she'll find him is in the garden, chatting among friends, because he doesn't know a single person there.

The iron gate is open, ready for the procession. Amy walks through its massive width and sees the town car, idling in the shade at the end of the street. Before she can signal, an arm extends from the driver's window and a palm opens. Immediately, the car moves toward her, slowing to a stop in front of the gate. The driver exits the car to open Amy's door but she's already opened it herself. She's already gotten in, already lowered herself into the leather seat and released the air she's been holding in her lungs.

Inside, Amy asks the driver to pull into the entrance and to the side of the house.

"Right there," she says, pointing past the garden to a small area to the right of the garage. In the cemented space, Theresa waits with Mrs. Leong, who holds a teacup in her hand.

As the car stops, the women approach and the driver bolts from his seat to open the door before they can. Theresa slides in first, to the middle seat, followed by Mrs. Leong, who steadies herself with the driver's hand, entering the backseat with her second hand extended, teacup first.

"Did you see him?" Theresa asks.

Her mother shakes her head.

"I knew he wouldn't come," Theresa mumbles, raising her eyes to the ceiling of the car. *Bastard*, she whispers.

*   *   *

From behind the windshield, the driver can see that it's almost time to start the procession. An old woman, her hair entirely white, enters the garden from the house, clutching a shallow silver bowl with one arm. She ushers the guests forward, past the garden and through the gates, all the while dipping her fingers into the bowl and flicking water around her, sprinkling it in their wake. It's salt water in that bowl; the driver knows this from the hundreds of Chinese funerals he has witnessed from his car. Salt purifies the space; it drives the spirits from the home. When the family returns, they will repeat the process. They will dip their hands in salt water, purifying them, giving them a clean start after death.

As the driver watches the white-haired woman, her trail of water widens; she rotates methodically from side to side, throwing the liquid in beads, extending her arm as if feeding chickens, advancing all the while. The driver stares, caught in something of a trance, hanging on her every movement like a siren's song, like a magician's final act.

Then, suddenly, the woman turns and looks directly at him, as if expecting him to be there, and waves him behind the hearse. The driver flinches, pulled from his strange thoughts. The woman looks through the windshield; her head and her arm move together in large swooping movements, which continue until the driver has pulled up behind the funeral car. The white-haired woman, still clutching her silver bowl, climbs into the backseat of the hearse and a moment later the car starts forward. They begin their steady crawl through the gate.

On the street, the mourners wait with fistfuls of paper money. As the driver passes them, they throw the squares of paper high into the air so that it rains gold and white, flitting left and right across the windows of the car. The confetti catches in the branches of the cherry blossoms, glinting beside the blushing petals. The driver keeps his foot on the brake, nervous with so many important bodies surrounding him, dozens of cars lining the road, and leans forward in his seat, wrapping ten fingers around the wheel as he maneuvers slowly through the crowd.

At the end of the street, they come to a stop sign. The driver opens his fists and feels the blood return. He shakes out his fingers and realigns them on the wheel. He breathes.

It's nearly noon and the sun sits directly above. The driver turns the dial on his air-conditioning and a cool, steady gust pushes through the vents. He lets it dry the sweat on his skin before adjusting the vents and sending the air behind him.

They leave Diamond Head and enter the valley, driving north to Manoa, when the driver senses something moving behind him. He looks in his rearview mirror and sees the oldest woman, sitting behind him, shifting her body from the front of her seat to the back, sliding anxiously about in the small space. Her face looks out the window; her fingers tap the frame. Nothing unusual, the driver thinks, and returns his gaze to the road.

"Lin," Amy Leong says, and the driver's eyes dart back up to his mirror. He looks again at the old woman's face but can only see her profile, slumped and agitated. "We're on our way to the cemetery. We're going to bury Bohai."

Amy Leong extends her hand across her daughter's lap to steady the woman and the driver nearly chokes. *It's Mrs. Leong*, he realizes. *Lin Leong*, back from wherever they've been hiding her. Every year, every spring, the public schools in Kaneohe paid tribute to her work with a fund-raiser in her name. They sent an invitation to the Diamond Head house, addressed to Lin, but every year Kaipo came instead, apologizing for his mother's absence, offering a check and no excuses, no specifics. The driver was told explicitly, on multiple occasions, that the Leong mother would not be attending the funeral. So when he saw the old woman, standing by the side of the house with Amy's daughter, he assumed that she was someone else. For twenty years, Lin Leong had not been seen in public.

The driver alternates his focus between his mirror and the road. Amy Leong leans across the middle seat, over her daughter's belly, and holds her mother-in-law's shoulder, trying to steady her. Lin

Leong has yet to respond, but her breathing has deepened; her chest heaves, rising and falling noticeably with each long, troubled breath.

"Should we stop?" Amy's daughter asks.

"I don't know," her mother says rapidly, shaking her head. "Lin," she says like a command, then again with more urgency. Both of her hands are on the old woman now, one on her shoulder, one on her knee, but Lin Leong continues to shift, back and forth in her seat, her eyes never leaving the window.

It's curious the way the woman moves, as if she's anticipating something terrible, unable to sit still with the sheer thought of what's looming. Certainly a funeral brings disquiet but there's something else, the driver thinks, his own heart beginning to quicken.

Ahead, they come to a stop light. They're on University Avenue, minutes from the cemetery. Any farther, the driver thinks, and he would pull over. He sees that the woman needs air. But they're so close. They're nearly there and where would he stop? The neighborhood is residential now, white plantation houses, wooden telephone poles, brick walls and private driveways—not a parking lot in sight. He reaches his hand to the air conditioner and turns it up once again. He steps on the gas and closes the gap between his car and the hearse ahead.

Behind him, the sharp clatter of something breaking. A low rattle of its pieces shaking against each other.

"Shit—Mom!" the daughter shouts.

The driver pushes himself up in his seat, digging his left heel into the floor so he can see lower into his mirror. Lin Leong's hand is closed into a fist; blood drips down her wrist. *Jesus*, Amy says, as she gathers the shards of white and blue porcelain that have fallen around her.

"Sir!" she calls to the driver. "Do you have anything I can use? A napkin—anything?"

Lin Leong's lap is stained with tea and specked with blood, but still she looks out the window. If anything her face is closer now, almost touching the glass. The driver has a hard time looking away; it takes him a moment to register Amy's words.

"Sir!" she calls again.

He shakes his eyes from the mirror and reaches to his passenger side. He opens the glove compartment and sees the three identical handkerchiefs, sitting limply next to his manual. For a moment, he hesitates, dumbstruck by the sight of them. In all his planning, all his predictions, never did he conjure a situation even vaguely like the one he's in. *Holy shit*, he whispers, grabbing the thin stack.

"Is she okay?" he dares to ask, passing the handkerchiefs to Amy, but no one answers. She presses two cotton squares into the old woman's palm.

They're so close. Ahead, the road forks and to the left and at the end of the street lies the entrance to the cemetery.

But Lin Leong is panicking again. Her hands jump from surface to surface, the window, the door, the back of the driver's chair. She touches these things as if she were blind, desperate to orient herself in a strange new place. Her head follows her hands, jerking in every direction but always returning to the window, where she holds her focus for a moment longer. The driver realizes she's panting, almost wheezing from effort. A single handkerchief sticks to her bloody palm, trailing her movements like a white flag.

"We need to stop the car," Theresa tells her mother. "She needs to get out."

The entrance to the cemetery is thirty feet ahead. The driver's foot hovers above his two pedals, pivoting on his heel, unsure whether to race through the gate or stop immediately.

"Stop the car!" Amy shouts, and the driver's foot comes down fast. Lin Leong's two palms slam against the inside of her window and she screams.

A high-pitched wail, a harrowing shriek from a terrible place. It fills the car like spiders, crawling along the skin, rattling the core. The strength in her voice is extraordinary, bottomless and raw, expanding into every crevice of the sealed car. The driver turns in his seat, unsure of what to do, and is met by something that rattles him further. Amy Leong, from across the seat, buried beneath the sound, is crying. Her eyes are closed, tears race down her face. She's whispering. *I'm sorry*, she mouths. *I'm so sorry.*

Lin

1942
DIAMOND HEAD, HAWAII

Two days after the wedding, Frank falls ill. It's the drinking, I tell him. He has to be careful, he's no longer young. But he insists it was the fourth course, the shellfish. All that money, he grumbles, and the lobster wasn't fresh.

The first day, he remains in bed without a fight. Hong makes soup and takes his temperature. He's running a fever; the heat from his skin leaves signs on his pillow, sunken and damp. On the second day, I find Frank in his office holding his head in the dark. When I turn on the light, he flinches. *Out*, I insist, out of the office and back into bed. He tells me he's fine, so I point to the bottle of painkillers beside him, the strongest medicine my husband will touch and even so with great infrequency. After that, he agrees, but he brings a stack of papers with him to bed. He ruffles through them to make a point.

Later that evening as I pretend to sleep, I hear Frank vomiting in the bathroom. He's not getting better, I tell myself. In forty years, I have never seen him ill like this. It's clear that rest is not enough; it's time to see a doctor. In the morning, I decide, I must call Dr. Lum.

But the next morning the space beside me is empty. Frank has already risen, so I go to find him, to scold him for his impatience. He's at the kitchen table eating toast with guava jam, dressed in a suit and tie, ready to leave for work.

"Absolutely not," I exclaim, removing the jacket from his shoulders. "Are you out of your mind?"

"I'm perfectly well," he smiles. "The sickness has passed entirely."

"I'm calling Alan Lum," I tell him. "You're making yourself worse."

Without a word, Frank stands from the table and walks into the pantry. When he emerges, there is a twenty-pound sack of rice slung across his shoulder.

"Look, Lin," he says, pacing the length of the kitchen. "Could a sick man do this?"

He squats and raises the bag above his head. His arms barely strain.

I shake my head, but strangely enough, Frank looks fine. He smiles like he's healthy, like the rest has done him well. It's a relief to see him like this, after two days of worrying, but still, I feel the need to protest.

"Tomorrow," I compromise. "If you still feel this way tomorrow, you can go to the harbor. But you need to rest for one more day—just one more."

"Fine," he groans, dropping the sack of rice to the floor. "But you'll wish I had gone!"

He spends the rest of the day repairing anything he can find, leaving messes and making noise with his tools from the garage. Tools I have never seen before, that I did not even know he owned. *Look*, Lin, he says, showing me a chair he leveled. A thin layer of dust covers every surface of the kitchen. The breakfast table is upside down. I know he's doing it on purpose, to show how healthy he is, how restless he feels. And I must admit, he makes his point.

The next day, I don't protest when Frank leaves for the harbor. I think of the tools and the mess and I let him go without a fight.

But forty minutes later, as I trim flowers in the basin, Frank returns. He tries to sneak through the kitchen door; he doesn't see me at the sink. I turn around as the door opens.

"What are you doing back?" I ask, dropping my flowers, walking to him. "Why are you walking like that? Frank, what's the matter?"

I reach out to touch his arm and he releases a sharp, horrible whimper. As if burned by a match, he pulls his arm away, clutching it to his body as he hunches further forward.

"Jesus Christ, Frank," I breathe, stepping backward. "Get in bed. I'm calling Dr. Lum this minute."

I try to move my eyes, but halted and alarmed, they will not leave Frank.

"I'm fine," Frank manages, shifting his weight between his legs, but that's all he says, nothing more. He moves past me with stubborn determination but even he cannot hide the difficulty in his stride. He handles his legs like toothpicks, as if they could easily snap in two. His arms swing limply. He takes small, swift steps across the living room and when he reaches the corridor, I remember the phone.

"I need you here immediately," I say to Dr. Lum. "It's Frank; there's something wrong. Please, as fast as you can—it's urgent!"

I hang up the receiver and start for our bedroom. Something tells me to run, so I do. I sprint down the corridor and never has it felt so long, so narrow and dark. I take off my shoes and run faster.

Finally I reach the bedroom door, but on the opposite side, the bed lies empty, perfectly made. I hesitate. The shower is running; I can hear it through the dividing wall.

"Frank," I call, moving through the room to the bathroom door. "Frank. Alan is on his way."

I open the bathroom door and step into a shallow pool of water. The shower is running; the shower door hangs open and Frank lies on the floor, completely naked. *Frank*, I scream, kneeling to him. He opens his mouth and little bubbles float through the water that's collected around his head, his face. In the light, in the water, his scars look swollen and gruesome, brand new. *The bed*, he whispers, so I pull his wet arms around my shoulders. Using my knees and all my strength I heave him to his feet. He cries out, broken and raw. He's helping the best he can; I feel him trying, can hear him panting in my ear. Our bodies stumble together through the doorway and I release him onto the bed. He falls face-first. His legs stick straight out from the mattress.

My body shakes as I stare at him and I feel like I might vomit.

I flee from the room. I run to find my sons, screaming.

*   *   *

He's in the bedroom, I yell as my sons sprint past me. They're faster than I am and reach him before I do. As I turn the corner, I see their horror. The scars, I realize. They've never seen them—not like this. I open my mouth to explain but Dr. Lum's voice shouts down the hall. A sound escapes me: a scream, a name, I have no idea, but his footsteps grow closer until they're beside me. He rushes to Frank's side and holds two fingers to his throat, two fingers to his wrist. He inhales like the air is freezing cold.

"Call an ambulance," Dr. Lum says, and I hesitate. Not one of us moves. He yells it a second time and I can't believe what I'm about to say—what I know my sons are thinking too.

"Alan," I say, "we can't." I'm shaking and it shakes the authority from my words. I hear how empty they sound, how foolish.

"He's losing control of his limbs, Lin! Do you see him! I don't care what he wants, I want him alive!" He stares at me like I don't and I almost give in.

"She's right." I hear Kaipo's voice. "We have to take him ourselves. We have to, we promised him—we all did."

"Jesus Christ," Dr. Lum says, pounding his fist into the bed, and I know we've said enough. Frank would rather die than be forced into a screaming ambulance, his naked body on display, his trauma a spectacle for all the island to see.

"Kaipo," Dr. Lum commands without looking up from the mattress. "Get something to carry him on and quickly! And for Christ's sake, Bohai, cover your father!"

They wrap Frank's body in the bedsheet and like the flip of a switch my thoughts return.

"Kaipo," I scream down the hall. "The table. Take a leaf from the table!"

Moments later Kaipo returns with the wooden panel beneath his arm. He places the board on the mattress and together the three of them lift Frank on top of it. He cries out in pain, like he's being

213

branded with an iron, and it takes everything I have not to run from the room.

"Bohai," I say, and I feel the bile rise, taste the acid on the back of my tongue, against the lumps that have risen. "You need to stay here until we get him to the car. Dr. Lum and Kaipo will manage. As soon as we leave, get Hong and bring her to Queens Hospital. I don't want her to see this—do you understand?"

He nods, looking at his father as he leaves the room. Swiftly, I guide Dr. Lum and Kaipo to the driveway and open the back door of Dr. Lum's town car. They slide Frank along the backseat, the sharp corner of the wood panel tearing at the leather. There are no seats left so I shove myself into the thin gap between the board and the front seats and squat next to my husband, my face hovering inches from his.

I'm here, Frank, I whisper to him. *I'm right here.*

He opens his right eye halfway and wrinkles the right side of his mouth, as if he's trying to smile. I bite down hard on my lower lip and taste blood.

It makes me think of red strings. The copper taste fills my mouth and I swallow it, feeling a strange, divine strength enter my bones. We're connected, I tell myself; we always have been. And if he is slipping away, being pulled into another world by an act of fate—I'll be right here to pull him back. I know the strength of our fate, and I'm certain it's enough to keep him here with me.

Just relax, I say. *We'll be at the hospital soon, and look, Frank, no ambulance.* I press my lips into a tight smile, my tongue running along the cut that I made, feeling fiercer with each sharp taste of blood. Frank squeezes his eye shut and tries to nod but his neck is too stiff. We race to the hospital, stopping at red lights only when absolutely necessary.

Through the back door of the emergency room, Dr. Lum sprints into the hospital and emerges with four men in blue scrubs pushing a stretcher. They pull Frank's body from the backseat and wheel him into the building, Kaipo and I chasing behind. At the end of the hallway, they push my husband through a heavy set of double doors, and when we try to follow, a man stops us. He holds out both arms like he's trying to catch us.

"Please have a seat," the doctor says, motioning to the waiting area. "You can begin to fill out the paperwork until we know what's happening."

I'm breathless and barefoot. I left the house without shoes and the linoleum floor is cold on my feet. I don't have time for this.

"Do you know who I am!" I yell at the doctor, pushing myself up to my toes. People in the hallway stop and stare. I have never once said these words but I don't know what else to do. I need to get through those doors, so he needs to know who we are. The doctor looks at me uneasily, like he should know but does not.

"My name is Lin Leong, wife of Frank Leong, the man who just went through those doors," I say, my voice lowering as my tongue clicks on each syllable, "and if something happens to him and I'm not there—"

The doctor is already punching his code into the wall. The double doors swing open. He says something but I don't hear him.

We run from door to door, pressing our faces to the tiny windows until a nurse points us to Frank's room. It's the last one on the hall; the blue door, she says. When we enter, Frank is in a hospital gown. He's sitting upright and his right eye is open again. They've already attached him to several machines, each one beeping at regular intervals. The room feels like gelatin. The air resists with each difficult step.

"I'm okay," I think he says, but it could be anything. Only part of his mouth moves.

"Mrs. Leong." The doctor in the white coat turns to me. "I'm Dr. Harris. Your husband appears to be in an early stage of paralysis. He's currently stable, but after these tests we hope to know more."

I say something back and walk farther into the tiny room. Kaipo is behind me and Dr. Lum is reading one of the machines. Dr. Harris is haole. He has light brown hair and blue eyes.

"I'll take these over immediately," he says, holding up three vials of dark blood, "and we should have word within the hour."

I nod my head and the doctor leaves. I turn to Kaipo and tell him to find his brother and Hong. I tell Dr. Lum to begin the paperwork. I want to sit alone with Frank and feel just him. I need to try to understand what is happening to my husband.

Alone, I sit in the metal chair by the bed. Frank's eyes are closed again and the room is still except for the beeping of the monitors. Softly, I touch my finger to his wrist and hope he doesn't cry out. The lids of his eyes are heavy and drooping; they look a hundred years old. When he doesn't respond to my touch, I place the palm of my hand against his. It's warm and swollen and feels like a stranger's hand—someone who's been sick all his life. I want to pull my hand away but instead I close my eyes. I leave it. I slowly wrap my fingers around Frank's, waiting for him to come alive for me. But he continues to lie motionless in his upright position—like he doesn't sense me at all. I squeeze and release, my entire body clenching as I do, but nothing happens. He doesn't know I'm there.

"Frank," I say like a tunnel of wind, lungs collapsed. He lifts his head suddenly, and slowly he peels his lips apart.

"I'm okay," I think he says again. His eyes are still closed.

I haven't cried yet but I know it's coming. I look out the window and focus my eyes on the sun, trying to dissolve the tears.

"Frank," I whisper, lowering my eyes again to his face, "you're going to be fine."

It sounds empty, meaningless.

"You have to be fine," I try again, my fingers still touching his, "because—"

I don't know how to finish this sentence. I don't even know if he hears me. I pause for a moment and tilt my head back. I feel the weight of what this man means to me—of all that he has done for me and all the ways he has made me better, and I feel every tiny hair on my body tingle.

"Because I don't know who I am without you."

The door opens as my throat begins to swell. Dr. Harris walks in with a clipboard.

"Mrs. Leong," he says, lowering the clipboard to his side, "I have news that I think will bring some relief."

I release Frank's hand and stand.

"What is it? Do you know what's wrong with him?" I move closer to the doctor.

"Your husband has been diagnosed with Guillain-Barré syndrome. Are you familiar with this condition?"

I shake my head.

"Guillain-Barré is an acute disease of the nerves in which they lose their outer protective coating—or myelin. It prevents the nerves from relaying messages smoothly or operating properly. Normally, it emerges from a common cold or virus. Did your husband suffer from flu-like symptoms before his nerve pain began?"

"Yes," I say, nodding my head impatiently. "Yes, just earlier this week. A day ago."

"Precisely," Dr. Harris continues. "Although his condition may seem quite serious—and it can be if left untreated—the vast majority of Guillain-Barré patients make a full recovery within a week. We'll put him on a regimen of antibodies and within a few days he should have his full body function back."

"So he'll be okay?" I exclaim, my toes curling beneath my feet.

"Yes, he should be just fine." Dr. Harris smiles and so I smile too. He takes his clipboard and removes two sheets of paper.

"These are for you." He hands me the papers. "Information on Guillain-Barré. I would suggest becoming familiar with the symptoms and the treatment. Perhaps now would be a good time to see your family and share the news."

"Thank you, Doctor," I say, electricity running through my veins. "You don't know how relieved they'll be."

Dr. Harris tells me that while I'm gone, he'll check Frank's breathing to make sure it's regular. Before they begin treatment, they'll have to be sure that his diaphragm is not going into paralysis. With his breathing stabilized, they'll give him his first injection of antibodies, which should do wonders, he says.

In the hallway I begin to read the list of symptoms. *Weakness of the lower limbs, numbness or tingling, respiratory difficulties, loss of tendon reflexes, difficulty with eye movement, unsteady or inability to walk, severe back pain.* The list goes on for half a page, each symptom eating away at my newfound confidence. I can't finish it. I put the paper to the side and look for the waiting area outside the emergency wing.

My legs move faster as I spot it. I start to jog, the papers flapping as I quicken my step.

"He's going to be okay!" I announce. "The doctor says he'll be fine!" I'm caught in an embrace of Hong and my sons. Amy is there too but she stands to the side, hands clasped together, relief in her smile.

A nurse tells us to go home and rest, that we can come back in the morning—but I don't want to. I'll sleep in the metal chair. I ask her for a pair of shoes.

That evening, I read to Frank from the newspaper. I find the business section in the waiting room and bring it to him. Every morning he reads the newspaper, so until he gets better, I will read it to him.

"Look, Frank," I say, "Wong's Meat Shop reopened yesterday. When you get better, you can have *char siu.*"

Frank grunts and it makes me happy. I skip an article about the rising cost of fuel and instead read to him about the new Plymouth cars for the army. "You'll like this," I say.

The next day Dr. Harris comes to give Frank his dose of antibodies. He hasn't improved, I say to the doctor. He seems the same. Dr. Harris assures me that by tomorrow, I will certainly notice an improvement. And so I wait in my metal chair. I read to Frank until I fall asleep.

I wake up the next morning full of hope; I open the window blinds and let the early light into the room.

When I turn, I see something strange.

Thick, horrible clumps of grey hair have fallen from Frank's head overnight. They're on his pillowcase, lying limply in small piles. I pinch a few hairs between my fingers and hold them up to the light. I can't breathe.

The follicles are jet-black. His face is pale and there's something slightly pink on his cheek; a rash that spreads like a starfish. His limbs don't move. I run to the heart monitor and grab the screen with both hands. It beeps and I shake it, rattle it for its answers. It beeps again and I run for a doctor.

On the other side of the door, I yell. A nurse pushing a metal cart stops when she hears me. I grab her arm and pull her into the room. I show her my husband. She's out the door before I can say anything.

I pace the room watching the clock, watching the heart monitor, wondering where the hell Dr. Harris is.

"He's coming, Frank," I say. "He's almost here."

Finally Dr. Harris walks through the door and begins to say something but stops when he sees Frank. His cheeks collapse. He rushes to Frank's side and sees the hair, sees the rash. He looks startled in a way a doctor never should.

"What the hell is going on?" I yell at him. "Why is his hair falling out?"

"Prussian blue," he stammers, turning to the nurse from the hallway. "Prussian blue, I need it immediately!" He's yelling now. He's putting on gloves. I can see his arms shaking beneath his white coat.

"What's Prussian blue?" I shriek, my hands reaching for the wall behind me as I begin to feel faint.

"Mrs. Leong," he says, "I need you to leave the room."

Frank gasps for air. His mouth opens and his neck convulses. He takes quick, sharp intakes of breath, each one making a high-pitched sound as he wheezes and coughs.

"Mrs. Leong, leave the room right now!"

"For God's sake, do something!" I scream, pushing him toward my husband.

He places his fingers on my husband's throat and massages his neck. He pushes his fingers upward and Frank begins to gag.

Dr. Harris reaches his arm to open a drawer. His fingers fumble within it; I register the sound of metal instruments clanging together as he searches for his tool.

"Look away!" he yells but I can't. I watch him find it; I watch him pull a thin, silver shape from the drawer. He raises the instrument to Frank's neck and I realize it's a scalpel. *It's a knife he's holding to Frank's throat.*

"Wh—what the hell are you doing?"

"Look away!" he yells again.

He draws the knife across Frank's neck and cuts a slit into his throat. Blood spills from the incision and a scream escapes from the deepest, most fragile part of my soul. My back is pressed against the wall and I'm sliding down it. I want to look away but I can't. He separates the skin with his fingers and punctures something below it. My hands seize my face, they tear at my hair. More blood, more blood than the gauze can carry. The beeping from the machines is pounding in my ears, so I scream over it. It's the fastest it's ever been.

I hear Frank take a deep, difficult breath. He's breathing, I realize. He's breathing from that hole.

The doctor holds the opening apart with his fingers; blood reaches to his elbow.

"Where the hell is the Prussian blue?" he screams over me. My eyes are drowning in tears and I can barely see. The doctor and my husband are dripping blurs.

A third blur enters the room. It's the nurse with the medicine—a bottle of dark blue capsules. She yells to the doctor; he grabs the bottle and shakes the pills from its mouth. His fingers fumble to grasp a pill as the beeping of the heart monitor stutters and flattens. The sound is crushed into an even, penetrating hum that stops the motion of the room, of the world.

I close my eyes and hear the smashing of glass against a wall. *Fuck,* someone screams.

I don't know how long I stay in that room. I don't know what happens after that. I wake up in a hospital bed of my own. No Frank.

There's a nurse. She asks if she can get me anything.

"Frank," I say, "Where's Frank?"

"Let me get your son," she says. "He's here."

Bohai enters the room but his face is different.

"Where's your father?" I say, sitting up in my bed.

"Mom," he says, putting a hand on my arm. "Dad's gone. We lost him this morning."

And then I remember the blood. The screaming. The knife.

"He killed him," I stammer, "the doctor, he killed him, didn't he? He slit his throat! I saw it!"

Bohai takes a deep breath. He puts his hands on the side of my bed.

"Not exactly," he says, pausing for a moment. "Dr. Harris misdiagnosed him. Dad didn't have Guillain-Barré. He was poisoned."

"Poisoned?" I echo, startled by the word. "But that's absurd! Who would *poison* your father?" I'm holding on to both his wrists.

"We don't know." Bohai's face is colorless, almost ghostlike. His eyes shift downward. "But it was thallium. The tests came back a few hours ago."

I become aware of my breathing. I fill my lungs and push it through my nose. I let the oxygen rise to my head and fizzle in the heat.

"Where's Kaipo?"

"He went home. He's looking through the phone records. He wanted me to ask you."

"Ask me what?" I repeat, barely registering the words that came before.

"The file Dad said he kept, of threats against him, was it real? Do you know where he kept it?"

It's too much. I have no idea what he's talking about. I don't care. I can't handle more, can't think beyond the blood-soaked gauze, Frank gasping for air as the knife drags across his throat, the drone of the heart monitor still crawling beneath my skin.

"Get me Dr. Harris right now," I command, rising from my bed, standing on my own feet. "*Now*, Bohai."

He nods once and leaves the room. Right away, Dr. Harris opens the door and I can't stop myself. I remember it all.

I scream at him in Cantonese. I call him every vulgar name I can think of, every name my father called me. *My husband is dead; his body is in a room somewhere; his heart is no longer beating.* I begin to cry violent tears, pulling at my hair and knocking over boxes of bandages, throwing metal cups of instruments, yanking at the roll of medical paper and ripping it apart. I open drawers and destroy everything I can: syringes and gloves and wooden sticks fly against the wall. Dr. Harris stands there quietly and lets me do it. I grab the stethoscope from his neck and throw it to the floor. He flinches but does nothing.

"I will have you fired," I gasp, my arms pulsing at my sides, my accent suddenly enormous. "I will have your medical license revoked and I will make damn well sure that you never practice medicine ever again." I slap my hand against the table.

"You killed my husband. Now get the hell out of my sight."

The next morning, the story hits the papers. *Millionaire Industrialist Dies from Poison.* I send Hong around the island. I tell her to purchase every copy she can find. I need to control the damage. I call my husband's lawyer, Mr. Lee, and schedule an appointment for the next day to discuss funeral decisions, and most important, to begin the investigation and my lawsuit against Dr. Harris.

At home, I lock myself in our bedroom. I want to see no one. Not Hong, not my sons. I curl up inside our blanket and sleep until I hear a knock. Mr. Lee is here, Hong says. It's already tomorrow.

I pull my hair together in a tangled clump and stay in Frank's black T-shirt and pants. I drag my feet across the bedroom and unlock the door.

Hong embraces me. We stay there for a moment without speaking, so much sadness passing between our bodies. Frank saved us and now he is gone, leaving something dead within us both. There's a warmth I've been saving in the folds of his T-shirt and Hong's embrace wraps me within it. I want to crawl inside and sleep again.

She walks me down the hallway and into the sitting room, her hand on my back, guiding me forward. It seems a lifetime ago that she arrived at our door. Suddenly, I know how she feels. I know what it's like to have your red string cut from your ankle. To watch your husband die before your eyes.

"Lin," someone says as I emerge from the hallway. It's Mr. Lee. Bohai and Kaipo sit on the couch across from him. They look exhausted.

"I don't know what to say," he says, standing. "I'm so sorry for your loss. For all of our loss. Frank was a very special man."

I nod and sit on the couch between my two sons.

"I want to file a suit immediately against Dr. Harris. Whatever it costs, spend it. I want him ruined," I say without emotion. "Then we will begin our investigation of the poisoning."

Mr. Lee looks uneasy. His face is twisted in a way that I cannot interpret.

"Before we start with the lawsuit, there's something pressing I need to speak with you about. And perhaps it would be better if we did it in private." His eyes avoid Bohai and Kaipo. He wants them to leave but I don't care what he wants.

"Whatever you have to say, you can say it in front of my sons. From this point on, they will run the business and the estate."

Mr. Lee's face grows more tense. He has something to say and I assume it's bad. But what could he possibly tell me that could make me feel worse? Frank is dead.

"Lin, I just think that—"

"Sam." I cut him off. "We've been through enough. Say what you have to say. If there's not as much money as we expected, it's fine. Money is the least of my concerns. I just need enough to support myself and my children. Everything else is—"

"Lin, there is no money," he says abruptly. It startles me at first until I realize the absurdity—the impossibility. I try to laugh but it sounds hollow and cruel.

"That's ridiculous," I say. "You know as well as I do that there's plenty of money."

Mr. Lee pauses and takes a deep breath.

"Lin." He looks at me and his eyes are glossy and small. Like pebbles under water. "Did you know that Frank had other wives?"

I don't understand; I remain perfectly still.

"In 1896, when he was nineteen, Frank married a woman named Ching Lan. Together they had two children. Both full grown by now, both girls."

I listen. My face begins to tighten but still I say nothing. The name Ching Lan echoes in my head and it sounds like traffic.

"In 1898, he married again. To a woman named Huan-yue. With her, he produced another girl. While he was married to them, he began his shipping business, which took off right before he did. In 1899, when his oldest daughter was three years old, he disappeared. He found you."

Mr. Lee stops. It's a horrible story he's telling and I want him to leave. This is not why I asked him to come. I feel the warmth beginning to seep through the fabric of Frank's shirt. It's leaking from my bones.

I keep my limbs as still as they'll let me.

"Sam, is this some kind of joke?"

Sam shakes his head, his eyelids heavy. "I'm so sorry," he whispers.

"Why are you telling us this now? Why would you tell us this now?" I wonder if it's me saying this but it's Kaipo. He's holding my hand and I'm overflowing onto him.

"Of course," Mr. Lee says, nodding at Kaipo. "Of course there is a reason."

The humming in my head makes it difficult to hear. I want to find the sound but I'm too afraid to move—too concerned that everything I've been saving will slip away.

"The vast majority of your husband's accounts are in China. When I called to change the rights on the account, I was told that they had all been frozen and were pending a transfer to his wife. When I told him that I was doing the same thing, we realized that our names did not match. And that's how I discovered his first two wives."

First two wives, *two wives. More traffic, more honking. I want to bring my hands to my ears but I don't.*

"Legally speaking, and tragically, there's nothing we can do. Your husband sent them money every month until he died. He provided for all their expenses. He sent all three girls to private school, then to college. There are receipts for American cars. As his first wives, in China where the money is held, they are entitled to everything."

What about a will? Kaipo is standing, but I don't want to look. I shut my eyes. *My father had a will!*

This, I hear, *is perhaps the most tragic part of all. From what I can tell, your father had no will—not officially, at least.*

Sam's words are melting in my ears. My husband had no will. Why does my husband have no will?

He always skirted the issue with me, telling me he had an old one that would do for the time being. I offered to write up a new summary many times, but he put it off. I realize now that he probably never had a will—you know your father, he thought he was invincible. And he did not want me to know about his other wives, which is why I could never be a witness. If a will exists, I don't have it. Right now, I have nothing in my possession.

I open my eyes. I look in his hands and there's nothing there. I forget what I'm looking for.

Wind blows from my right and it's Kaipo again and his hands are moving like tree branches in a storm. It echoes to the left and it's Bohai in a shadow and I see a girl with grey eyes lying on the floor. It's Hailee and I close my eyes again.

When I open them, she's still there, lying in the pile of toxic sheets she died in. But now there's a red string around her neck and it's my fault. I know where it leads. It's Bohai in the shadow, the string extending from Hailee's neck to his, cutting into his flesh and tangling around his limbs. I see hands extending and I realize they're mine, the fingers fumbling with the knots, groping to find the end but it continues; the string extends past my son to another shadow, and as I see Amy's face I begin to grow frantic, tugging at the knots, but it only pulls their bodies closer together, the friction making them bleed.

I release my hands and shut my eyes. I try to breathe.

What's left? *It's Frank's voice and he's asking me but someone else replies. Funeral costs, he says, and the sound is lower than I expected. Other than that, the women haven't offered anything.*

The tree branches rustle to my right and I bring my hands to my ears. I remember a song that we would dance to. The humming comes from my stomach and it vibrates through my neck and I sway to the music.

You will receive seven thousand dollars, he says. What's left in the account.

I see Frank in the traffic. He's wearing the same suit. I try to open the car door but it's locked. I yell to him but no sound comes out. Everything is buzzing like static on the radio. He's running frantically and I know he's looking for me. Over here, I'm trying to yell, but there are a million cars and they're smoking. It's billowing from underneath and he's coughing now. The horn. I remember the horn and I lean against it and Frank turns. I leap forward and bang on the window with both fists but something is stuck.

Additionally, you are entitled to what you already possess—that is, your house, your cars, the funds from your charities.

I pull on my foot but it's closed in the car door. My leg is on one side and my foot on the other. I look out the window and follow the trail of blood, under cars and over hoods, wrapped around tires and dripping down windows. The smoke carries it into the air.

I'm so sorry, he says.

To the north. I must go to the north, he says, and I know. Now blood is inside the car. It's on the floor, a little puddle but growing. Collecting, beginning to rise.

You have the option of going to court, but I fear it will be a long and difficult battle. Branches rustle, a shadow falls over the car and suddenly it's freezing.

When blood spills onto the seat I reach for the roof. My fingers touch the soft underside and I think of the lotuses in our front yard. They need to be watered, I say to Frank. They're dying. He's outside the window but he won't open the door. He smiles while the car fills with blood.

I hear birds calling from the kitchen. Third wife, they call me, and they think it's my name. A knife, they say. Use the knife to be with your husband.

If he could only hear me he would open the door.

I open a drawer and reach inside.

CHAPTER 8

November 1964
HONOLULU, HAWAII

As quickly as the screaming began, it retreats—all at once—as soon as the driver opens his door. He hesitates in the new calm, but still he decides to get out and help the old woman, to give her some air.

The driver is met by three faces, all turned to the left, all facing in his direction as he opens the rear door. Farthest from him, Amy Leong's tears have stopped but her face is tinged red across her nose and cheeks, her skin swollen. She takes deep breaths as her eyes dart upward, absorbing their wetness as she tries to calm down. Beside her, her daughter's expression is absolute desperation. She seems disoriented by the chaos, both startled and suspicious of the sudden silence that has fallen over them. And Mrs. Leong, closest to the driver, sits calmly now, hands clutching the underside of her seat, frowning at him passively, quietly.

"Get Hong," the daughter says. "You need to get Hong."

"What—who?"

"Hong." Her voice shakes. "White hair—just ask for her, please!"

The driver knows exactly which woman is Hong. He looks again to Amy Leong and when she nods, he turns and begins to sprint, in his best suit, up the road to the entrance of the cemetery. His legs thrust forward impulsively, from sheer adrenaline, the sound of her screaming still hanging in his ears, pushing him onward.

When he arrives at the sign, a red pagoda with a jade roof flanked by a pair of snarling stone dragons, the driver turns right and begins to climb, with considerable effort, up the winding, rising asphalt that curves through the hundreds of gravesites around him. He follows the red ginger and scarlet ti leaves that guide his path up the sloping hill, twisting with the cracked road, its crevices filled with streaks of bright green grass.

Thin, weeping trees kiss the ground, offering him flashes of shade, fluttering softly as he passes. The driver's pants strain with each forward stretch of his leg, gathering at his knee and falling stiffly back down. It crosses his mind that they might tear, but he doesn't slow. He runs as fast as he can, inhaling deeply, exhaling with forceful determination, feeling better with each stride he puts between himself and his car.

At last, at the top of the hill he can see the funeral car parked beneath the enormous banyan tree, twisted roots falling like ropes from above. Warped shadows, like lengths of knotted cord, fall across a statue of a child Buddha; they reach east, across a pair of granite pagodas. The white-haired woman stands below the banyan, beneath its glossy leather branches. She no longer holds the silver bowl.

"Hong," the driver pants, slowing, slumped with exhaustion. "Hong, they need you. Mrs. Leong. She's screaming. They asked for you." He points down the long entrance of the cemetery, toward where he left the car.

Hong's face stills and she nods, once, in a way that makes the driver feel instantly melodramatic, excessive in both his pace and delivery. Hong nods as if she had expected him to say this, like she knew it would happen before Mrs. Leong could scream, before Amy's daughter could think to ask for her. She nods as if it is perfectly reasonable, nothing extraordinary.

"Okay," Hong says, and she begins to jog, arms held tightly into her body, the skin on her cheeks shaking loosely with each landing on the pavement. Ten feet ahead of him, she turns. "Come," she says, beckoning him with her head, before continuing her steady jog down the pathway. The driver starts forward, following her white hair, her white clothing, thankful at least for her authority, relieved to be moving downhill.

Hong's pace is difficult for the driver to match. Her feet take small, tight steps, but they move swiftly; her body makes more vertical movement than forward progress. The driver tries to jog but feels ridiculous, running in place behind the old woman. Walking feels even stranger, lunging downhill after her. He settles on a kind of march, arms tight to his side, feet moving with adequate urgency as they reach the bottom of the hill.

They turn left and see the car. Amy and her daughter have exited the backseat. They stand by Mrs. Leong's open door, pacing, guarding her passage.

"Oh, thank God," Amy breathes as Hong approaches. "I'm so sorry, she just started panicking and I didn't know what to do."

Hong raises a palm as she slows beside the car.

"It's okay," she says, inhaling three times, her chest expanding and collapsing. "I'll take her to the house. You two go. Be with Bohai."

Neither of them responds, unable to accept or deny Hong's instructions. Two more cars pass as they stand along the side of the road.

"Go," Hong repeats. "The service will start. Don't worry. It's okay."

Amy walks toward Hong and wraps her arms around her shoulders. She pulls her body into Hong's and remains there for a few moments, her face buried in Hong's neck. *Thank you*, she whispers. She wishes she could stay there. She wishes she could go with them, back to the empty house, an empty room, a chair, a cold drink. Her muscles stiffen; she has a hard time letting go.

At last, Amy releases her. Hong walks to the open car door and squats in the space, facing Mrs. Leong. Without a single word, Mrs. Leong slides over and makes room for Hong, who gets in and shuts the door softly behind them.

"I'll come back," the driver says, looking at Amy. "I'll take them home and I'll come right back for you."

"Okay," she says. "Thank you."

Alone, Amy and Theresa stand on the road. The afternoon breeze whips against their faces, which helps, Amy thinks, to erase the marks of distress.

Without a word, they begin to walk in slow unison toward the cemetery entrance. Their heels fight the uneven, broken pavement. They don't look at each other.

Past the entrance, they begin their climb. They hold their eyes on anything they can: the canopy of green, the engravings on the tombstones, the offerings placed before them, the cracks in the pavement, the flat blades of grass, a ladybug, a stick.

Silently, they approach the top of the hill, where twelve marble statues, pristine and white, stand guard on a wall. The animals of the zodiac, the entire ensemble, perch above the most coveted gravesites; those highest in elevation, the most expensive, plots with six-foot pagodas, with thick slabs of solid marble and colored photographs set into gold. The women are met with the sound of a man's voice, carried on the wind. It's a greeting, breathy and heavy with deep, pronounced vowels. The service is beginning. The kahuna has begun to speak and Theresa knows what comes next. She's been waiting for this moment; it's the only ritual that excites her, the only part of the day that makes perfect sense. The smoke and the lights and the burning of paper—the Chinese ceremony was allegory for Theresa, traditions from a generation not her own. But the Hawaiian rites, the idea of *talking to the dead*, of being granted a final opportunity to speak to her father before he's lowered into the ground, of having a last private moment—Theresa wants that chance. Shrouded in this sacred place, in the tranquility of the rising hill, among the gentle sounds and sweet smells of the island that raised him, Theresa truly believes that her father is nearby.

"What are you going to tell him?" she asks, turning toward her mother.

"What?"

"When you get up there, what are you going to say?"

"Don't be ridiculous."

"What?" Theresa halts. "You're not going up there?"

"Theresa, why are you doing this to me?"

"*Jesus*, Mom," Theresa explodes. "Are you serious? Maku's dead because you couldn't get it together—because you played the victim for six *ridiculous* months and now it's your last chance and you're doing it *again*?" Theresa laughs. She can't stop it. The cruel, broken sound rises from the back of her throat, pushing its way out, momentum from the entire day.

"It's classic, really. I should have known." She's shaking her head; her fingers, laced together, pulse with the intensity she's trying to contain. Theresa takes a breath and slowly, doggedly, she speaks to her mother like she is a young child.

"This is your final chance—do you understand that? If you waste this, you will not get another one. You will *never* be okay; you will *never* feel right about what happened, about what you did to him, because Maku will be gone. And because of what?" Theresa's pace quickens, her breath shortens. "Because you're too proud? Or is it because you're too weak? Sorry—you never did tell me what role you'd be playing today."

"*Theresa.*"

"*Look*, I'll never say anything because of Maku, not because of you— but for God's sake, just be honest with him. That's all he wanted. He wanted to know what happened between the two of you, what *actually* happened. Tell him the truth, tell him that you weren't involved. Protect your husband, Mom, not some stranger. Some spineless pathetic stranger—"

"*Theresa.*"

"The last thing," Theresa commands, raising a palm, "and then I'm done."

Amy nods, full of shame that these words are her daughter's. That somehow, her daughter, pregnant and confused and nineteen years old, has more insight, more tenacity when faced with disgrace than she does.

"Let it go," Theresa says. "No one will hear you but him. No one will think less of you, no one will know if you tell him the truth. It's only now that I realize how many years of your life you've spent wishing for something else. You think it's so unfair what happened to you? Well, bullshit. He loved you. He loved you so much and you're still doing *this*. If I end up with a man who loves me even a fraction as much as Maku loved you—which I won't, which you know—then *Jesus Christ, Mom*. I hope like hell I don't waste it the way you did."

Theresa looks straight into her mother's eyes. She wonders if she's said too much. She doesn't care. Theresa leaves Amy on the pathway. She turns and walks toward the service, her strides long and determined, where she can see Kaipo standing at the coffin, his head lowered, both hands resting on the wooden surface. She walks around the crowd and to the front. She stands by the kahuna; their eyes meet; she's next. She absolutely must go next.

Alone on the asphalt, Amy hasn't moved. She's thinking about Theresa. She's softening her heart, fighting to let the words penetrate, fighting the impulse to write them off completely. *Her daughter's words, she doesn't know anything*, Amy's mind fights back. But she can't write it off. Not this time. She's immobilized by how much Theresa sees without even knowing the extent of her accuracy. How many years, Amy thinks, how many decades has she wasted feeling cheated? And how, she pushes herself. *How* had she let the disappointment become her, come to define her?

Amy thinks of Mrs. Leong and understands exactly where she lost control. She remembers the day that she first took the bait. She found her excuse; she never let it go; she followed it down a road that ended in this, in today.

Amy

I was alone again, in the backyard, where I had spent the last few days trying to make sense of the wreckage that had fallen upon this house. How everything had gone so horribly wrong, so implausibly wrong, in less than a week since the wedding.

Dr. Lum was here again, but this time it was for Mrs. Leong. Bohai had come to tell me, had called my name from the lanai and found me in my hiding spot, a shaded curve of rocks near the waterfall. His face was sallow and stricken, the whites of his eyes clouded with broken blood vessels. He looked terrible in the light, shading his eyes above me. Pale and thin in a crumpled shirt, he looked like the sun could evaporate him entirely, could cripple him with a single beam. He squatted and put his hand on my knee.

They were in the sitting room, Bohai said. They were meeting with their lawyer when he had told them something terrible. His father had been keeping wives in China, two of them, both with children. There was no will, he said, and his father's entire fortune would go to them.

As I tried to digest this startling fact, standing, opening my mouth to verify what he had said, Bohai told me something else—something perhaps worse, but who could tell at this point, as disaster trailed behind itself, eclipsing only the one that came before it. Mrs. Leong stopped responding in the middle of the conversation. She got up silently and walked into the kitchen. They called to her, Bohai said, but they hadn't followed. And when they did, just ten minutes later, they found her unconscious in a pool of her own blood, her ankle slit in four places.

I didn't know what to say. It had been days of not knowing what to say. I'd been going crazy in the yard alone, hiding within the crater, trying to mourn the death of a man who was more real to me in black-and-white photographs than in reality. When I saw his picture in the paper the day before, in the piles of newspapers Hong had collected from around the island, I had the strangest sensation of nostalgia. Not for Mr. Leong's life, but for my own, when his picture in the paper brought excitement, or even further back, when it meant nothing to me at all.

It seemed wrong to be with Bohai and his family during this time. Even at the hospital I felt like a fraud, pretending to be part of a family I barely knew and to whom I could offer nothing. I had no words of comfort, no memories, nothing sincere enough to be worthy of saying.

And now Mrs. Leong was falling apart. I had seen her that morning, walking to the sitting room with Hong by her side, her thin body withered beneath a black T-shirt and pants. It was then that I had cried for the first time, seeing how damaged she looked, how shattered and frail. Thinking of her in that puddle of blood, her mind warped, her sadness folding in on itself, growing thicker and denser with each crease, I brought my head to my hands and pulled my knees to my heart.

What had I done? What had I chosen?

Henry's face appeared in my mind. I hugged my body tighter, held myself closer. *His entire fortune will go to his wives in China.* Bohai's words echoed in my head and they wouldn't stop. I couldn't stop; even the morning's tragedy could not displace the dark, stubborn seed attaching itself to my thoughts, poisoning everything.

I tried not to think about the money. I really, really tried. Bohai was a good man, I told myself, and I could still find happiness with him. Despite what was happening to his family, we would manage. But as I watched him walk away, across the yard and back into the house, I knew there had been a terrible shift in my mind. Repulsion had risen from beneath the water; once calm and impenetrable, a sheet of plastic, that liquid surface was now a sea of bodies floating slowly to the surface. Bohai was one of them, and I could feel the current pulling me as well. Pawns. Hostages. That's what it felt like, and because Mr. Leong was dead, and because I felt no connection to him at all, I let my repulsion linger on my husband.

My husband. Another word that inflicted so much pain. How stupid had I turned out to be? How pathetic? I'd sold my life to a man panicked by his own voice, a man with no friends, with no life of his own. I thought of a lifetime with Bohai—his slow words, his tidy bed, his wire glasses—and I began to panic.

I looked up. I imagined myself running; I could even feel it. In my mind I sprinted around the house, out the iron gate, across the island to my bed in Kaneohe, where I could begin my apology to Henry. I'd tell him I had made a terrible mistake, that I desperately wanted him back, that I hated myself for what I'd done. Perhaps it wasn't too late. It had only been three months since Henry left: a single season, not even enough time for the fruit trees to ripen, for the schools to reopen, for anything to be irreversibly changed. Only three months.

And then, reality. I hadn't been unfaithful. I hadn't messed around or had a fling or gotten caught up in a moment I now regretted. I was *married*. To the most prominent family on Oahu, front-page news, fireworks, three dresses, nine courses, all of it a sham. Henry would have to be as stupid as I was to even consider it.

But would he? The question remained.

I let my mind wander, casting a wide, thick shadow with its recklessness. I felt my conscience thrashing on the inside, banging in my ears, begging me to stop. I had chosen this, it screamed, and if the money was gone and I wanted to leave, what the hell kind of person did that make me? What kind of empty, rubbish person would be thinking about money when their father-in-law had just been murdered? When their mother-in-law was lying in a pool of her own blood?

I shook my head, harder and harder until my skin became numb, trying to wipe my mind of its toxins. Who was to say that Henry would take me back? He probably hated me now—his whole family probably cursed the day I had entered their lives. And Mrs. Leong had given me so much. The last three months, I reminded myself, they'd been spectacular. She had treated me as if I were her own, as if I belonged. With her, I'd never looked back, not once.

Thinking of her now, trampled, defeated by her husband's final secret, I wondered if she'd have done the same for me knowing how it would all turn out. If I would even be here if we knew that Mr. Leong would die, or if she would have made different decisions—not just about me, but in her own life—trading her privilege to avoid the horrific agony she felt now. It was a terrible game to play, a dangerous game. What-ifs. And here I was, twenty-one years old, looking back on my life as if it were over.

Or maybe, I thought for a moment, looking at the waterfall and the fat koi and the perfectly manicured trees that surrounded me—maybe, in the end, looking back on the good years and the bad, it was still better to be a Leong than nobody at all.

I thought of my own parents. How they had suffered a lifetime of mundane sorrows and would continue to live this way, the dice never falling in their favor, until the day they died, their bodies buried in a concrete block of regular people. Mrs. Leong's life was at least extravagant, and it seemed as if this extravagance would never leave her, even now, as she crumbled under the elaborate lies of a man who lived excessively.

Bohai and I had our whole lives ahead of us. We could learn to love each other and overcome the difficult legacy his father had left behind. The Leong name did not have to die with this man. We could rebuild it. It would take time, but things could get better.

Or maybe they wouldn't. The thought crept back into my mind like a disease, mutating and expanding, making me wish for things too horrible to say.

If Henry would take me back, would I go? The answer rang in my ears, filling me with self-hatred and hope.

Dr. Lum instructed us to let Mrs. Leong rest. Kaipo called their lawyer, Mr. Lee, and postponed his visit until the next morning, when they hoped Mrs. Leong would be of sounder mind. I told Bohai I needed air—that I'd be back by dinner, I just needed to walk. He insisted that I take his car, which made my stomach wrench with something thick and oily.

"Take your time," he said, handing me the keys, "and be careful. I can't lose you too." He smiled for the first time since his father passed and I nearly changed my mind, feeling caught under the weight of his sincerity. But instead I took the keys. I took the keys and walked out the door.

"I will," I replied, "don't worry about me."

Henry had taught me to drive before he left. Not well, but enough to get me away from Diamond Head and slowly across the valley floor. I came off the hill and passed through downtown, taking in streets that should have felt familiar but didn't. As hard as I tried to extract its comfort, it refused to come. I should have felt something, back down on the surface where my real life took place, and I grew frustrated as nothing came, just more resentment, more desperation.

The streets were busy, buzzing with people untouched by tragedy. Their days would be easily forgotten, I thought to myself, my chest expanding with envy. A month from now they would not remember where they had been, what they had been doing at this moment; only that it was a regular day, and perhaps that they had been happy.

I drove past my street and thought of my parents. I considered stopping; telling them of the destruction that had swept through the Leongs' house that morning. But what would that accomplish? I could picture their faces processing my words, attempting to comfort me but really thinking of themselves. My dad would fall silent and my mother would cry, asking questions like: *All of the money? Are you positive?*

No. I shook my head, my fingers clamping the wheel. They would find out soon enough.

Behind the wheel of the car I felt free—like if I drove fast enough or long enough, I could leave it all behind. But I suppose that was the problem. I didn't want a new beginning, I wanted to rewind; to delete the last three months and prove to myself—to Henry—that I was a better woman than I had turned out to be.

I turned onto the final street and slowed, feeling more hopeful than I could possibly justify. As I pulled into the small parking lot, I closed my eyes and said a prayer. I told God that I knew exactly what I deserved, and while it wasn't happiness, I hoped that it would at least be a chance at redemption. I told Him that I was better for my mistakes. That I was no longer as selfish as I had been three months ago.

But there I was, parked outside the pharmacy, about to make a plea perhaps more selfish than any I had ever made. I opened my eyes and looked through the sunroof, up at the sky, knowing that I had no business asking any god for anything.

I lowered my eyes, about to apologize for wasting His time, when I realized there was someone standing in front of my car, staring at me through the windshield.

I fumbled with my keys and opened the door. Henry's brother, Paul, stood perfectly still, his dark eyes penetrating me.

"What the hell are you doing here?"

"I—" I stammered, closing the door behind me. "I don't know. I just wanted to say—"

"What, Amy? What did you want to say?" He moved closer, his voice growing harsher as I pressed my back against the car door. "Did our wedding invitation get lost in the mail?"

I was going to cry. It was coming; there was no stopping it.

"I don't know," I sobbed, the backs of my thighs burning against the heat of the car. "I mean, no," I stammered. I willed myself to stop. *Please please please*, I begged myself. This was not how it was supposed to happen.

"You're pathetic," Paul said, turning his head and spitting on the hood of Bohai's car. "You have some nerve, you know that? Coming here in your Mercedes, like we'd have anything to say to you. You mail us some bullshit apology, you don't even tell my brother. You're the worst kind of woman—you know that, don't you?"

"I made a huge mistake," I pleaded, tears falling down my shoulders.

"Well, look at that!" He kicked the front tire with his foot and I jumped. "You finally got something right."

He laughed, staring at me with cold eyes. "But guess what? You're not welcome here anymore. You see, Amy, family means a lot to us Wongs. We may not have a garage full of cars or a mansion with servants or any of the other shit that made you fuck over my brother. But do you know what we do have, Amy?"

I shook my head, feeling so foolish. He was enjoying this, watching me cry, shaming me in my own neighborhood. And why not? Didn't I deserve it? My vision clouded as he moved closer.

"We have souls, Amy. We have consciences. We have *hearts*."

We stood there in icy silence, his face so close I could feel his breath on me. For a moment, I thought he might hit me. I lowered my eyes to the ground and tried to breathe.

"We're done," he spat. "Get off our property."

He shoved my shoulders against the car with both hands. I let him. Then he turned around and walked back into the pharmacy, where I could see Henry's mother watching through the shop window.

She held her hands in front of her apron, her face exactly as I remembered it, but vacant. It was clear that she'd been there the whole time—that she'd seen the whole thing and hadn't stopped it. My heart broke into even tinier pieces, so small I knew I might never find them again. She was my last hope, but she felt the same way. She wanted me off her property, erased from their life.

I opened the car door and got inside, wanting to crawl into the backseat and melt until there was nothing left. But they were still watching me, I knew they were. I started the engine and pulled out of the parking lot without any idea of where I would go next.

I drove for two more hours, through small side streets that reminded me of home, and then along the highway, where I was finally able to breathe. I drove until I was almost out of gas and realized I had no money. No money and no place to go but Diamond Head—to the place where I least belonged. I took it slowly, watching the valley floor disappear behind me, finally understanding that this was it. Right before the Leongs' street, I pulled off to the side of the road and placed my head against the wheel, promising myself that no matter what happened, I would remember this feeling. I would never forget how I hurt at this moment; hollow and broken with a single option left. And if I continued to behave like this, always searching for something better, never satisfied, soon I might have nothing left at all.

This is it, I said to myself, my shaky voice filling the car. *No more running, no more regrets. This is your life now. Be happy.*

The next day, Mrs. Leong was still in a fragile state. Physically, she was fine. The cuts on her ankle had begun to scab. Her blood level was healthy and stable. But mentally, she couldn't focus for longer than a minute or two, and Mr. Lee had to repeat the terrible events to her several times before she responded with a single sentence.

Sell the house, sell everything. Then she closed her eyes and went back to sleep. Hong left the room immediately after. It was almost impossible, excruciatingly difficult for me to watch the two of them together. Mrs. Leong would flicker out, close her eyes and retreat, and Hong, so unlike herself, would leave. She would stand up or turn around and exit the room at the first sign of pain. It was the first time she seemed without a solution, without the capacity to make tea and place a hand on Mrs. Leong's back, to simply sit with her, wordlessly as they so often did.

Over the next few days, Bohai and the others decided on an auction, which their lawyer said would be the least painful way to get rid of the house. Whoever offered the highest price would be handed the keys straightaway, and we would find a new place to live with Mrs. Leong. But two days before the house was to be released to the public, Kaipo changed his mind. He came to us first and we came to an agreement. And then, knocking on his mother's door later that evening, he gathered us all in the sitting room and began to speak with a sincerity and sorrow that I never knew he possessed.

"I'm resentful," he began, his voice dipping between two pitches, neither of them his own, "like everyone else in this family. I'm angry that we've been left like this and I don't know if that anger will ever go away."

He paused for a moment and looked at his mother, who was rubbing her fingers along the hem of her shirt. Her eyes were unfocused, disconnected. She was wearing the same black T-shirt, the same black pants. I had seen very little of her since they'd found her in the kitchen, but whenever I did, I looked away. She was managing her grief in the most devastating of ways, and it felt disrespectful to witness her so vulnerable, so changed from the woman I had known.

"But if for some reason it does," Kaipo began again, "I can't help but feel that selling the house to a stranger would be a mistake. One that might surface after the resentment has subsided. Which I hope, with time, will be the case."

I looked at Bohai, whose expression remained the same, knowing that he felt very differently. A few nights before, after I returned from my drive, we had sat in the kitchen together, drinking whiskey into the morning hours and speaking more openly than we ever had. If I was going to live this life, if I was going to learn to be with my husband, then we had to get to know each other; something we had overlooked amid the excitement of our wedding.

He had told me about his birth mother, a teenage concubine who died back in China. Bohai had no memory of her. It had always eaten away at him, he said, that he was different, that half of him belonged to another woman, to a frightened girl. And now, with the discovery of his father's first two wives, he felt completely isolated.

"I feel like one of them," he told me. "Like I should have been left in China, just like them. I keep thinking, had I not been born a boy, then what? I would have been just another secret child, another skeleton in my father's closet."

I listened. I had tried so hard to listen and care and feel something stir within me for this man. But all that came was pity. It made so much sense. He was the oldest son, but Bohai was not the first son. What a sad life, I thought, what a tortured existence. I searched the deepest folds of my heart, trying to find some sympathy, a sliver of encouragement for the man before me, my husband, but I couldn't. What could I offer him? What could I say when this sorrow, this burden was my life, too?

And then, without waiting for a response, Bohai took my hand from across the table. He had leaned in as if he had a secret, and he had said something else.

"But it's not all tragedy, because I have you. I can't wait to spend the rest of our lives together. We have a chance to be just us, ordinary people, unpolluted by the lies my father told."

He looked so happy when he said it. The exhaustion in his eyes gave way to the hope he held for our future, and it took all my effort, everything I had left, to smile and pretend that I, too, wanted to be ordinary.

"I know why you can't live here," Kaipo continued, looking at his mother, his eyelids heavy with grief. "I do. But after many sleepless nights considering the situation, I've decided that I can't leave. This house is my oldest memory. It's where I took my first steps, where I chased geckos, where I want to return after a long trip. This is where everything important in my life took place." He took a slow breath. "Mom, I want the house. Not because of its ties to Dad, but for the significance it has in my own life. I want my children to grow up here. I want to pass it through the generations."

Mrs. Leong looked up at Kaipo with the same expression that made me look away each time; blank eyes, hollow cheeks, each feature more lifeless than the next. She spoke only in whispers now. She was suspicious of everything, worried that a display of emotion might tip the scale, that a single outburst might shatter her fragile bones.

"The money," she whispered. The sound came from her throat, cracking under each new syllable. "We need the money."

I looked at Kaipo and knew it took all of his strength to continue. I had never witnessed such a disturbing transformation in a person. Mrs. Leong no longer ate meals with us. She refused them. She ate from the pantry now, forbidding us to shop for fresh food. When Hong had stocked the cupboards earlier in the week, Mrs. Leong had scolded her in Chinese and made her take all the groceries back to the store. The two of them together, they spoke only Chinese now. I was the only one who couldn't understand them, the only one unnerved by their linked regression, the only person who felt the house shift into a different world, a different era, the Oriental rugs now imperialist and stifling, the red door no longer modern or warm.

Mrs. Leong ate dehydrated peas and strips of preserved cuttlefish straight from the plastic bag, and when those things ran out, she ate cans of cold corn and kidney beans. The rest of us had stopped eating at the table, stopped eating together entirely because it upset her so much. I think I was the only one who didn't mind. For me it was almost soothing, sitting cross-legged on my bed, eating leftover rice alone from a single bowl.

Last week, Kaipo had found his mother in the kitchen, frying up pounds of pomfret—a strange flat fish that no one had ever seen in the house. It had a stale, assaulting smell that rose through the floorboards. The hot oil burned, and smoke sailed from room to room like a warning. Mrs. Leong sat on the kitchen floor and ate the fish with her hands—I saw it out of the corner of my eye—and when she was finished, she passed out on the greasy tiles, tiny bones and bits of flesh still stuck to her fingers. Every night, she slept on the floor of whatever room she ended up in, with no pillows or blankets, refusing help of any kind. She cut off chunks of her hair and hid them at the bottom of trash cans; Hong would find them and show Bohai and Kaipo.

Mrs. Leong could still walk and bathe and respond to certain questions. She wasn't completely gone, not yet. But it was clear to us all that we needed to get her out, that she was rapidly deteriorating within the house that she had built with her husband.

"Mom," Kaipo said, placing his hand on her knee, "we're going to take care of you. I'm going to buy the house, for whatever price you think is fair. And with that money, we're going to find you a new home. Whatever you want, Mom. Whatever makes you happy. Just say the word and it's yours. Don't worry about the money. I have plenty saved and so does Bohai. We're going to take care of you."

Mrs. Leong stared off into the corner, above Kaipo's shoulder. She said nothing.

"If it's okay with you," Kaipo continued cautiously, "Bohai and Amy will move in with you, to your new house, to help take care of you. Would you like that?"

Mrs. Leong began to hum. A forceful buzz escaped her mouth, the uneven sound pushing through tightly shut lips. She didn't look at Kaipo; she didn't look at anything. It was as if she barely knew we were there. I was afraid that she might faint. She hadn't stopped for air and the sound kept pushing, growing, retreating but never stopping. We looked at one another but no one moved, not even Hong. There was something satisfying about her humming, something decent, as if she were purging herself of the pain. I hoped it was working. I watched her, the sound beginning to penetrate me, to reach into my bones and twist, and I begged God to please, *please* allow this woman some relief.

Bohai and I were given the task of selecting the house in which we would live with Mrs. Leong. It was Bohai who had first offered to be his mother's caretaker, and I agreed, feeling closer to her now, as things fell apart, than I had before. It was a new beginning for Bohai, I told myself, and for me as well. We would have our own place, the constant reminders of his father left in the past.

We knew she needed a complete change of scenery—the exact opposite of the house in Diamond Head. We looked at properties on the beach. We even considered moving her to the calm of the North Shore, but in the end we decided it was too far. She needed the strength of her entire family—needed to be close to both of her children, to Hong. So the minute we saw the house in Hawaii Kai, with the open marina and the dock out back, we knew. She could have the peacefulness of the water, the privacy of the dock, the distance from downtown, and the proximity to Kaipo and Hong. It was a beautiful house, simpler than I had imagined but perfect in almost every way. It reminded me of old Hawaii with its moss stone wall and assortment of low bushes and skinny palm trees. The shape of the house, like a horseshoe, gave us privacy at the entrance, a place to breathe as we sorted things out. A cast-iron gate, thin and discreet, guarded the house from the outside world. We bought it immediately with a portion of the money Kaipo had given us for his father's house, and moved in the following week.

So badly did I want my family back, but of course, we were different now; my father and I, our days together were over. After Mr. Leong died my parents backed away, perhaps unintentionally, but without my in-laws, without the money, they were terribly uncomfortable around Bohai and me, around Hong and Kaipo. They asked about the investigation, about Mr. Leong's business and state of affairs, or else they asked about nothing. It was as if I were the acquaintance and Mr. Leong their flesh and blood, the shipping business their investment and I their oddball daughter, a girl they had trouble looking straight in the eye. I no longer trusted them; Bohai and I both, we feared that his father's secret, so closely guarded by Kaipo, would be betrayed. Soon enough, I stopped missing them.

Not Kaneohe—I missed my old life every day—but my parents, I thought of them less and less.

Kaipo was alone in his investigation of Mr. Leong's murder. He managed to trace phone calls to Germany, dozens of them in the final weeks of his father's life, but what could that prove? According to the police, it meant close to nothing. Without a threat letter or a confession, without a clear motive, a clear idea of what exactly Mr. Leong was doing abroad, they had very little to go on. Kaipo had yet to find the file. He needed help but he wouldn't go outside the family, wouldn't risk exposing his father's last endeavors, dirtying his family's name. The investigation went slowly, hitting one dead end after another as Kaipo realized that for the most part, his father did as he pleased. Kaipo had the kitchen staff from the wedding interrogated; he had their backgrounds checked; he searched for ties to science labs, pest exterminators, glass manufacturers, anything that might tie back to the thallium. But they all came back clean, and Kaipo began to realize it was a futile task trying to compile every bite of food and sip of tea his father put into his mouth, trying to trace its distant origins.

With the hospital, there were small victories. Dr. Harris had been fired, his medical license under scrutiny of the state. Mr. Lee was in the process of negotiating a settlement out of court, as neither party wanted to risk public exposure. An agreement had yet to be reached, but it was going well, Mr. Lee told us. With them, we had the upper hand.

Despite asking Bohai on countless occasions, trying to persuade him in a dozen different ways, Kaipo was also alone in his decision to carry on with his father's shipping endeavors. Mr. Leong's wives in China had no interest in taking over the business, so it went to Kaipo, who continued his work as if his father had never passed. For two weeks, Bohai agreed to help his brother. He showed Kaipo the company's paper infrastructure, how shipments were processed and billed, recorded in the books, training the young accountants Kaipo had hired. When he was finished, Bohai told me something that I wish I'd never known. He told me how quickly money was building in the company bank accounts, how swiftly the business would get back on track—it was simply a matter of years, but Bohai wanted nothing to do with it. He was relieved that his burden was over. Kaipo would be fine, he'd keep the house, his life would continue almost exactly as planned. It seemed likely Bohai would not be needed again. We were free to begin our new life.

Bohai was hired right away at Punahou, his old school, teaching mathematics in the seventh grade. He stayed up all night creating lesson plans for weeks in advance. He had his briefcase embroidered with his initials and the Punahou hala tree. More than anyone else in the family, Bohai began to create a new life for himself, burying his grief with his father and moving forward happily, eagerly.

For me, it was more difficult. The fact that I had no college degree limited my choices—but even more challenging was the fact that I had never before had a real job. It seemed somehow inappropriate for me to resume cleaning houses for the neighbors in Diamond Head, and I refused to go back to work for my father. So I relied on the only other skill I had, and offered my services to the various dress shops in Waikiki. When all of them said no, which I expected, I thought I might have to travel farther along the island to find work. But then Hong told me of a small shop at the end of a residential block that she had used before. I went the next day, wearing a dress I had made myself, and I asked for a job. There were three women, all of them middle aged and plump from sitting, and after a short assessment of my stitching and a few questions, they hired me on the spot.

I left the shop feeling surprisingly gratified; I was light and calm and strangely pleased with myself. Not that I'd ever dreamed of becoming a seamstress, but it was something that made me valuable to the real world. After weeks of feeling useless, it was a welcome surprise that I was, at the very least, qualified to work an actual job. In some small way, I could make it on my own.

But on my first day of work, that pride was quickly trampled. The way the other women were constantly smiling in my direction and asking me questions and disappearing into the back room two at a time—by the end of the day it was clear to me that they recognized my face from my wedding pictures in the paper. It was obvious that they knew I was the newest Leong, and that they were either still excited by the family name or, more likely, that they had continued to read the papers and they knew how the story ended—that they had hired me out of pity and curiosity. But they were the only shop who had offered me a paycheck, so I put aside my pride, what little of it remained, and focused on my sewing. I really had no other choice, and I continued to remind myself, each morning as I entered the shop, that it wasn't so bad. That things could be much, much worse, and so I began to occupy my mind with those things. Death, war, starvation, disease, they all helped me get through my day.

Clumsily, then, and with mixed emotions, the three of us began a new life together. I woke up at six each morning to prepare breakfast, and when the dishes were cleared and drying on the rack, Bohai and I would set off for our new, regular jobs by eight.

We left Mrs. Leong alone during the day, encouraging her to spend her time as she pleased. We told her to use the dock or walk to the neighborhood park or to rest all day if she needed to. We assumed that Hong would visit often. We gave her a key. But every evening when we returned home, we found Mrs. Leong alone in the same position, sitting fully upright in a chair or a stool or on the floor, and we knew that she had been there for hours, trapped in the stillness that was polluting her mind. It was as if she couldn't understand that her surroundings had changed; that she had moved houses, that she lived with us now, that things were different. Mrs. Leong continued to sleep on the floor; she still refused hot meals; she spoke only in whispers. Even Hong could handle only so much; I understood completely.

We exchanged words of encouragement, despite the obvious. Mrs.

Leong was not getting better, not at all. Our house had become a sad place, our four walls a kind of casket as we watched her fade, the slow pull of death always present. She wasn't dying, not physically, at least. We weren't witnessing the death of a person, but the death of a spirit that would never, could never return. Mrs. Leong was sixty years old when her husband passed, too old to look to the future and imagine a different kind of life. She'd experienced too much to believe in renewal. And as the thought passed through my mind, I realized that I could say the same thing about myself. There was a punishment for indulgence, I saw it every day. It happened in the mind; there was a breaking point. It seemed to me that Mrs. Leong chose stillness, punishing herself for guilt or extravagance or stupidity. And wasn't I punishing myself as well? Why did I stay with Bohai? The answer was immediate. I had taken too much. I had been greedy and selfish and there was no way, no way I could see to give it back.

It was me who found her that Saturday in May, wrapped in newspapers on the kitchen floor. I had just come home from a long shift at the dress shop, having stayed late to help with an order of a dozen *muʻu muʻu*. I couldn't wait to get home. As I opened the door, I heard a rustling sound from the kitchen and went to greet my mother-in-law.

I found her shivering in her undergarments, newspapers wrapped around her shoulders like a shawl, sitting in a mess of corn kernels, grains of uncooked rice, and their torn packaging. She was freezing.

"Tell my husband to turn on the heat," she whispered to me, picking a grain of rice from her thigh and putting it into her mouth.

"Okay," I said, carefully offering Mrs. Leong my hand, "I'll tell him right now. But first let's get you in a hot bath. It will make you feel much better."

She slapped my hand away and I took a long, slow breath.

"No!" She wailed. "Just tell Frank—he'll know what to do. This rice tastes terrible." She spat it onto the floor.

I steadied myself against the counter and gathered all my strength so I wouldn't cry. I forced the rising resentment back down into my chest but still, tears welled; a vengeful warmth pressed against the backs of my eyes. I looked at Mrs. Leong, waiting on my kitchen floor for her husband to save her, still waiting. A husband who had lied and deceived her, who had escaped to death without any concern for the time she had remaining. I tried not to think of him now, knowing that it would only make things worse, that it would only stir up anger and hostility. But I couldn't help but wonder how it felt; to love so tenaciously that the world could crack and fall around you, that everything you believed could be a lie, and yet you continue to wait. You continue to wait, full of hope, for someone who would never arrive.

I tried two more times to get Mrs. Leong off the floor, and each time she refused. So I kneeled and I sat with her, in the mess of damp food, telling her that Frank was on his way. That he'd be here soon to turn up the heat. I didn't know what else to do.

I pretended to shiver with her, wrapping a newspaper around my shoulders despite the fact that it was eighty degrees. I excused myself to the bathroom and called Bohai at Punahou. My voice cracked as I told him to get home quickly and to call his brother. There was something terribly wrong with his mother.

When Bohai arrived at home that evening, Kaipo and Hong five minutes behind him, his mother could not remember either of their names. She called Kaipo Frank, and scolded him for leaving the house so cold. When Dr. Lum arrived later that night, bringing a specialist with him, she could not tell them what year it was. She could not tell them what she did that day or any other day that week. She said she had gone fishing with Frank, that they had caught a golden mahimahi. The specialist suggested a small clinic on the North Shore, in Waialua, where they specialized in senile dementia. It was an intimate home, he told us. She would receive constant care and be ensured privacy from the press.

Waialua. My heart slowed when he said it, everything did. Of course, it had to be Waialua. There were dozens of quiet towns that lined the North Shore but only one where Henry and I had met. Only one where I had memories buried in the sand, tears floating in the ocean. So this was how I'd return, I thought to myself, almost laughing from the revulsion that filled me. What destiny. What a piece of shit it was.

Bohai refused at first and I thought we might be okay. He didn't want to send his mother away. He said that he would quit his job and look after her himself. But after the purchase of the new house, Bohai and I could not survive off my wages alone, and he refused to live off Kaipo's earnings. He looked to Hong then; he asked her for help.

"I know it's not your burden, but my mother trusts you more than anyone, she loves you. You could live here, we have plenty of space. You would have everything you needed, anything at all."

Hong's gaze met the ground, her face tortured. Her eyes, already so narrow, strained with distress as we looked to her, waiting for her verdict.

"She is sick," Hong said finally, holding her stare below her, her arms shaking gently. Her voice was hoarse, her accent overpowering. "I am a not doctor. I do not know how to take care for her. Soup, tea . . ." She paused. "It cannot fix this."

She barely finished her sentence before pushing forward in her chair, stumbling on her tangled feet, her body hunched forward as she made her way from the room, wiping the moisture that ran down her face. The rest of us, we looked at each other and knew what had to be done, because if Hong had lost her faith, then how ludicrous it was to think that we could keep ours.

The next Saturday, we packed two cars and drove Mrs. Leong to Waialua.

It was all the same.

The dirt was still red, the roads still narrow, the old sugar mill still there among the overgrown grass, the rusty silo, the Waianae Mountains wrapped in mist. The sight of these things hurt, literally hurt like a lit cigarette being pressed into my skin, over and over again. I felt treacherous the entire time, but against whom I didn't know. Henry didn't know I was there. Bohai didn't know what the place meant. And me, I was holding all the secrets, gorging on these sights like an addict. I sat in the front seat with Bohai, sunglasses concealing my stare, fearful the entire ride that I was leaking, that my glasses could not contain all that I felt.

We parked in front of a yellow house with a wooden porch that wrapped around the front. Inside we were greeted by a Filipino woman who offered us cans of guava juice, showing us down the hallway to the last door on the right. The walls held pictures of tranquil things: sunrises and hills with flowers and a wicker basket with a litter of golden puppies.

We settled Mrs. Leong into her new room, the four of us crowded around her single bed, and did not discuss how tiny it was. We did not talk about how the window did not open. We did not speak of how immensely depressing, how horribly sad it was in this sterile shoebox, how appalling it was that the four of us were so marred by the year that we couldn't come to a different solution, that we could not find a better fate for the matriarch of our illustrious house.

With the decision to send Mrs. Leong away, faced with an enormous bill that would recur each month, we reached an agreement in the lawsuit with the hospital. Bohai and Kaipo, refusing any profit from the death of their father, asked the hospital to pay their mother's medical bills. Anything she needed, any expense related to her health or well-being would be provided for as long as she needed it, no stipulations. A life taken, a life restored, that was the way we put it to each other, knowing full well we could have asked for something else. Could have used the money to care for her ourselves, could have found a way to keep her closer. But not one of us suggested it, not even a mention, not Bohai, not Kaipo, not Hong.

It was then, as I left the room, apologizing to the others, that I promised myself—I swore to myself on absolutely everything I valued, threatened myself with a fate worse than this reality—that I would visit this woman once a month, my oath good until the day she passed. I shut the door quietly behind me and found myself squatting against the wall in the narrow hallway, head lowered into my hands, elbows balanced on shaky knees. Breathing.

I hated that even in death, Mr. Leong had this kind of power. I hated that I had fallen under his spell—that we all had, and now we were left to suffer, to contemplate what the hell we had done to deserve this.

How does it *feel*, I thought to myself, to love this strongly when it's so devastatingly wrong? Was this fate, or was it a punishment for eluding it? Something that people hoped was fate as they neared the end of their lives; as they tried to come to terms with all the mistakes they had made and all the clues they had missed but now understood.

This was not fate, I told myself; it was the furthest thing from it. This pain was intimate, deeply, sickeningly personal, and as I closed my eyes and lowered myself to the ground, I knew that it had all been created. The tangles from one generation to the next, the mistakes passed from mother to daughter, the lies from father to son—it wasn't fate, who could call that fate? These things were within our control, outcomes not linked to our flesh, and all of us, every single one of us, had played a hand in this destiny.

CHAPTER 9

November 1964
HONOLULU, HAWAII

Theresa places her hands on her father's casket; she closes her eyes, filled with intention, and does not know how to begin. I'm sorry. That's the first thing that comes to her, the words she's thought so often, almost every time she thinks of her father. But the apology is loaded; it's more complicated than that. She's sorry she got pregnant, of course she is. She's sorry she disappointed him. She's sorry about her mother's selfishness, sorry about the letter; she still feels deeply, maddeningly responsible. But she's also sorry that her father did not rise to the occasion. She's sorry that he could not defend himself, couldn't fight harder against his own insecurities so that he might live past this.

No, Theresa thinks, quieting herself. She will not say sorry; that will not be the first thing her father hears from her.

I love you, she thinks, but even that sounds strange. *Love* was not a word she and her father used often, not because they didn't love each other but because they shared so few words between them. *Love* felt too serious, too demanding for every day, for informal greetings. But now Theresa wishes she had said it more. She feels ashamed for so many reasons, but there's one that plagues her more than the rest. She never knew her father, not in any truthful way. All these things she's learned since his death, all these heartbreaking, noble details about his life, while he was her father, while he was alive, Theresa didn't know a single one. She never thought to ask.

There's a barrier between them, something keeping Theresa

quiet. Every time she considers speaking, she thinks of her mother. She thinks of how, without her mother, there is very little she can say, very little that will matter.

Without her mother, Theresa's burden is enormous. She feels the need to comfort her father, to say the things that her mother should be saying but is not, because she's not there. Because she is a coward, Theresa thinks, because she's still on the cemetery road, still feeling sorry for herself, still rewriting history to favor her delusions.

Without her mother, Theresa must find a way to say it herself.

"She told me everything," she begins suddenly, leaning into her father, each word like a magnet drawing her closer. "Since you left, she's been telling me everything she knows about you. About your real mom. About NaiNai."

"She knows a lot about you, Maku. I know that doesn't mean much now, but she does. She remembers everything; she remembers more about you and your time together than she does about anyone else. And that's the truth. You were her life—you and me."

"I don't understand what happened twenty years ago, I don't and I probably never will. But in the last six months she changed, Maku. *She* changed—not what she felt for you. She's still not the same; she's still acting like an idiot and I can only assume that she's confused and . . . she misses you."

Theresa pauses. She hears what she must say next and loses her momentum; she whispers now.

"Do you want to know what gets me the most? It's not Mom. It's not the letter. It's not the way you went. What kills me the most, what I can't stop thinking about, is how well I know you, how much I understand you now, now that you're gone. All these things Mom's told me, all your bravery, all the odds you weren't meant to beat— you're *remarkable*, Maku. You're the strongest person I've ever known, and I didn't know it until now, until this week. We've gone all this time, all my life never really understanding how much you took care of us, how much your strength held the three of us together. You chose to leave; I get that now and I don't blame you. It was us who pushed you away, Mom and I who were unworthy of you. You deserved to make this choice, I sincerely believe that, and I'll never think less of you for it."

Theresa inhales, folding her lips inward, feeling her father's presence beside her, wishing he could respond, knowing that he never will.

"But I wish you hadn't. For the rest of my life, Maku, I'll always wish you had stayed."

Theresa places her forehead against his casket, her eyes still closed, her words blowing warm air against the wood. There are so many things she'd like to say, a mountain of fears she'd like to share with her father. She wants him to know how panicked she feels, how terrified she is about being both a wife and a mother. She wants to tell him how, with every minute, with every step, she feels his absence. She feels how easily she could topple, and fears that without his steady hand, there will be no one left to help her find her feet, to help her stand. She has never learned to help herself and that, Theresa realizes, is her greatest fear.

The sun beats against the back of her exposed neck. She considers staying there, never opening her eyes, letting them carry her away. She thinks of her father within the casket; she remembers him on his final day, drained of emotion, withered beneath his hospital gown and then, finally, Theresa finds her point. She sees him with his suitcase, walking out the front door, and it comes to her; the only thing that matters, the one thing that was never said.

"She loved you," she says decisively, because she means it. "She loved you, Maku. I really believe she did."

Theresa takes a deep breath, drawing the air slowly to her lungs. She raises her head and opens her eyes.

Her mother stands before her, on the opposite side of the coffin.

Her eyes squint beneath the afternoon sun. They can barely contain their moisture, which collects along the bottoms, reflecting the light. Theresa looks at her mother and feels the first relief of the day; it swells within her like a balloon, a lightness she has almost forgotten. She presses her hand to the casket and breathes again; she says good-bye to her father; she leaves her parents their final moment.

Theresa

1943–1964
HONOLULU, HAWAII

Maku's love for my mom was the most genuine love that I have witnessed in my lifetime. Every morning that he woke up next to her,
I know he felt alive, lucky to find such beauty beside him. He knew
everything about her; he remembered every detail. On my mom's
vanity, where she does her makeup every morning, there is a vase that
once held birds of paradise. Every week, for as long as I can remember, Maku would replace them for her. He would rinse out the vase
for the next bouquet; he would trim the stems to an angle.

When we could afford only one car, it went to my mom. Maku
biked to work that year; he said he enjoyed the exercise. They had a
table at the Pacific Broiler, my mother's favorite restaurant, where
they had dinner every Friday. Even after they became regulars,
when there was no longer any need to make a reservation, Maku
still called. He would ask the hostess to put aside a crème brûlée;
he would confirm that they still had a crab cake. On the weekends,
I'd walk with my parents downtown and my mom would point in
a window. *How pretty*, she would say, because that was all it took.
Within a week, usually less, a gift-wrapped package would appear
on the kitchen counter. He'd write her name on the card, as if we'd
mistake it as a gift for someone else. And there was always a card,
something generic but lovely; an old-fashioned touch that he never
once forgot.

My mom turned thirty and Maku took her to Paris, to drink champagne in its birthplace, he told her as she stared at the tickets. It never
once occurred to me that my parents weren't in love. I thought my
mom was modest, self-conscious perhaps. The fact that they never

hugged or kissed, that they never held hands, it didn't bother me. These things, until recently, had never crossed my mind.

Ten months into her marriage, long before I was born, my mom tried to leave Maku. She told me this the week after Maku died, I believe, to make a point. She wanted to show me how long, how many years she had spent unhappy.

She told me she called a lunch that day. She invited my Auntie B and two of her girlfriends and when they had ordered, she made her announcement.

She was unhappy, she told them. She was unhappy and she wanted a divorce.

My mom assumed that her friends would encourage her decision, that they would tell her to flee her hopeless marriage—so when her announcement was greeted by a long, uncomfortable pause, my mom was not prepared.

"What?" she asked, her eyes stopping on each averted stare. "What? You don't agree?"

Obviously, I thought to myself, they would not agree. Thinking of my mom and her newly charmed life, thinking of my Auntie B and the *tita* girlfriends they knew from back home, this surprised me not at all. She couldn't see the departure of their lives? She didn't hear the arrogance in her announcement? I held in these questions, I simply listened because the answer was clear to me. Even ten months into her marriage, my mom was somewhere else. She lived so much in her head that while her life transitioned around her, her thoughts had stayed behind. She was not yet a Leong; in the space where she lived, in her mind, there was still hope for something else, something better.

It had been three days since Maku died and I had so much anger, so much resentment toward my mom that I knew whatever came out would be purposefully cruel. I held my tongue for selfish reasons; there was no time, no energy for another fight and I needed her to finish. I had my own point to make, and while I couldn't be certain, I placed my bet on the reluctance that had suddenly come over her.

"So what did they say?" I prodded. "Your friends, they must have said something."

My mom was caught; I could see it. She knew she couldn't end the story there, knew that she had not made the case she had set out to make. She inhaled slowly through her nose, her eyes resting in her lap where her hands sat quietly.

"It was your Auntie B," she said, pausing, taking a second breath.

"She told me I was wrong. She told me I was wrong if I thought there was something better out there. *Don't be stupid*, that's what she said."

Her sister's words. My mom had suppressed them, but she had never forgotten. She continued the story as if it came all at once, forcefully, a part of her memory that had been silenced for decades.

That day, my mom looked across the table at each of her childhood friends and found the same nervousness in their eyes, the same hesitancy on their lips, because it mattered nothing at all to them that her husband was a stiff and her marriage shaky and they no longer lived in the largest mansion in all of Oahu. These women, these girls from my mom's past, they were all still single, all still living in their parents' houses, still working jobs that required uniforms and name tags and bottles of all-purpose cleaner. They all wanted to be married, to own a house in Hawaii Kai with a man who took them out for dinner, shy or strange or otherwise. It didn't matter. They grew up poor together—all of them courted by the same overinflated, big-bodied mokes who ended up in jail or knocking you up, running away. My mom had left Kaneohe, she had escaped that fate and they marveled at her good fortune. They coveted her life.

"Is it really that bad?" her sister asked. My mom looked at my Auntie B and considered her words. Beverly, without a doubt, would marry her on-again, off-again boyfriend and raise her family in the Palama projects where they already lived. She would not go to college, nor would any of her children. Her boyfriend had already been to jail—twice. The path she was on had very few exits.

I felt the defeat in my mom's voice, even as she told the story twenty years later. I know that if she had her way, if she could have rewritten this conversation, her friends would have said something else, or she would have had different friends—girls who had been to the top of Diamond Head, to the height of the Pali and looked down on the world as she had, who saw the fragility, the urgency to live for something spectacular.

But she didn't, and in the end, she couldn't explain it.

So feebly, and with tremendous effort, my mom embarked upon the strange task of trying to love her husband, of trying to *feel* lucky. She went home that night and made lists of all the good things that she admired in Maku. Responsible, she wrote at the very top, followed by generous, kind, and patient. The lists were long and comprehensive, the most important of the traits made bold by dozens of strokes of her pen. She decided that she liked the way he smelled when he got out of the shower—how the woodiness of eucalyptus lingered on his shoulders. She liked the way he ordered wine; with authority, swirling the first sip in his mouth, actually knowing what he was tasting. Lastly, she liked the look of release in his eyes when he came home to find her sitting on the couch at the end of the day, sewing or watching TV—so thankful that she was still there. But I suppose for my mom, all this wasn't enough. It would never be enough. The lists and the eucalyptus and the constant doting did not add up to a happy marriage.

Sometimes I joke to my friends that I was a mistake, but I know now that's wrong. Everything about my birth was planned, everything about my life, my purpose, was considered for years before I was conceived. I was a last-ditch effort to save my mom, a final attempt to validate her life and her marriage, and only now do I see how terribly I failed.

It took my mom two years of marriage, two years of emptiness and mental isolation to decide that she was ready to have a child. Maku asked her regularly, attempting to talk her through her apprehensions but their talk went in circles, my mom never able to reveal to him why she resisted. But Maku wanted a child so desperately, and as the second year of my parents' marriage came to a close, my mom could no longer find a reason to deny him. So the following Friday, over crab cakes and crème brûlée, my mom acquiesced. She told Maku she was ready, finally ready to be a mother.

I was born in June 1945, to a parade of well-wishers. My Uncle Kaipo was newly married but still childless. I was the first of a new generation; a fresh start, an untainted life.

I'm told I was a beautiful baby. Seven pounds, seven ounces, twenty-one inches long with a full head of hair. I arrived via emergency cesarean, thirteen days late. I came out smiling, my mom smiling back at me, her eyes shining from tears and anesthesia and happy anticipation. She said it was the greatest joy she had ever felt. She told me that day, seeing me for the first time, she was certain that she would be better, that she would find a way to be happy. The name Theresa means to harvest, to reap the rewards of hard work. My mom, she was the gardener and I was the crop. Even before I was born, she put her faith in the power of sweat. She believed that if she gave enough effort, if she paid enough attention, her daughter would grow and flourish. My mom trusted in the end, that with time, she would harvest the good that she had planted.

From kindergarten through the twelfth grade they sent me to Punahou, the best private school on Oahu. I was a lifer, a rarity—one of the wealthy kids whose parents got them into Punahou early.

I've come to realize that school in Hawaii functions differently from many other places. Private schools here are for education, solely and out of necessity. It doesn't take a mastermind to look at the public schools and understand that the way to get an island kid into college is through the golden gates of Punahou, but it does take money, thirteen years of it—an amount that could send four kids to college.

Even as kids, we talked about it. We knew our school looked nothing like the ones down the street with the rusty chain-link fences and the sad sprinkling of brown grass, the tetherball poles with just a rope, the basketball hoops with no net. We wore uniforms. We went to services in a chapel lit by stained-glass windows. We had a carnival with games and malasadas with mango chutney and hula with live music and a man who juggled fire.

When parents got divorced or a dad lost his job, I watched my classmates leave for public schools closer to their dad's new condo on the windward side, in the country. It was normal, it happened every year, but not once did I fear this would happen to me. And it wasn't because Maku was a teacher at my school. My parents were planners; I understood that early on. Breakfast was prepared the night before, cereal and a banana lay beside my empty bowl, set on the table with a napkin and a spoon. Scraps of paper with lists of groceries and chores and errands littered every surface of our house, emptied from every pocket when we did laundry. And laundry was done twice a week: clothes on Wednesdays, towels and linens on Sundays. The idea of divorce, it never crossed my mind. For a divorce there had to be fighting, there had to be a degree of spontaneity, and in my house I felt a calm assurance that our days would be the same, even certainty. Our lives would run on schedule. My parents planned for thirteen years of Punahou, the best education they could buy—and barring some unforeseeable disaster, I knew it would unfold exactly as they planned.

My mom kept her job as a seamstress. From kindergarten through the fifth grade she would make my clothes by hand, taking my measurements, letting me choose my own fabrics and patterns, shortening hems and adding sleeves on demand. I thought about our time together all during my days at school; I couldn't wait to see my mom in the parking lot, to decide what we would make that night, what we would eat, what we would listen to. I sailed into her arms, actually running to her, my classmates lingering in the hallways, my excitement to see her never diminished. My mom dazzled me with her ability to make anything I wanted; anything I saw in a window or a magazine was mine after a short trip to the fabric store, my favorite place, the bolts of cloth calling out to me with such ambition, my faith planted firmly in my mother's able fingers.

Then, at home, her foot on the tan petal, the steady pump of her heel, the whir of her machine—that sound, that even hum of my mother's diligence, it's all colored differently now. She kept the clothes. She never told me but I found them, unlabeled, as if it were shameful that she preserve the proof. My mom and I, there was a time when we were everything.

All through lower school, for five years, twenty seasons, we had matching outfits. Cotton *mu'u mu'us* with crocheted collars, bright floral holokus, papaya-colored shifts, an absurd creation of velvet and floral fashioned into overalls. We spent a hundred weekends sitting together in her sewing room, listening to the radio and eating kaki-mochi rice crackers with nori and sesame, with sour, powdery li hing plum, each other's only friend. With the exception of my Auntie B, my mom had no friends, and for the longest time it seemed perfectly normal because neither did I. I wonder now if she intentionally kept me for herself—if that's how desperately she needed a companion. But it's not true. We fed off each other, needing each other in the same way, for protection and validation and understanding. I was an awkward child, if not innately then because I was poorly socialized. I talked only of chain stitches and slip stiches and buttonholes, and when the kids at school looked at me with bewilderment, I would try to explain in detail. They teased me, and after a while I began to break. The words of others, the judgments of girls wearing clothes with tags, with labels and zippers with logos that you couldn't buy in fabric shops—without warning, they began to put cracks in my world.

I turned twelve and it became abundantly clear that no one else at school wore handmade dresses that matched their mom's. My mom stood in the parking lot that day after school and I stormed past her, infuriated, humiliated by her teal dress, my own in a trash can, ripped at the neckline where I tore it from my body, hysterical. I was furious, betrayed that she had allowed me to be taunted until I found myself in the nurse's office, tears and mucus running down my face, begging for a set of gym clothes. It was the first time I had ever been mad at her and it was dizzying, nauseating to the point of panic. I felt out of control, blindsided by the collision of my two worlds. The popular girls, their questions came at me from nowhere; they struck me like pellets, rapid fire, relentless and hard. For seven years we'd been going to school together. Their moms knew my name and they knew my mom's—I'd been to one of their birthday parties, had swum in one of their pools. That day they sat at my lunch table, smiling, two other classmates sitting with me. It caught me entirely off guard.

Theresa. Does your mom really make all of your clothes?

Yes.

Really? Even your underwear? Can we see?

No!

Are you even allowed to buy normal clothes?

Yes. I mean, I think so.

They asked their questions, six more, eight more, question after question—it startles me now that I answered them all, not knowing what else to do, not knowing how to lie or even omit. They probed me until I was entirely rattled, bruised from their jabs, pushing myself from the table as I felt the tears. My name, the laughter, the blur of the hallway as I tore past the older kids, the bright doorways streaking by my vision, colors running down my face.

My mom, she felt terrible. I know she did because immediately she backed down. I demanded that we go to Liberty House and buy new clothes and my mom reluctantly agreed, paying three times as much for the brand-name, factory-made crap that everyone else was wearing. I threw a tantrum in the dressing room when she told me she could easily make all these clothes. I called her poor. I told her she came from the country and she would never understand me. I told her it was her fault that I had no friends. She was selfish. She was weird. I said some horrible things and I remember them all, because they hurt me as I said them. I didn't know if it was true. I didn't know if she was the reason I hated myself that day but she was all I had and I knew that no matter how out of line I was, how cruel, she would never look at me the way those girls had. I took pleasure in that fact; I purged myself within her safety.

Walking through the racks of synthetic materials and stamped-out patterns, grabbing at anything with a price tag larger than I knew was reasonable, this is the moment I point to when I think of what went wrong—with me, with my mom and me both. That day, I asked to be homogenized. I begged her to let me be like everyone else, to help me erase the beautiful peculiarities that knitted me close to her—and she didn't fight me. She couldn't. She could never say no and I knew it well.

Things changed after that; I changed. I wanted friends. All I could think about was how to be liked, how to be envied, how to never, *ever* feel that searing nausea of humiliation. The day I wore the teal dress, I heard my family's name in a way I never had before. *Are you really a Leong? So why does your mom make your clothes? Aren't you rich? Aren't you from Diamond Head?* The popular girls said it like they'd been wondering for a while, like tiny grown-ups lording a secret over me, their question loaded with such intention. It made me feel at once exposed and protected by my last name. It was my first glimpse of what made me important and interesting and in that instant, heat arriving at every inch of flesh, I considered the spread of my family. I thought of the strange ritual we performed each year, driving from Maku's side to my mom's, from Diamond Head to Kaneohe, a day unlike any other of the year, a stretch of hours where my parents had parents and we

were Chinese and I had a family so large, so mismatched and con-
trary that never once had I seen them together.

I thought of my uncle's house in Diamond Head and, even at
twelve years old, I began to understand that there was something
very strange about my family. That there were things meant to be
held up to the attention of the world, things to be admired from the
outside, and things that were better left in the darkness, in the safety
of my mother's sewing room. But at twelve years old, without the
knowledge of my family's history, I had the two entirely confused.

As the day approached, I could feel it coming. A week before, my
mom fluttered around the house, her hands busier than normal, the
house immaculate, everything she sewed some variation of red. The
three of us, we got our hair cut. We got new toothbrushes, new towels, new socks.

We woke up early on the eve of the New Year. Downtown, in the
shops of Chinatown, we filled white paper boxes with flat, brown
rice cakes cut into shimmering squares that jiggled when shook. We
picked the fattest mandarin oranges from a heaping pile, holding
them in our hand, one by one, to check for a good weight. The flower
shop, where Maku spoke Chinese to the old lady with long, wrinkled
fingers, arranged plum blossoms and narcissus into a silvery bouquet,
the whites of the petals lit up by specks of crimson and apricot.

Each year my mom complained how difficult it was to find gifts
for Maku's family. All the delicacies they sold in Chinatown, Hong
already made by hand. The red paper lanterns that cluttered the
shop doorways, my Uncle Kaipo made new ones each year, except
his were made of fabric, of silk with gold characters painted on the
front. These things—the items made from paper and glue and plastic
confetti and bits of string—we bought for my mom's family, for my
Grandpa and Grandma Chan. These things my mom bought without
ceremony, without checking for quality or weight or blemishes. We
barely saw her buy them, scooping up a handful of red envelopes or

noisemakers from a bin and paying quickly, never asking our opinion. These things went into a separate bag.

After I turned twelve, Chinese New Year was the only time I allowed my mom to make my clothes. I understood how important it was to her, how hard she worked on each of our outfits, how complicated her patterns were, how fussy the material: a dark crimson shirt for Maku with thin strands of silver running vertically through the silk, a steamed collar, buttons made of koa; a ruby dress for me with a short skirt, pleated generously, full from the waist with a thick gold zipper that ran up the back; a sheath for my mom, long and thin with a slit up the side, a deep shade of scarlet. In our house, as we stood before the mirror, a trio of red shimmering in our extravagance, we looked ridiculous, the backdrop of our house entirely unsuitable. But I knew that as soon as we crossed through the gates in Diamond Head, our clothes, polished and slippery, would help ease us into an evening that seemed to drop from another world entirely.

The year I stopped wearing my mother's clothes, I counted down the days to my uncle's party, my plan fully formed. There would be a triumphant end to the sixth grade. I would gather details that I never thought to remember, things that never seemed important until that year. We were rich, I was sure of it but I needed evidence. The house in Diamond Head looked different every year, which made it almost impossible for me to explain it to the girls at school. I sounded like a fraud: one year there were dark wooden horses lined up along the garden path, another year there were snakes with neon-colored scales, fuchsia and teal, rising from the ponds, which were lit from below. I felt so stupid when my mom explained to me later. They were the signs of the zodiac, matched with the year's element. Horse and wood. Snake and water. We'd learned these things in school; if only I'd put it together before that day in the cafeteria, they might have believed me. Had the universe tilted in my favor that day, perhaps I would not have wasted the following years searching for my in, trying to make up for it.

As we drove through the giant iron gate, I thought about how passing through that gate felt like being swallowed by the volcano, how it wrapped around everything and, once the gates closed, how there was no seeing out.

The Eve of the New Year, we learned at school that we were supposed to eat a fish. We saw pictures of Chinese families from around the world gathered before a steamed fish, a simple table of dumplings and rice wine. Perhaps there was a melon carved into a bowl, but nothing in those pictures compared to the five-foot lanterns that lit my uncle's garden, shaped like monkeys, the towering candles flaring from their open mouths, their gaping eyes. Sleek red canopies dipped above us; they caught the candlelight and reflected it back down against the dark depth of the ponds. Between the canopies I looked up to see the ridges of the crater, the walls that surrounded us, powdered gold in a silhouette of flames. The effect was immediate. We were within a pit of fire and as light touched the golden surface, it blazed. Music poured from speakers I couldn't find and my Uncle Kaipo's voice called out above it, yelling my father's name, then my mom's, and finally mine.

"Every year, I always think you'll cancel on me, Bohai, but here you are! And I couldn't be happier to see you."

"You've really outdone yourself this year," Maku said, hugging my uncle. "I barely recognize the place."

"Well, you wouldn't, would you? You never come to visit!"

My Uncle Kaipo hugged my mom and leaned down to hug me.

"I'm sorry I still don't have kids," he joked, always trying with me, but it was never natural, articulating slowly, overly animated. "Not a lot of kids here—still, Hong is excited to see you."

Every year, it was all adults: men dressed in tuxedos with women on their arms, the backs of their red dresses slit entirely open, thin flutes of champagne balanced between fingers. But unlike the years before, I didn't care.

"Where's your mom?" My mom smoothed her dress.

"In the back," my uncle said, pointing, "in the sunroom. I think she likes the gold flames, because she's been looking at them all day." He grinned and my uncle was so handsome, so unlike Maku. I remember the thought frustrating me.

"It's great to see you, Kaipo." Maku patted him on the back. "We'll just get a drink inside and say hi to Mom, then."

My NaiNai, I thought. She never said a thing to me; she responded only to my mom. Every year my mom would say my name, slowly, as if introducing us for the first time. Some years my NaiNai looked at me, looked me clear in the eye and said nothing, while other years it was as if she couldn't hear a thing, couldn't see me right in front of her. That year, I tried to stay with her for as long as I possibly could but there was something in her face that I couldn't take. Simply glancing at her features, the quiet trauma that seized her, made her presence unbearable to me. I said my hello and I left.

Thankfully, Hong appeared, as she always did, sensing my discomfort through the walls and the noise. She swept in and kneeled, hugging me first, always me first, even when I got older and she no longer needed to kneel. Hong was the only one who felt like a relative, how I imagined a relative should feel. An aunt who you see just once a year, someone you hardly know but who is so pleased by the sight of you. Who knows what it is you need as soon as you need it, who senses the exact moment that you need saving, whisking you into the kitchen to wrap dumplings, to fill the boxes of sweetmeats.

The counters would be lined end to end with rectangular silver platters covered in fish, adorned with flowers and fruit and sprigs of green and lavender. The smells of chili oil and vinegar, they returned to me. The lofted windows of the kitchen, the copper pots hanging above the stove, the abundance of clean, polished space, of a dozen men dressed identically rushing in and out, replacing their empty trays with new ones, and Hong, pulling out the bags of dried lotus root and coconut, melon seeds and carrots for me to distribute among the porcelain boxes—dozens of them, one for every guest.

At midnight a gong sounded, thunderous and sudden, and we rushed together to the backyard to find the adults crowded together, looking up to the sky. My mom and Maku were in the back drinking, their cheeks flushed even in the dark, my NaiNai in a chair beside them. From above, from the golden ridges that surrounded us, missiles of color shot into the night sky, crackling and popping as the adults shouted, raising their glasses, cheering for a happy new year.

The next morning, we slept in. When we woke, we dressed in our normal clothes, the regular things we wore to work and school, and my mom grabbed the plastic bag she filled in Chinatown and we drove to Kaneohe. We went to see her family.

Back then, I knew just one thing about my mom's childhood. The house we visited each year, the tiny whitewashed home with rust stains along the bottom panels where the wood met the dirt—it was different when my mom was younger. She grew up in the basement, the space below that I'd never seen, but now her parents lived on the top floor, the ground floor. The year my parents got married, my grandparents bought the whole house.

The front yard was cluttered with people—*my cousins*, my mom called them without ever explaining how we were related. I was exhausted that day. I had no interest in going to Kaneohe. I complained when I woke up, told my parents that I was sick, but I was dragged anyway.

The sprinklers were on and my cousins ran through it, shirtless, even some of the girls, red dirt molded to their feet, plastic hula hoops left in their wake, half-eaten plates of food littering the ground. Smoke from a barbeque drifted sideways, into my Grandma and Grandpa Chan, who sat in folding chairs, their arms crossed across their chest.

"Is that who I think it is?" my grandma called out to me, lifting a hand to shade her eyes. "Is that my Theresa?" She stood from her chair as we approached. I waited for her to tell me how big I'd gotten, and she did.

"It must have been some party last night! I think we could see the fireworks from here. Did Kaipo tell you that we ran into him last month? I thought he might invite us but it's okay. We're old folks now. Too old for a party. Nothing to wear."

"Hi, Mom." My mom, she did this with my grandparents. She didn't answer their questions. She said something else. "There's lisee for the kids." She handed her the plastic bag. "Gung Hee Fat Choi."

"I hope you didn't wear this last night! You know, you can dress up a little when you come here, too. No, you look great. I'm just joking. I saw a blouse just like that at Sears."

"Is B already here?"

"Inside."

My Auntie B had six kids. She forced them to play with me, to include me every year. She said it like that, too. Play with Theresa. Include Theresa. It never bothered me until that year. In fact, I remember enjoying their company, poking sticks into the muddy stream, chasing the wild pigs that ran through the back fields, stealing sips of their parents' warm, leftover beers. But that year I took my auntie's orders as an insult, an assumption that I had no friends, and so I tried to impress my cousins with tales from Diamond Head and they hated me after that. I understand why now. I can hear my twelve-year-old voice saying *silver platters* and *golden flames* and *servants*. When they found out I got pregnant, when they heard there was no boyfriend, I'm sure they all felt some degree of satisfaction. The irony is that those stories, about how we used to light bottle rockets and explode them into the neighbors' bushes, how they set chicken traps and hog traps and picked up chameleons by their slithering tails, watching their bodies detach and run—at a place like Punahou, these were the stories that could have defined me.

My Grandpa Chan, he avoided me like I avoided my NaiNai. A pat on the back, a *Good girl, Theresa*, that was about all I ever got from him. I understood his relationship with my mom was strained. There was something he wanted from her and Maku, a list of contacts, something my Ye Ye had promised him before he died. My grandpa wanted their names. He wanted to take their photographs and it seemed my parents didn't want him to.

We ate on our laps, all of us sitting on folding chairs with woven nylon seats. Huli huli chicken, macaroni salad, chicken long rice. It was hot and greasy and spilled between the compartments of my plastic plate. Chicken bones were thrown to the floor, for the dogs who weaved between our legs, sniffing us, waiting for more.

We left before the sun went down, and in the car, my mom released her air as if she were a balloon, slowly deflating, sinking into her seat until she'd emptied her lungs.

"Once a year," my mom whispered to Maku.

"Once a year," he repeated.

My plan worked slowly. Little by little, over the next year, I made my way into the circle of girls who had made me cry. I learned to talk like them, how to talk about others and how to talk about myself. I established myself as a Leong, the only heir to a fortune I knew nothing about. It was assumed that I was wildly, unfathomably rich. I made excuses for Maku's unremarkable appearance. I said he dressed like that only at school, that he had to at least pretend to be a regular teacher. Our family's name, it held so much weight, it seemed preposterous that we'd worry about money, but our reality was very different.

Every cent from Maku's time working for my Ye Ye, from the sale of his house to my Uncle Kaipo, my parents saved in a high-interest bank account, sustaining themselves, their needs, their wants, with their two modest paychecks. All the presents for my mom, all the dinners on the marina, Maku saved for them. Every bottle of wine, every plane ticket, every single bird of paradise came from hours in the classroom teaching seventh-grade math. The money accumulating in the bank account, it was all for me. Private school, summer vacations, hula classes, a bike, a car, anything I could think to ask for. For years, it seems, they had been saving, planning, waiting to say yes.

When I got to high school, I began to get glimpses into my family's history. It wasn't through my parents, who continued to tell me almost nothing, repeating their vague explanations, coming to each other's rescue when I began to ask questions. They told me my Grandpa Chan was a drunk, my Grandma Chan an enabler, my Uncle Kaipo too busy to be bothered with us. They knew I was scared of my NaiNai so they made no excuses for her, but the general consensus in our house was that we were better off without them. Still, I couldn't help but notice it was my Uncle Kaipo who called Maku to have dinner with him every month, who came to the house to pick him up, who seemed happy to see me when I answered the door. It was a collective effort, the way my parents avoided their families, how they kept me away from both Diamond Head and Kaneohe. And somehow, it worked. For the better part of my teenage years, I grew up thinking it was normal, sharing an island with relatives I saw just once a year.

It was through my friends and their parents, their chatter, their rumors, that my parents' smoke screen finally broke. The effect was overwhelming, changing me overnight. I couldn't believe how important we were, how famous. My Ye Ye built this city; charities were named after my NaiNai; my Uncle Kaipo was considered the most eligible bachelor in all of Oahu. I became a nightmare, a mean kid, but I was popular. I threw my Ye Ye's name around like I knew him, as if I'd met him, as if he hadn't died before I was born.

But my mom soldiered on, not letting my bad attitude get in the way of her plans for me. Until recently, her objective was staunch, unwavering: to stay close to me, to remain in my inner circle as I grew into a teenager, to always keep the door between us open, the conversation flowing. She refused to tell me what to do, how to feel, who to like. She wanted me to blossom on my own, never steering me in any one direction, never projecting her own failed goals onto me—

I see that now. She took pleasure in the possibilities she was able to offer, never pushing one in front of another, simply happy that she had made this happen. I was popular. I was happy. She had given her daughter a better life, and it seemed that was enough.

Every summer we vacationed on Maui, at a small beach house in Lahaina where I had my own room. I was allowed to bring friends, as many as I wanted. Maku would grill steaks on his hibachi and drive us to shave ice, handing us the car keys as we got older. We trailed sand through the house and left our dishes on the table, our towels on the floor. My mom, she never said a thing. She'd sweep behind us, clear the table, wash the towels. Put the dishes away, she'd ask, and I'd tell her I'd do it later. But later, it was already done.

My parents shielded me from anything difficult, either purchasing the solution or sweeping in and smoothing it out, fixing it themselves. I remember in the ninth grade, when the popular girls had Pan Am bags to carry their schoolbooks, my mom drove me to the airport and bought me one, at what expense I can only imagine. I remember hearing her talk with the airline director, telling him that she was not flying that afternoon but if he would check the flight records, he would see that the Leongs flew Pan America frequently, first class, worth at least a dozen of the bags she was willing to pay for.

I don't remember saying thank you. I don't remember being grateful. How my mom allowed this, how she continued to give for as long as she did, for me that's the biggest mystery of parenthood. Does it happen innately, this kind of stubborn, reckless love for a child? Will I be capable of loving my child, of loving anyone this way? And why—between the two of us, he so much worthier than I—why could she never find this love for Maku?

Fortunately for everyone, things got better my junior year, when I got an accidental A on a test and discovered that Maku had passed something on to me—I was good at math. It was those last two years, before I got pregnant that I began to change. It occurred to me for the first time in my life that I might be good at something. Numbers came effortlessly: learn the equation, solve the problem. And that's exactly what I did, collecting As and small glimpses of myself, my real self, along the way.

Maku was my biggest supporter, his own numerical mind trying to light the fire in mine. He would write unfinished equations on a note card and leave them on my door, slip them into my locker at school, challenging me to solve them. They got more and more difficult, moving from simple algebra to more complicated statistics and probability—my favorite numbers game. He tried so hard to make his questions relevant to my life, to make math fun.

You drive to Sandy Beach and there are thirty cars in the parking lot. Ten are Fords, twelve are Chryslers, and eight are Cadillacs (the Series 62 that you like). If the Fords are three times as likely to leave as the others, find the probability of a Chrysler leaving first.

He was funny like that, always trying to trick me into learning, not pestering me to finish his problems, but waiting patiently until the card showed up under his door or on his desk at school. But it wasn't Maku I was doing it for. I wanted it on my own. It was the first time in my life that my mind was being used for something that wasn't stupid. I joined the Math Club that spring, lying to my friends and telling them I was at my hula *halau*.

There was a certain understanding between me and the rest of the math nerds that I did not belong there. This was their time to be free from kids like me—the kids they'd known for years, who'd been taunting them since middle school. They assumed I was there because of Maku, and I was fine with that. It was funny, sneaking around to draw bell curves and find their standard deviations, the only kid in the room wearing designer clothes. But soon enough, they warmed up to me, realizing that I was for real—that I could outscore them all on the math SATs. They respected me, not for my name but for my mind, and I'll admit, it felt damn good.

I felt something that spring that I haven't felt since, a feeling that I fear now happens only once in a lifetime. That spring, I felt the world beginning to open up to me; I felt the weight of my life about to begin and the endless, boundless possibilities that lay ahead. I think of myself in the math room, serious and competent, and I know I might never forgive myself for what happened next.

My senior year at Punahou was a whirlwind. I was voted Prom Queen, I scored high enough on my SATs to get a full ride to the University of Hawaii. I think even my parents' relationship improved that year—their spoiled daughter finally showing some real potential.

The summer before I started college, my parents sent me to Europe for a month with a girlfriend, paid for us both. We were supposed to see three countries, but I couldn't tear myself from Italy. The architecture took hold of me as soon as I stepped off the plane in Rome. Everything seemed to be a math game; the symmetry of the cathedrals, the proportions of the columns, the geometry of the city. I sat on a bench in Pisa for three hours, staring at the leaning tower with a notepad and pencil, copying numbers from my guidebook and scribbling ratios, trying to get it to make sense. Italy was—is still—the oldest place I have ever been, and its history made me stop and think about things that had never before crossed my mind. Like how hundreds of years before I was born, when Hawaii was barely on a map, Italy was doing math. They were doing math and constructing perfect buildings that would teeter for a thousand years but never fall. When Captain Cook stumbled upon the Big Island in 1778, the Romans had already built Saint Peter's Basilica—*twice*. And as I stopped to consider these foreign things, I was introduced to yet another unfamiliar sentiment: insignificance. No one in Italy gave a shit that my Ye Ye shipped things from China to Hawaii three decades ago, no one cared that my family's name appeared periodically in the *Honolulu Star-Bulletin*. Looking back, I wish that I could live that moment over and over, adjusting my narrow perspective of the world until I got it right—until something really stuck. But the weeks flew by and the moment would only last for so long, giving me what I thought would be enough inspiration to be better, to remove myself from the axis of the universe and learn some basic humility. When my month was up, I found I was ready to go home. Not because I wanted to leave Italy, but because I was ready to start my own career—to construct my own perfect buildings. And I was confident that I would return; I threw a thousand lire into the Trevi Fountain.

I'd be lying if I said that college was easy for me. Math was easy, college was not. I wasn't popular in college. No one knew who I was; no one thought I was smart. I was good at math but other than that, I was just like everyone else. It wasn't like Punahou. I was no longer a faculty daughter; no one took a special interest in me like before. I studied hard—I really did, but there's something about living on an island that shrinks your perspective. I still believe that, having only been abroad once. *Everything you need is here—why leave?* It's easy to imagine an island as the entire world, not able to get in your car and drive for miles in any direction just to see what's at the end. There's a certain doubt that begins to creep into your mind: *why leave, why search for something else when paradise is home?* You begin to associate the mainland with isolation and loneliness, and your island with comfort and stability, beauty and fortune. So the memories of Italy faded as I fell back into my old patterns. I wanted a boyfriend. I wanted to bitch about the workload at school, to call my teachers unfair and their grading practices biased. My perspective shrunk and shrunk until there was little left. Until I was back to the old me—to the island girl who wanted nothing more in life than to be an object of petty jealousy.

By the time spring came around last year, my grades had already dropped. They weren't terrible—I could have still turned it around. It would have taken a final push, a week of studying to ace my finals, but I wasn't willing to do it. I wanted a break and there was a dance—

some annual party that the university put on that took all my attention, all my efforts. For weeks, as my books remained in their Pan Am bag, as I dragged their idle heft from class to class, I could think of nothing else but that goddamned dance.

I didn't have a date. Despite my attempts at popularity, no one had asked me and all the good choices were quickly pairing off, waiting for each other in the hallways, their coy smiles driving me slowly insane. I begged my friend to introduce me to her brother who was home from college in California. His name was Roy. He was twenty-one with a car of his own, she told me, and when he agreed to the date I was beside myself, my delirium larger than ever. I became obsessed with the idea of an older man, a stranger. He had gone to Iolani, Punahou's rival school, and after twelve years of seeing the same kids, the same faces, I reveled in the idea that we had never met.

I went immediately to buy a dress. My mom asked to come and she said she would pay, which I knew was an offering; she would not ask to make it. I spotted the dress right away, on a mannequin in the Liberty House window. Short and black, the straps as thin as the stroke of a pen, it was closer to a negligée than something fit for spring. But I wanted something I could look sexy in, experienced, and my mom didn't seem to mind. She paid for it without complaint. She hadn't gotten my grades yet.

The night of the dance, Roy picked me up in a Cadillac Series 62 and I almost fainted. He was exactly who I wanted to take me to the dance—exactly who I'd been dreaming of as my mind wandered in class. Roy was slim and muscular, his black hair thick and wavy. His teeth were perfectly white, his skin golden. I swear to God his eyes sparkled. He met Maku and my mom, shaking their hands and thanking them for letting him take their daughter to the dance. He spoke to them with authority, a head taller than them both; he made Maku laugh, asked him if he could pull some strings and get him into Punahou. My mom smiled approvingly—told him how handsome he was.

Roy opened the car door for me and I slid in, instantly encased in soft black leather. The underside of my thighs sank luxuriously into the seat and I felt suddenly sexy, intoxicatingly glamorous. Maku had a station wagon, a Chevy Corvair in olive green, the most practical car in the most practical color.

"So you like the car, huh?" Roy asked, raising an eyebrow, starting the ignition.

"Is it that obvious?" I giggled, nodding my head, my smile entirely out of control. I was so far gone, clinging to a single thought, hell-bent in my determination. I would not screw this up, I warned myself. I would be everything he hoped I would be, every bit as dazzling as my family's name, as sensational as the prom queen he was promised. At the very least, the bare minimum, Roy would feel the same desire I felt for him.

Roy drove fast, the muscles in his wrist contracting as he shifted gears, revving his engine at each new green light. He cast sideways glances at me, his muscular neck, his square jawline protruding from the collar of his shirt, crisp and white. It was simple, getting him to want me. In that dress, my mouth painted a scarlet red, my eyes emboldened by dark, smoky liner—I was a flawless version of myself, I saw it in his stare. He looked at me in a way that no man had before, like I was a perfect, delicious object, his glassy eyes penetrating me, causing me to look away. My smile turned to pride, to vanity, to shameless delight. I remember thinking how easy it was, how powerful I felt, as if being beautiful that night could mitigate my grades, my self-esteem, my hardening reality.

When we arrived at the dance, once again, Roy walked around the car and opened my door, whistling as I stepped out into the parking lot.

"Let me look at you," he said, and I relished in his stare. He took my hand and spun me around in my heels. I couldn't get enough. My entire body felt lit up, rapt with excitement, filled with expectation. He put his hand against the small of my back and led me into the ballroom, his fingers pressing through the silk, the heat of his touch reaching to my skin.

Everyone—I mean *everyone* was at this dance. I recognized so many faces of pretty girls I'd seen around campus and they were all looking at me—or rightfully, at my date. He was gorgeous, that was obvious, but these girls seemed to *know* him.

"Hi, Roy," they'd whisper as they passed him, completely ignoring me. "What's it like in California?"

"A lot of blondes," he would reply, "I like it much better here." Then he would wrap his arm tightly around my waist and smile. The girls would throw out a phony laugh and walk away. I could have died happily right there, could have drowned in the glow of my spotlight.

I asked for a drink, which Roy gladly retrieved for me. The more jealous stares I received, the more I drank, the happier I became, the closer I let myself get to Roy, the more convinced I became that this would be the greatest night of my life. I was not used to drinking and the vodka hit me hard. My head blurred and suddenly, all I could do was follow Roy around and smile, clink my glass against his and move to the music when he wanted to dance. When the last song had played, Roy took my hand and led me from the ballroom and through the parking lot. He opened his car door and I got in. It felt so good to sit down. I remember taking off my shoes, rubbing my feet together where they felt sore. I was sure he was going to drive me home. He headed in the direction of my house, toward the marina, but he stopped short, pulling into the small lot that overlooked the inlet. He turned off the engine.

"What are we doing here?" I asked, letting my body sink into the seat. I had seen this view a million times, but that night it was spectacular. The water was still, all the boats tied up to their docks, their tops covered as if tucked in for the night. Light from a handful of houses, those still awake, reflected faintly against the perfect calm. In the distance, Koko Head rose beyond the water, its rugged silhouette a shade darker than the midnight sky.

"I love this spot," he replied, turning the radio on, adjusting it until he settled on a song. "Sometimes I come here and think. It really clears your head." It was Skeeter Davis, I remember thinking. "The End of the World."

I remember hearing the song, wishing that my head were clear. I wanted to enjoy the moment, there with Roy, but I was having trouble holding on to any single thought, my eyelids heavy with liquor and exhaustion. Skeeter Davis's voice, its sweet nasal pitch, I felt it in my veins. I knew I had drunk too much and this might just be the end of it and then, all of a sudden, Roy leaned over the divide and kissed me.

All I could feel were sensations of hot and cold. His lips against mine were warm, breathing hot air into my mouth as they parted and closed. His hands on my bare thighs were cold, slowly warming as they moved up and down. He raised my arms and my dress came off; cold, so cold until his entire body came over the divide to warm me up; hot. He pulled my underwear down. I let him. He kissed my neck. The leather under me was becoming so hot under the weight of two bodies. I wanted more cold. And then I felt him, the pain of my first time subdued by the vodka tumbling in my body. I lay there frozen, trying to relax myself so I could try to enjoy what I knew was happening. My hands clutched the soft leather of the underside of the seat. He breathed into my ear. He was panting, harder and harder until I heard him release. I barely registered that it was over. The weight of his body collapsed on me, his skin sticky with sweat.

I fell asleep. He re-dressed me and drove me home, kissing me on the forehead when we reached my driveway.

"You fell asleep, princess. You're home. Do you want me to get you some water?"

I looked up at him and barely recognized the face that was looking back at me. I needed to leave; I needed to be alone.

"No, no," I replied. "I'll be okay. Good night," I said, stepping out of the car, feeling empty, disgusting.

"I'll call you," he said as he pulled out of the driveway. I didn't reply.

I unlocked the front door and walked straight to my bathroom, clutching at the walls of the hallway. I caught my reflection in the mirror and froze, leaned in closer to study myself, to make sure it was real. Black eyeliner spread beneath my eyes like oil spills, dragging them down, making their redness so much more shocking. My lipstick, my perfect mouth, was gone except for a chapped ring that clung to the outline. I touched my hair, the strands that had come undone matted to my temples, when I felt him drip from between my legs. I collapsed on the toilet. And I cried. I took a shower and scrubbed my body raw. I hated him. I hated myself.

Roy called a couple of times over the next few weeks but I ignored his messages. My mom couldn't understand why I would reject such a handsome boy with such good manners. I couldn't explain it to her. I told her he was an idiot.

I spent three weeks locked in my house trying to forgive myself for what I had done, for my own stupidity. I had trouble sleeping; every time I closed my eyes, I felt the weight of his body on mine and I couldn't breathe. I stopped seeing my college friends, all of them wanting to know how it turned out with Roy. I hated Roy—I couldn't believe that there were men out there who would do that. I couldn't forgive him. I couldn't forgive myself. I needed to wash him from my life and my mind, which is exactly what I set out to do.

But five weeks passed and my period never came. On Tuesday of week six, I ran to the bathroom and threw my head over the toilet, panicking as I clutched my nauseated stomach. I choked into the water. It wasn't possible, I told myself; I was *nineteen*, only nineteen. These things, they just didn't happen on the first time. It took years for people to have a baby, a hundred tries without a single pregnancy. I raised my head and breathed, the acidity of my own vomit burning at my throat. My fingers, clamped down on the edge of the bowl, began to shake as the tears came. There was no way, I fought myself, no god that would allow this.

There was a knock on the door, followed by my mom's voice.

"Theresa, my God. Are you all right?"

I looked at her as she walked into the bathroom. I saw her concern, her obliviousness, and I closed my eyes, returned my head to the toilet and breathed. I counted to five and then to three.

"I could hear you from the kitchen," she said. "What's the matter? I didn't know you were sick."

She kneeled and put her hand on my back. Almost immediately, I gave in to her touch. I crumbled into her lap and let my tears fall down her legs. I couldn't stop crying. I needed to tell someone, but not her. I couldn't tell her.

"Did you eat something bad?" She ran her hand down my back, stroking my heaving body, trying to relax me. "It's okay. Just tell me what's wrong."

I couldn't hold it in any longer. If not my mom, then who would I tell? Maku? The idea of telling Maku I was pregnant—I couldn't finish the thought. I reached up for the toilet and puked again.

"*Theresa*, tell me," she begged, her hand still stroking my back.

I took a deep breath and raised my body up to meet her gaze. I wiped my mouth with my palm.

"Mom," I whispered. "Please don't hate me."

"Hate you, why would I—"

"I think I'm pregnant."

My mom's hand stopped. Her body stiffened as she pushed back to sturdy herself against the bathroom wall.

"Well, that's ridiculous," she stammered. "How could you possibly be pregnant? You don't have a boyfriend, you haven't been out of the house in we—" And then she paused, as if the answer had hit her right at that very moment, mid-sentence. "Ohmygod," she whispered.

"Mom." I whimpered, moving toward her. "I'm so sorry. I'm so, so sorry."

I reached out my hand but she pressed her back firmly against the wall, eyes narrowed. She looked as pale as I felt.

"You're *sorry?*" she said, her voice turning icy. She began to laugh, tears falling from her eyes. She reached her hands behind her and grabbed the wall, lifting her body from the floor, her arms shaking softly.

"Oh, Theresa." She laughed again, high-pitched, frantic. "Sorry doesn't even begin to describe what you're going to feel. Sorry is for children who can correct their mistakes, but *this. This* you will live with for the rest of your life! You'll understand that sorry has nothing to do with it! *Damn it*, Theresa, I tried. I really did. I gave you everything I could—absolutely everything! And look what you've done."

She shook her head and left the room, shutting the door behind her, leaving me alone on the bathroom floor. I sat there in desperate silence; my tears refused to fall. I curled up on the bathroom rug and closed my eyes. I prayed, really prayed for the first time in my entire life. Let it be a mistake, I begged.

That was seven months ago.

My mom told Maku three days later, after a visit to the hospital confirmed it was true. For three days, we kept the secret from him, hoping that we would be wrong.

After she told him, they called me out to the living room, and the enormity of heartbreak on Maku's face, the way he looked at me, his eyes deeply burdened, the curve of his lips weighed down in defeat, it regularly keeps me from sleep.

He didn't say anything when I sat down, but I could feel his teeth clamped together, could feel the horrible tension in his jaw.

My mom was the only one who spoke.

"You've disappointed us both," she said. "You've disrespected us both."

I nodded. I thought, *and myself.*

"You must know by now that your decision carries serious consequences."

"I do," I said, and I thought I knew what she meant.

She paused to look at me, to really look at me. She shook her head, staring me straight on, as if to express her seriousness, her severity. As if to say, *I won't clean up after you, Theresa; not this time.* Seven months ago. That was the first time I saw this face.

"You want to be an adult, Theresa? You want to make adult decisions? Fine."

Fine? I thought. It was the last word I would use to describe what was happening. Fine was the opposite of what I saw on my parents' faces.

"You'll marry him," she said decisively, her eyes still held mine. "I've spoken to his mother and she agrees."

"What?" I exclaimed, rising in my chair.

"What?" my mom shot back. "You think you can raise this child without a father? Or did you think your father and I would raise it for you? Is that it? There are consequences, Theresa! You made the choice to do this—you made this choice!"

My mom's face was stricken, flushed with effort and anger. She meant what she said; the way she said it, it terrified me.

"Maku?" I pleaded, turning to him for the first time. "Maku, please, you can't think this is right. He's horrible—he forced himself on me, he forced me!"

"Enough!" he called out, raising his hand in the air. "Enough."

I went silent. There was so much discomfort obstructing our conversation, so many words that we weren't saying, words we had never said to each other before. We wouldn't say them, I knew we wouldn't. We weren't that kind of family. In our house, we spoke of math, we spoke of food.

"It doesn't matter what I think," Maku said. "I stand with your mother. You made your choice, Theresa, and you chose wrong. Now it's out of your hands."

"I can do it myself," I begged, looking to each of my parents. "I'll do it myself, I can do it; I know I can. Let me do it on my own, I can't—I can't marry him."

"It's not up for discussion, Theresa."

I looked to my mom and could barely believe it was her speaking, her voice saying these words, her face, stern and decisive. My mom, who had given me everything, then sat calmly through my tantrums when I told her it wasn't enough. *My mom*, who had entertained a thousand requests for designer clothes and tennis racquets and vacations around the world—who gave me full use of her car when I turned fifteen. I had crossed the line; it hit me suddenly. I had hurt her in a way that could not be undone.

"What did you tell Roy's mom?" I demanded, trying to send my fears elsewhere. "She didn't tell him, did she? Jesus, Mom—*did she tell him?*"

As humiliated as I felt, there was a desperate part of me that hoped she had told Roy. There was a part that hoped Roy was sitting in shame at that moment, in repentance, thinking about what a bastard he was, what a fucked-up thing he had done.

"I told her what happened, Theresa, and she's dealing with it just as we are. The best she can. She's a widow, did you know that? What am I saying, of course you didn't. She lost her husband two years ago. Roy is her oldest. She has four more, all girls."

"And I assume he knows," she added. "We want the wedding before you begin to show."

"This isn't happening," I breathed to myself. "This can't be happening."

"It'll be a small ceremony. We'll have it here, in the backyard. Nothing fancy."

"Mom, *please*."

"And we won't say a thing about this, Theresa," she said, eyes narrowed like a warning, a challenge to defy her again. "No one has to know about your condition."

"Jesus, Mom," I burst out. "My *condition*?"

"Your *condition*, your *situation*—I'm sorry, Theresa, I've never had a pregnant teenager before! How would you like me to say it?"

"Fine."

"Fine *what*, Theresa?"

"It's all fine with me!" I cried, standing from my chair, waving my arms furiously. I couldn't stop; I couldn't stop myself.

"Fine to marrying the bastard who stole my virginity while I was drunk—yes, that's right! He just did it, and I had no idea what was going on and I hate myself for it and now I guess you both can hate me too. *Fine* to spending the rest of my life with a stranger. *Fine* to giving up a real boyfriend, a real husband, so that I can be with *Roy*, the man I hate most in this entire world, the filthiest person I have ever met, who I met on the stupidest night of my life, which I think about *constantly. And the worst part?* Do you want to hear the worst part? I can barely remember that night. I can barely remember the moment that is destroying my entire life. You don't think I would take it back if I could? You don't think that I'm sorry? That I don't understand what I've done? I relive that night in my mind and I run from that car, I spend the rest of college alone, studying, being the woman we all want me to be, but I *can't*—don't you see that? I can't do anything about it because I'm pregnant and I'm getting married and everything is just fucking *fine*."

I stared at my parents, crying, panting, waiting for them to react. They would take it back, I told myself, they had to. They had to know how wrong this was, what a ridiculous, disgusting demand they were making.

But as hard as I stared, as hysterical as I looked, neither of them said a word. I know Maku wanted to, but he couldn't. All my life, Maku gave me whatever I wanted, with the exception of what my mom did not. She was always his first priority, forever his final word.

"Maku," I tried. "Please. What about red strings? What about my happiness—*my destined match*?" I pleaded frantically; the words came to me suddenly. "He's a knot, Maku; he's a mistake. You'll tie me to him for the rest of my life."

Our eyes connected, just for a moment before he looked away. He turned to my mom and shook his head.

And then he stood up and walked from the room.

The wedding was scheduled for the middle of June, giving us a month to prepare our home and our minds for what would come. My parents met with Roy's mother, Mrs. Lo, but I had yet to speak with Roy. He didn't call and I didn't want him to. The less I heard from him, the less I thought about him, the easier it was to pretend that the wedding wasn't happening. That perhaps my parents and Mrs. Lo had called it off, realizing the absurdity of forcing us together for the rest of our lives.

But with or without Roy, the wedding was being planned. During the first week, a case of white napkins arrived at our house, then a crate of champagne glasses and fifty folding chairs, stacked one on top of another on the lanai. During the second week, little red envelopes cluttered our mailbox, RSVPs from our fifty guests. I refused to check the mail. I knew if I did, those little cards would be thrown in the marina, eaten by the bottom-feeders, never to be found.

I was to wear my mom's wedding dress, the gold cheongsam she wore to her banquet. She never offered her ceremony dress, the white dress, and I didn't ask. White was for virgins, not teenage brides, pregnant and lying at a shotgun wedding. She didn't have to say it; I understood perfectly. Almost every day, my mom asked me to try on the cheongsam. It wouldn't fit, she said, we had to alter it before the wedding. But I refused that as well. I would wear the dress as it was, made for someone else. I had no interest in looking beautiful, not for Roy or for anyone else participating in the charade.

During the third week, my mom stopped asking. She stopped showing me forks and pictures of cakes, stopped insisting that I speak to Roy. At first, it was a relief, a small victory. She had finally realized that I would never be interested in the details of the wedding, that I couldn't give a shit if my shoes matched my dress, *her dress*. There was a distance that crept up on us, something quietly unsettling that I tried not to acknowledge. But then, slowly, its breadth reached past the wedding; my mom's remoteness, emotionally and physically, began to appear everywhere. There were no groceries, no clean laundry, no greetings or goodbyes—not even for Maku. That was the first alarm. When my mom was mad at me, she would withhold these favors for a day, maybe two, but never from Maku. Even during difficult times, for as long as I can remember, my mom was a wife, dutiful and considerate. If she didn't cook, there would be leftovers warming in the oven. If she was gone, there would be a note. But during the fourth week, as the wedding loomed just days ahead, I knew something had changed, something was wrong.

For three days, whenever Maku was away, my mom spent hours, literally hours locked in their bedroom. She would sneak in and out, locking her door for half an hour at a time, only to emerge and continue about her day until she disappeared again an hour later. For three days, Maku went to run errands, to jog, to grade exams at school, and my mom would disappear, lock herself in their room. Normally, I would have asked. It was a simple question, *what are you doing in there?* But in the last few weeks, everything about my mom and I had become complicated, difficult and strained. I no longer spoke to her voluntarily. When I responded, it was a yes or no. Casual questions, conversation, they had been eliminated from our relationship. I spent all my time in my room—but she didn't. My mom was not one to stay in her room; happy or sad, she was always busy, always doing something, and that locked bedroom door began to worry me.

Perhaps even stranger, when Maku was home, my mom would be gone. She'd go shopping for new clothes. She'd come back with her hair cut and dyed jet-black, something she had never done before. At first I thought it was for the wedding. She wanted to look nice for our guests—but what was she doing in her room? Why was she avoiding Maku?

I couldn't help myself; with the wedding so close, I had to know. Did Maku not want the wedding? Were they fighting because he tried to call it off? The next day, I waited for her exit into the bedroom, and immediately, I left through the front door. I walked around the side of the house, to the back window of her room. The curtains were pulled closed but there was a gap in the left corner where the fabric had been pulled too far. I squatted and closed one eye, focused the other.

I saw my mom at her vanity, her profile. She was closing the drawer where she kept her jewelry, locking it behind her. She walked to her bed and I noticed a piece of paper in her left hand, folded in three. She held it so gently, like it might melt if touched in too many places. She sat on her bed and unfolded it, raised it to her face.

She stared at the paper for twenty minutes.

I must have looked at my watch fourteen times, wondering how she was still reading, still staring at that single sheet of paper. I looked back at the vanity and searched for clues, examining her pots of makeup, her hairbrush, her perfumes. They were a mess, I realized suddenly, bottles of lotion pushed into a pile, tubes of lipstick scattered across the mirrored surface, the vase of birds of paradise suspended precariously off the edge. My mom was adamant about organization, about keeping everything in its proper place, and I had never seen her belongings in such disarray. I looked back at her and she was so still, I wondered if she was breathing, wondered if she had made that mess herself, still startled by the sight.

She stood up suddenly. Without warning, her legs straightened below her. I watched my mom fold the paper and walk to her vanity, unlock the drawer, and replace the letter. She locked the drawer and left the room, the small key safely in her pocket.

Squatting at the window, my knees cramping below me, my mind buzzing with possibilities, the only thing I knew for certain was that

I needed to read that paper. It was the only hope I saw; in that paper, I thought that maybe, just maybe there was evidence that my wedding had been canceled, that it was all a plan to terrify me, to set me straight.

So I began to watch the paper as if it were a bomb, ready to interfere at any moment. The plan was simpler than I imagined; my mom's neurosis gave me an easy opportunity. That evening, she moved the paper. I watched her put it in her purse and I grabbed it out as her bag sat on the counter. She was going out—*just out*, she told me, not even looking in my direction. But the phone had rung; she went to answer it. I walked swiftly to the adjoining room and slid the paper between the cushions of the couch, to the left of the armrest where I knew there was a gap. I went immediately to my room. From my door, I listened for her to hang up. I walked to my window and saw her get into her car, her purse on her right shoulder, watched her drive away.

I ran back to the couch and pulled the paper from the cushions. It was a letter, I realized as I unfolded it, handwritten in short, square writing. The corner read July 2—a week before. My eyes raced across the words, so many words. I devoured them standing up.

Dear Amy,

I know this letter may come as a surprise, and I'm ashamed to be contacting you like this after so many years. I suppose this is my attempt at an apology, about twenty years late, but I couldn't find a way to do it any sooner. I found your address in the Punahou directory. I'm not following you, I promise. I just need to get this out. I need to tell you this now, before I lose my nerve, so that I might finally have a chance at moving on.

I was in Palermo when I found out you were engaged to Bohai Leong. My brother wrote me a letter. He included the newspaper article and he was so angry. Amy, I went crazy when I read that letter. I had just found you and already, you were gone again—

had committed your life to another man. I was furious with myself. I shouldn't have left when everything was so uncertain. I should have written more, should have given you a better ring. I started drinking every day. I stopped showing up for my assignments. I even thought about ending it all. 1500 volts to the head. An end to the misery.

But then, selfishly, I decided to hurt you. But it wasn't that easy, Amy, and that's what you must understand. I loved you more than anything and I just wanted you to know what a huge mistake you had made.

Every letter I exchanged with my brother made it worse, pushed me further and deeper into my head. He knew how I felt about you. Since we were kids, he knew exactly how I felt about you and in a way, I think Paul felt betrayed as well. The year had already been so shitty for my family and Paul was in a bad place, a really dark place, and I just—I followed him into that hole.

I knew it was the money you were after. I don't blame you— you made the choice you had to, but to come home and see you driving a Mercedes and living in Diamond Head with some other man . . . I couldn't handle it. I couldn't bear the thought. So I did something stupid, something loathsome that ended in catastrophe. On the day of your wedding, Paul was there. It was too simple. Black shirt, black pants, and no one knew the difference between him and the rest of the restaurant staff. He said the party was rowdy and it was easy enough; a couple drops of thallium in a teacup, just enough to make him sick, to make you question your future, to shake your confidence.

But he put too much in, Amy. It all went wrong. He swore it wasn't our fault—said that it must have been something else but the newspapers confirmed it. They said it was poison, a murder, and I have never felt more disgusting in my life—not at war, not ever. Amy, please know that I have never hated myself more than when I realized what we had done.

I was positive we would be caught—I almost hoped we would be. We waited, week after week, for that knock on the door. But it never came. The investigation began and then it ended. I was dumbfounded, skeptical of our luck, but then I found out what happened to you.

I ran into your father at the bar on Kawa Street, a month after I came home. He was drunk, yelling at the bartender when he recognized me. He called me over. I asked about you and he said he didn't know. He said he hadn't seen you in a while and we got to talking and he was so drunk, emotional and angry, and I sat there, Amy, just letting him talk, listening to what I had done.

If I had known about your father-in-law's other wives, I would have never allowed it—it would have been too risky. Believe me, if I knew how much you would suffer, I would have let you go. All I wanted was a minor tragedy, something difficult you could interpret as a sign, a reason to come back to me. But you never did, Amy. You stuck with your husband, and so I've been keeping this secret for twenty-one years.

I understand that you must be repulsed by me and that this letter could put me in jail for a very long time—that my penance could come at any moment. My brother moved to Vancouver six years ago; he couldn't handle being here. His life was crumbling; the guilt was eating him alive. It's the same for me, Amy. I think about it constantly, morning and night, and I think about you. If we're telling the truth now, I should tell you that I'm also married, for eight years. It took me twelve to even imagine being with someone else and it all still feels like a sham. She's a wonderful woman, but I haven't been fair to her. I haven't been fair to anyone, especially you.

I need no response. All I can hope is that one day things will be right, be it now or in the afterlife. I still love you. I still think about you. Please, please forgive me.

Henry

Reading that letter was like being held underwater. When it ended I came up for my first breath of air, panting, disoriented. *Who the hell was Henry?* He had murdered my Ye Ye, that part was clear, but he was also in love with my mom. He was engaged to my mom. My mom who read the letter eight times a day, who took it with her wherever she went, who dyed her hair black, who no longer talked about the wedding. *What the hell was going on?*

Then, right then, as if God had been waiting the entire time, finger on the trigger for the perfect moment to punish me, Maku walked through the front door from his afternoon jog.

I had a physical reaction. I smashed the letter between my fists and sat on it, practically threw myself on the couch. Maku caught me mid-epiphany, at the worst possible time, as the avalanche of significance was still falling. I had just begun to realize what it all meant and my hands could not keep pace with my thoughts; I was too slow. Maku saw me hiding the letter, and in his newfound mistrust of my decisions, he insisted on knowing what it was.

I bumbled around; I told him it was nothing. I raised my empty hands into the air like an idiot. I could have come up with something better but there wasn't time. I got trapped. I ran out of excuses and he wasn't going anywhere. He stood over me, his hand extended. *Theresa,* he said, *now.* I had to give it to him; I couldn't see another way.

He took it. I watched as he read, the silence between us so large, his hands shaking gently against the wrinkled pages. In my head, I screamed at God. Why the hell would you send Maku in now? What was the point? What the fuck were you thinking?

"Where did you find this?" Maku asked, looking up for the first time. His knuckles were white; everything about him was white, stern, quietly distraught. The look on his face was devastating. I should have ripped that letter apart, should have brought a match to the corner—something, anything to avoid the damage I saw now, so irreversible, unforgivable.

"Maku," I whispered, too afraid to answer his question. "I'm so sorry. I had no idea."

Maku nodded at me, once, as if that's all he had left. He set the pages on the coffee table and walked back out the front door.

The wedding was postponed. It was not canceled, my mom continued to remind me; it was postponed. We told our guests that Maku was sick. I couldn't believe that was our excuse. Maku, of all people, was not well.

But in the end, I suppose it wasn't a lie.

At first, in those first few days after he confronted my mom, Maku began to look at her differently. It was as small as that, but I noticed it immediately, the distance and severity in his eyes. It was unsettling in a way that no amount of screaming, no amount of fighting could ever be. My father, who loved my mother more than any big-screen romance, more than any fairy-tale cliché, could no longer bring himself to look at her.

They did not go to dinner that Friday, nor any Friday that followed. The birds of paradise died; they were not replaced.

A month passed like this. My parents entered and left the house like strangers, not speaking unless absolutely necessary. Maku's pillow stayed on the couch, folded blankets left permanently on the armrests. The folding chairs remained stacked on the lanai; the case of napkins still on the table. When the phone rang, no one answered.

Then there was fighting. Three months of it, my stomach showing by then, my pregnancy unmistakable. My mom would scream, she would cry. The guilt, it was eating her alive; I could see it, but I couldn't say anything. I couldn't help her—it was larger than that. The whole story, it was enormous, torrential, anger and bitterness and jealousy that I could not begin to understand, buried since before I was alive, before they even knew I would exist.

Why would I have told you? What would it have mattered? My mom's defense lacked any trace of sympathy, any sign of an apology.

It would have mattered. Maku, more solemn than ever, would raise his voice. *You know it would have mattered.*

That was the most incredible thing to me. In all their fights, in all their yelling, I never once heard them mention my Ye Ye or his death. Naturally, my mom would not bring it up because it was linked to her, a crime committed in her name. But for Maku, I realized his despair had little to do with his father and everything to do with my mom, his wife, his everything. He waited for her to come to him, to explain that she loved him most, that Henry was simply a man from her past, his crime unprovoked. But she never did. She withdrew; she grew defensive. All these years, Maku believed they were fated, he and my mom, that her love was as fervent as his. But now the glass had shattered and it was clear, at least to me, that he could never again see it the same way. The window was closing; as weeks became months with no resolution, no explanation, it was becoming harder and harder for him to forgive.

Five months passed and I took myself shopping for new clothes, bigger clothes. My mom didn't offer; she didn't spare me the shame of shopping in public, a pregnant teenager all alone. The only time I saw her was when we went to the doctor, and even then, we barely spoke. I hated her and she hated me. She wanted to know the sex of my baby, Dr. Ho's prediction, and I wouldn't tell her. I held the information back as a punishment; I said I'd tell her when she stopped being such an asshole, when she found a way to apologize to Maku. We blamed each other for everything, for Maku, for my pregnancy, for the wedding, for the lonely desperation that had consumed our house, ripping a hole through our lives.

And then Maku's hair began to fall out. It collected in the drain of the guest bathroom, limp, spidery piles. He lost so much weight, nearly forty pounds in the final two months. He didn't shop for new clothes; instead, he quit his job. It seemed that every day he grew weaker, right in front of my eyes; he lost himself in silence, in the dark shadow that had been cast over all of his memories. We ate meals separately. I talked to my baby by then. Secretly, I had named it. In a way, being pregnant made it all feel less solitary. When I ate, I knew I was feeding the baby, too. As I slept, the baby was right there with me. I told the baby about my day, I read out loud. I told the baby I was scared. I told it I was terrified that Maku would die.

It overwhelmed me, the thought of him dying, the way I couldn't stop thinking of it, fearing constantly that he would be gone. I was certain that Maku would die. Somehow it felt inevitable, unavoidable that he wouldn't make it through the year. It was a horrible, destructive thought, but watching him fade like that, watching my father wilt before me, each day a bitter, unbearable battle, I just—I couldn't see another way. I couldn't find a solution for my father, the master of solutions, the unshakable rock.

Slowly, excruciatingly, I watched Maku lose everything about him. His hair, then his appetite, his voice, the color in his skin, his smile, his job, his glasses, his love of reading, the movement in his hands, the expression in his eyes, simple pleasures of any kind.

And then, after six months, six long, heartbreaking months of screaming and lies, of miserable, penetrating silences, Maku chose not to stay. He checked himself into the hospital. Of course we went with him, but it wasn't our idea; we barely knew what was happening. We practically chased him through our front door, trying to figure out where he was going with a suitcase in his hand.

Two days later, he was gone. Just like that, like he'd timed it, as if he'd run the numbers on his death and solved the equation before he left.

I was getting coffee down the hall. The doctor found me, led me back to the room where Maku lay in his medical gown, his eyes shut, his face as pale and thin as ever.

Congestive failure, *a weak heart*—that was the doctor's diagnosis, his first words, and only then did I understand what we had done.

CHAPTER 10

November 1964
HONOLULU, HAWAII

From his rearview mirror, the driver watches. Dismayed, he sees what he has done.

In the backseat, Hong sits in rigid deliberation, silenced. Her eyes, blank from the outside, grow narrow. They focus inward as they search. Her lips move faintly, noiselessly, summoning a voice that has yet to arrive.

The strange effect of his words, the disquiet that's arrived, the driver does not know how he managed it, how his single phrase, his careful proverb finally uttered, triggered such a reaction.

It was out of habit that he said it, from thirty years of repetition. His mother's favorite adage, he liked it for its simplicity, its ability to touch but not intrude. As he drove from the cemetery, the two women behind him, it had come out. *What is fated to be yours will always return.* He said it confidently, offered it courageously, turning around in his seat. After sprinting up the hill, after delivering Hong to Mrs. Leong, the driver felt somehow worthier of the day. He felt, for a fleeting moment, the importance of his position, the necessity of his presence.

Hong raised her eyes to meet the driver's. She studied him, taking long, slow breaths as her gaze ripped through his confidence. She frowned.

"I'm sorry," the driver apologized, steadying his foot as he braked for a light. He said it again, because he could think of nothing else to say. Immediately, he knew he had struck something terrible. His words, his nine words hung miserably on Hong's face.

The light turns green; a car honks behind him and the driver turns in his seat, back to the road. He is pushed forward with the traffic, his hair damp against his temples.

The fact that it's Hong makes it so much worse. Hong, who is commanding and dexterous and effortlessly graceful. The white-haired woman on whom the others rely, the keeper of solutions, their steady hand—the driver has done what the day could not. He has upset her. For the first time that day, through his rearview mirror, he sees her hesitate; he watches her panic.

Hong turns to Mrs. Leong. She opens her mouth and turns away without a sound.

She does this twice, then a third time as they leave Manoa. With each failed attempt Hong grows stranger in movement. Her breathing deepens, her lips buzz, her fingers twist slowly together. What she holds lies on the tip of her tongue, on the brink of release, but she holds it in.

Beside Hong, Mrs. Leong waits. She faces her friend. She's listening.

Hong exhales before untangling her fingers. She peels them apart, extends their wrinkled length.

"Sometimes," she says, turning to Mrs. Leong, her brow heavy with concentration, "we are distracted by fate. So much, sometimes, that we lose our chance at destiny."

The driver blinks. It is the last thing he expects.

"This car," Hong says, interrupting the driver's thoughts, lifting her eyes to the ceiling. "Fate is like this car, shiny and new, soft on the inside. Some people are born into cars like this and that is their fate. Bohai and Kaipo, your children were born into cars like this one. Brand-new, comfortable, safe."

Hong lowers her eyes; they settle on Mrs. Leong.

"Others," she says, "are born into rusty cars. Cars with engines that need time to start. They need attention. You and me, Frank, Amy, our cars had no leather. Our cars had no driver, no radio, no heat for cold days. That is our fate. This is what we are given. There is no way to trade for a different car."

Hong's voice carries no anger, holds no bitterness at the observation she makes. Her thoughts come fluidly in quiet surges; like the stroke of a painter, she glides until she runs short of ink. She dips her brush and the strength returns.

"But destiny has so little to do with fate. If fate is like this car then destiny is the road we take. And this road, it is ours to choose. We make the turns, we speed and slow, we decide when to stop, when to go. This is destiny. No matter what car we drive, the road is open to us all. All of us, we are given the chance to make what we can. With whatever car, whatever fate, we choose the road."

Mrs. Leong listens carefully. A single line of perspiration glistens on her brow. She makes no sign of acknowledgment but it's clear that she's present. Her mind pushes; she wants to listen.

"I have forgotten this," Hong says. "I have confused them. I have placed too much on fate, on chance, and not enough on destiny, on the difficulty of choosing. To take me into your home, to come to Hawaii, to send you to Waialua—this is not fate. These are choices we made. These things, they draw us closer to destiny. The choices that bring fear, that make us turn to fate . . . this, in fact, is destiny. This, for good or bad, we can control."

The car has grown warm; it has shrunken in size. Hong's words are like an ocean's tide, developing silently in the distance, being pulled by the moon, gathering momentum as she reaches the shore, as she looms just before her point.

"I knew," Hong's voice crashes. Her lips press inward as tears form, a glossy dampness along the width of her eyes.

"I knew about Frank. I knew before I met you. I knew, Lin, and I never told you."

Hong's eyes overflow; upsetting her speech, arresting her rhythm. She brings a hand to her mouth, containing herself. She stares at Mrs. Leong as she holds herself steady.

A moment passes.

The rumble of the car is the only sound; the shifting of the gears, the gentle revving of the engine. They have begun their ascent to Diamond Head, rising along the hill as the sun lowers. It casts a brilliant glow that slices through the windows, catching in Hong's tears, lowering her eyes.

"Frank spoke to me," she whispers. "The week you took me in. Shen knew, so Frank assumed. I promised him I wouldn't say a thing. He said it was better for everyone, that he loved you best. He said he would take care of it and I saw no other option, Lin. I knew so little of you at the time. I could not imagine how close we would grow, how much like sisters, how heavy a burden it would become. When he died, I told myself it was fate. The way it unraveled, I told myself there was nothing to be done." Hong shakes her head.

"I couldn't face you. I let them take you away. I chose again and I didn't stop it."

A tear falls, the first sign that Mrs. Leong understands. The driver watches, his foot pressed against the gas pedal, his overwrought limbs fighting to stay steady. Beneath his foot, he can barely feel the metal. He does not understand what he is witnessing. His mind feels like jelly, his bones like cold steel. He thinks of the morning, mere hours before, of his first trip to the mighty crater and wonders if it was really him, awestruck, lit with a desire to pry, to know. He feels none of these things now.

"Every day," Hong says, reaching for Mrs. Leong's hand, silencing her tears, "I miss you. Every day I wish you were here. I wish that I told you. I think of you alone, every day alone in a strange place, and I am so sorry," Hong breathes, both hands wrapped around Mrs. Leong's. "Every day, Lin, I regret."

The women stare at each other. Their sadness aligns. An understanding passes like a shadow, dark and cool, and it carries relief. It sweeps through the car, returning the driver's eyes to the road, replacing the air stale in his lungs.

"I made arrangements," the driver hears. "I found a room. It's near the beach, five minutes from you. The house belongs to a nurse at the clinic."

Ahead, the gates of the great house come into view. The stone lions, atop their mighty pillars, cast long, sideways shadows across the empty road. The car passes through and the light flickers.

"I'm so sorry," Hong says. "I'm so sorry it took me this long."

Theresa hears her name. She turns back to the casket and sees her mother, still squinting beneath the lowering sun.

"Theresa," Amy says again, her voice fainter than she intended. "Stay here." It sounds like a command; she corrects herself. "Please, Theresa, will you stay?"

Amy is trying. She is overflowing, trying to gather the pieces before allowing herself to release.

"Please," she says again, fighting against her daughter's ambivalence. "You deserve to hear this, too."

As she returns to the casket, Theresa's expression does not change. Her face holds no sympathy for her mother; she has no intention of easing her task. She dreads being present. If Amy fails, if she comes up empty, Theresa fears her own reaction.

"Go ahead," Theresa says, nodding at her. "I'm listening."

Amy feels like she might vomit. The gaze of a dozen onlookers, her daughter's disdain, her husband's body, a final moment to do the right thing. Amy fears, once again, that she will choke; her courage will escape her yet again.

Amy closes her eyes.

She sees herself on her thirtieth birthday. She sees the birds of paradise, their thick, shiny stalks, their tangerine blossoms. She sees the card beside the vase, on her mirrored vanity. *Happy Birthday*, it says. *Meet us in the kitchen.* She walks to the kitchen and there they are, making breakfast. Bohai's wearing an apron; Theresa's licking a spoon. *Don't look*, Theresa says. *You woke up too early!* Amy sees them on the dock, eating pancakes and fruit salad, the three of them, their bare feet, the morning sun. She's talking to Theresa about mangoes, about how to cut them, how to slice around the stubborn pit. Bohai's wearing a baseball cap; he's leaning back, resting on his forearms. It's a perfect day; she remembers it so. The three of them, they had dinner on the marina, outside on the deck by the boats. Theresa had questions about the boats, the water, and Bohai had the answers. Amy sees her husband smiling, teasing their daughter. She hears his voice. *It's a bimini top, Theresa, not a bikini top.* She sees their faces above her birthday cake, a single candle flickering between them, lighting up the whites of their teeth.

Behind her eyelids, there is proof of her happiness. There is a glint of how it might have been.

Amy doesn't open her eyes; she can't, not yet. She places both palms on the casket and breathes.

"Bohai," she says, just louder than a whisper. The sound of his name on her lips, on her breath, Amy feels her husband's presence in the silence that follows.

"It's difficult to explain how you changed my life. You appeared at such a strange time, when everything was changing. The world was changing, I was changing; I was just beginning to understand the limitations of being myself, of coming from where I did, of having nothing. It scared me enormously, the thought of ending up in that same place. All I wanted was to be better than my parents. They were so unhappy, so broken by the way their lives turned out—and I've never told you any of this." Amy pauses; her arms shake softly against the casket.

"Twenty years we've been married and you've told me everything and I've told you nothing. Nothing at all. You asked, you always asked me and I brushed it off. You let me be. The thing is, Bohai. The truth is that I didn't want you to know me then. I didn't want to confirm that I was so beneath you, so changed by your presence, better by simply being around you. Because I was.

"Before I lived in your family's house, I was cleaning them. Months before, I was wearing the same gloves and the same house shoes as the women who cleaned your house, and all of a sudden, Bohai, I wasn't anymore. I was *living* in the house. They were making *my* bed. They were doing *my* wash. I can't tell you how much that ate at me. We were married and I hadn't told you any of this. You had no idea who I was. And then your father passed and even more so, I felt completely useless, completely out of place.

"The first two years, before we had Theresa, I think I was waiting. I was waiting for you to realize I was a fraud, to see what different worlds we had come from, to tell me it wouldn't work out. But you didn't, and so we decided to have Theresa and I was sure that feeling would go away, that I would be somehow more secure, more in control. But again, I was wrong.

"It had become second nature, Bohai, hiding that part of me. I told myself it had been too long; I couldn't say something now. How would it sound? I knew how it would sound. I was certain you would see me differently, that you would think less of me.

"So I never allowed you to become my real life. I never allowed myself to love you the way I should have. And the absurdity of this whole thing is that you probably knew all of this. Your mother probably told you that I lived in a basement and my siblings ran around like animals and my parents hated each other. You probably knew. But I didn't want to believe that. You gave me every reason to trust you, to open up, and I chose not to. I chose instead to protect myself and look what happened. I failed us all; I jeopardized our entire family, everything we worked for.

"I have a money box in the closet, Bohai. There's almost a thousand dollars in it. That's how real it felt. That's how deluded I've been, how unfair I've been to you. I feared, after all this time, that one day you would wake up and leave us. You would go back to Diamond Head. You would see through me."

"So." Amy hesitates; she chokes on the word. "So when that letter arrived, when I read that letter, I felt everything about myself that I never wanted you to know. I married for money. I ruined so many lives. I was responsible for a death, for a *murder*. I was every bit as terrible and selfish and deceitful as I feared and I just, I completely lost control. I'm still out of control. I still don't trust myself to be honest, to do the right thing, to be the mother that I need to be."

Amy breathes. She opens her eyes and is met by Theresa's stare. She looks directly into her mother's eyes, still as glass. Below her, Theresa's lips have formed something of a smile, pressed tightly together, the hint of a curve. Amy fights the impulse to reach for her daughter, to pull her in, to apologize for the things she couldn't say, to retract the words she said instead—but she doesn't. She searches for strength from within; she finds it.

"The last thing," Amy whispers, drawing her eyes from her daughter. "The most important thing. The heaviest burden."

Amy looks up now; she focuses on the sky above.

"You, Bohai, were the great love of my life. You always have been. You are the greatest man I have ever known, the only man who never let me down, the man who loved me unconditionally, who never gave me reason to doubt. As the man who taught me to love, who showed me how love should be, I will always love you. And despite my flaws, my vast, enormous flaws—every day I will feel blessed to have been your wife."

Theresa reaches across the casket and places her palms on her mother's hands, presses them against her father's heart. The lowering sun lights Amy from behind, her honesty radiant, her face shrouded in shadow. Theresa leans into the rounded wood and something heavy, something luminous shifts within her.

Across the valley, over the Koolau Range, a mighty volcano darkens below a blistering sky, breaking from gold to amber; a dormant silhouette.

Below Theresa's skin, beneath her lungs, her son stretches his limbs.

ACKNOWLEDGMENTS

When I embarked on the journey of trying to write a novel, I had no concept of how many people it takes to nurture a book, both editorially and emotionally. I worked on this novel for five years, growing socially weirder and more deranged as time progressed, and my saving grace was consistently the people who surrounded me, who pulled me from the depths, who quieted the crazy and pushed me forward. I have been extraordinarily blessed by the people who have donated their time and their brilliance to help get me here, and I am truly grateful for all they've done.

Before I even knew I was writing a novel, I think Mary Gordon did, and her faith in my work was the fuel for this book. Generous with her time and her knowledge, Mary continues to be one of the sagest women I know.

To Genevieve Gagne-Hawes, a razor-sharp editor and perfect stranger who stuck with me and this book for years before anyone believed in it, when no one wanted it, when I paid for her editing with bottles of Lambrusco and rides to Newark Airport.

To my agent, Meredith Kaffel, whose steadfast vision and dazzling tenacity have turned my dreams into reality. Charming and warm and effortlessly talented—every day, I feel blessed to have found her.

To Maya Ziv, the kind of editor that makes a writer's job luxurious. Her clear eye has added depth and precision to every page of this book. I rarely disagree with Maya, and when I do, I'm usually wrong.

To my parents, Kono and Susan Wong, who are two of the coolest, most encouraging parents in the universe. They've trusted me every step of the way and have been selfless in their support, resolute in their belief that life should be lived to the brim. My mom, the wisest woman in the world, taught me what it means to be fated to my dad, who is kind and hilarious and a rock to us all.

To my Grandpa and Grandma Wong and my Popo and Gung Gung Hee, whose generous stories have been integral to both my life and my book. I am lucky to come from such a genuine and bighearted lineage.

To Stephanie Sisco, Emily Hathaway, and Allegra Sachs—three of the best girlfriends a writer could ask for. Champions from the beginning to the end, these extraordinary women read years of drafts and rejections. Their unwavering enthusiasm for a book that might never be published was hugely important to me.

To Ashley, Galen, Lindsay, Mason, Rachel, and Saranya—friends who read drafts, who offered insight and encouragement throughout the years.

And finally, to Read, the man behind everything. I can't count how many breakdowns Read has endured with impossible grace, how many threats to give up and set myself on fire. Read is the reason this book is a book, and his stubborn faith in me and my story is what makes me believe that fate and destiny are well within reach, if only you are willing to fight for it.